GUNNER

BRACKEN RIDGE REBELS MC

MACKENZY FOX

Copyright © 2021 Mackenzy Fox

All rights reserved. No part of this publication may be reproduced, distributed, or transmitted in any form or by any means, including photocopying, recording, or other electronic or mechanical methods, without the prior written permission of the publisher

Please purchase only authorised electronic editions and do not participate in, or encourage, the electronic piracy of copyrighted materials. Your support of the author's rights is appreciated.

This book is a work of fiction. Names, characters, places, brands, and incidents are the products of the author's imagination or used fictitiously. Any resemblance to actual events, locales or persons, living or dead, is entirely coincidental.

Cover by: Mayhem cover creations
Formatting by: @peachykeenas (Savannah Richey)
Editing by: diannegi
Proofreading by: Dakotah Fox

AUTHOR'S NOTE

CONTENT WARNING: Gunner is a steamy romance for readers 18+ it contains mature themes that may make some readers uncomfortable, including violence, possible triggers (Gunner's child abuse, while it is not graphic or detailed it is mentioned, it may cause triggers in some readers) a lot of cursing and HOT steamy love scenes.

BRACKEN RIDGE REBELS M.C. RULE– Enter at own risk…….

Bracken Ridge Arizona, where the Rebels M.C. rule and the only thing they ride or die for more than their club is their women, this is Gunner's story:

Gunner: She's always been there, it's not like I haven't noticed, I have. I wanted her once, long ago, but it's forbidden, she's off limits; a club sister, *Steel's* sister. The more I try not to think of her or want to touch her, the more I can't stop. She's under my skin. Clawing at my heart. I know I have to stay away but she's like forbidden fruit, the one thing I can't have and the sinner in me wants to corrupt her in every way I can; taint her like only I know how. And I will, at least for a while. I always get what I want. Always. Even if it means breaking hearts.

Lily: He's within reach but always so far away. For the longest time I've watched and waited, admired him, ached for him, all from a distance. But now my time has come. It's now or never. He's all wrong for me, I know that. I've always known, but it doesn't stop me wanting him, it never will. The question is, can my heart ever recover or beat again the same way when he's finished with me? Or will I live to regret laying my heart on the line and baring my soul to the one man who has the power to shatter me forever.

NB* Gunner refers to himself as Joshua and his sister Summer as Amanda in the flashback scenes when they were children, they changed their names when they were adopted.

1

LILY

5 YEARS EARLIER...

Nothing much has changed as I glance around the clubroom, except tonight it smells more like testosterone on steroids than stale beer.

The usual Saturday night party is in full swing; loud music blares, some guys are playing pool, scantily clad women are strewn around here, there, and everywhere, and Ginger's behind the bar serving drinks like nobody's business.

This is not the place for somebody's little sister; my brother being the Sergeant at Arms, the protector of the club, and it's definitely not the place for an underage girl. Not that the brothers would do anything sinister, more like they'd send us packing out of here quick smart with an ass whooping. But if I do run into Steel; my night will be over. He takes being an overprotective big brother to a whole new level. Where I'm concerned, he has no boundaries.

I haven't seen Gunner since I was eleven, now he's back in Bracken Ridge prospecting for the club.

I guess you can take the boy out of the town but there was no taking the town out of the boy.

When Deanna, the club President Hutch's daughter, told me Gunner was back in town I knew I wanted to spend spring break back home so I could see him, secretly, just a glance, anything to look at those beautiful, beguiling eyes again and see his warm smile.

He's always been sweet and kind to me, never treated me like a child, and he's drop dead gorgeous, obviously, even though it's been years I bet he's just gotten better with age.

Deanna tugs on my arm, gabbling in my ear. I don't know how long we'll hold out before we get caught and kicked out. Everyone seems too absorbed in their Saturday night of partying to notice us, but I don't care, just getting a look at him is worth the punishment of being yelled at.

However, I don't dare to think what will happen if Hutch catches us, that'd be a different story. Deanna told me he's not going to be here tonight, hence why we're being so cavalier. The only thing scarier than my brother telling us off is Hutch. That would not be fun.

But Deanna walks in like she owns the place.

I wish I had her confidence, she exudes it, her long raven hair with blue tips waving behind her as she walks, legs that go up to her armpits and curves in all the right places.

I'm a good deal shorter, petite with chestnut hair and long bangs, blue eyes and I'm more of a 'fake it till you make it' kinda gal when it comes to being assertive.

"We shouldn't really be doing this," I whisper for what feels like the hundredth time, my heart racing in my chest.

I glance here and there as we walk but I don't see Steel, *please don't let him be here.*

"Relax, nobody will question it if we look like we're invited and belong here," she says over her shoulder.

She's probably right. When you're the MC President's daughter, nobody questions anything.

We get a couple of nods from a few of the guys who don't

know any better. Ginger stops and gives us a pointed look as she pours a beer, but we ignore it and pass by quickly before she can stop us.

"Crap, Ginger just saw us," I whisper worriedly, once we're safely past her hawk eyes.

"Just be cool, Lil," Deanna reassures me as she keeps walking, completely unaffected.

Famous last words. And it's okay for her, she's twenty-one and old enough to drink and be in bars. I'm not.

"What's the big plan anyway?" I wonder, hoping she has one.

"You want to perve on Guns and I want to see Amelia and party, snag some beers, dance with some cute guys, and get wrecked."

Urgh, I hate beer. And I've never been wrecked, the thought of getting drunk repulses me. And dancing with cute guys, well I've never done that either. Since I go to an all-girls school, I rarely get any chance to interact with boys.

Amelia is Brock's younger sister, the Vice President of the club, she's a few years older than me. She's been away at college and we rarely ever get to catch up unless it's spring break, Thanksgiving, or Christmas.

We find Amelia pretty quickly; she's standing with a group of older girls who are all dressed in an array of revealing and blush-worthy outfits. They have lots of makeup on with drink bottles in hand, but that's typical around here. Anything goes.

We get slipped a beer and I try not to hide my disgust as I pretend to sip it, hoping to blend in.

The girls at my school don't party like the girls here. I've made some good friends at boarding school and I know my mom is trying to give me the very best for my future, but my future has always belonged in Bracken Ridge.

This is my home; these are my people. I don't know how

3

I'm going to tell her that I want to come home after I graduate. I don't want to go to college, I want to go to beauty school, but mom has big plans for me, as does Steel; plans they seem to want to make without my say-so.

"Don't look now..." Deanna says in my ear above the music, nudging me; I follow her subtle nod over to one of the tables behind me.

The first thing I see is the back of a Prospect cut and a mop of blonde shaggy hair.

Gunner.

His cut is sleeveless and he's wearing a tight fitted Henley underneath. His hair's longer, still sunshine blonde but it's tied back off his face. He moves around collecting empty glasses into a large container and he turns to the side, giving me a better look.

Both sides of his head are shaved, so he has a mohawk thing going on. His eyes are still cast down, concentrating on his job. My breath hitches in my chest as he turns front on, unaware he has an audience.

And there he is.

In all his beautiful glory. As gorgeous as ever.

Unlike me, he's not a teenager anymore, he's definitely changed, and it shows in all the right places.

His skin's slightly tanned from the outdoors. He's taller, broader, his arms fill out the tight sleeves of the Henley well, and he's got heavy, silver rings adorning his knuckles and chains and beads hanging all around his neck and up his arms. He's also grown a small goatee, I really hope he doesn't decide to grow it too long and cover up that beautiful face, that would be a shame.

He is the epitome of everything a man should be and everything I know I can't have.

I can't keep my eyes in my head as I watch him move around.

A biker shouldn't be that pretty. I think he's even trying to look badass with the mohawk thing he's sporting. My eyes linger and travel down his body...*I can't even.*

I hear Deanna giggle next to me. "You've got it bad," she laughs, nudging me with her shoulder.

I shove her back, my eyes still on him, "I do not."

"Uh huh, yeah you do."

"I haven't seen him in a while that's all, I'm allowed to look," I mutter.

Like a siren call, his eyes flick up toward me suddenly. I've been caught staring like a stalker.

Shit, shit, double shit.

He bites his lip and a slow smile spreads across his face as he gives me a chin lift followed by a cheeky wink. To my disappointment he doesn't wave, or say hi, or come over.

I know he's busy and he's working but still, he's known me since I was born.

He's a prospect, I remind myself. That means he *can't* come over and socialize; he won't do that until he's been dismissed from his duties, which may be never, tonight it looks like he's Ginger's bitch and she's keeping him on his toes.

I look away, embarrassed, and when I get the guts to look back again, he's moved on to another table and begins the glass collecting ritual all over again.

My heart hammers in my chest at the mere sight of him, his crystal blue eyes are like sparkling topaz, full of promise, full of mischief.

Now I realize why I'm not interested in any of the guys I know, because nobody compares to him.

He's bad ass, through and through.

As the night proceeds, every now and again I get a glance of him as he passes by tidying up, moving around unnoticed, and every now and again our eyes meet across the room and he smirks, each time I look away.

After a while the girls want to dance; Deanna and another girl, Stacey drag me out onto the dance floor and we begin to shake our groove. It's dark and the music is blaring, some of the guys nearby watch us and whistle and cat call as we dance. It's probably not a great way to keep ourselves off the radar but they can't shoot us for having fun.

Being wild and free is a far cry from the afternoon tea parties I have at boarding school; if only my Headmistress could see me now, she'd be horrified. That only makes me grin even wider at the thought.

I look up across the crowded room and see that Gunner is staring at me. I keep moving as I watch him; I raise my arms up in the air and move my body to the beat. His eyes drop and rake down my body, they linger on my breasts in my tight tank top and move slowly down; *he's checking me out!* I feel a thrill run through me that warms my insides.

He should not be looking at me like that but hot damn I love it.

Holy shit balls. Breathe.

I break eye contact and I have to excuse myself quickly to go to the bathroom, I have to splash cold water on my face before I combust. When come back out of the ladies' room a few moments later, I run right into a brick wall. I look up to see who I've collided with and all the air leaves my lungs.

It's him. I gulp as he looks down at me, smirking to himself in his sexy way.

"You're beautiful," he shouts over the music as he stares down at me, "what's your name?"

I laugh and look down momentarily, then I meet his gaze quickly; he's waiting for a reply.

What the hell?

Is he for real?

I think about it for a millisecond... *is there a chance he really doesn't know who I am?*

I mean, I was a kid the last time I saw him, I definitely don't resemble an eleven-year-old now; I'm eighteen, a lot has changed.

And curiously, he's not looking at me like he knows me, if he knew it was *me*, he'd have hugged me by now and then most likely marched me right on out of here back home.

Suddenly a plan hatches in my brain. I want to applaud myself for my quick thinking.

He has no idea who I am... so I can be anybody, somebody he might want to make out with for example. Huh.

If he finds out the truth, he won't touch me with a ten-foot pole; I'm practically his surrogate sister... That's an awkwardly weird and creeped out thought...

"Marie," I tell him before my brain catches up with my mouth, well, it *is* my middle name so it's only a little, teeny, tiny, white lie.

He leans closer to me. "You're gorgeous," he says, he leans back and frowns a little. "How old are you?"

My heart is beating so fast it could jump out of my chest right now, I know I'm digging a big hole for myself, but I can't seem to stop.

"Twenty-one," I lie, hoping he believes it.

His eyes graze down my body again and when he brings those blue eyes back up to mine, I'm lost. The way he's looking at me is scorching hot and leaves nothing to the imagination for what he's got in mind.

He leans to my ear again. "I'm on a break, you wanna go somewhere quiet?"

Say yes, say yes, say YES!

I nod, feeling like I'm in the twilight zone. My legs feel like jelly, I hope they don't give out on me, that would be embarrassing.

"What did you have in mind?" I reply, looking up at him, trying not to sound nervous.

Shit, I hope he doesn't say up to his room. I've never done it with a guy; I've never even gotten to second base. While he's gorgeous and I'd love to make out, I don't know if I'm ready to have sex, that's completely terrifying.

I mean, what if I'm no good? Sex does seem pretty basic but I'm not experienced enough to know.

Calm down already, he's not even asking for sex.

"Wanna go make out?" he gives me a lopsided grin.

Or maybe not.

I find myself nodding because I seem to have lost my powers of speech and before I can change my mind, he grabs my hand and pulls me with him toward the store cupboard where they keep the kegs of beer.

I glance back and see Deanna's startled face as we disappear down the hallway. She has the audacity to give me a thumbs up, it's the last thing I see before we're out of view.

His hand is warm in mine, it feels tight and secure and strangely intimate.

When we're out of the crowded, noisy space, he turns to me.

"Couldn't hear myself think in there." He grins, pushing the door open. He sweeps his arm out in front of him, "Ladies first."

I step inside and he kicks the door closed with his boot.

I turn around and he's staring at me with twinkling eyes full of trouble. Desire is written all over his face, and I know I'm playing with fire.

Breathe Lily, just breathe.

He comes toward me as I step back further and stop when I hit a keg. He brings both of his arms up to rest against the shelf above us, effectively caging me in, his eyes studying me carefully. He smells delicious too, it's a spicy heady mix combined with bourbon and cigarettes.

"You sure we never met before?" he asks quizzically.

I bite my lip, I can't lie to him again, I just can't, so I change the subject instead.

"Shut up and kiss me," I murmur. The fire I have going on inside me feels more like a volcano about to erupt. I've waited a long time for his kiss and I'm not wasting any more time.

His eyebrows shoot up and his eyes dart down to my mouth. "You've got a very pretty mouth, little girl." His voice is sexy and low, his eyes are eating me alive as they trail over me. "I can't wait for you to taste me."

My eyes go wide as he moves in and kisses me. It's soft at first, gentle in fact, and he still doesn't touch me with his hands, but his lips feel like magic against mine, the bristles of his goatee feel prickly and I imagine his mouth somewhere else. It sends sensations right through me right down to my toes.

Unlike him, I don't have the same restraint; I clutch his cut and pull him closer, he grins against my lips and deepens the kiss, all of a sudden he's pushing his tongue in my mouth and it's the most beautiful, amazing feeling I've ever experienced, my insides turn to mush.

I've kissed guys before but not like this, *never* like this. It's obvious he's had a lot of practice and it's definitely paid off.

He pulls back and his arms come down and clutch my face. "Fuck you're beautiful, Marie."

He moves his mouth to my neck and kisses me there, biting softly as I clutch his biceps to hold myself up. I'm so turned on that I want him to touch me wherever he wants; reckless abandon floods me and I feel my cheeks heat up at every touch, every kiss, every nip.

His hands move down my arms and one rests on my hip, the other makes its way up my torso and sweeps over my breast as he squeezes gently through my tank top, *holy mother of god.* My head falls back in absolute pleasurable agony as he fondles me, the intoxication of his kiss is too much, the sensation sends me into a spin. His mouth finds mine again and his tongue sweeps inside once more, leaving no doubt that he's into it because I can feel his erection pressing against my stomach.

"Babe," he groans as he moves his body closer to mine. His other hand reaches around to grab my ass and he pulls me further into him, grinding his hard cock against me as I wrap my arms around his neck.

All of a sudden, he lifts me by the hips and rests me down on top of the shelf and he moves in between my legs.

"Gunner..." I whisper in his ear as his mouth assaults my neck again; slowly heading south, his hands are everywhere, kneading me gently as I clutch onto him for dear life.

"Yeah babe?"

"You feel so good." I continue breathlessly. I don't want him to stop, even though I probably should – I'm a liar after all- instead I grip him harder.

Both his hands move to my breasts as he moans into my mouth. "Jesus these are fuckin' hot." His thumbs find my nipples through the fabric as I squeeze my eyes shut.

Things are escalating very, very quickly.

I didn't come here expecting this; to actually be making out with him and him touching me places I've never been touched before. I just wanted to get a look at him, anything on top of that is purely a bonus.

You're a liar, Lily.

I shove the thought away to a more pressing one; *what if he actually does wants to have sex?*

I internally chastise myself once more. Of course he does, he's as hard as a rock. He didn't bring me back here to play patty-cake.

I never imagined my first time would be up against a keg of beer in the back storeroom in the clubhouse.

"Touch me," he says, breaking our kiss. He shoves his cut off his shoulders and I waste no time in running my hands up the inside of his Henley and up his bare chest onto his warm skin, feeling all of his hard muscles. He's breathing heavy and that makes me smile, hopefully that means I'm doing it right.

He curses as he watches my hands moving over him. He moves one hand up my skirt to the inside of my thigh and my blood runs cold; shit, he's going to touch me there.

I instinctively grab hold of his wrist, stopping him from moving in that general direction.

He pulls back and looks at me gently. Bikers are not supposed to look at anybody like he does, I know from being around the club that they take what they want, girls fall at their feet. The girls are all up for it, sure, but this is Gunner, he's different. "You okay babe?"

"Yes," I pant. "I'm just nervous…"

"You gonna let me in?" he presses against my forehead with his.

Shit. He wants in.

"Here?" I exclaim, I can't keep the panic out of my voice.

He glances around as if reminded of where we are. "You're right," he agrees, as if just realizing, "this is no place for a lady, let's move it upstairs to my bedroom, doubt anyone's gonna miss me out there."

A lady. I can't help but smile. I'm glad he doesn't think I'm a skank like some of the other girls that hang off him like the sweet butts do; they're the girls in the MC who sleep around, and they don't care who it is.

My eyes go wide and he notices. "You okay with that?"

I bite my lip.

Noticing my hesitation, he narrows his eyes. "You sure you're twenty-one?"

I nod. "I'm a late bloomer, that's all." Ain't that the truth.

He leans toward my ear. "Good, this whole virgin act is really turning me the fuck on, babe."

His dirty words go straight to my core, not that I need any more heat down there.

I feel his dick twitch against my knee and we both look down.

I've never gone this far with a guy and we're still both fully clothed.

Who the hell am I?

"You wanna touch me babe?" he nuzzles into my neck, his voice low.

I know where he means and I find myself nodding, it's not like I haven't thought about what it would be like, what he'd look like naked, but I can't bring myself to do it. He wastes no time in grabbing one of my arms from around his neck and swiftly plants my hand on the hard bulge in his jeans.

"Holy shit," I splutter.

He grins.

God he's so hard.

"That's what you've done to me staring at me across the room all night." He moves his face between my breasts and sighs contentedly.

I stare down at my hand grasped over his bulge and our eyes meet as he looks up.

He edges back and smirks.

"Move your hand like this," he tells me, holding his hand over the top of mine, he begins to stroke himself through the material. He closes his eyes for a second and tips his head back slightly, it's the most erotic thing I've ever seen. I'm making Gunner lose control. *Me.*

I should feel ashamed of myself, I'm a good girl. I'm not a girl who bangs bikers up against a keg, but with him I have no sense of decency or restraint.

I stare at my hand as he watches it too, making appreciative noises, none of which help keep my control in check. He's hard in my hand, and thick and big, and I'm scared shitless.

You can do this, keep your mouth shut and don't tell him anything.

But I can't do it.

I have to tell him that I'm not Marie, even if a devious part of me wants to see his reaction when he realizes the truth.

I want more though, just a little bit.

My hands move to his belt buckle as his rest on my hips, one hand moves up my thigh and over the lace of my panties. *Oh God.*

"You've got beautiful tits," he tells me as I look up at him, he moves his head lower and down to my breast and sucks me through the material.

I groan and grind myself into him, all the senses in my lower half feel like a wild fire out of control. I feel his fingers brush over the front of my panties and I hold my breath; I'm throbbing so hard that one touch will send me over the edge.

"Holy fuck," he curses as he rubs me through the sheer lace of my panties and then pushes them to the side, touching my bare flesh. "I can't wait to taste your sweet honey."

The thought of his head between my legs is all that it takes for my first orgasm to rip through me, it's so intense and happens so fast, too fast. I call out his name in a rush of ecstasy with my head thrown back. He has barely touched me and I've lost complete control.

When it's over I open my eyes and he's grinning like he owns the world.

I pant, trying to catch my breath and stare at him wildly.

"Babe that was so fuckin' hot, but we need to get upstairs

before I take you on the bench." He kisses me again urgently but before he can lift me up the door swings open.

"Shit sorry man," Brock says and swiftly shuts the door, our eyes meet briefly over Gunner's shoulder.

Oh holy mother of god.

Brock just saw me.

The door swings immediately open again.

Brock stares at me for a few awkward moments.

"Hey," Gunner calls without looking around. "Kinda busy here, dude."

Brock stands there and slowly puts his hands on his hips as his eyebrows raise dangerously, kicking the door shut with his boot, it slams hard, shaking the rafters.

Yeah, Brock knows exactly who I am.

Gunner immediately looks over his shoulder.

"What the fuck are you doing, Liliana?" he barks before Gunner can say anything more.

Oh no, and things were going so well, leading me to wish we should have escaped out of here the first time he'd suggested it. Too late now.

Time stands still. It's one of those moments that I actually hope the ground will open and swallow me whole right here, right now.

My moment of ecstasy is over. Gunner's startled eyes turn back to me in confusion as I stare back at him like a deer caught in headlights as he fits the pieces together.

Now I have two pairs of pissed off eyes boring into me and I've nowhere left to run.

My life is officially over at eighteen.

2

GUNNER

LILIANA?

I turn back to the girl in my arms and stare at her, her hand still on my dick though she's stopped moving it thank Christ.

What the fuck? Why's he calling her Liliana?

A cold rush of blood sweeps through my body as I pull back, I think I know the answer to that. There's only one Liliana I know.

I turn back to Brock, he's eying not her, but *me* speculatively, and he's furious. Neither of us say anything. Neither of us move.

I turn back to look at Marie/Liliana and then I see the guilty look in her eyes. I take a step back like she's burned me with hot coal.

Oh holy fuck.

She's just signed my death warrant.

He takes in our disheveled state and shakes his head. I take it back; he's beyond furious, lasers may shoot from his eyeballs at any second. I'm royally fucked and there is no doubt about it; this is gonna hurt.

"For Liliana's sake and decency, if there's any left of that, I'll give you about thirty seconds to get your shit together before I come back in here." He turns and walks out the door, slamming it hard behind him, so hard the hinges my fall off from his anger.

I take another step back.

"Liliana?" I say like I'm trying out the words for the first time. "As in Liliana Steelman?"

Please say no, please say no, please don't let this be Steel's little sister.

"Gunner, I'm sorry, I was going to tell you…" she trails off anxiously. "But one thing led to another quickly…"

I step further back and run both hands through my hair, panic sweeps through me, then horror swiftly follows. She doesn't look like how I remember her.

No shit dummy, that was like seven years ago, she's not a kid anymore.

"Why did you tell me your name was Marie?"

She looks up from her hands. "It's my middle name."

I close my eyes.

It's official; I'm a dead man.

"You nearly let me fuck you against a keg?" I burst out, and I know my words are harsh, but she has no idea what she's just done.

Brock's going to kill me, then Steel's going to finish me off.

I'm a dead man at twenty-three, finito.

So what if I had hopes and dreams and wanted to get somewhere in life? That's all gone flying out the window now, not to mention my short-lived stint as a prospect.

I wonder suddenly how far it is to the Mexican border and if I'd be safe there, but who am I kidding? I can't run from the M.C. for one I'm no coward, and secondly, they'll find me anyway, most probably skin me alive for not taking my punishment like a man.

"I wasn't going to let you do that," she says, unconvincingly. "I just got lost in the moment."

Lost in the moment? Like that's an excuse. I give her a doubtful look before another alarming thought runs through me. "How old are you really?"

Please for fucks sakes say over eighteen... maybe then they'll let me keep my balls.

"Eighteen," she stammers. I try not to sag with relief, not that it's anything to be proud of.

I mean way to go, I need a pat on the back, I almost defiled not only Steel's baby sister but a freaking teenager who's technically a minor, this is an all-time low even for me.

She's fuckin' hot but that is no excuse. I didn't know eighteen-year-old high school students looked like that, I'm sure they didn't when I was in school.

Her big blue eyes, looking at me for salvation, are the one thing that hasn't changed. The rest of her; yeah, she's transformed from a child to a woman in those few short years.

I should have known.

I let out a rushed breath then look back up at her.

"I want the truth now," I say, my tone serious. "I mean it, Lil."

She nods, eager to get back in my good graces.

Oh please god, I don't want the answer to this...please don't let me look like a complete and utter creep.

"Are you still a virgin?"

Her eyes go wide and her face falls about the time it goes bright red, I know the answer immediately. Of course she is. Unlike the girls I usually screw, Liliana's a good girl. She's still in high school and clearly not messing around with boys in *that* way, she doesn't even go to school here. I thought that whole virgin act was such a turn on, seriously, kill me now.

It's official; I'm going to hell, and I'll have a tomahawk stuck in my back as I ride through the pearly gates, a farewell gesture from my club.

Jesus, fuck.

"Liliana," I breathe. "You shouldn't have done that, it's not mine to take."

She reaches for me. "I've always wanted you, Guns," she blurts out. "Since forever."

"Always?" I roll my eyes. "You're only eighteen for God's sake, kids your age don't know what they want."

"I'm not a kid." She rolls her eyes petulantly.

"I hate to break it to you sweetheart, but technically you are, and the last time I saw you, things were a little different." I wave my hand down her body like it's not already obvious.

Her eyes narrow, the famous Steelman temper may be about to raise its ugly head, that's all I need.

"This is bullshit!" she spits. "And you weren't just treating me like a kid with your hands all over me and your tongue down my throat!"

I bite my cheek to keep from laughing, this isn't funny by any means, but Lily really mad is a delight, she's even sweeter than I ever imagined.

My merriment is short lived because a flashback of all the dirty things I just said to her and the places I had my hands and mouth invade my thoughts. There is no doubt I would've taken her up to my room and nailed her. I pale at the thought.

"You've no idea what you've done," I tell her quietly. The blood still hasn't resurfaced from the front of my jeans and it's actually getting painful, I wonder when it's going to go down, I hope before Brock returns and sees it.

"He'll go easy on you, won't he?"

I smile sadly. "No babe, he won't."

Her eyes go round. "They won't kick you out, will they? I'll tell them the truth; that it's all my fault!"

"It won't make a difference."

Her face falls and I move closer and tilt her chin up with my hand.

"It's not that I don't want to, you're gorgeous, a knockout." I smile. I think she needs to hear it. "You're just too young, and Steel's little sister, obviously that's not a good idea, not to mention that I like my balls hanging freely; this isn't right sweetheart, and you shouldn't have lied to me."

Her face falls again. "But it felt right," she mutters. "It felt *really, really* right."

I breathe heavily. "Just promise me when the time's right, with the right guy, you won't give it up on top of a keg in an MC clubhouse…"

I don't get to finish as the door bangs open and Brock enters again, looking just as mad if not worse than before. He's like a bull, a wounded bull, not a good combination.

Here we go.

I turn and move as far away from Lily as I can. He moves closer and I don't even see the swing coming but it feels like my head may come off my shoulders at any given moment; that's gonna hurt tomorrow.

I hear Lily scream.

"Brock!" she yells.

He points a finger at her, stopping her from running over to me. "Be quiet," he gruffs. "I want an explanation and fast, you've got approximately ten seconds."

"It was all me!" she screams, I don't need to look to know she has tears streaming down her face. Oh Lily. "I lied and said I was Marie and I was twenty-one, he didn't know."

"It wasn't," I cut in, holding my jaw. "Don't listen to her." I don't want her in trouble as well. I don't want her taking the blame, even though she technically did lie to me.

"You mean you brought her in here knowing full well she was Steel's underage sister?" He's turned into a raging bull now, with steam coming out of his ears; getting up in my face, he's large and bulky and he could kill me if he wanted to, maybe they'll bury my body out in the desert somewhere, now is not the time to tell him I want to be cremated.

"I lied!" Lily rushes out. "He didn't know it was me, it's been years since we saw each other, I was just a kid, I've changed since then, please Brock!"

Brock turns to me. "Is this true? Don't go trying to cover for her, you'll only make it worse for yourself."

I let out a long sigh, I don't want to drop Lily in the shit, but lying to my V.P. is not an option either.

"She told me her name was Marie," I admit. "I didn't know who she was, I haven't seen her since she was like eleven that's the truth."

Brock's murderous glare turns back to Lily and she literally cringes and steps back further.

"Liliana? What were you thinking?" he barks. "More to the point what are you even doing in here? Does Steel know you're here, out lookin' for strange?"

She wipes her tears away. "I obviously *wasn't* thinking, and I wasn't looking for strange! I just wanted to catch up with the girls and have some fun. Please don't tell Steel, he'll kill me!"

I see his jaw visibly tighten, *not helping Lily.*

"Did you…?" he asks, pinching the bridge of his nose like he doesn't really want to know the answer but has to ask.

"No!" we both shout at the same time.

At least we're consistent.

He looks momentarily relieved but I'm not a fool to believe that will last.

"You're not going to tell Steel, are you?" Lily gasps again

before he can say anything else. True, unbridled panic runs over her face about the same time as mine.

He rubs his jaw with one hand like he's thinking, plotting my demise. He's probably weighing up how to sneak my body out of here without anybody noticing or how many pieces he has to cut me into, to make it easier to carry. All kinds of crazy thoughts run through my head right now and none of them are good.

"I should go get him right now just to teach you both a lesson, one you'll never forget."

Oh shit, nobody needs any of Steel's lessons on right hooks, the man used to torture people in the military. He's built like a freak and takes no crap from nobody. Being on his radar is like hurtling towards the devil himself. I'd never survive his beating.

Lily jumps forward, startling us both; she clutches Brocks meaty arm.

"Please don't," she begs. "It isn't his fault, and nothing happened anyway, we were just kissing; that's it, I swear to God!"

She's a little liar, but boy she's convincing.

Christ, if only he knew what I'd just given her. How she called my name while she came and I didn't even get around to penetrating....I feel like I need to purge or repent my sins or something. I wonder if it'd help.

He looks down at her hand clutching him but she doesn't let go.

I think about me telling her how beautiful her tits were and I cringe even more.

He turns back to look at me. "You've put me in a very compromising position, prospect!" he barks, turning back to Lily with disgust he glares at her. "He's going to have to pay now for what you've done, hope you're fuckin' happy."

"It's not her fault," I interject but he just holds his hand up to stop me talking.

"But I was the one who lied," she cries. "Please Brock…"

"That doesn't matter, he should have known better and if he doesn't then that's nobody's problem but his own. High time you started thinking with that head on your shoulders instead of the one between your legs, isn't it prospect?"

It's not Brock's fault either, he has to punish me, it's how this works. Prospects are scum, lower than garbage, what kind of a V.P. would he be if I got off lightly?

There is no way out of this and we both know it.

"What are you going to do with him?" she stammers, all hope in her tone is lost.

"That's none of your concern," he barks, then thumbs over his shoulder. "Now beat it."

She shakes her head. "No, I'm not leaving."

"Lily…" I begin. She's only gonna make it worse. "It's alright, do as he says."

She looks over at me, her eyes full of tears and regret, I give her a chin lift to let her know it's okay. I forgive her, I just don't know if I can forgive myself.

Brock however, isn't so patient. "Liliana, don't make me tell you again, do you want me to go find Steel?"

Her eyes go round and she shakes her head. "No," she whispers sadly.

My gut lurches, poor kid. I feel bad for her, but not as bad as I'm gonna be feeling after having my face rearranged. I have to take it like a man, I'm good at that, I can take a beating. They'll never break me. Nobody can.

"Get gone," he tells her again.

She smiles at me sadly and mouths 'sorry' and quietly leaves the room.

I watch her go, then I take a steely breath.

Brock turns to me like thunder.

"I don't know if it's any consolation but it was a genuine mistake," I say holding up my hands, like that's gonna protect me.

"Happy to throw her under the bus?" he sneers.

"No." I shake my head. "She's a kid, she doesn't know any better, hormones and all that shit."

He lets out a slow breath. "For what it's worth I believe you. Girls that age are trouble, especially her with that blood in her veins; but that's no excuse, you should be smarter, you should have realized she was with Deanna and Amelia, a bit of a giveaway."

Realized? The last time I saw her she was a child for pete's sake. Now she's a full-blown hottie with the lips of an angel and a body made for sin.

God, I may never get her out of my brain.

At least I'll have the memory of her, if I have any brain cells left after this that is.

"You know what I have to do, and just know this, I don't want to do it, you're a good kid, but you fucked up and in this club there's no room for mistakes like that. It's how the world works, prospect, it's how the club works, you know all of this. I expect better from you."

Okay, he's not gonna tell Steel then, that's hopeful, I think.

"It won't happen again," I blurt out quickly. "I promise." My heart thunders that my club may kick me out for good. It's all I have. This club saved my life. I'm nothing without it.

"I know it won't."

I shove the panic down.

I've been in worse places than this. Oh yeah, I've got demons alright and compared to that shit, this is nothing.

"Can you just go easy on the face?" I wince, bracing myself for impact, it's gonna happen any moment.

He grins. "You don't get to call the shots, princess."

I nod in agreement. "Okay."

"This is between us," he adds. "But I won't be very lenient if we wind up here again."

"We won't," I assure him.

The relief that runs through me is palpable. I'd do anything for this club, anything. I don't want to disappoint anyone, much less him.

"And we're never gonna speak of it again."

"I appreciate that."

"Shut up."

"Sorry," I mumble.

"Don't worry, there's plenty of little has-beens waiting out there to fix you up afterwards, ones that aren't in high school, that might soften the blow."

It won't, but I don't tell him that.

If only he knew; the only girl I'll be thinking about from here to eternity is little miss Liliana Marie Steelman and what I just did to her, and what other things I wanted to do.

Her beautiful eyes looking up at me like that, full of wonder. I should be mad with her, I *should* be, but that was just the sweetest thing that's happened to me in a long, long time, it might even be worth the smack down I'm about to receive.

She's pure. Innocent. Everything I'm not.

Yeah, that'll be my private little fantasy from here on in, nobody has to know. It doesn't escape me that I can still smell her perfume on me, sweet and soft, like her.

I close my eyes.

I'm royally fucked, that's all I know.

Let the blows begin.

GUNNER

I WAKE UP WITH A GROAN, pain engulfs me from all angles. To make matters worse, a stream of light beads through the curtains blinding me, making me wince. *Ouch.*

One thing's for sure; Brock doesn't hit like a girl, oh no, he could never be accused of that. My face hurts; I dread to think what I look like. He had to purposely keep hitting me in the face, my money-maker, couldn't take most of the blows to the body, oh no. My body can be covered for a while, my face however...

I groan out loud.

Not even the aftermath of having the girls paw over me later was worth it. One of them, Serena I think, patched me up and put me to bed but I couldn't even get it up for her, I was in too much pain. How embarrassing.

I wince again.

Shit. I hope he hasn't damaged me permanently down there. I reach down and pull my underpants elastic out; it's still attached at least and doesn't feel sore, thank fuck.

I sink back down onto the pillows.

I have a flashback of knocking down a bunch of shots and being dragged up to bed half cut, I definitely didn't finish the job, how could I, my body hurt like hell and she wasn't Liliana Marie, nothing about her ever could be. Poor Serena, she would have left pouting.

My mind flashes back to Lily.

Jesus, she's so hot it should be illegal. And the fact she's still a virgin has me shuddering in all kinds of ways I shouldn't. I shouldn't be thinking about her like that, but I am, I fucking am. The fact nobody's been there with her makes my dick jump and stand to attention.

I remember our kisses, our tongues, my hands all over her, her hands on me, rubbing me, fuck – I got her off.

I grin at the thought, *ouch.*

Remembering her face as she came undone has my dick

hardening even more. I've never seen anything so satisfying as watching her lose it, God that was raw, her pink cheeks flushed and her lips swollen, I imagine her lips around my cock and groan.

I'm definitely going to hell.

If I weren't so sore, I might think it was all some sordid, delicious dream I just conjured up, but my aching bones remind me I'm a fuck face and that's why I'm in pain.

I'm glad that at least my dick's not damaged permanently, my face and body will heal.

I rub my hand up and down a few times just to be sure, glad that the blood circulation is alive and well, what with my brain being so damaged. I sigh a long breath of relief.

But I have to stop fantasizing about her. She's only eighteen and she's not available in that way, ever.

I mean, I've known her since she was in her mother's stomach. That's disgusting. If some guy was moving in on my sister, one she'd grown up with and trusted, I'd hang him from the town square and let him bleed out.

Am I a sick son-of-a-bitch? Maybe I am, but I'm not dumb enough to move in on her, I don't have a death wish. I like my life.

I close my eyes and think about my hands running up her tiny little waist and squeezing her tits; fuck they were nice, and how wet she was when I rubbed her slick swollen flesh.

I imagine how tight she'd be and I let out a groan. Jesus, I wanted to do so much more.

No fuck face, no, just stop.

But I can't stop, no matter how much I try to not think about it that's all I end up doing.

I realize nothing is gonna make it stop.

I reach to the top drawer next to my bed without even looking and dip my hand inside, feeling around for the baby oil.

Yeah. There is one thing I need to do to get this out of my system once and for all. It's wrong, so very wrong, but I'll do it once and that'll be it, she'll be out of my head. I reach my other hand down into my pants and sheath my dick.

Nobody has to know. It'll be mine and my palms' dirty little secret. Yeah.

Just once.

Then I'll be done.

3

LILY

PRESENT DAY

"Hey Lil, where do you want these boxes?" Colt bellows from the backdoor.

Ever since Steel put Colt on my watch after my drink was spiked at the Stone Crow about a month ago, he's kind of taken it upon himself to help me out from time to time, usually it's with all the heavy boxes I get delivered for the salon.

He's a good-looking guy, solidly built, with dark, short cut hair, nice hazel-colored eyes and just the right amount of facial hair. I realize though that I hardly know anything about him, he's only just been patched in and keeps to himself a lot. He's a real sweetheart, I know that much.

"Just in here," I call back.

He picks a stack up and carries three of them up the hallway toward me, I push the store cupboard door open for him to dump everything. "Thanks," I say as he passes. "That's super nice of you."

"No problem."

"You know you don't have to do this anymore," I remind him. "You're technically off the hook."

"I don't mind." He shrugs. "Plus, I get to keep an eye on you so it's not all that bad."

He gives me a wink as I roll my eyes, he kids around a lot and he flirts a bit, but it's completely platonic between us. I mean, it would be so easy with him, but we've become more like buddies than anything romantic, not that he isn't nice to look at.

I shove him in the ribs. "You mean the girls in the salon?" he looks over my shoulder at the two hairdressers who work for me, Katy and Miranda, and wiggles his eyebrows, a clear smirk on his face.

"Which one is into me again?"

God men are so disgusting. "Neither! And you can't go breaking any of my girls' hearts because then their work will suffer, which means *I* will suffer," I reply matter of factly. "And we can't have that, so play nice."

"I don't intend on breaking their hearts." He winks, placing a hand on his chest while trying to look innocent, he fails miserably.

"No, just breaking them in," I mutter, shoving him again as I make my way down the hallway toward the rest of the boxes.

"You have a very low opinion of me Lil," he laughs following me.

"Stop staring at my ass," I retort without turning around.

"What do you say when you go into a store and buy a skirt like that, I'll buy that tiny little scrap of material so nobody will notice me?"

I turn and poke my tongue out. "Ha-ha."

We both turn as a loud motorcycle sounds and then pulls around the back and my heart lurches in my chest.

It's Gunner.

I shouldn't know the sound of his bike but it's a testament to how pathetic I am that I know everything about him.

He parks next to my car, pulls off his brain bucket and tears his goggles from his face and bounds toward us in a couple of steps.

This is Gunner, always in a good mood, like a ray of sunshine.

"Sup guys?" he gives Colt the usual handshake, shoulder bump thing they all do and he turns to look down at me.

"Hey Lil."

"Hey," I reply turning to him, he doesn't come and hug me like he normally does which is weird, in fact, he's been acting weird for a couple of weeks now, ever since he got back from out of town with Steel and the boys on some business they had to take care of with Sienna.

Normally he flirts openly, puts his arm around me and asks me about boys and other impromptu stuff, but lately he's done none of those things. I can't think of what I've done and he's not acting pissed off at me or anything.

"You good?" he nods at me.

"Yes." I shrug, turning away from him, picking up one of the small packages. "What are you doing here?"

He and Colt go to pick up some more large boxes and follow me back through the door.

"Just came to grab Colt, going out to the depot and I need him to help me off load the trailer."

The depot is the industrial shed of junk that Bones and Brock run at the scrap yard, a few miles out of town. It's a pretty weird place to find the most unusual shit, if you're after metal and tires and rusted, old car parts nobody wants then that is the place to find it.

"Glad to see you're making yourself useful," I say with an eye roll that he can't see.

"Hi Gunner," the girls coo after him in unison as he comes up the corridor.

Oh god help me, it's like this everywhere he goes.

I'm sure if girls could just follow him around worshipping his every move, kissing his feet as they go and get away with it, they would.

"Hi ladies," he replies with a lopsided grin as he follows me in and asks me where I want the boxes.

I point to the corner. "Just down there, thanks."

Colt dumps his and goes to get the last few, he always has his head in the game, unlike Gunner.

Gunner turns back to me and I honestly just can't help myself.

"Hey, is everything alright with you?" I ask, subtly blocking his exit.

He glances up at me as he stands. "Yeah babe, why wouldn't it be?"

I glance behind me to make sure Colt isn't coming back.

"You don't seem yourself that's all," I whisper quietly.

He gives me a lopsided smile, but it doesn't reach his eyes. Just as I suspected, something's up. I know every inch of his perfect face and I don't know this look at all.

"I'm fine, just had a long week and I haven't been feeling well or sleeping."

He can't lie for shit either.

Miranda comes barging in, much to my annoyance, and this is what it's like; I never get five seconds to talk to him alone about anything, heaven forbid if we had two minutes without interruption.

"Oops sorry," she says half-heartedly, yeah right. "I just need some more foil."

I move aside as Gunner grins at her and gives her a wink. "You baking a turkey sweetheart?"

She giggles and I roll my eyes, I feel like making a gagging noise but somehow, I refrain.

"No silly, I'm dying Mrs. Smythe's hair two different

colors, speaking of which, isn't your big photo shoot coming up?"

Oh, I forgot about that. Gunner has been commissioned to pose for some raunchy women's magazine called Sizzle. He also wants to use the publicity to promote his jewelry piercing line too.

Come to think of it, Gunner hasn't mentioned it for a while and Deanna and I are meant to be getting him prepped and ready. This is a big deal and could well earn him a lot of money as well as new exposure. Any excuse I get to see him stripping off his clothes is a good one. Maybe he's just nervous about that? It seems odd because he's never nervous about being a show-off, he was born to have people gawking at him.

"You think I need some highlights?" he laughs, running his hands through his scraggly blonde hair. God I've seen him with short, long and no hair, and he suits everything. Bastard. I watch him watching her, oblivious to anything.

"Not at all," she smiles, grabbing a small box of pre-cut foil off the top shelf where she has to reach up high, his eyes are on her ass. "You're perfect as you are."

"A girl after my own heart," he laughs as she passes by, he tries to swat her on the ass and misses as she darts past him, giggling. I watch deadpan as his eyes stay glued to her behind and she disappears back the way she came. I muster every power of strength I have not to throw something at her head. Colt comes back with the last box.

"This is it," he announces.

"Thanks Colt, I really appreciate it."

"We better get going," he says and retreats again out the door. "Yell if you need me again this week, Lil."

"Thank you honey," I call back.

And then we're alone again.

Gunner looks at me. "You got any appointments for me tomorrow?"

Gunner has just started piercing at the salon and let's just say he's booked out weeks in advance; all the teenagers, Instagram chicks, hot mommies and anything in between come to get their ears, noses, and navels pierced. Even little girls with their moms getting their ears done for the first time love him, he just has a way with women, all women, even five-year-old's with pigtails.

We thought we would trial it since nobody else in town is offering piercing except Angel's Ink, and Angel's isn't the type of place you'd take children, being primarily a tattoo parlor.

"Booked out tomorrow, your first appointment is at eleven."

He reaches out and nips my chin gently with his thumb and forefinger like he can't help himself, he still doesn't hug me. "I'll see you at eleven then."

He doesn't wait for me to answer, he takes off down the hall as I sigh out loud and go back to the front to drink my cold cup of coffee and set up the waxing station.

Something is definitely up.

∽

"You've been such a big brave girl," Gunner says to miss eight-year-old Lyndsay as her mom watches on proudly on the stool next to her. "I've never seen anyone so brave."

He's right, she didn't even cry. I remember having my ears pierced and I cried my eyes out, and I was older than her.

He hands her a love heart-shaped lollipop. "I don't give these to all the girls you know," he says with a conspirator's wink.

"Thank you, Gunner," she beams happily, with tears in her eyes but smiles at him like he's an angel sent from heaven. I watch as he glances up at her mom, she's looking at him like she wants to eat him for lunch. *Puh-lease.*

At the salon he insists on wearing one of the T-Shirts we all wear with the slogan; Liliana's Beauty Parlor on it, along with black ripped jeans and a bandana. On anyone else wearing a Liliana T-shirt would look slightly odd, but he's ripped the sleeves off his shirt so it looks effortlessly cool of course. It also shows off all his tattoos laced down his arms which is a bit of a no-no in this kind of establishment, but funnily enough nobody seems to mind it, nor do they care.

"You are such a sweetheart," Lyndsay's mom coos, she touches him on the upper arm as he smiles at her. "Really Gunner, thank you for being so good with her."

His face turns pretend serious as he hands mom the antiseptic spray and some swabs for later.

"Now for the important boring stuff, make sure you leave the studs in for two days but spray her ears front and back, then take them out and soak them in the solution overnight before putting them back in, they should heal in about ten days."

She nods eagerly, hanging onto his every word and I glance down at her jiggling boobs. I don't think she needs to wear a tank top that low, this is a reputable establishment, not topless afternoon Tuesdays.

I pretend to work on the computer as he comes toward the counter with the client in tow to ring up the sale. God he could sell ice to the Eskimos.

Lyndsay happily sucks on her lollipop without a care in the world as mom hands her credit card over and she's all smiles.

I should be happy that we've got a new, happy client, but instead I'm like a green-eyed monster.

"Thank you for making this so comfortable, I was so nervous for Lynd's, but I needn't have been," the woman gushes, clearly flirting. She's already said thanks fifty times, we get it.

"Well now, that's my pleasure, there's plenty more lollipops where they came from."

I don't need to look up to know he's just winked at her, she's grinning from ear to ear, her hand playing with the ends of her hair, god she's touching herself, *get a life you old hag!*

He hands back her receipt and her credit card.

"Say thank you Lyndsay," she calls, as if realizing she actually has a child in tow.

"Thank you, Gunner," Lyndsay replies sweetly.

"Look after those ears, my favorite girl." He leans on the counter as they move away toward the door.

"See you around," mom says hopefully as they exit the salon, she gives Gunner a little wave for good measure, I try my hardest not to choke on my own vomit.

I shift my eyes to the side and watch as Gunner looks down at something in his hand then slips something in his back pocket.

I don't believe it.

"Do not tell me she slipped you her phone number?" I can't help myself now that we're alone.

He laughs. "It's not my fault, I don't ask for it."

"Sure you don't," I mutter going back to the computer. I'm supposed to be putting new codes into the system for some of the new accessories that have come in. They need to get on the shelves pronto, but the system doesn't seem to want to work today, but maybe it's because I'm always distracted when he's around and where other women are concerned.

"She wasn't bad though, for a mom."

I stare at the screen unmoved. "She had ten years on you

or more, somebody needs to tell her to keep her runaway tits in her bra so she doesn't scare people in the street."

He guffaws at my tone then turns to look at me. "Someone's cranky today."

Yeah, I am, he's been flirty and lovely all day to everyone, and yet to me he's been distant and hardly said two words. Sure, he's talking to me, but it's more out of obligation than anything, and now I'm just acting like a sulking five-year-old.

"I'm just tired," I lie.

"You need a vacation."

I laugh. "Yeah right, when I've paid this loan off in two thousand and fifty-five, then I'll take a vacation."

He studies me for a moment and I decide to let him know my plans, not that he'd care. He's probably going to go and bone Lyndsay's mom later.

"Anyway, I'd love to stay and chat, but I've got a date tonight that I've got to go get ready for."

He visibly frowns. "Oh, who's the lucky guy?"

God, I wish he'd act a little bit jealous. "Wade someone or other, he's a friend of Amelia's."

Amelia lives out of town about an hour away but is back home on the regular, visiting when she can, she said this Wade guy is really nice, he went to college with her and he's apparently smart, funny and he likes motorcycles, not that I care about that.

It's been forever since I went on a date, I've been too busy adulting, which just goes to show how dull and pathetic my life is. I'm looking forward to having some fun for a change.

He looks at me for a few moments as I pretend to keep working on the numbers I'm failing to input properly.

"Does Steel know about this?"

I roll my eyes and sigh loudly. "I'm twenty-three-years

old. Steel doesn't need to know what I'm doing or who I'm doing it with or who I'm sleeping with for that matter."

He stands up a little bit straighter. "You're sleeping with him?"

The truth is I'm not sleeping with anyone, nobody has had any kind of appeal in the way that I'd consider giving my body to, I don't know why. The thought of a one-night stand turns my stomach. My last Tinder date disaster almost led to me being date raped.

"No," I splutter. "I hardly know him, it's just a phrase. Steel doesn't rule my life even if he thinks he does."

He continues to look at me for a long moment, I wish I knew what he was thinking.

"Just be careful, especially after the last date, I worry about you, there's a lot of weirdos out there, most guys only want one thing and will say anything to score, just remember that."

He worries about me? Hmm.

"Yeah, you would know," I mutter. "You're the love 'em and leave 'em type so how does that make you any different?"

He purses his lips, unsmiling. "Cause I don't fuckin' lie about it."

Well, I suppose he's right.

Instead of agreeing I just sigh loudly instead.

I feel him glance at me again. "You really are cranky today, aren't you?"

He doesn't care that I'm going on a date, while crushing, it's not surprising. When am I going to get it into my thick head that he just isn't into me? Maybe he never was.

"Well, if it's good for the goose?" I shrug like it's no big deal. "Then maybe I'll try my luck, take a leaf out of your book, huh?"

He sits down on one of the stools on wheels and pushes off the ground to wheel closer to me.

"You know what I mean," he continues. "You're not like that, you never have been, don't do anything you don't want to, and if you do want to, then make him work for it, you deserve that kind of respect."

I cannot believe we are having this conversation.

He's one to talk, it's not like he's Mr. Respectful-of-the-year or chivalrous in any sense of the word. Added to that is the fact that he doesn't actually care if I sleep with anybody else, it's like the final nail in the coffin.

"Do you make all your girlfriends work for it?" I fire back, trying to sound a little playful.

"Girlfriends?" he coughs. "Well, they know what they're there for. I don't date, babe; all that shit's too complicated, you know I'm not made like that."

He's admitted it out loud numerous times and why I know we can't be together. His bedroom is a revolving door and that there is reason enough to not want to touch him with a ten-foot pole.

Maybe I do need to get out there and sleep with someone. The thought terrifies me, especially with everyone constantly reminding me about the almost date-rape thing.

Heaven knows he's got unlimited options where he spends his evenings.

"I think I'm gonna call it a day," I sigh when I can't think of any other reply to that comment.

"I'll lock up babe, you go get yourself ready."

I live in the apartment above the shop. Imagining him down here securing the premises while I go upstairs and take a shower and get ready for the date that I don't really want to go on makes the butterflies in my stomach even worse.

Why doesn't he notice me?

I was good enough for him when I was eighteen and he thought I was Marie. I can safely say he's never looked at me like that again, and we've never spoken of it since. We've sort of just dodged around it and pretended it never happened.

He's the reason I still wait in the wings with hope, why I can't seem to give myself over to anybody else. I've tried. But I'm just not made that way, I wish I could be.

Maybe I will really like Wade, maybe he will take my mind off things, like a welcome distraction. If only I really believed that were possible then this all would be so much simpler.

"If you're sure?" I say as he gets up off the stool to go and get the sign in from outside and lock the front door.

"Have a nice time, and remember to take the pepper spray," he says as he disappears out the door. I stare at his back as my mood plummets.

It's official.

He doesn't give a shit.

I'm just like a little sister to him.

That's all I'll ever be and it's like the kiss of death.

4

GUNNER

AGE 7

I stare at the ceiling. Nobody told me being seven-years-old would be a drag. But that's how it feels.

No birthday party, no presents, not even a happy birthday from anyone except my baby sister. She would never forget.

Mommy cries all the time these days. She doesn't know what day of the week it is; she doesn't know a lot of things.

We take ourselves to school most days and I make sure Amanda gets something to eat, even if I don't.

I don't ever say his name, the man mommy has come over, he's been gone for a few days. I like it when he's gone, I wish every time that he'd never come back.

It's not long after that I hear the front door slam and I sit up suddenly.

My heart plummets into my chest as I hear his voice.

Please no.

Not today. Let me have today.

"Where is the little shit?" I hear him bark loudly as he approaches my room. It's worse when he's been drinking, it's always worse.

Amanda is already asleep in the wardrobe. On nights like this, when I don't know his whereabouts, it's safer that way. There is no need to put her in the firing line as well. I'll do anything it takes to shield her from this chaos.

When Tommy told me about his dad playing ball with him in the backyard, I wondered what that would be like. To be able to run into his arms instead of running away, having him give chase. To laugh and play like all normal kids instead of hiding somewhere, anywhere. I've learned that it's best to not hide, that only makes him madder.

This is my normal. This is what we do every day.

I suddenly hear mom's voice and then I hear him say something, but I can't make out the words, they stop near the door and I hear heated but muffled words as I strain to listen. A few moments later I hear his boots as he stomps away. I don't know what happened but relief floods through me and I realize I've been sitting on my hands, unable to stop them shaking. I don't want him touching me. I don't want him anywhere near either of us. But what I want doesn't matter.

I'm seven today, and nobody noticed.

∼

I WAKE UP SUDDENLY. A searing pain hits me between the eyes and I'm in a tangled mess of sweat and sheets. Then my dream comes back to me and I run a hand over my face.

All the torture of my childhood comes rushing to the forefront of my mind as I press the heel of my palms to my eyes.

I shouldn't drink so much. When I drink excessively it only makes the flashbacks and nightmares worse.

The night terrors and waking up in a panic have always plagued me, but it's the recurring unwanted dreams that are new, something I can't seem to shake.

Being sexually and physically abused by my stepfather is

something I've learned to live with, it's something I try to forget each and every waking moment, but sleep is one of the few passages of time where I have no control over it. My sister Summer, she was called Amanda then, is younger than me and I tried to shield her from everything; I tried to get in the way where I could so he wouldn't hurt her. I tried and failed.

I saw a therapist once, for a long time, not long after we were removed from that place. Nancy was her name. She got me through the first few years of not talking; though I liked talking to Helen sometimes, Steel's mom, and Kirsty, Hutch's wife, they were kind to us.

I think back to when I was almost eight and Lily was being born, I remember Helen being pregnant with her. I don't know why that flashes before my eyes, maybe because I've been thinking about her a lot lately, in actual fact I can't seem to get her off my mind.

When they brought Lily home from the hospital, Summer and I had been adopted by our new mom Gloria. She couldn't have kids of her own and had been trying to adopt a kid for years. I'm still forever grateful that they kept us together, not that Helen, Kirsty, or even Hutch would let anybody split us up.

So much went wrong in my early years of life, but so much turned out right and that's what I try to divert my thoughts to when I turn to the dark side. I count all of my blessings every day that Hutch did what he did.

Still. My mind wanders a lot.

My birth mom's boyfriend put a gun down his throat when he got caught, or so the story goes. But I know better. I was there that night. Our birth mom, well, she died of an overdose not long after, I like to think that she took her own life over her guilt of being a fucking shit parent. But I know better about that, too.

I blame her for everything, though I know she had a shit life herself, the cards she got dealt weren't what you'd call blissful.

Still, I find it hard to have any sympathy for her when she let it happen. She fucking let it happen. No matter what your upbringing or how shit you've had it, surely you know right from wrong? Surely you know children shouldn't be put through that. There's no reasoning with a junkie though. There's no point in even trying.

Which brings me back to the Liliana dilemma.

Ever since Sienna, Steel's 'ol lady, told me that Lily still has feelings for me I've not been able to think straight. I thought that was all dead and gone, I thought we'd buried this a long time ago. And anyway, it shouldn't matter, she's off limits.

I can't have her.

Sometimes I wrestle with the wild thought of what it would be like, but I've never acted on it. I reason with myself that she's like a sister to me and therefore she's definitely in the 'no go zone.'

I used to have women issues, back when I started prospecting, but Hutch beat that out of me, literally. I needed it. Nobody came into this club and disrespected women.

Sure, the guys all slept around, mouthed off a bit, and did what they wanted with the sweet butts, but nobody got rough with them. You'd have your ass handed to you if you did.

Hutch is big on that. Women know their place, but if you stepped over the line, like Angel's old man had, man, you'd wish you were never born.

A few weeks back when I'd been stone, cold drunk at my mom's grave, Lily had seen me at my absolute worst. Steel hauled my ass home and Lily stayed to take care of me because I was so drunk, I couldn't stand upright. I wonder and fuckin' hope nothing blurted out of my mouth that night, cause I tend to get real chatty when I'm drunk off my face.

Nobody knows about mine and Summer's past aside from Hutch, Kirsty, Helen, and Steel, and I plan on keeping it that way.

It was bad enough Steel seeing me like that at the gravestone, but Lily. Christ no. The shame of it is almost too much.

I'm still angry with my birth mom, maybe I always will be. It's not like I can ever forgive her. I still hurl all my unbridled anger at her and then there's him, I can't even deal with that bastard. Numbing the pain is how I deal with it.

Nancy said the pain will never fully leave you, but it will lessen. I guess she's right. I bury a lot of it down deep where nobody can get to it or ever find it. It's safe there and only comes out in my nightmares, and when I'm really drunk.

I promised myself all anyone would ever see was sunshine. It's part of my façade, and I play the part so well.

Lovable, stupid, devil-may-care Gunner.

Nobody questions it, why would they? I'm fine on the surface. Nothing to see here.

That's how I like it.

I'd die before Lily ever knew.

What would she think of me?

I shudder at the thought, not going there.

It actually disgusts me. I know that it's not my fault; I was a child, I was innocent, but that part of my life is so bad that her knowing would make me want to plummet off a bridge. I don't want her sympathy, God that's the last thing I would ever want. I can't even stomach the very notion of it.

Lily's so beautiful and special to me that the pedestal I've got her on is so high even I can't reach it.

But the truth is, I can't stop thinking about what Sienna

told me; Lily is still interested in me. Her words have stuck in my brain for weeks like a bad hangover and I can't seem to shake them.

It's made me view Lily in a whole new light, and, truth be told, I've avoided her where possible because I've no idea how to act around her. She doesn't know that I know.

She doesn't know that this changes things.

The rational part of my brain tells me I need to pretend I know nothing at all. Do nothing. Leave it be.

But still, it makes my mind wander and that is a very, very bad idea.

I need to let it go.

Ignore it and hope her date goes well.

But there is a sick, twisted part of me is intrigued to know if it's true. I mean, there must be some truth to it; girls talk, and Sienna wouldn't just blurt something like that out for no good reason. She told me in no uncertain terms to stop dicking Lily around and either do something about it or make it clear it's never gonna happen.

I had no idea I had to do either of those things up until now.

Do I really dick her around?

I mean, I flirt a lot, it's in my personality. I can't help it. I get on with women a lot better than I get on with guys, they're easier to talk to, nicer, and they listen, well, most of the time.

Lily's everything I'm not.

Pure.

Kind.

Beautiful.

Funny.

Everyone loves her.

When she walks into a room it lights up just by her presence. I'm proud of her too, for making something of herself in this town, for being a success, and mostly for having her own mind. She's worked hard and it's paid off. She should be proud of herself.

I remember Brock and the beating he gave me that night five years ago when he'd caught us making out, man he got me good, I was sore for weeks. All I did was think of her night after night and that didn't help my healing one bit.

I think about that night a lot. It still gets me hard. I imagine what would have happened if he hadn't caught us. It's too delicious to imagine.

The way we'd kissed. It was so urgent, so full of lust, and I realize now that it was so full of innocence, on her part obviously, not mine. She'd let me touch her places nobody else had, and I'd felt that nagging torture inside me of something feeling so right, pieces fitting, it wasn't just lust and us being horny, it was something so much more.

That's how I know I'm cursed. Because I shouldn't be going there, but I can't stop my mind from wandering and devouring every single second of that night. I secretly wished I'd done more. I wanted to fuck her so bad.

But she's Lily.

Too pure. Too good for me. Too lovely for anything I've got to offer.

I don't like complications. Women are messy creatures, I know this, I've been with enough of them to know they have baggage and most of it ain't pretty.

I wonder what baggage, if any, Lily has. I know she's barely dated anybody and that strikes me as strange.

I know I didn't feel too good when she declared she was going on that date. It shouldn't bother me but for some niggling, annoying reason, it does.

I wonder if her date led to sex.

Hell, I've never been on a date so what would I know. My

nights with women in my company always lead to sex, it's what we're there for.

It's what I do. I'm good at it.

But as much as I'd like to imagine it, I can't douse my flame with Liliana, no I can't do that. She deserves better.

I like being single. I like all my ducks in a row. No expectations, nothing to live up to, nobody to disappoint. I'm a commitment-phobe through and through but at least I can admit it.

I like sex and a lot of it. And Lily would hate me if I slept with her and couldn't be exclusive. It would feel cheap, nasty, she deserves better than that. She deserves the world.

My body may react to her every time she pouts in that way of hers, hell it always has, but I have to push the illicit thoughts away because it's too dangerous to pursue it. There's too much to lose.

She's always been different and I like that about her. She isn't easy. She doesn't chase. She's not like other girls. Yeah, that pedestal is really fuckin' high.

Still as I glance around my shithole of a room, I feel the emptiness creep in.

Oh god it's empty.

Nobody I've ever been with makes me feel anything, it's true what I said about it being just sex. It is just sex, something to get me off, to get them off, everyone's a winner. But with her everything feels foreign, everything comes alight in all the wrong sorts of ways.

When I think of her, I know she's the ray of sunshine that I can never have.

I don't want things to be weird between us and I need to stop being a dick. She can't hide from me, I know she likes my flirting and our hugs, but now it feels wrong; and I have Sienna's voice in my head reminding me I'm apparently leading her on.

I have to snap out of this cause' it's eating me alive.

I can still hug her. Friends hug, right?

Nothing is going to happen. I won't let it.

Maybe if I keep telling myself that then I may actually start to believe it. For once in my miserable life I need to do the right thing.

I need to stay the hell away from her.

It's that simple.

Surely even I can't fuck that up.

5

LILY

I JUMP UP AND DOWN, squealing in excitement with the phone pressed to my ear.

"When is the big day? Tell me everything!"

"Next month!" Crystal gushes down the line. "It has to be, I'm starting to show."

Crystal is one of the newly appointed ol' ladies at the New Orleans chapter, her old man is Ryder, the V.P., and he's finally making an honest woman of her after knocking her up.

"I'm so happy for you babes, I really am! OMG you're gonna be so fat!" I can barely contain my excitement.

"Oh God, tell me about it," she groans.

Crystal and I have been friends since we were little, she's always been destined to be part of the M.C. in some way, shape, or form. Like me she's grown up within the club, it's all she knows and she loves being an ol' lady. I just didn't expect her to move to New Orleans in order to find Mr. Right but it happens, and Ryder is a good guy, I like him.

I miss her though; we had some good times together

running amok when we were teenagers and getting into trouble.

"Next month doesn't really give you much time," I say, balancing my phone from my ear to my shoulder as I place my cup under the coffee maker and select a pod.

"I know, that's why I'm calling you, I would love you girls to come down, Summer and Deanna too, please say you'll come!"

I squeal again with delight as I push the button on the machine. "That sounds amazing, you know I wouldn't miss it for the world, I can check with D and Summer, we'd have to book flights, ooh do you have anyone to do your hair and makeup yet?"

"Are you kidding? I've barely gotten around to telling everyone," she sighs. "I didn't realize how much went into planning a wedding, I'm telling you it never freaking ends, from place cards to flowers to the freakin color of napkins! I mean, who really cares about shit like that?"

"Some people," I admit. "But I've just had a genius plan, I could come and do it for you and your bridesmaids, whatever you want baby cakes, hair, makeup, waxing, I can do it all."

"Lily, you would do that for me?" she gasps.

"Of course," I laugh. "God it feels like five minutes ago we were in detention for looking at naked guys on the internet, remember when Mrs. McCluskey totally took the phone from us so she could have a dirty old perv herself?"

"God she was such a bitch!"

Those were the days.

"We said we'd always marry really hot guys too, remember, you always wanted a guy with lots of ink and long hair, seems like you got your wish."

"He just walks by me and I get pregnant," Crystal giggles. "Like seriously, we should be locked up."

"Eww."

"What about you, how's your love life?"

"Urgh," I moan. "Non-existent, you know me, I'm a workaholic, I went on a coffee date the other night, it wasn't so bad."

"Did you make out?"

I laugh and though she can't see me, I wrinkle my nose. "It was a *coffee* date."

She laughs again. "You'll know when you meet him babes, trust me, you won't be able to keep your hands off him."

"I can't wait for the day," I sigh. Really, it can't come soon enough.

"You know, when you come down you can let loose a little bit, nobody knows you here, and there's plenty of hot guys in the club, they're not all Neanderthals, I promise."

"Famous last words," I laugh. "I recall you saying you weren't going to New Orleans to fall in love, either."

"You got me there." The warmth in her voice makes me so happy, she deserves this. She's from a broken home like me and had a pretty rough life growing up.

"Well, you deserve your happy ending Crystal, and not before time. I'm so glad Ryder's not a douche."

"You're going to make me cry if you keep it up, I'm already so hormonal with the baby, what I'd give for a shot," she laughs, I can just picture her rubbing her belly. "God knows I need it, I also have to pick out some pretty invitations so people will actually show up, apparently it's courtesy to formally invite people these days."

"Who knew?" I snicker.

Ryder treats her well and I'm glad about that, he's a tough son of a bitch like my brother, but that's how the brothers of the club are in all things. Over-protective assholes.

"Send me the deets, if you need anything before then let me know," I add excitedly. "I mean it, I am the queen of organizing after all, and I'm at your beck and call, so use me up."

"You sound so dirty," she snorts. "And thank you for offering Lil, I love the girls here, but they aren't exactly wedding planner material."

I giggle too. "Call me if you get stuck with invitations, I can help via facetime."

"I've got you on speed dial babes."

"Later."

I hang up feeling elated, and of course a plan is already brewing in my head. I smile as I pour my coffee. This is going to be fun going with the girls, letting our hair down in an amazing city like New Orleans. I have a spring in my step just thinking about it.

Getting to New Orleans could be tricky if Steel has anything to do with it, he could make things difficult because he's not only an over-protective asshole but a kill joy as well, fun goes to his house to die.

Luckily, I know how to handle him and work it to my advantage and I've got Sienna on my side, us girls have to stick together. Steel may blow a gasket about us going, but D and Summer sure are going to be excited when I break the news.

I buzz around my messy apartment, shove a load of laundry on and text Deanna to see if she wants to have a catch up before work so I can share the excitement, Summer isn't an early riser since working late nights at the club and she's now doing some shifts at the Stone Crow; I try not to text her before noon out of courtesy.

"Oh my god I love New Orleans!" Deanna claps her hands together when we meet at the Coffee Bean half an hour later and I tell her everything, she does a happy dance at the table.

"We are so overdue for a girl's trip." I agree. "And I said I'd do Crystal's and her bridesmaids' hair and makeup as a wedding gift, she's so excited."

"That's nice of you Lil, she'll love that."

Deanna orders the biggest stack of pancakes on the menu; I have no idea where she puts it.

"Well, it'll be nice as long as we get to go," I grumble, thinking about the men in our lives who make things difficult. "You know how they all are; you'd think I was twelve the way Steel acts, he's such a caveman, he's always looking down his nose at me and what I wear."

Although we're grown women, we're still obligated to get permission to go into another Chapter's clubhouse, and this is where my annoying brother comes in, as well as Hutch.

"Don't worry about Dad," Deanna smirks, sitting back in her chair tapping her nose. "I know how to get what I want, worst case scenario is he'll send a couple of the guys with us, no big deal."

Hutch is known not only for being hard-headed, but he comes from the school of hard knocks and he definitely takes no prisoners. Deanna is the apple of his eye so that could work to our advantage; she's right, she always gets what she wants.

"Hey I forgot to ask how the date with Wade went?"

I shrug my shoulders. "Not much to tell, he seems nice, wants to come to the clubhouse, in fact it's all he talks about, he likes motorcycles. I don't know if I'll see him again though. He's cute and all but I'm not sure if he's really my type."

"You mean he's not blonde, covered in ink, and can't keep his dick in his pants?"

I throw a piece of bagel at her and she dodges it, smirking.

"I'm not sure what that's supposed to mean but whatever

happens, Steel's gonna embarrass the hell out of me one way or the other." We both know that's true; he can't help himself.

"Well, I'll talk to dad and explain the situation with Crystal, and he'll call the club and sort it out with Cash, it'll be fine, you worry too much."

Cash is the President of the New Orleans Chapter, him and Hutch go way back and are on good terms.

"I could talk to Sienna, get her to try and keep Steel away. I can put up with Bones or Brock babysitting us but not my brother."

Our coffee arrives and Deanna heaps two teaspoons of sugar into hers and stirs it around. "Good plan. While I do think Steel's only got your best interests at heart, he is definitely going to hinder any or all attempts at us picking up hot guys."

I shake my head. "I'm not going down there to pick up hot guys."

"Have you even heard yourself?" she gasps. "Did you escape from the nunnery or something?"

I sip my coffee and look at her over the rim. "Ha-ha, very funny."

"I'm actually serious, it's time Lil, you're not still pining over lover boy, are you?"

Of course, Deanna's known from day one about my feelings for Gunner, none of its changed, we just haven't talked about it for a while.

I look down into my coffee. "I'm not pining, D."

"No but you're not exactly jumping off the roof about Wade, are you?"

"I didn't realize it was a crime to not like someone on a first date, isn't that why it's called *a date?*" I raise a questioning eyebrow as she studies me from across the table.

"Don't be a smartass, you know what I mean, you've been on quite a few first dates that led to nowhere," she reminds me. "I get it, you have to feel a connection with someone, but if you're still hung up on Guns then you're never going to let yourself really explore the possibility of someone else, the guy never really stood a chance."

I gape at her. "Thanks, Dr. Phil, just when I thought my mom was done lecturing me, you pull a zinger out of your ass."

She rolls her eyes. "If I were you, I'd either quit this shit with Guns or finally fucking accost him, for my sanity alone."

"I'm not even going to dignify that with an answer."

"You know what your problem is Lil?" she asks, leaning over the table in a hushed tone.

Here we go. I can't wait for whatever truth bomb is about to explode out of her mouth.

"I only have one?"

She ignores that snide comment and launches into turbo mode. "You care way too much about what people think. I get it, Steel's all overprotective and cock blocking at every turn, not to mention you're the baby of the club which doesn't help, so everyone kind of looks out for you regardless, but you've got to stand your ground Lil, go out and get what's yours, if you really want it, take it."

I stare at her.

My genius plan of luring Gunner to New Orleans and testing the waters seems so juvenile compared to Deanna's balls deep approach.

"I don't know if I can just go out and get…"

She holds up a hand to stop me speaking. "He was hot for you back then, I don't see what could have changed, sure, he's put you in the 'friends' zone' but that's only because you're Steel's sister, not cause you're not hot, you're smokin' right now Lil; I'm not even kidding, you're in your prime, if I were a lesbian I'd so go there."

I almost choke on my bagel.

"You have such a way with words girl," I laugh. "Like seriously, so poetic."

"That's why you love me." She winks. "But seriously, you need to bone Guns and get it out of your system or ditch this whole idea and move on."

I literally do now choke on the bagel.

"Shhhh!" I chastise, looking around me. "Advertise it to the neighborhood, why don't you?"

That earns me another eye roll. "See what I mean, you care way too much."

When I've finished coughing into my napkin, I take a big gulp of coffee. "For your information I've got a business in this town," I scold. "So, I don't need you screaming out shit like that for everyone to hear, I've got a reputation to uphold."

We both sober up as Deanna's extra-large stack of pancakes arrive, when the waitress is gone, she continues. "You know what you should seriously do?"

"Shove my head down the toilet and repeatedly flush it?"

She ignores me. "You need to accost him, well and truly. I'm serious, throw it in his face, amp it up so he notices you, which won't be too hard, he's a walking pogo stick, and then fuck him out of your system, voila. Problem solved."

"Problem solved?" I look at her like she's actually gone mad. "You forgot the part where not only does Steel and the rest of the boys kick the shit out of him and bury his body out in the desert, but I don't actually want to be just another notch on Gunner's belt and we both know I would be. Things would be weird between us, we can't do the friends with benefits thing, it just wouldn't work."

"Yes, that's because you have him on a pedestal and it's high time you took him down a peg or two." She tucks into her pancakes offering me some, I shake my head and keep picking at my bagel. "You also worry too much about Steel.

Guns is a big boy, he can handle it, and if he can't then that's not your problem, you're grown adults. Steel can't rule your life forever, they can go stick their archaic bro of club rules up their asses."

"Are you done with that outburst?" I laugh, shaking my head.

She's quiet for a second because she's shoveling pancakes into her mouth, so I get a moment of reprieve.

I think about one of Gunner's regular squeezes, Chelsea, and wrinkle my nose, just the sound of her name makes me want to hurl. The last thing I want to do is think about Gunner with other women, lord knows he's slept with more than I care to remember over the years, which means yes, obviously he knows what he was doing in the bedroom, and it should disgust me that he's been with so many women, it *should*, but with Gunner nothing shocks me.

My infatuation with him makes absolutely no sense, even to me.

"There's just that one small detail being that obviously he's just not into me!"

I don't get sympathetic eyes; this is why I love Deanna. She always gives it to me straight, whether I want it or not.

She looks up under her lashes and shakes her head. "You know, I don't really believe that, and like I said, you'll never know unless you take charge and put it out there, these boys act so macho, but they wouldn't know what to do with a woman who actually goes after what she wants, he's no different."

I know she has a point.

"He's not exactly boyfriend material," I mutter. "He's had more girls than I've had hot dinners, and that is a really disgusting thought."

"So what, and who's talking about *boyfriend material*? And I'd like to point out one distinct advantage; you're way prettier, smarter, funnier, and hotter than any sweet butt or chick he's been with," she blurts out. "Plus, he adores you Lil, that's no secret, if you do skate down the 'friends with benny's' lane then I have to warn you to be prepared for things to potentially turn a little awkward, it ain't all roses."

"What do you mean?" My heart races, even though I don't like the idea of friends with benefits. Too much can go wrong.

She gives me a pointed stare. "I don't think men and women who do the dirty on the regular can be friends; feelings happen, especially where you're concerned. I don't want you to get hurt, Lil, that's another thing to consider because it isn't like he's monogamous, as long as you know that and keep your feelings at bay then you can let your hair down and enjoy it. Bone him, get it out of your system, move on, repeat my words."

I almost laugh. "Monogamy? I'm not an idiot D, I know what he's like."

"As long as you do, and if you do pursue him you have to be prepared to see him with other chicks, can you really handle that?"

I swallow hard, we both know the answer to that. I know my heart would never recover from seeing other chicks draped all over him. Not now, not ever. She's right, I'm too invested.

"Yes, if I'm allowed to punch them all in the face."

She laughs. "So, just use him for sex then, that way you stay in control."

I let that sink in.

"I've never done the one-night stand thing." Hell, I've never done a one-night anything. "I don't know if I can be all those things, I don't know if the using him for sex thing is me D, he means more to me than that."

"You don't know that until you've tried it." She smiles, this time she does have a little sympathy in her eyes. "You've always felt too much, girl, and maybe that's my problem, I don't feel anything, maybe when I meet the right guy, I'll only want to be with him and I won't be giving you bad advice on how to not get your heart broken."

"I wish I had your confidence," I admit. "Then this wouldn't be so hard."

"Haven't you heard the saying?" she laughs. "Fake it till you make it?"

I laugh as well, then I sober as I consider her words for a few moments.

Could I actually do it, proposition him? Do the one-night thing?

I'm not a complete nun, I know how to work it and get a man excited, the trouble is Deanna's right, I do feel too much. I always have.

But maybe this is the perfect solution, as long as I stay away from church and don't see him with other women, that is. The thought churns my stomach, I'm already set to fail.

"The big thing is going to be getting his mindset off me being like his sister, I need to get out of the friend's no-go zone, and onto being a sex kitten," I say, a spark suddenly lighting my tone. "Not an easy feat, especially when he knew I was going on a date and didn't bat an eyelid."

I have to break this curse.

"Cause he doesn't know yet what you want, if he knew he was gonna pop your cherry, I think he'd be throwing you over his shoulder and taking you up the stairs two at a time, I heard he's hung like a fucking cobra by the way."

My eyes go round. "Eww."

She laughs. "You're not supposed to say eww, Lil, you're supposed to say something crude back like; get in my pussy."

I slap my forehead "If I was as dirty as you, I'd be hitting a home run instead of sitting here wallowing in self-pity."

She laughs again. "If all else fails, you could always start making it *really* obvious, start flirting, work your magic, and why don't you bring Wade to the party this weekend? Nothing like a little competition to get things stirred up."

My gaze falls on her. "To rub it in his face?"

"No, but if he sees another guy is going to get it then it might stir something in him, wake his cobra up, nobody's seen you with a guy at church, this could be really perfect."

"That's because Steel will pummel my date into next week; and for the record, Wade isn't going to get it, and I don't think using him to make Gunner jealous is very kind."

"Sex kitten, remember," she reminds me. "Keep all feelings at bay."

"Ah," I say, nodding. "Sorry I forgot, maybe it could be my walking mantra? I can think about patent leather and slutty crop tops every time I'm about to lose my nerve."

She taps her fork on the table. "I say bring Wade, he likes the club, and you might even get to know him a little better, test the waters, so to speak."

I try not to wrinkle my nose. It does seem a little mean leading him on if I don't plan on it going anywhere. Then again, I've not really given him a chance, and he was kind of sweet. I just don't want to use him to get something else.

My brain toys between jumping Gunner and letting him go once and for all, I need to get off this merry-go-round.

"Perfect, operation get Lily nailed starts today, we'll begin by picking out all the revealing things you can wear to drive him wild."

I shake with laughter. "You really are a toolbox D, and I don't own anything revealing enough to make him notice, I can't go to church with my ass hanging out."

She gives me a wink. "That's why you have me babe, wardrobe vulgarity extraordinaire, just leave it up to me, don't you worry, I'll have you sex kittened up in no time."

"I dread to think." I roll my eyes. "And I'll think about

asking Wade, he has been asking about the club and seems genuinely interested in me."

"There you go, ye who have little faith!"

I shake my head and wonder what the hell I'm doing.

Friends with benefits?

It's so not me, but Deanna's right, I can't go on like this.

I need to either take the plunge and let him know or forget him altogether.

6

GUNNER

"What do you mean they're going to New Orleans?" Steel is his usual jovial self at our weekly meeting at church; I swear the dude could radiate fire from his nostrils if he gave it half a chance. He's always been larger than life but when he's mad, he's unstoppable.

"I need to talk to Cash first," Hutch gruffs like he's got better things to talk about than whatever this is that I've walked in on. "Nothing's been decided yet."

"What's in New Orleans?" I ask, taking my seat next to Brock. Everyone's already here and I'm late again, not that anybody seems to notice.

Brock does a double take. "Why are you so... *brown?*" he assesses me with narrowed brows.

I roll my eyes. "The shoots coming up." I shrug, hoping he'll leave it be and that'll be the end of it.

He looks across at Steel then back at me when Steel offers no help. "What the hell happened?"

"It's fake tan," I admit. Trust him to notice, it's meant to be dark in here, obviously not dark enough.

"What the fuck bro?" he shakes with laughter.

"I've heard it all now," Hutch mutters, unimpressed. "What the fuck did you go and do now, Guns?"

I don't know why they're all so shocked; they should expect this kind of crazy shit from me by now. It's what I do, nothing's off limits.

"They said I'm too white."

"That's discrimination," Bones says across from me, trying to keep a straight face. "Seriously, don't put up with that shit."

"He has been looking a little pasty lately," Rubble pipes up, assessing me. "Bit of color kinda suits you Guns, though I'm not sure the instructions said to apply the whole fucking bottle to your face."

Of course, I expect nothing less from them and knew I'd be subject to their taunts and jibes when this went sour, still, I don't think it's that bad. I run a hand slowly down my face.

"You need to get Liliana to fix that shit brother," Steel says with finality. "Chicks know how to apply it so it's a little more subtle and not so obvious, they have machines and shit to ensure an even finish."

We all look over to him in unison.

"What?" he questions like we're the ones who are all crazy.

"Sienna's really got you by the balls," I laugh as a cough into my fist. "Next you'll be lecturing us on waxing and tinting and the benefits of sunbeds."

"It's girly shit," he replies, waving a hand around like that explains everything. "Which is why you're the asshole applying it."

"Someone woke up on the wrong side again," I mutter, giving him a big grin because I know that'll just annoy him all the more.

He levels me with a stare. "And don't you be worrying about my balls, they're quite nicely taken care of night after night, in fact, what's it been now Guns? A couple of weeks without any pussy? That's a record for you, isn't it? At least I'm getting a hot piece of ass every night, when I want it, how I want it."

I roll my eyes, for once he can brag that he's getting more sex than I am, but he's right about one thing; Sienna is one hot piece of ass. I'd been totally into her before lover-boy came charging into the rescue when Sienna had first come to town.

The reality was that I never stood a chance. It struck me as an even weirder anomaly that Steel did, and now he's sticking it to her every fuckin' night and rubbing it in all our faces. He deserves to be happy; I concede that, even though I'd never admit it out loud.

She got him good and proper.

The only way to win is with words, and while it's never smart to piss him off, I can't help but to enjoy winding him up just a little bit cause I'm a sadistic son-of-a-bitch.

"I've been busy with my Instagram following going off the charts, not to mention the
piercing and jewelry launch breaking records, in fact it's sold out online. Oh, and the photo shoot I'm being paid thousands of dollars for and all I have to do is show up and drop my pants, but you're right about one thing." I smile at him across the table. "You definitely have one hot piece of ass waiting for you at home."

"Watch it." He points at me.

And we're off.

"What? You said it yourself, Sienna's a smokin' hot babe, it's no wonder you're never around anymore; but one can hardly blame you, bro, I'd let her have my balls and do her every chance I got too if she were my ol' lady." I try hard to keep a straight face.

Steel isn't laughing, oh no, there's only been one smile

and that was when his beloved rescue pit-bull Lola became a qualified therapy dog and earned her stripes, oh and the time he finally boned Sienna, he was all smiles that day too.

"Just keep fuckin' talking, Guns," he says, shaking his head. "You won't have any teeth left in that pretty mouth of yours if you keep it up."

I shake my hands in front of me like I'm scared.

"Speak for yourself," Rubble grumbles. "I've got a raging lunatic of a hormonal wife at home, not only was she taking all those hormone injections when we were first trying to conceive, fuck, she had me performing on que like some trained circus monkey. But now that she's pregnant the mood swings are like living with Jekyll and Hyde, I never know which one I'm gonna get. You think you got problems? Bite me princess."

We all groan, not this again. We've heard quite enough about his and Lucy's bedroom escapades to last a lifetime. I have more information about the female reproductive system than I care to know about, and now I can't erase some of that shit from my brain.

It's really ridiculous that we have to sit here and listen to him complain when he's got the best ol' lady you could wish for, especially since it *has* almost been two weeks for me since I got laid, that is definitely a record, one I'm not proud of.

Maybe I'm coming down with something?

"Better watch out Steel," I smirk, sitting back with my hands linked behind my head. "Sienna's been hanging around Lucy a lot lately, she'll be nagging you soon for babies, it's only a matter of time, my man."

I love poking the bear, or maybe I just have a death wish after all.

Steel noticeably pales. "Would you like me to rearrange your face?" he asks like I would even have a choice in the matter if he were serious, and of course I wouldn't like that arrangement, he's a big guy and he hits hard.

"Not before my photoshoot," I retort. "They need me in pristine condition."

That earns a chuckle from the others.

"I'll give you a pristine condition imprint of my knuckles on your fuckin' forehead," Steel offers.

"God everyone's so touchy around here," I moan, sitting back like the cat who got the cream, when really, I got nothing. "You got the best girl in town and you get sex on the regular, think yourself lucky, you could be like Brock over here using your palm every night cause Angel's sticking it to some other guy and you won't do anything about it."

Everyone looks at him as he gives me a side eye that could cut glass.

Well, he and Angel have been fighting this for years.

They were high school sweethearts a long time ago. She now owns and operates the local tattoo studio in town, he never really got over their split, despite what he says. She has a gorgeous little girl called Rawlings who's the sweetest thing, they've had a shit time of late but Angel's a survivor.

He punches me hard on the arm. "What Angel does or doesn't do and who she does it with, has nothing to do with me, fuck face. And we're talkin' about *your* dick falling off from neglect brother, not mine."

"Will you shut the fuck up?" Hutch barks, before I can retort. He usually shuts us down a lot sooner than this; clearly, he has a lot on his mind right now. "We're discussing New Orleans when you bitches have finished. Deanna, Lily, and Summer have been invited to Crystal and Ryder's wedding, which leaves me in a predicament I'll need to discuss with Cash; but if I let them go, they won't be going alone. I've known Cash and most of the boys for years, but that doesn't mean I trust any of them with my girls."

Summer hasn't told me anything about this which is typical, and neither has Lily.

"Some of us should attend," he goes on. "Out of respect and to keep an eye on the girls."

"Count me in," Rubble pipes up, anything to get away from his wife's hormones for a few days.

There's a whole lot of ungratefulness going on around this table.

"And distract you from Daddy duties, wouldn't dream of it," Hutch replies, earning snickers from around the table. "Brock, Bones, and Guns can go with the girls, just because they're the New Orleans chapter and I know them well don't mean shit, and you know what Deanna can be like, she'll lead the others astray."

Yeah, she's a real wild child that one.

"When's the wedding?" Brock asks.

"Two weeks, Deanna has all the details."

"Will be pretty wild," Bones puts in. "Jett's a good guy, we can trust him to look out for the girls, Tag too, he's a straight shooter. Nothin's gonna happen to them." He looks over toward Steel who's noticeably silent. After the whole Lily drugging situation, I know he'll want to come because he's been torn up over that since it happened.

"Steel?" I say, as he glances over to me. "What's up, you worried about Lily?"

"Of course I'm worried about Lily," he barks out like it's obvious. "She was drugged and almost date raped, in our hometown, behind a fuckin' dumpster, I can't even imagine what kind of trouble she'd get up to in fuckin' New Orleans for Christ sakes. You know what she's like, trouble seems to find her a whole lot quicker than common sense does, lookin' out for her is a full-time job."

"We'll look out for her, for all of them," Brock agrees. "Nothing's going to happen, we won't let it."

"No, it won't, because I'll be going."

Great, the fun police get to tag along. Just awesome.

"Speaking about that night and that asshole in jail," Hutch interjects, referring to the fuckhead who drugged Lily. "I have some news from county."

We all turn to look at him.

"Fucker was found hanged in his cell a few nights ago, seems he has a rap sheet a mile long and drugging and raping young women was just one of his many specialties, nasty piece of work, they're looking into links for human trafficking and illegal prostitution amongst other things."

Holy shit.

My blood runs cold. Steel's eyes flick to mine.

Being a survivor of child abuse, this hits close to home, except I didn't have the luxury of being drugged when it happened to me over and over, I was fully awake each and every time. While Steel and Hutch know about my past, the other brothers don't, and I wish to keep it that way.

I shift in my chair uncomfortably.

"Who was on the job?" Rubble asks.

Hutch shakes his head. "He took matters into his own hands unfortunately; pity, I had plenty of sleepless nights lined up for him in the state pen, a couple of guys owe me, too bad he won't get to suffer, that's what really pisses me off."

My mind tries to wander but I don't let it, I don't ever let myself go there willingly. This guy made his own bad decisions, I had no control over what happened to me and Summer. Which is one of the reasons I'm still so angry, we were fucking kids.

I let out a slow breath and try to calm my beating heart.

"I'll kill anyone who tries to hurt her, or Summer or Deanna or any of the girls for that matter," I blurt out of nowhere. Well, it's the truth, not only would I do anything for my club and my brothers all sitting at this table, but the club girls too. They're my family.

All heads turn to face me. This is something close to my heart. I've been my sister's shadow for as long as I can remember, she keeps to herself a lot, I worry about her.

I wish she'd go back to school instead of working at the bar but she never finishes anything, there's always excuse after excuse.

"I'm still going, to keep an eye on things," Steel says to Hutch. "It's gonna be wild and out of control and we can't take any chances, need I remind everyone it's my job as the enforcer of this club, and where Liliana is concerned, that's all my business."

God it's no wonder Lily doesn't have a boyfriend or anyone permanent on the scene, come to think of it she's not had that many boyfriends at all. I guess one look at her older, scary, badass brother and you'd be shitting your pants. Who could blame a guy? I'd probably run a mile too and I've plotted my own escape many times over the years.

"Nothing's going to happen, Steel," Hutch reiterates. "Cash will make sure of it, you think I'd send my own daughter down there if I thought they'd be in danger? And nobody is going to stop you, if you insist, but I don't want any trouble."

"Look how we party," Steel counters. "Need I say more."

Shit yeah, he's got a point.

The girls are far too pretty and vulnerable at another clubhouse; some of the guys who don't know any better will be trying their luck for sure. My blood curdles at the thought of someone touching any of them, it seems like Steel isn't the only son of a bitch who's protective.

"*Used* to party," Bones offers. "Past tense, you've been broken in now bro, it's all downhill from here."

"Glad someone finally said it," I laugh.

"Fuck off," Steel replies, he's not having any of it today. Something's pissed him right off.

"Letting them go is the right thing to do," Brock agrees, ignoring our banter. "If we resist or make it harder than it needs to be, they'll only find a way to go regardless, at least this way we have full control, nobody has to get their panties in a knot over what they're doin', and things won't get out of hand."

I'm glad he's so confident.

"I don't like it," Steel mutters.

"He's right," Hutch agrees. "You know what the girls are like, between the three of them they're as thick as thieves, that can only brew trouble."

"Speaking of babysitting duty, how's Cassidy going?" I ask Steel across the table. He looks up with weary eyes.

"Ask Colt." He nods sagely. "She's formed some kind of attachment to her 'rescuer'."

I glance at Brock, this is new.

Cassidy is Sienna's cousin who was kidnapped by Sienna's ex-boyfriend and held at ransom, the guy was completely off his rocker, he almost killed her. He's dead now, a tragic car 'accident,' terribly sad. The club took care of it, or rather Steel and I finished off the job when he took an unexpected fall after Steel punched him out. He deserved all he got after what he put Sienna through, and from what I saw of what he'd done to Cassidy; the guy had it coming. The world is less one more crackhead.

"What'd he do? Ride in on a white horse or something?" Rubble chuckles.

Brock rolls his eyes. "This would be funny if the situation wasn't so fucked up, the chick won't leave him alone though, I think he's genuinely scared."

I can't help but to laugh. Colt is newly patched in and can hold his own just fine, but this is kind of out there.

"Wait, he's not like… tapping that, is he?" Bones asks, genuinely curious.

"He better not, he's living on my couch most nights," Steel mutters, unimpressed.

"She feels safe with him, he's the one who picked her up after the ropes came off her wrists and ankles, he took her to the safety of the car," I interject. "She's got Florence Nightingale Syndrome, it's a thing."

"Didn't know you were so sentimental, bro." Bones kicks my shin under the table.

"Oww fucker, it's obvious to me, she probably needs to get some help if she's latching onto him."

That earns me more curious looks; it's a bit insulting they all think I'm so dumb. I did complete a degree in digital marketing and graduated with honors, something Hutch made me do before I was allowed to patch in; but nobody cares to think about that because I take my clothes off for a living and pierce kids ears as a sideline.

"Since when are you an expert on kidnapping victims?" Brock asks, genuinely surprised.

"I watch a lot of cable." I slap him on the back. "I know a good therapist if you're interested in working any of your shit out."

"I got no shit to work out," he gruffs.

We both know that's not true.

Hutch rolls his eyes then turns to Steel. "How bad is it?"

He doesn't look impressed. "Bad enough that he's around *a lot*, and it's starting to affect my down time, he's slept on the couch four times this week. It's got to fuckin' stop at some point, I get that it's traumatic for her, but for fucks sakes."

"Jesus Christ," Hutch says. "Why didn't you say something?"

"I really think she's permanently damaged," Steel grumbles. "Sienna's looking into therapy but it's hard with what happened, we can't have her revealing any of that shit to anybody cause it'll get back to the pigs."

Hutch deliberates for a moment. "Kirsty knows someone," he says. "I'll send her details over later; we can trust her."

"Appreciate that." Steel nods. "I've got her helping Sienna in the office for the time being to keep her mind off things, it's worse at night when it's quiet. She was beat up pretty bad, I feel sorry for the kid, but she needs help."

It has been a few weeks since the whole kidnapping incident, and judging from when I saw Cassidy last, I could tell she was a world away from being okay.

Hutch shakes his head. "Keep me informed on her progress. I'll talk to Cash later today, anyone else got anything important to say?"

"Yes," Bones pipes up. "Can we please do something about Gunner and that weird ass orange color permeating from his skin, it's giving me the creeps."

Everyone laughs and I flip him the bird.

Hutch bangs the gavel down; the meeting is over. I get up to leave and shove Bones with my shoulder for the hilarious comment.

"Maybe if you spent more time doing actual work than doing stupid ass shit you wouldn't be having to go get my sister to bail you out," Steel says.

I turn to Steel because I'm only half-way done with getting a rise out of him. I never really grew up or lost my stupid sense of humor, some may say I subconsciously try to make up for the childhood I lost. Or maybe I'm just a glutton for punishment.

"I don't mind her bailing me out, but I've got a better idea, if you're gonna be out of town then maybe I should stay home and swing by to keep Sienna company for that weekend? A change is as good as a holiday, so they say."

He goes to elbow me in the ribs but I dodge him, knowing his signature move well by now.

"You'll be coming dick cheese, that's if Lily doesn't kick you out of the salon for scaring the customers away lookin' like that."

"Ah that's alright, I'm not worried, they line up round the corner like moths to a flame," I interject. "A little off-color fake tan won't put them off, trust me, a bomb scare wouldn't deter those soccer moms."

He mimics my voice in a try-hard girlie tone which just isn't even passable as an imitation.

"I wouldn't trust you with my ninety-year-old Grandmother," he adds as we head across the main foyer floor.

"That's because she has impeccably good taste and she knows a good lay when she sees one."

I just dodge his fist to my face as he shakes his head and calls me more obscene names under his breath.

One thing we can agree on is that I have to go see Lily tonight, even though it's late. She can clean up the mess I've made, she'll know what to do.

This is what I get from avoiding her when she could have just done it in the first place.

I don't want to go to her apartment, she'll laugh at me, but she's my only hope right now. The gig is in two days and I doubt they want an orange-colored buffoon on the front of Sizzle Magazine. I can't jeopardize this shoot, I've a lot riding on it.

I smirk to myself. I'm gonna be rolling in dough, and all I have to do is strip and pose in several suggestive positions, they even want a shot of me on my motorcycle. I also get to use some of the footage on my Instagram and Facebook stories with a link to buy the magazine and images online. I have a separate 'Gunner After Dark' page with a fans' only subscription. I'm not gonna go full frontal or anything but some of the shots leave little to the imagination. This is gonna be serious pay dirt.

"Hey dick face," Steel calls to me as I mount my sled in the lot. I give him a chin lift as I pull my helmet on. "I know you meant it about protecting the girls, especially after what Lil's been through, that means a lot that you have her back when I'm not around."

"Lily's a good kid," I say, and I mean it. "I'd do anything for this club, for you, all jokes aside, you know that."

He nods. I lean over because I can't help myself and offer him my fist, I've done this since I was seven, he fists pumps me back.

"Later, Guns."

"Yeah, later dude."

Then he glances back and shakes his head for the hundredth time. "Go sort out your fuckin' tan, you're scaring the shit out of me."

I laugh as a roar my sled to life and take off like a bat out of hell.

7

LILY

I stare down at the text message and my heart races in my chest.

- *Babe, you around? Need your help ASAP. Emergency.*

Gunner rarely texts me unless it's to do with work.
I quickly text him back.

- *Hey, are you okay?*

- *Yeah, but I kind of did something stupid.*

I stare at my phone. I hope he's not drunk again, oh no. I really don't want to be the one making sure he doesn't choke on his own vomit like the last time, once was enough.

- *Did you drink too much again?*

Please say no.
A reply bounces right back.

- *Completely sober. I'm on my way.*

I dread to think what kind of emergency could have him hightailing it over here at this hour of the night but I'm not going to argue.

I also just got off the phone with Wade, he actually asked me about the party on Saturday at church, he seems really into it, but not exactly what you'd call potential biker material. I've taken Deanna's advice and taken a stand. I mean, she's right, Steel can't go around telling me what to do forever.

I quickly run into the bathroom to assess my appearance; disheveled hair, pajama pants with one leg not rolled all the way down, fluffy socks, and a sloppy Snoopy t-shirt, this won't do. I don't want to scream sex kitten tonight but still, standards people. As fast as the speed of light I brush some bronzer on my cheeks, add a swipe of cherry lip balm to my lips, and drag a brush through my hair, slinging it up in a high ponytail. I quickly run to the bedroom and throw on the first pair of jeans I can find and drag on a Metallica t-shirt, ripped in all the right places, just as I hear the familiar sound of straight pipes getting closer.

A few minutes later there's a heavy thump at the back door.

I pick up several things scattered on the landing as I pass and dump them in the hallway cupboard. Thank God I tidied up earlier, the rest of the living room looks presentable enough if he comes up. I don't want him thinking I live like a slob.

I run down the stairs and peer through the peephole of the back door. I take a couple of deep breaths, hoping it's not obvious that I ran, and I begin to free the locks, all three of them because Steel insists on overkill.

I'm thrilled, when I eventually open the door, to see he

really isn't drunk, and he doesn't appear to be bleeding or anything either.

"Gunner?" I say questioningly, wondering where the fire is.

"Yeah, it's me babe."

"What's wrong?"

I move aside to let him in.

The minute he steps inside I see the problem.

"Oh shit!" My hand flies up to my mouth as I cover it.

He turns around and looks down at me.

"Yeah, yeah I know, I already got a ribbing from the boys, go on get it out now if you really must."

"I have no words," I say honestly. I bite my lip and hold back an outburst of laughter as I turn my back on him to bolt the door behind us.

Fake tan? Gunner used fake tan? I can only imagine the amount of shit he would have gotten at church.

"Hope you checked the peep hole before unlocking that," he states; he hasn't moved from the doorway.

He's wearing a black long sleeve Henley, his usual cut and jeans that fit in all the right places, his eyes a sparkling blue mixed with a hint of cheeky. He's a force of nature, even though he's the wrong color right now.

"I did," I say, turning back to face him. "Overdid it on the tanner then?"

"No, I love going out in public looking like this just for kicks."

"Jesus Guns."

"Is it really that bad?" he frowns as I stare at him.

"I wouldn't pay for it," I laugh.

"Luckily, I didn't, home job, very cheap. Go figure."

I shake my head. "I can tell. Honestly Guns, I don't know why you didn't just come to me in the first place."

Yeah Guns, I'd be happy to have you strip naked and spray tan your entire body. The very thought sends tingles down my spine.

He leans back against the wall, in no hurry to go anywhere. "You cost a fortune," he says with a wink. "Can't afford you." It seems playful Gunner is back, yippee.

"I wouldn't have charged you for heaven's sakes."

"I don't expect shit for free." He pushes the hair grazing his forehead back with one hand. He smells so divine it should be illegal. "You're worth every penny."

"You're just saying that because you need me to fix you."

His mouth twists into a smirk. "Touché."

He pushes off the wall and prowls towards me.

He has this look in his eyes that's very predatory, I've not seen this in quite some time.

An alarm bell goes off somewhere in my head telling me he's like this with everyone and he's just flirting because I have something he needs. This is what Gunner does and he does it well.

"You sound like you're flirting with me, Liliana Marie." The way my full name sounds on his lips is nothing short of orgasmic. My mouth goes dry, but I hold my own, stepping back as he comes towards me.

"I wouldn't dream of it, but I do need to take you upstairs," I fire back.

His lips curl into a smile.

"Sounds a little taboo, baby doll. What do you plan on doing with me?"

"You need to exfoliate; it's the only way to remove the tan and in order to do that we need my bathroom."

My legs hit the counter as he stops right in front of me, too close; he smells like musk, cigarettes and nighttime. It's so intoxicating that I grip the bench behind me with brute force.

"Exfoliate?"

"It's a product with little granules, or usually a glove, it'll get it off without it being patchy."

"You know your shit, I'm impressed," he says. I hope he doesn't notice the rapid rise and fall of my chest.

"Well, I didn't go to the most expensive beauty school in the country to learn bad techniques." I roll my lips inwards. "So, you up for it?"

He purses his lips. "Someone's in a naughty mood."

I know I'm flirting back but I really don't care. I've earned this.

He brushes a lock of my hair off my shoulder with his fingers as his beautiful eyes study me. My skin feels like it's on fire when he touches me. I'm momentarily stunned out of my diatribe.

Why is he touching me?

He's been so strange for a few weeks, barely speaking to me, and now he's all Gunner on steroids with the compliments. *Don't read too much into it...*

"Get your mind out of the gutter. If I don't remove the tan then all of your girlie fan club will be so disappointed if the shoot gets cancelled, we don't want that now, do we?"

He smirks again, his eyes drop to my lips. "Girlie fan club? I'll have you know my main following is stay-at-home mommy types who drink turmeric lattes and have made yoga pants a fashion statement, it's a force to be reckoned with," he laughs. "And rich, over-the-hill old women with too much time on their hands come a close second."

"You're impossible," I sigh, pretending my heart isn't racing in my chest at his close proximity.

"Fine, you can take me upstairs." He grins. "But no funny business."

Don't read too much into it... don't read too much into it...

I break away from our reverie. "Of course," I say,

sashaying over to the door that leads upstairs to my apartment. "I'm sure I can restrain myself."

I hear him laugh behind me.

"I've never been in your apartment," he states, as his heavy boots thud on each step behind me.

"Well, it's pretty small, we can do the grand tour in five seconds. Do you want a coffee or anything?"

"Won't say no." He follows me into the kitchen.

I turn the coffee machine on that sits on my counter.

My apartment is pretty small but it's cute and comfy and it has all I need.

I grab a couple of cups from the overhead cupboard.

"How do you take yours?"

"Straight up."

"No sugar, cream?"

"I'm sweet enough, aren't I?" he laughs, I turn to look at him over my shoulder as he grins.

"Do you say that to all the girls?"

He smirks. "Only the ones who are going to de-tan me."

I feel a flutter in my chest, and I know it's stupid. "I should charge you double for being on call after hours."

Little does he know I'm watching Vampire Diaries on Netflix.

"I'll make it up to you," he promises. "You know I'm the best re-gifter ever."

"I can't argue with that," I reply, the hot liquid filling one cup. I change the pod and make another, adding milk to mine. "Let's go into the bathroom then so I can assess the damage."

I carry our cups and he pushes off the counter to follow me. It's only now that I'm noticing just how much smaller everything feels now that he's in my apartment.

"You did the place up nice, Lil," he tells me, looking around.

"Thanks, it cost a bomb, was a real shit hole when I moved in."

"You've done well for yourself."

"Yeah, well the bank certainly thinks so, I'm in their debt for about thirty years so I plan on being here a while."

I shove the bathroom door open to reveal my shower/bath/toilet combo, there's barely room for me, let alone him. He follows me in, taking up *all* of the space.

I ignore his proximity and rummage through the cupboard behind the mirror until I find what I'm looking for, the glove and the bottle of tan remover.

I turn to face him. "Sit."

He moves around me, smirking. "So bossy Lily, I think I like this side of you."

"Ha-ha, park your ass."

He shrugs off his cut, lays it over the towel rail and sits down on the side of the bath, spreading his legs wide. His Henley is tight and clings to every perfect muscle on his body, which I try hard not to notice.

"What are you going to do with me?" he asks, one eyebrow quirks in question.

Why does everything he say sound so sexual?

"I'm going to patch test it first as the last thing we want is you coming out in a rash, so you'll need to remove your shirt."

His face almost pales at the rash comment, I doubt it will, but it's best to test it first.

"Now you want me naked?" he teases.

I wait with my heart hammering in my chest, pretending I don't care, averting my eyes.

"Just the shirt's fine, you can take the bottle home once I show you what to do." I have no idea how I make the sound of my voice even. I've not seen him shirtless for years.

He grabs the hem of his shirt and swiftly lifts it over his head.

I'm met with a flash of color. I forgot how many tattoos he has under there and he's added a lot more since I saw his chest last. I take the opportunity to study his body, he's so ripped it should be illegal, no wonder he's stripping for a women's magazine.

He has a smooth chest, but he does have a trail of hair south of his belly button that disappears into the hem of his jeans. I can't even think about that, good grief.

He's bulked up a lot too, in fact, he's goddamned perfect, his torso is a gift from heaven... and it's then I realize I'm staring.

"Liliana Marie, my eyes are up here," he murmurs.

Oops.

I snap my attention back to his face where he gives me a lopsided look.

"You got more tattoos," I say, my mouth dry as I try to sound normal.

He throws his shirt over my head where it lands on the floor. "Yeah I did, you know me, I'm a sucker for pain."

Play it cool, god damn it.

"You also have a really bad tan application," I add as I shake my head, assessing the damage further.

"Rash aside, you can fix it right?" he sounds a little panicked, I know this shoot means a lot to him.

"Shut up and hold still." I turn and move to the sink, wet the glove under the faucet, then apply the remover and move back towards him.

Jesus it's so cramped in here, it's like he's everywhere.

"I don't bite," he says when I try to keep an arm's length away from him.

Does he even know any of my inner turmoil?
What's more; does he care?

I'm a coward at the end of the day, an insufferable coward at that.

I step between his legs and touch his left pec with my free hand to hold it taught, I then move the mitt around in circular motions with my other hand. He grips onto the side of the bath.

My eyes shift to his and I feel my heartbeat accelerate.

There is complete silence as I work.

"It's coming off," I say after a few moments. I feel like I have cotton wool in my mouth.

"Lily," he murmurs as I purposely don't look at him.

"Hmm?"

He moves his hands to my hips and holds them there ever so gently. I don't know why he's touching me; this doesn't help my raging hormones.

"Do you ever think about it?" he asks softly.

Oh.My.God.

What? He did *not* just go there.

"Think about what?" I reply, as if I have no idea.

I see in my periphery his head move to watch my hand working on him, touching him.

"You know what."

"If you mean *us,* that's ancient history, remember?" We've never really addressed it, truth be told.

"I know, but it's a pretty simple question." He removes his hands and places them back on the side of the bath. "Do you ever think about what we did?"

I breathe in and out slowly. "You mean what we *almost* did?"

He laughs. "I gave you your first orgasm, if I remember correctly?"

My cheeks heat at his words.

"Gunner…"

"What? Just answer the fuckin' question."

I purse my lips. I can't lie to him.

"It was too long ago," I whisper, afraid of baring my soul to him. He'll break me.

"I do," he tells me softly.

He tips his head back and looks up at the ceiling for a long moment as silence falls between us.

I stop what I'm doing.

"I shouldn't." He brings his crystal blue eyes back to me. "But sometimes when I'm alone and it's quiet or I need to settle my mind, I let myself go there and…"

I wait as he trails off, his eyes squeeze shut for a second.

"And what?" I ask, feeling like I have no air in my lungs.

"And it feels like fuckin' paradise."

My eyes go wide. I don't know if I'm still breathing but his eyes drop to the floor.

"Gunner." I can barely whisper his name.

He looks back up at me. "Fuck you're beautiful Lil, I just want you to know that…"

I blink once, then twice. His hand moves to lift my chin, so I'm looking at him.

"But you know why we can't, don't you?"

And there it is. The age-old excuses he's about to throw at me.

My stomach plummets.

I know he feels it too, his eyes look hungry, or maybe that's just what I want to see. I don't know any more.

"Nobody has to know." The words leave my lips before I can stop them.

"Lily…"

"Well." I shrug. "It's the truth, we could."

"You say that like it's so easy."

"Right, because I'm Steel's sister and you can't go against the unwritten bro club of ethics?" I laugh without humor, shaking my head.

"That's not the only reason."

Oh great, that makes me feel so much better.

"Just take this home and use it twice in the shower," I reply. "Wet the glove fully and just move it around until the tan starts to come off, don't scrub too hard, it'll make your skin red and dry…"

"Babe please, I can't handle you being mad at me, Steel trusts me, I can't do that to him, there's lines you can't cross in the club. You know that, I wish things could be different."

I shake my head; I want to hurl the bottle at him. How humiliating. "Can't do it to *him*," I mutter.

Tears threaten, but I won't give him the satisfaction. I've wasted too much time already and I refuse to let him get the better of me. I'm going to bring Wade on Saturday night and maybe *he* won't care about anything to do with my big brother, Gunner, and club rules.

"Don't be upset." He goes to touch the side of my cheek and I pull away.

"I'm not upset," I defend harshly. "You're right, let's not overcomplicate things, right? I'm not exactly a revolving door like you are, so it should be fairly easy."

He winces at my words. I don't know why, he's the one known for the most notches on his belt, the only one he doesn't want is me.

He pulls me closer to him, holding my elbows.

"Gunner, don't."

"Look at me!" he says firmly.

I bite my lip because if I don't the tears will flow and I won't be able to stop them.

"I didn't know you still felt that way until recently, but with *us* we'd be crossing a line, one that's been drawn and one we can't get blurred. We're friends, *fuck*, we're like family, and in the club we're brothers, he's my brother and bedding you would be a betrayal."

I won't give him the satisfaction of crying in front of him. I'm not a child. "It's fine, I'm not good enough, not loose enough, you don't want me like that, I get it loud and clear."

He puts both his hands on the side of my face so he's looking directly at me and I can't squirm away. He grabs one of my hands suddenly and places it over the very hard bulge in his jeans.

"Does that feel like I don't want you?" he hisses.

I'm so shocked that I gasp at the contact. "Holy shit," I whisper. He's rock hard.

"Don't ever say anything like that to me again you hear me? *You're* too good for *me,* that's the problem, that's always been the problem. I've had to stop myself from wanting to do so much more than I'm able to over the years. In the end we both know I'm not capable of more Lil, I'd hurt you without meaning to, I fuck up everything, you know this about me." He sounds bitter, his thunderous eyes glitter like a raging storm. A small shiver runs up my spine, not that I'm afraid of him, but the depths of despair I see there haunt me.

I stare back at him; he truly does look distressed.

A traitorous tear escapes my eye and I could kick myself. He frowns when he sees it, releases his hand and brushes the fallen tear away with his fingertip, studying it carefully.

My heart is doing somersaults at his revelation. Everything else is blurry and uncontrolled. It's best to stay still and pretend none of this is happening.

I move my hand against his hard length and he groans.

"Lily," he pleads. "We can't."

I move in closer, my lips against his. "Yes, we can, you put my hand there for a reason and you're the one making excuses, not me."

I move my lips to his and I kiss him gently, softly, and all those memories of years gone by come flooding back.

"You're driving me mad, woman," he murmurs. His lips

find mine and even though it's slow and controlled, its hungry too, passionate. His lips are soft, sensual, beautiful. I feel his tongue enter my mouth and I groan incoherently.

"We need to stop."

"No, we don't."

"It's for the best," he groans, still kissing me, our lips part then meet again, and again.

"Say it like you mean it." I throw back at him, my hand still rubbing him through his jeans.

His eyes bore into mine. "Technically you kissed me first, and you shouldn't have done that, babe."

I don't reply, there's no need.

He looks down at my hand and then, as if he's reluctant, puts his hand over mine to stop me. My body, however, burns like a volcano about to erupt. He's lit the fire in me once more and this time it can't be contained.

"I wanna know something," he whispers against my lips.

I have no words, so I just nod.

"Why haven't you found anyone steady?"

Because of you, you stupid dummy.

"Now that you mention it, I'm bringing my date to church this weekend," I tell him, hoping for a reaction. "He's really quite nice, respectable, a good Catholic boy." I add all the sarcasm in the world to my tone.

He pulls back to look at me. "And you're kissing me?"

"It's a second date, we've not even touched."

He purses his lips as he studies me and he's about to say something else when suddenly his phone chimes in his back pocket. He pulls it out swiftly, reads the text and looks back up at me.

"I have to go babe, but listen, I don't want to fight with you, got me? We'll talk about this later, in the meantime behave yourself and stay outta trouble."

He stands up and leans over to get his cut, adjusting

himself in his jeans. I bite my bottom lip with my teeth knowing I turned him on.

Oh, if only my dear, old brother could see him now.

He looks at me like he doesn't know what to do with me and he's probably right. He takes the bottle of tan remover and the mitt from my hands.

"You have to give me a visual, when the tan's all gone," I say, looking up at him as sultry possible, hoping I pull it off.

"Liliana," he warns. "I gotta ride home with this raging hard on, no need to make it worse."

I glance down to his groin and I can't help the smile on my face.

The jolt of electricity between us when we kiss is undeniable, I feel the heat radiating from him, he can say what he likes but I'm going to make sure that he and his archaic band of brothers will re-write the rule books.

Too bad if they don't like it.

8

GUNNER

I MOUNT my sled and glance up at the window to Lily's apartment and close my eyes for a second.

What was I thinking?

I'm in half a mind to go pound the door down, get her to let me back in, then I can take her to bed and keep her big, beautiful lips, her hands and pussy busy all night. The way her mouth felt against mine, her small, tight little body… holy shit, *I'm fucked.*

Then I remember that just an hour ago Steel fist pumped me and thanked me for looking out for her.

Jesus Christ.

What have I done?

Why did I kiss her back and let her fondle me? I mean, placing her hand on my cock? What was I thinking?

Well, I know why, she's drop dead gorgeous and I was in the moment.

It doesn't help she's got a body built for sin, her tits… hell, I could spend eternity there and never resurface; her soft, full mouth, those big blue eyes looking up at me…*no, no, no…* this isn't good, not good at all. I should have stopped it, not encouraged it.

Starting something with her would be suicide, I know that, but another part of me doesn't give a fuck.

I want her.

I've always wanted her.

Ever since Sienna dropped the truth bomb, I've been in a daze because I didn't think it was possible that she still thought of me like that. I figured it was just puppy love back then, nothing more.

I'm not exactly a revolving door like you are, so it should be fairly easy. I cringe at her words.

Okay I've been with a lot of women but that was chilly, hearing it from her lips; devastating. It's got me all tied up in knots and I don't like this feeling, I can't identify it, it's like I can't control myself.

I run a hand over my face and try to shake off all of what just happened.

I try to dig deep to understand why I don't just take what I want, screw what Steel thinks, he can beat me into oblivion then we'll be done, I'll recover. But I know the answer and it kills me to admit it.

Fuck it. I respect her.

A small part of me knows that I'm bad news and all wrong for her, I've got too much baggage. Lily deserves better than that.

Our brotherhood at the Rebels is strong; we have bonds that can never be broken. We keep each other's secrets; we'll take shit to the grave. It's not just a club, it's a family.

What do I honestly have to give her when all's said and done?

Except my body, yeah, I could give her that, I could give her that all night long, but I doubt it would quench my thirst.

I can't give her my soul because that's broken, and I don't

know if I even have a heart, I mean it beats and all, but it holds resentment and a whole lotta hate. That's a bad combination for somebody like me, someone so volatile.

I care about her, sure, but I destroy everything without any purpose or intent, it just happens. It's like I radiate darkness, it creeps into my bones and suffocates me. It's why I prefer to sleep alone, I can't put anyone else through my nightmares, that would be unfair and then I'd have to explain. I can't let her see into any of my past. That's a no-go zone.

My shame stays only with me and even if it lurks close by, threatening to overcome me, I won't fucking let it.

I can't because I know I will break her, even if the sinner in me doesn't give a shit, a rational part of my brain takes over and reminds me that I'm nothing and she's well out of my league. It screams at me to walk away.

Lily isn't like other chicks, she's smart. She doesn't need a man to prop her up or look after her, she's doing what she loves, gotta respect that, too.

I had to let her know, though. That she had it all wrong. That old saying *it's not you, it's me,* really is true; in this situation it explains everything, even if she doesn't understand.

So why am I sitting here outside her apartment with a huge hard-on that won't quit and a racing heart beating out of my chest like a runaway freight train?

What is this exactly?

I don't know, I've never had such strong feelings before; it's making me all sorts of confused.

I feel connected to her.

She gets me.

She's never looked at me like a piece of meat like the other girls do, clawing their nails into my back and inevitably trying to get my pants down. She looks at me like I've got something intelligent to say, which I rarely do, but that's how it is with us, how it's always been. She actually gives a shit. And here I am thinking all kinds of dirty things while manhandling her and leading her down a slippery slope.

I can't take that kiss back now and I don't want to. It was perfect, just like her.

I think back to when we got caught by Brock and he'd kicked my ass, how later I'd even googled the distance between Arizona and Mexico to see how far I'd get on my sled. Why he hadn't ratted me out I'll never know, but he'd beat me up bad enough so I'd never even look sideways at her again. And I didn't.

Now I've led her on, *again.*

Me and my big mouth. I just don't know when to quit.

When I'm in the moment, I just can't help myself. I blurt out the truth because that's who I am. And it almost always gets me into some kind of trouble. I should know better; you'd think by now I would have learned something valuable in all the years I've been alive.

I gun the engine and pull my helmet and goggles on, maybe the cold night air might do something for my sanity; it might bring me back to fuckin' earth instead of up in the clouds acting like a mad-man; like I can just do what I want, with her I can't.

No. It's best to just forget all about this and keep busy, stay away from Lily for a while. Except now she's bringing her fuckin' date to the party on Saturday night, the thought rattles me for some reason. I feel a surge of protectiveness and not just that, I feel infuriated imagining this guy touching her and I've never even met him.

I've never been the jealous type, but after having her lips on me and imagining doing all kinds of nasty things to her, it has me reeling.

I've got to get control of myself.

I rev my engine loudly and take off down the alleyway, skidding as I turn onto the main street.

Two weeks ago, if a woman had me pent up and frustrated like this, I'd go hunt down a sweet butt and fuck her senseless, that's how I roll.

Not this sweet shit with Lily. Soft, sensual kisses, her hand gently caressing me, both wanting to do more.

I think back; has a woman ever been gentle with me? *Hell no.* But my body can't deny that I like it, I like it a whole damn lot. Now I've got a piece of iron between my legs that doesn't appear to be getting the memo that the night's over, and the thought of going to Chelsea disgusts me.

I've never let chicks get to me like this, they don't get under my skin, and they don't get any piece of me except my body.

No one gets my mind, no one.

Nobody gets my heart, like I said; I don't even have one. It's tarnished. Shattered. All kinds of fucked up.

I can't be fixed.

And I intend to keep it that way.

～

"Beautiful, a little to the right, chin up a bit... now tilt towards me, yes that's it... perfect! And back to me, a little attitude, yes!" The photographer is hurling orders at me left, right, and center, and I'm following along okay, I think. This isn't my first rodeo though it is my first naughty shoot.

I'm actually kind of calm on set, cool on camera, and 'acting' like I've done tons of these shoots before, when in reality this is my first big paid job, and I've got no clothes on.

I realize 'Sizzle' isn't exactly anyone's life-long dream, but I got plans, and those plans cost money and this pays more than laying bricks and tinkering with cars which is what I've been doing lately, I've never used my degree unless it's marketing my side lines.

If people wanna pay to look at the goods then so be it, they can pay and look. It's just my body and a pretty face, may as well use it.

The first round of snaps were kind of tame of me shirtless on my sled with my jeans unbuttoned out in the lot of the Sizzle HQ.

Thank god the awful tan is gone, replaced by something more subtle that Lily gave me that washes off. On these kinds of shoots though they want to put makeup on you, which you have no say in, and my hair is so thick with gel it may never come down from sticking up on end. I don't want to look like a fucking pretty boy, I get enough ribbing for my baby face from the boys as it is.

I'm not shy, I never have been, especially where my body's concerned, but I wonder what Lily will think of the photo's when they inevitably get *out there.* She'll see them soon enough.

Deanna runs my website, Instagram, Facebook, and the jewelry line I'm launching. I'm hoping that the attention I get from this might boost some sales.

Deanna is trying to launch into interior decorating herself and she's pretty good at it, I help her out while she's in between the jobs she gets. She's the only one who doesn't judge me and I dig that about her.

"Gunner, honey, you're doing great," my agent Teresa gives me two thumbs up. She's a Texan ball-busting, big haired scary woman who would cut you if you got on the wrong side of her. She's only small but wears six-inch stilettos and though she's over fifty she'd give women half her age a run for their money. She keeps herself well. She took me under her wing and gave me a chance with no modelling experience.

She likes me. And I like to keep her onside.

I've always had this way with women. It's no secret, I don't know what it is.

With her it's not sexual, Christ she's old enough to be my mother, but I've been told I have this endearing quality about me, something that pleads to the heartstrings. Women want to fix me, or some shit.

Teresa has grown sons older than me so she's definitely not trying to fix anything, just her bank account. Making coin off my ass has been long awaited scratch for her too. I mean, I love her and all that but for a good pay dirt she'd sell my organs on the black market for scientific research.

I move over to the bed and this is where things get a little raunchier. I'm not totally nude in the photos but I may as well be, it doesn't leave much to the imagination. My brothers are going to give me so much shit about this I can just see it now.

I'm in boxer briefs lying on my front, then I lie on my back. I have to look at the camera like I want to eat it, according to the photographer. Every now and then I get told to move my head this way, move it that way, look up, look down, but the photographer says I'm a natural. I wonder if she's just being nice because really, I look like a loser.

They want a side shot of me in the buff with me holding my briefs over the goods, and that obviously means removing *all* my clothes. It's kind of weird but I'm cool with it, I didn't take this gig and expect to keep my clothes on.

I hope to god these photos look alright though, the last thing I want is Sizzle changing their minds and dropping me off the cover and no centerfold. That would be embarrassing. I'd never live it down.

Still, I strip in a room full of strangers because I need the cash.

I hold my discarded briefs over my junk and face side on.

It's a tough gig, you gotta remember to hold your stomach in, flex, smile or not smile, look mean but don't grimace, look cheeky, look sexy, look fuckin' bewildered but not scared, and hope to god you don't look like an ass. I certainly feel like one.

It feels like this last part is just dragging on and I should be having more fun than I'm actually having, I don't like taking myself so seriously.

When we're finally done, I get handed a robe and I slip it on gratefully. Teresa, who's been here the whole time watching, has now just seen me naked, awkward. She slaps me on the back like a Quarterback coming off the field after a good innings. Maybe I should start calling her coach.

"We're gonna be rich, cowboy," she whispers. She's got long, colorful nails and her eyelashes are longer than my... *never mind.*

"I fuckin' hope so," I whisper back. "Please tell me that was okay and I didn't look like a complete asshole."

She shakes her head in disbelief. "Better than okay sweetie, it was fabulous; it's gonna be their biggest issue yet, that last shot in black and white, it's gonna be the money shot. I'm telling ya that was cookin' Gunner, I told ya I'd make you a star."

She fans herself while grinning like a Cheshire cat, that is Teresa talk for *Fuck Yeah.*

"I hope so, I need the scratch, babe."

"It'll come, don't worry."

"You think?"

She leans in. "Well, if I wanna go home and do bad things to my husband Trevor after watching that, then I'm pretty sure all the other girls who read Sizzle are going to love it."

I glance at her momentarily stunned. "You sly woman you, glad I got you goin'." *Go Trevor.*

"You're always doubting yourself," she goes on, wagging a finger at me. "I've said it before and I'll say it again; I knew it when I first saw you, Guns, I said he's someone, he's something, you've got a look, a niche, it's unique, don't be surprised if by this time in two weeks when the magazine launches my phone is inundated with more jobs, come on, what hot-blooded female doesn't love a tatted up biker babe in flannel!"

"Or without," I mutter, there was plenty without.

"Give the fans what they want, sweet cheeks."

"You're like a magic genie," I say, shaking my head. At least she's enthusiastic, that gives me hope. "I owe you for lining this up, but I'm sure you'll take it out of my commission."

"You've always been my favorite." She gives me a wink and I know she's shrewd but I do like her.

This is why she gets paid the big bucks.

"I bet you say that to all the dudes with their asses hanging out."

She gets signaled by one of the Sizzle execs and pats me on the arm. "Be right back darlin'."

Oh yeah, she's lovin' me now.

I should be happy. I should not feel anxious like I'm feeling right now. I don't usually get nervous but knowing these pictures will be out there for the world to see, well, I don't want to be a laughing stock, no matter what Teresa says.

I wonder what Lily will think and why the fuck would I care?

The more I think about her date, the more I don't want to think about her doing anything with him, with anyone, unless it's with me, and that is very, very dangerous.

I wish I could stop thinking about her, I'm like the same song on repeat.

I go into the dressing room, disrobe, pull my jeans and ripped t-shirt back on, and check myself in the mirror. I look different. The makeup chick put fucking eyeliner on me, it's subtle, brings out my eyes, but I hate all this shit. I want to wash my face and take off. I want to go home and I need a stiff drink or two, I think I've earned it.

More to the point I need to wash away any thoughts of Lily and that kiss and where her hand was located.

I'm a dumb fuck, I should never have encouraged her like that, why can't I just keep it in my pants? Why did I let her kiss me?

Just the thought of her… I look down at my bulge and sigh. "Not today champ, not ever with her."

I need to get a grip, and fast, before I lose control for good.

9

LILY

"Get your ass over here pronto," Deanna says, the minute I answer my cell.

"Are you alright?" I ask, stopping in my tracks at her urgent tone. It sounds like I'm in trouble or something. I'm taking towels out of the dryer and I dump them in the laundry hamper.

"I just got Gunner's Sizzle shots through to my email."

"Holy crap."

My mind wanders to Gunner in all his glory.

"I know it's poker night but come now so I can show you before the others get here."

We have poker night once a month, it keeps the boys off our backs and gives the girls an outlet to get out, gossip and have some fun. We don't play for real money but sometimes we truth or dare the losers with shots.

"I'm leaving now." Nothing could be better than having a sneak preview of Gunner's shoot, I'm so intrigued to see how the photos came out.

"I suggest you bring your fire extinguisher," she laughs wickedly, and I know right there this is going to be good.

"Be there in five." I waste no time in jumping in my Camaro and hightail it over to Deanna's apartment across town.

She's on the sofa when I let myself in, her head buried behind her laptop.

I plonk down next to her and look over at the screen.

"Hey!" I say when she doesn't bother greeting me.

"That was fast, did you run all the red lights?"

"No, but I brought wine." I hold up the bottle and she grins.

"Now we're talking."

I look back at the screen but don't see any Gunner. "How much out of ten would you rate him as a model?" I ask.

"Fucking five thousand."

I cannot contain my giggle. "Jesus, hurry up would you, I'm growing old here."

She double clicks a file icon and we wait impatiently for it to open.

"He's allowed to use a couple of shots for the gram with Sizzle's website in the link, so he's sent these over to see what I think," she tells me. "I'm gonna upload whichever ones he wants later, I wanted you to see them first."

"Does he know that?" I watch the screen, a little thrill of excitement running through me.

"Hell no."

"He isn't coming over, is he?" I look around nervously.

"No, and why are you acting all weird?"

I haven't told anyone about my and Gunner's little make out session in my bathroom from the other night. Best keep that to myself until we figure this out, not that there's any *we*.

"I'm not."

The file finally opens and my eyes go wide as I see Gunner lying on his back, he's on a large four poster bed clutching a sheet that covers the lower part of his man parts.

He's looking directly at the camera, his blue eyes staring back at me. They look hauntingly beautiful.

His golden blonde hair is slicked back off his face; he looks different, like an angel.

A fallen angel.

He's so perfect; his eyes, his body, his physique, his tats, that wanton look he's sporting, damn it, he's the whole freaking package.

Deanna smirks when no words come out of my mouth. I'm in stunned silence.

"Told ya."

"Holy shit," I whisper.

"Yeah, no kidding, I got a bit hot under the collar looking at these myself and I don't even think of him like *that*, eww," she says, disgust filling her tone.

She clicks onto the next photo, same backdrop but he's on his front now, the back part of him is slightly faded out but you can see his bare ass. The look in his eyes is a mixture of sex, lust, and a whole lot of attitude. I mean, he's gonna break hearts just by the smoldering look he's got going on. It's off the charts.

My throat goes dry. I'm certain these are going to launch him into some sort of overnight sensation. He definitely has the whole model characteristic down pat, along with all the right sexy poses.

"God he's so photogenic."

"And ripped too, those abs are ridiculous."

"Right," I agree. "He's always been pretty to look at but this is insane, if he got any hotter, he'd burst into flames."

"That's because he's naked," she says, like it's obvious. She has a point, I guess.

Thinking of the almost innocent but illicit kiss we shared taunts my every waking moment. It's all I've been thinking about.

I shake my head, as if that will help. "That should be illegal."

She laughs. "Well lucky for us it isn't, and the Sizzle customers are going to get their money's worth this month." She continues to slide show through the file, the pics seem to get raunchier as we go on.

Him straddled on his bike with a black leather jacket on but no shirt, his jeans are loose and unfastened. There are plenty more with him shirtless in various poses, in some he's dazzling with his trademark smile, in others he's serious. I like the one where he's leaning against his bike looking over his shoulder, wearing only his tight boxer briefs.

He could be an underwear model, there's no doubt about it. He could sell anything.

His tats look epic too, smattered all over his skin like a fine work of art. I've never seen him with his hair slicked back but he suits it, they've also put liner around his eyes and smudged it, so he looks like some fallen cowboy/bad boy rocker/ sexy biker all rolled into one.

He's glorious, just when I thought he couldn't get any hotter he knocks one out of the park.

"But wait for it." She pretends to do a drum roll. "This is the cover shot, I'm not allowed to use this one but he attached it to see what I thought."

She opens it and I let out a squeak as the black and white picture of him completely naked springs on the screen, he's side on with a muted background. He's holding his underpants over his crown jewels while pouting at the camera cheekily, like he's all that and he knows it. His muscles are flexed, his tatts on display, his skin glowing. I've never seen anything so intense, outwardly provocative and sexy in my life.

"I know," Deanna sighs. "I may need to go hit my vibrator later, seriously, it disgusts me to even say it."

GUNNER

I bite my lip. "I'm impressed, it's his first big shoot and it's like he's literally made to do this, he's going to sell a million copies." I'm only stating the truth, albeit if not a little biased.

"I know, not bad for a day's work, he gets paid per view on top and if people subscribe from the link, he gets a percentage."

Suddenly the doorbell sounds from downstairs and we both jump, it's like we've been caught doing something we shouldn't.

"That'll be one of the girls," Deanna says.

"Oh, are you gonna show them the photos?"

She shakes her head, getting up to look at the monitor, then she presses the button to let Sienna up.

"Nah, gotta keep this under wraps babe, Gunner will kill me if he knows I showed you."

We hear Sienna on the stairs and I'm still staring at the black and white cover picture.

"When's it out?"

"Two weeks, quick shut it down." Then she looks up at Sienna at the top of the stairs. "Hey Sienna!"

"Hi!" Sienna's holding a bowl of something and has a bag of corn chips under her arm, she hugs Deanna then comes over to the couch. "I made chili con queso, oh holy crap, what's that?"

Deanna and Sienna are both looking over at me. I've clicked the x button at the top of the screen but the laptop's frozen. Deanna slaps her forehead.

Sienna moves forward. "Holy shit balls, is that *Gunner*?"

"Yes." I nod, whoops. "Sorry D, the screen froze."

"She's glued to it; I need my vibrator and I'm not meant to be showing people."

Sienna moves over closer to the couch. "Oh, his big shoot was yesterday, right? Looks like things went well." She snickers as I giggle too.

"Yep, he's going to be insufferable," Deanna complains. "As if his head isn't big enough already."

"I may need a cold shower." Sienna sits down next to me and leans closer. "Are there anymore?"

Deanna laughs. "Oh yeah."

"Tons," I add.

"Let's see them then, I won't say anything."

"You'd better not," Deanna says, plopping back down on the other side of me noisily. "Especially to Steel and definitely not to Gunner, he'll hand me my ass."

"Steel can eat dirt," I mutter, I'm so sick of worrying about him.

She waves a hand at me. "He won't find out, and anyway, I'm allowed to look at the menu, as long as I eat at home."

Deanna wrinkles her nose. "Please never use that phrase again."

"Yeah, like TMI," I agree.

I click onto the next picture and we all lean closer simultaneously. We spend the next few minutes looking through the photos again, each one better than the last, each time we all make suggestive remarks that shouldn't be repeated in public.

"God, he's so hot," Sienna marvels, like she's only just noticed.

"He also wants me to set up Gunner After Dark, that's where he gets subscribers to sign up to his monthly subscription service and they get exclusive pics and content that you can't get elsewhere, the photos are a lot saucier in After Dark though."

"Saucier?" Sienna and I chime out in unison.

"Just more revealing stuff, no full frontals or anything, calm down." Deanna takes the dish Sienna is still holding and puts it on the coffee table with a bag of chips she's holding in the other hand.

It's been four days since our make out session and he hasn't texted me or said anything.

Typical jerk face behavior, I've come to expect it, but I try not to let that hamper tonight.

'Sometimes I let myself go there and it's like fuckin' paradise.'

I remember his words, hell I've got them ingrained into my brain.

He's just so into the club rules and I'm just so not. Unspoken law my ass, he's making this way more complicated than it needs to be.

The club sees me as the baby as I'm the youngest and that comes with complications, like everyone is always treating me like I'm a child. I hate it, I'm not a kid anymore, I have my own business and adult responsibilities, but none of them see it that way.

And in any case, Gunner didn't seem to think I was a child when he had his tongue down my throat and his hands all over me, so he of all people can cut the crap with the *you're Steel's sister* mumbo jumbo.

"When the boys see this..." Sienna says, breaking my reverie. "They are gonna flip out."

I shake my head. "Oh, I know, they're going to die, jealous fuckers."

The door buzzes again.

Deanna jumps up. "Ooh, it's Lucy and Summer."

She lets them in and doesn't get me to shut the laptop down or even attempt to, sworn to secrecy has all gone out the window.

"What's everyone doing?" Lucy asks, sharp as ever as all of our faces are turned to the laptop screen. Then she sees what we're looking at. "Holy mother of God!"

Deanna turns to her. "Yeah, but you can't say anything to Rubble, I'm not supposed to be showing anyone, now everybody knows!"

"Oh my god I'm going to be sick," Summer cries, she puts a platter of celery sticks, carrots, and dip on the countertop and moves closer with her nose wrinkled. "I'm gonna need bleach to erase that image from my brain, kill me now."

We all laugh.

"Holy cannoli, what the fuck?" Lucy exclaims. "He's got some buns on him, hasn't he? So tight. Jesus, Mother Mary, and Joseph, look at those abs, I could eat off them. Why am I so late to the party on Guns in the nod?"

Summer shakes her head and pretends to gag.

"Well, you have been busy getting knocked up," I remind her. "That'll do it to you."

"I only just got the photos," Deanna explains. "And I mean it when I say close your big mouth, if Gunner fires me, I'll need to find another part-time job."

"He's not going to fire you," I laugh.

"I'm just wondering why you'd even wear clothes at all?" Sienna says, fanning herself.

If only the brothers could hear them now, they'd have a fit.

"Umm because living relatives don't want to see their sibling's bits hanging out and their ass on display." Summer places her hands on her hips and points a finger at Sienna. "Thanks for *that* visual, I'm repulsed beyond belief, you've all probably scarred me for life now."

"He's allowed to put some of these on his Instagram page." I fill them in. "D's supposed to help him decide which ones make the cut."

"Well, he'd better pick the least naked one for the gram or they'll boot him off for indecent exposure." Summer is still averting her eyes and looking unimpressed. "Do you really need to sit here ogling the screen, I thought we came here to play poker?"

We all ignore her whining.

"Just imagine if it were Jett," Deanna, ever the big mouth, puts in helpfully. "Then you'd be all over it in a nanosecond."

We all turn to look at Summer. Jett is one of the brothers from the New Orleans Chapter, he came here last month to help the boys with the new security system for the Stone Crow after the whole drugging incident. And nobody missed the interested eyes he'd thrown her way. He's quiet though, nothing like any of the boys in our club. He's dark, handsome and very mysterious, it gives him a sexy edge that begs to know more.

"What did I miss?" Lucy says, almost choking on a celery stick.

"Nothing." Summer rolls her eyes.

"He was so into you," Deanna singsongs in a high-pitched voice. "Couldn't keep his eyes off you all night at the bonfire. He didn't go upstairs with anyone either, good looking guy like that could get anybody, maybe he's abstaining cause he's lovesick." She cackles as we laugh along with her.

"He's so hot," I agree. "Broody, mysterious, gagging for it, what more could you want? And D's right, he only had eyes for you."

"Yeah, and he lives in *New Orleans,*" Summer reiterates like we're all stupid. "Did you forget that small detail?"

"Like that matters." Lucy rolls her eyes. "For a one-night thing who cares? And he's got a tight ass too, bet he'd go for hours with those hips, you can tell a lot from a man by the way he walks, if he's got a swagger, you know he's gonna kill it between the sheets."

Gunner definitely has a swagger.

More nods and yeah's go around the room; honestly, these chicks are worse than the guys.

We all know Summer doesn't do one-night things; she doesn't even do one-year things. She's worse than I am when it comes to dudes and dates.

"I like to get to know a guy first," she defends, busying herself with something in the kitchen. "Call me old fashioned but if I don't like the guy and he can't make me laugh then he ain't getting any of the good stuff."

"Old fashioned!" Lucy calls out, going in for more dip. "You chicks overthink things way too much, give the guy a break."

"Shoulda just shook him all night long," Deanna chimes in. "Gave him something to pine over when he left." She's always been more than comfortable in her own skin; she knows how to get the guys and keep them interested.

Summer mutters something from the kitchen that I can't make out.

"Did I ever tell you guys the story of how me and Rubble met?" Lucy says, shoving more chips down her neck.

"Yes!" we all groan at the same time. God, if I have to hear one more time about Lucy giving Rubble a lap dance because the stripper at the club he was in sucked, then I'll go mad. Granted, she wasn't stripping at the time, which is what makes the story so epic, but still. Overkill. We do not need to hear it again.

For Summer's sake I quickly change the subject back to the topic at hand and off Jett.

"Gunner's ass though, guys."

"I have to admit it's a fine specimen," says D. "I don't know which I like best though, gonna be hard to choose."

"It could be a wonder of the world." Lucy could almost wipe the drool from her mouth. "If I weren't married, I'd tap that all night, I don't care if I'm ten years older than him and his surrogate sister, whatever."

I almost choke on the chip and dip I'm eating.

"It should be," Sienna agrees. "His body's like a temple, wonder how many sit ups he does to get abs like that?"

"Assholes, were probably born that way," Lucy grumbles. "Why is it they can eat anything they want and not count calories, I just look at cake and I blow up like a Macy's sale float."

Deanna jumps up and comes back with wine glasses in her hand and pops the bottle of red, omitting Lucy with a large lime and soda instead. "Guys suck so much."

"Right, that's it!" Summer threatens, she leans behind me and slams the laptop screen closed. Rude.

We all groan our complaints at the same time. "I came here to play poker, not stare at my brother's dangly bits and his bare ass all night. If we're not going to play, I'll go home, and I'll take my guacamole with me."

I lunge for the dip in question and hug it to my chest. "Looks like the guac's staying, babe."

"Calm down," Deanna laughs. "Don't get your knickers in a twist, we're gonna play."

"Speaking of poker," Lucy interjects. "Some of the brothers were wanting to know what we're getting up to having a girl's night every month. Rubble actually thinks we're going to light up cigars when I told him about poker, he nearly had a heart attack." She rolls her eyes and rubs her belly at the same time. "Stupid fucks."

"He's just concerned about you," Sienna retorts, always the peacemaker. "I'm surprised he didn't come with you and want to play, though."

We all laugh at that. He has been a tad overprotective where Lucy's concerned.

Lucy snorts. "You're way too nice and still new around here honey, trust me when I say, they try any which way they can to control us with their big ol' domineering ways, well I told Rubble to mind his own damn business and I'd be home when I'm good and ready and not to call me every five minutes, do him good to fend for himself for a night."

"Sure you did." Deanna shakes her head.

We all know that no matter what she says, Rubble, like

most of the guys, will say we're too lippy for our own good and then try to take their balls back by trying to control us, the key is only giving them an inch, not a mile. So I'm told.

"Fend for himself?" I laugh, shocked.

"Well, I left his dinner in the microwave, I'm in the nesting phase, sue me."

Deanna frowns. "Hope I don't have him coming up in here checking we're not all smoking cigars."

"Why are men so annoying?" Lucy complains.

"Hold up." Sienna raises a palm. "In the first few months I got here, all I heard day and night was you being 'so in love' with your old man and how you did it on every random surface ten times a day." We all snort with laughter. "Now he's stupid and annoying?"

"He's less annoying when he's driving it home honey," she drawls.

Sienna's eyes go wide. "Guess I asked for that."

"He never stopped whining about all the sex he was getting at church when you were trying." Summer joins in. "Any man would be bragging about that shit, not moaning about it."

"Oh, he moaned alright." Lucy waggles her eyebrows. "Let me tell you, now I'm pregnant he won't come near me, says it's not good for the baby."

"Wow, is that true?" I wonder, sitting up, I don't know much about babies and being pregnant.

Lucy shrugs. "My doctor says it's fine, it's healthy even, but Rubble's grossed out that the baby's like inside while he's... you know..."

I wrinkle my nose. "I kind of get his point."

"TMI," D says, pretending to jam her fingers in her ears. "Bet he's secretly got baby names all picked out, kids got a good chance of being adorable, if it takes after you, anyway."

Lucy plops next to me on the couch. She's almost four

months and hardly showing a bump. "He says if it's a boy he's gonna be Axel, if it's a girl Rain or Storm, though God forbid we have a girl."

"Bet he thinks he only shoots out boys." Sienna rolls her eyes.

"Yep, you betcha he does, it'll serve him right if it is a girl."

"What do you want?" I ask.

She smiles. "I honestly don't care, long as he or she is healthy... and looks like me."

I snort and pass her the chips. "Married life sounds so blissful." My tone is purposefully sarcastic.

"Gotta get under their skin," she tells us knowingly. "Know what makes them tick, once you do that and it sticks, it's all over... *for them.* They think they make all the decisions and hold all the cards, but pillow talk is a very underrated commodity. Y'all should be writing this down by the way, don't believe for a second that the women of this club don't hold power and we just do what they say, we hold more than you think."

"Jesus, where were you when I needed you?" Sienna throws her hands up.

"I told you; treat them mean, keep them keen, you'd do well to remember that Lily." She points at me.

"Thanks for the advice," I say, rolling my eyes. "But I'd rather swallow razor blades than put up with half of their bullshit."

Sienna meets my eyes. Well, maybe she sees through my bravado. I'd wear Gunner's cut tomorrow if he asked me to be his ol' lady but they don't need to know that.

I decide then and there that on Saturday if Gunner doesn't bat an eye my way then I will abandon this whole idea of us, not that there is an *us*.

I'm a Steelman. If he doesn't want what I have to offer, then screw him. Seriously.

I know that if it comes to it; I have to let him go, as much as it will kill me, I can't keep playing this game.

"You say that now," Lucy replies with a wink.

"I brought chocolate mud shake shots," Summer interrupts. "Who wants one?"

"Me!" D and I chime together.

"I'll stick with vodka, thanks," says Sienna.

"This is the downside of being pregnant," Lucy grumbles. "I can't get drunk and I can't get any dick."

I sputter out half my wine and then choke on it.

Lucy side eyes me. "Seriously girl, be smart, stay single."

"You don't mean that," I laugh. We all know she loves Rubble to death but it's equal amounts of love and hate mixed with downright irritation.

"You're right, I don't! Be smart, have your own harem, don't settle down until you've experienced at least *one* threesome."

I slap my palm against my forehead.

"Oh lord," Deanna groans.

"Eww." From Summer.

"You're kidding me? That's just gross." I crinkle my nose at the thought.

Lucy just smiles and I know we're in for a long night, she's worse when she's sober.

And it's only nine o'clock.

10

LILY

My skirt is too short. It's black pleather and leaves nothing to the imagination. I paired it with a Ramones tank top with a slit down the front and sky-high black ankle boots.

I've spent a lot of time on my appearances tonight. I've gone the whole nine yards and I'm waxed within an inch of my life, not that I expect anything to happen, but a girl's gotta feel good all over. I also curled my hair so it's wavy on the ends and hangs halfway down my back.

I don't want to look as easy as can be, but I do want Gunner to notice.

I know Steel will tell me to cover up if he gets sight of me, but that's just Steel. He does it to all the girls and he's worse with me.

Steel has been through so much in his life, given up so much to make sure I had the best education after our Dad died just after I was born. I never knew him so none of that holds any significance. I know Steel only does what he does out of love, and I try to remember that when I want to choke him.

I meet Wade out in the front parking lot of church. He's

never been here before, but he knows a few people who have. Friends of club members are allowed on invite, but they aren't exactly allowed to pick up the sweet butts or take anything that may belong to the BRMC, those girls are for the patched members only, even the hang-arounds, you don't want to be caught chatting any of the girls up unless you're a patched member and want your face rearranging. The boys see it as the girls who come to church to party and drink their booze, eat their food and hang around their club have to pay for it somehow. It's sexist and kind of in the dark ages, but the girls that come here don't seem to think so, they're lining up to get in line to screw a bad, boy biker.

Gunner included, I think about all the women he's been through, being the best looking he's never short of women falling all over him. I'm so used to seeing it that I barely notice it anymore, I kind of just turn a blind eye to it. That was before we made out though, now the thought of seeing him with girls all over him makes me feel a little jealous, okay, *a lot* jealous, but I've got a fool-proof idea of making *him* the jealous one by being on Wade's arm all night.

Wade's in university completing a second major, I should know, it's all he talks about. I never realized on our first date how much he likes to brag. Aside from his grades, he also likes to rabbit on about motorcycles and hot rods. I should remind him this is an M.C. not a hot rod convention; if anyone hears him, he may be wearing his smile on the other side of his face.

Wade's not bad looking, he's dark haired, has nice eyes, built like a quarterback; but he isn't really the type I go for, for one he isn't blonde and beautiful.

Tonight, there's a bonfire outside in the back field behind the clubhouse and someone's set up loudspeakers in the neighboring trees. The boys don't need an excuse to party, oh no, just any random old Saturday night will do and by the looks of things, the party's in full swing.

We hold hands as I cross the threshold, a few of the regulars give us nods and I notice a few appreciative glances coming my way, I take that as a promising sign.

Deanna and Lucy spot me and I introduce them to Wade, not that they can hear over the throng. I keep his hand in mine as we go inside to get some drinks.

Inside the club is thick with bodies, people playing pool, dancing, hanging at the bar.

I don't need to look to know where Gunner is, his usual place on the couch. He'll have girls on either side of him, he always does.

Sure enough, our eyes inadvertently meet across the room. He's got his arms slung around two sweet butts, one of which may as well not even be wearing a tube top; it's barely covering her inflated, very fake looking breasts. I ignore his chin lift as I drag my date along with me to the bar. I make sure to sashay my hips in full swing all the way there, I know his eyes are on me and I like the odd look he's giving me, like he disapproves.

I do feel bad in a way because deep down I know I'm stringing Wade along, but the minute I turn to him he starts babbling about the Harley Davidson picture on the wall. I should be happy he isn't droning on about hot rods. He hasn't even commented on how I look or my outfit, and I know I look good tonight. He's barely noticed me; maybe I'm not as hot as I think I am? I guess I won't feel so mean should things not work out between us, which they won't. One look at Gunner and I know that I'm not attracted to Wade in *that* way.

I pretend to be interested in the picture as he gets us some drinks; he doesn't even ask me what I want. My ass buzzes as my phone goes off. I reach around and pull it out from my purse that's strapped across my body.

I read the text with bug eyes.

It's Gunner.

- That's a pretty short skirt.

I can't help the sly grin I have on my face, hmm so he *has* noticed. With my back still to him I respond.

- Oh, hello to you too.

Not like he's been in touch these last few days either, it's like our kissing and fondling never happened, maybe he's hoping now -in the light of day- that it didn't. I wait a few seconds and sure enough another message pings.

- That's your date?

I roll my eyes, what is that supposed to mean? Wade's cute enough and well dressed. He's normal, not that Gunner would know any of that, but he doesn't look like a freak.

- Yes, isn't he cute?

- Oh very.

I can't help but to feel his sarcasm just a little bit, who is he to judge? He's got two girls slobbering over him.

I drape an arm around Wade's shoulders. He's oblivious to my touch. I look down at my phone and send Gunner another message.

GUNNER

- Which one are you taking upstairs tonight, or should I say, which two?

The thought of him doing two chicks just about sends me over the edge. Wade passes me my drink, a vodka martini, and I down it in one gulp. He looks at me sharply.

"Long day," I mouth as he frowns then goes to order me another one. It's best he thinks I'm an alcoholic, so he doesn't get too attached. I rub his back flirtatiously, then turn around looking out across the room, avoiding looking over where Gunner is. I lean back against the bar and my phone pings again.

- Who says I am?

I roll my eyes, just for his benefit because I know he's watching me.

- I know you, revolving door, remember?

Ouch. That's gotta hurt.
He replies instantly.

- Maybe you should be concentrating on your 'date' instead of me and what I'm doing?

Okay, fine, I can play this game.

- Oh, I will be concentrating on him later 😊

I look up at him deliberately and smile. He doesn't look impressed. Oh no he does not. Good. *Suffer in your designer boxer briefs, asshole.*

It's juvenile, but I continue to touch Wade, my hand

117

gliding up his back. Gunner's eyes flick to my hand as he sips his beer. I shift my eyes to the left of him, Chelsea, typical, she's pretty enough but she's been with all the guys in the club because she's easy and she likes to brag. She's also oblivious to our little exchange across the room, she's prattling on to the girl next to her. My eyes flick to his right, the girl with the 'barely there' tube top, she leans over and whispers something in his ear, jabbing a finger in his chest, he smirks and gives her a chin lift.

What did she just say to him?

My eyes narrow as his eyes flick back to me; he keeps that goddamn smirk on his face. If he's deliberately trying to piss me off then he's succeeding, but instead of going over there and tipping my drink on her head, I roll my eyes and turn back to the bar.

I have to keep a level head. Keep calm; don't let him think he's getting to me. That's the plan and I have to stick to it, if he doesn't like me flirting with Wade or having a date with him then he needs to come over and do something about it.

My phone beeps again. I laugh at something Wade says, when he looks at me expectantly, I realize he's asked if I want to go outside. Oops, I need to pay better attention. I nod and we move away from the bar, I read the message as we walk.

- Since when do you drink vodka martinis?

I link my arm through Wade's as we make our way outside and toward the stage where the band is playing. Hmm, didn't know that Gunner was now Mr. Observant too.

I type back as we make our way across the back courtyard to find Deanna and Lucy. I'm glad I haven't spotted Steel yet.

- Maybe you should be concentrating on one of your dates, if you can call them that.

My phone goes silent for a long time as we mingle around. I don't even want to think about what Gunner is up to in there. Now that he's had his lips on me, it seems I've become a green-eyed monster. If I do anything reckless tonight it'll be his fault, not mine, and if these vodka martinis keep slipping down the hatch, I may not be responsible for what I'm gonna do next.

He doesn't reply and I don't care.

I dance with Lucy and Deanna. Sienna shows up a little later, which means Steel is now lurking around, I'm hidden amongst the crowd so hopefully he'll just mind his own business. My date's talking to some other blow in that he's made friends with and Colt joins them as they start talking bikes.

After what feels like an eternity of dancing, I need a drink of water. Sienna and I skip to the bar and I admit, I've had a few martinis but I'm not drunk, just a little tipsy. We pass by Steel on the way, he's talking with Hutch and Bones. He gives Sienna a squeeze of her ass on the way past when he notices me and frowns a whole lot, I tug on Sienna's arm, so she doesn't stop.

"Slow the bus," she says in my ear.

"Can't, I'm trying to go unnoticed."

She looks down at me. "In that outfit?"

I roll my eyes. "No, from Steel."

"Ahh." She nods. "Good plan."

"I may need you to go distract him for me."

She grins slyly. "Oh yeah, what are you scheming?"

I bat my eyelids innocently. "Who says I'm scheming?"

She glances around then her eyes come back to me.

"You're asking for trouble, I can tell."

"My middle name's trouble, haven't you heard?" I smile as we get to the bar. Ginger's slinging drinks and Summer and another girl called Stevie are busy making cocktails and all kinds of weird concoctions. Sometimes they like to get creative.

"And anyway, it's time I let my hair down, let loose a little, have some fun, like what Lucy said."

Nobody should ever take advice from Lucy.

Sienna looks down at me, concern crossing her face. "Have you spoken to him yet?"

I shrug. "He says we can't. Same shit different day."

Sienna rolls her eyes.

"I know right," I go on. "Pathetic, he's more worried about Steel pounding his face in and their stupid rules, so that tells you everything."

"What a schmuck, he needs to grow some balls."

"Totally, he thinks he can just get away with murder because he's so god damned pretty, well he can't anymore, and I'm over him anyway, I've got… Wayne." Lies, it's all lies.

Sienna turns to me again with a pointed look. "Isn't it Wade?"

I slap my hand over my mouth. "Wade, yes! My date *Wade*. I know his name, speaking of date, where the hell *is* he?" I look around, I haven't seen him in over an hour, like I even care.

"Last time I checked he had a boner for Colt's Harley, they all went to look at it out the front, he put new fenders on it or some shit."

I roll my eyes. "Lame, I mean seriously, look at me Sienna. I'm wearing a skirt that's illegal in several countries and he's out the front looking at a Harley frickin' Davidson!"

Sienna laughs. "It's probably for the best he's doing that if you're not into him."

"Wait, who says I'm not?" Have I made it that obvious?

She shrugs. "He isn't Gunner."

Don't I know it.

I turn and look for him on the couch but he's not there,

my heart sinks. He's probably up there now in his room, banging those chicks into next week, the thought churns my stomach.

I'm used to him doing this. I'm used to seeing him with other women. It was stupid to think we could ever be anything more. I'm an idiot.

I act like I don't care, maybe tonight I really don't. Maybe I am actually done with him.

He doesn't deserve my loyalty anyway; he can go to hell.

We each order a Pina Colada, because that's what you do at a biker party at BRMC and we go back to where all the action is at the front of the stage, we dance until my legs feel like jelly. Lucy's gone home; she can't take not drinking and partying without alcohol, but Deanna's in full swing and my friend Katy has joined in too.

We link hands, dance, carry on like crazies, and all the while nobody approaches us, not even my date, he's probably off somewhere banging an exhaust pipe by now.

Every now and again I see Steel on the outskirts of the crowd, he keeps looking over at Sienna and every now and then he runs both hands through his hair. He's got it so bad.

I never thought Steel would get tied down after his divorce, he's the toughest guy I know, and look at him, he's got an ol' lady and she runs his office now, probably bosses him around behind closed doors too, he'd do anything for her. Nothing caved down on his head because he decided to commit, and Sienna's awesome, she's like a cool big sister. If he screws this up, I'll kill him myself.

I pull Sienna towards me and shout in her ear. "My brother's seriously boning for you."

She laughs out loud then looks up and over to where he's leaning on the post near the side of the stage and blows him a kiss.

"Need me to go distract him yet?"

I look around but don't see Gunner; he's probably still upstairs getting a hammering.

"No, it's fine, probably gonna go home soon anyways."

"With your date?" she smirks, she knows the answer to that.

"Definitely not."

"Don't worry, there's plenty more fish in the sea."

"Yeah." I hide my disappointment well, I'm good at it. "I'm sure someone around here owes me a dance before I go."

"Better wait till I drag Steel upstairs."

I wrinkle my nose. "Eww, you wouldn't."

"It's not *that* bad, he's a neat freak, remember."

Oh yeah, I forgot that.

"How did you tame the wild beast?" I wonder sipping my drink with a laugh. "I mean seriously? I'll keep it on the down low if you tell me."

She shakes her head smiling, clearly just as smitten as he is. "He's really a pussy cat behind closed doors, we didn't exactly click at first, but he persisted, the more I pushed the more he pulled. Now I can't imagine my life without him."

I almost choke on my drink at her admission but don't get time to answer because Steel's bee-lining towards us, his eyes on Sienna. When he reaches us, he snakes one arm around her waist and the other around her shoulder, and she slinks her arms around him, under his cut.

"Hey big guy," she murmurs.

He looks down at her, doesn't smile but his eyes crinkle in the corner.

"What're you two scheming?"

She flutters her eyelashes innocently. "Nothing."

He snorts and kisses the top of her head. "That, I definitely don't believe." He turns his attention to me and frowns.

"It ain't Halloween till November."

"Steel!" Sienna slaps him on the butt.

He ignores her and raises a brow at me.

"It's called *fashion,* dear brother; you may want to try it some time."

He grunts. "Burn that skirt when you get home, it's too short, your ass is hangin' out for everyone to see."

I roll my eyes. "That is exactly the point and why I bought it," I reply like he's stupid.

He ignores me. "Where's that pencil dick you brought in here?" he looks around but of course Wade is nowhere to be found.

"Don't worry about him, he prefers Colt to my company anyway."

He looks from me to Sienna. "What's that supposed to mean?"

"I'll tell you later," Sienna giggles into his chest.

"Where've you been hiding him?" Steel goes on, not letting up.

"I only let him out of the dungeon on weekends," I drawl. "He likes to be tied up."

Steel's eyes go wide.

"She's kidding!" Sienna insists. "Right, Lily?"

I slap my thigh as I laugh. "Oh my God, your face, Steel!" I know I'm poking the bear but he's being an ass wipe.

"How much have you had to drink?" he grumbles, pecking Sienna on the forehead.

"Now may be a good time?" I suggest to Sienna smiling sweetly, through gritted teeth.

He gives me a pointed look. "Now may be a good time for what?"

Sienna crooks a finger and he leans down, she reaches up to his ear and whispers something and his eyebrows shoot up.

"We gotta go," he says two seconds later.

I snort a laugh and give her a wink. I like having a big sister to get rid of Steel when I need to, it comes in very handy.

"You need a ride home?" Sienna asks. "We can wait."

Steel snorts again. "Says who?"

"No, I'll get a ride with Deanna."

"She's been drinkin'," Steel says sternly, looking over the top of my head out to where the girls are still dancing. "Get one of the prospects instead or come with us now and we'll drive you."

"I'll get a prospect."

"Don't be looking for strange, either."

Sienna rolls her eyes, already down on the biker lingo.

"Steel!" I almost choke, I feel my cheeks coloring. "I came with a date and I'm going home dateless, how more pathetic could I be?"

"Best it stays that way."

Sienna rolls her lips, trying not to laugh.

He gives me a head shake, just in case his warnings aren't enough.

"Be safe alright?" he adds, a little softer.

Sienna one arm hugs me as Steel ruffles my hair annoyingly and then leads her out by the elbow, they stop to kiss a couple of times on the way.

"Get a room!" I yell after them.

Steel turns and gives me one final head shake as I laugh at him.

I flip him the bird behind his back. Thank God he's gone.

I take my drink and head back toward all the action to go find Deanna.

The night is still young after all and I'm not done dancing.

11

GUNNER

I stare at Lily in her hot as fuck outfit and wonder how I ever kept my eyes in my head before when she was around.

I don't know whether to laugh or cry. Now I know she's interested and has been for some time. It's changed things. It's all I can think about.

I watch her dancing with the girls, moving her hot little body to the music as just about every dude in the place checks her out. There's a good turn out tonight, I should be getting drunk and going upstairs with Chelsea and Tiffany but instead I'm leaning against the side wall of church checking out Lily like some freakin' stalker.

I'm not alone for long. A heavy thud on the picnic table next to me alerts me to the fact that Brock has just landed. He tosses me a beer.

"What you doin' out here by yourself, you feelin' ill?"

"Nah." I shrug. Truth be told I've had a headache all day. "Just kickin' back."

He follows my line of sight. "Who you checkin' out?"

"Nobody, just watching out for the girls."

He gives me a look.

"What?" I say innocently. He's always been good at reading me, his bullshit radar is almost as good as Steel's.

"Knock it off, you had that new hot chick all over you earlier and you're still down here looking like somebody just told you there's no Santa Clause, what gives brother? Why are you not up there nailing' her ass?"

I sigh. I can't confess to Brock, he already kicked my ass once over this whole Liliana shit, even if I was a prospect then, a nobody. I know he can't exactly kick my ass now and if he did, I'd be able to fight back, but still, the brotherhood is ingrained into my soul.

It lives there rent free.

"Just been feelin' out of sorts," I admit.

"Why's that?"

I shrug and sip my beer, watching Lily and her ass grind into some random dude, my heartbeat accelerates and not in a good way.

Brock swings his head back and laughs. "I know what it is."

I look at him sharply. "You do?"

"Yeah, you got it bad for someone bro? That's why you can't get it up, right?"

I roll my eyes. "I can get it up, fucker, it's up all day, every day. I got no complaints and I had a very nice blow job earlier." That's a lie but I have to keep up appearances.

He follows my line of sight.

"You and Lil?"

I look away and down at my boots. "Nah."

I can feel him watching me. "You tellin' me you're not tapping that?"

"Swear on my life I'm not."

"She wants you, that it?"

Why's he so goddamn observant? "She's a club sister, it wouldn't matter if she did."

He watches the gaggle of girls along with me.

"She needs to cover up though." He observes after a moment. "Brothers all eyeing her up tonight like she's a prime piece of Scotch fillet."

Ain't that the truth. "She knows it too," I mutter. "Shakin' her ass for anyone who'll look." She looks hot, but yeah, she's getting a lot of attention.

He snorts, then sobers just as quickly, something is definitely on his mind.

"Not a prospect now, but out of respect for Steel you should really approach him first, should lookin' turn to somethin' else."

I take a sip of my beer slowly.

"Nothin' to approach for, nothin's goin' on, she's too pure, always has been."

He watches her too. "Yeah, but she loves this club, obviously she's gonna end up with a brother at some stage, it's in her blood, you can't fight that shit when it's ingrained into you, may as well be you. Grow some balls for once in your life, take matters into your own hands if that's what's got you all up in knots."

I stare at him. "You've changed your tune all of a sudden, but it ain't like that."

Great, now I'm lying to him too.

"Come on Guns, can you say you haven't thought about it over the years? She's beautiful, smart, has a good head on her shoulders, and she's a good girl, don't make many like that anymore. Surprised it's taken you this long to work it out."

"Yeah, you kicked my ass the first time, remember, and that's the problem, she's too good, too good for me, anyway. I haven't got shit to give her."

"You talk shit," he chuckles. "I remember kicking your ass,

those were the days man. But you were a dog turd back then, it was my job, it made you stronger, didn't it?" He flexes his fist at the memory.

"Oh yeh, I fuckin' remember alright."

He side eyes me. "So, you thinkin' about it now?"

"Be lyin' if I said I wasn't, still have a dick, don't I? But I've been doin' what I should be doin' and nothin' more than that."

"Oh yeah and what's that exactly?"

I run a hand through my hair. "Lookin' out for her, for all the girls, bein' protective and shit."

Brock snorts. "I think most of them can take care of themselves."

"Sienna got herself in a pickle," I remind him. "Lily too, not so long ago, it's like the girls of this club just attract bad attention, they get into trouble faster than you can blink."

"Not wrong there, brother."

Damn the way she moves her body; the guy she was dancing with now has his hands all over her and I want to rip his arms out of their sockets. I don't know what this emotion is because I've never felt it before.

Jealousy?

Whatever it is, I don't like it.

"You gettin' lucky tonight?" I need to switch the topic off me and Lily. I'm hard enough as it is, and I need it to go away so I can get up and walk off with my dignity intact.

"Gonna go have a look around," he smirks. "Couple new girls around, since you're not interested."

"You know me brother, I like to keep my options open."

We clink beers and when Brock gets up to leave, he turns and points at me.

"Think about what I said, talk to Steel if you wanna do somethin' about her."

Shit. This is all I need. So much for keeping it on the down low.

"Thanks for the pep talk too, old man."

He pretends to dodge then fake punches me in the stomach and saunters off laughing. Some girl from nowhere comes up to him and he wraps an arm around her.

That was me a few weeks ago, now I'm all mixed up in the head, fucked up more like, and I don't like it.

The shoot went awesome, I should be celebrating, the launch is next week and already Teresa is calling me for another shoot for Tattooed Ink magazine, they want shots of my tats and it'll definitely help Angel out with free advertising since she did most of my work. I share the love around when I can.

I drift my eyes back to the girls. Deanna is laughing and draping her arms around the back of that Katy chick's shoulders as they do the loco-motion, *wild chicks*, even I find it hard keeping up with them.

My eyes flick to Lily. The guy behind her has his hands on her hips and he's holding her far too close. I look around, Steel's gone, he wouldn't be happy with this, hell, *I'm* not happy.

Before I can even think, I'm pushing off the wall as I drain my bottle of beer and head right for her. When I reach her, I grab her elbow and push the dude backwards.

I don't know who he is but he's not the guy she arrived with. He looks momentarily stunned then looks at my cut and shuts his mouth. Smart move. I'm in the mood to rearrange his face and one word will have my fist down his throat.

Without warning I yank her off the dance floor, not that anyone else even notices because they're all too drunk and disorderly to care. I don't stop until I get around the side of the clubhouse where it's dark and quieter and nobody can see us.

She yanks out of my grasp.

"Gunner!" she yells at me. "That was so rude! Get your hands off me!"

I roll my eyes as I corner her, she backs up against the wall and her palms hit the bricks as I cage her in.

Everything I just said to Brock is all about to go out the window.

"You like that guy with his hands all over your ass?"

She shrugs, cheeky little thing. "Why, it's not like you care."

She's had a few drinks and she's got that fighting spirit that I haven't seen for a little while, looks more like liquid courage but it's delightful all the same.

"Why all the attitude?" God her mouth looks so perfect, her chest heaves after my hauling her across the courtyard, my eyes go to her very ample cleavage.

"What attitude? This is me, Guns." She spreads her arms wide then places them back down on her hips and narrows her eyes. "I'm single and I wanna mingle."

I shake my head. "Right, you're just your own crown of thorns aren't you, Lil?"

She frowns. "What's that supposed to mean?"

I fight the urge to take her mouth, to press my body up against hers and make her come with a dry run, right now, against the wall. That'll shut her up.

"Lettin' guys touch you up like that, do you even know him? He's not the guy you arrived with."

She looks momentarily flabbergasted then narrows her eyes. "So what? You're not my keeper, I can do what I want, maybe you should just butt out?"

"I'm lookin' out for you, especially after what happened at the Crow."

Her eyes go wide and sadness falls over her face suddenly at the memory.

Fuck. I don't like being the one to make her look sad.

She averts her eyes to the floor.

"Lil, I'm sorry, I didn't mean..."

"It's alright," she says quietly. "Just another reminder of how I always fuck up, can't do anything right, can't even get my date to make out with me..." she trails off.

"You're crazy."

"I'm not, he's more interested in looking at all the sleds out in the lot and getting a boner over exhaust pipes."

"Well, he's a fuck face then, you can do better than that asshole anyway."

She sighs and looks up at me with those big blue eyes. "I'd like to go now."

"Why?" I look down at her lips again, she doesn't look like she wants to go, she doesn't attempt to shove me off.

"Because there's nothing else to say."

"You really wanna go home with him?"

"I was never going to go home with him!" she huffs adamantly.

I look at her quizzically. "Really? Why's that?"

"I don't screw just anybody, Gunner! I have to actually feel something for them to get that far, unlike *some* people, it's called a connection."

She's hit the nail on the head with that one.

I stare at her, then I clench my jaw. "You're getting really lippy, anyone ever tell you that?"

Her eyes flick to my mouth, she bites her bottom lip leaving an indentation there. Fuck she's so goddamned beautiful.

"Yeah, what are you gonna do about it?" she taunts. Something about her defiance excites me, but who am I kidding? *Everything* about her excites me.

I should get away from her, she's intoxicating. I *should*. But my feet don't move, they stay right where they are. I lift her chin with my hand and we stare at each other.

Every muscle in my body is telling me to take her and take her good, yet that very small part of my conscience is telling me to run before it's too late.

It seems I'm not very good at listening.

I close the gap and kiss her brutally. A shocked gasp escapes her as her lips part and my tongue seeks entry and I know I shouldn't, I fucking know, but fuck me, I do. And it's like heaven, sweet, sweet heaven.

I move in closer, my hands gripping her hair as I press my body against hers, my cock's so hard it's painful. I'm relieved to know it's finally working again. I could do her right here right now and not even feel bad about it. That's how far she pushes me, to my limits.

She moans into my mouth as I assault her senses, the sound only spurs me on. I eat her mouth like a starving man and when I pull back, she's breathless and panting.

"You wet?" I breathe.

She nods.

I glance down at her and frown. "Skirt's too fuckin' short."

"Don't you start," she mutters.

"Don't want you wearing that again."

She looks momentarily annoyed. "Since when can you tell me what to wear?"

"Since now."

"Shut up." She pulls me back in and we kiss again; it's frantic, hot, perfect, forbidden, so wrong, but oh so very right.

I push my dick into her stomach, Jesus I need her. I need her in all sorts of ways, all of them sordid and none of them decent. She smells like cotton candy and it sends all the remaining blood in my body rushing to my dick.

"Feel that?" I mumble in between the onslaught.

She makes a strangled noise in the back of her throat.

"That's what you do to me," I say, pulling back ever so slightly. "That's what I've been livin' with all week since the other night, you got me all stirred up, buttercup and I don't fuckin' know what to do about it."

God, her throwing herself at me like this is almost intolerable. I can't remember a time when I've ever been so excited and wanted to fuck so badly.

"So? Take it then."

"Babe, you shouldn't say that." Even I know it sounds halfhearted. I'm not a decent person, a decent man would walk away, not keep sticking his tongue in her mouth and dry humping her.

She looks up at me, her eyes narrow slightly. "Did you do anything with those other girls tonight?" she asks, her chest panting.

I'm stunned at her question, she shouldn't question me on anything, but I don't have the heart to feel annoyed. Lily could never annoy me even when she's being a pain in my ass.

"No babe."

She's still holding onto my cut. "Why not?"

I grunt. "You think I'd give you sloppy seconds? Please Lil, give me some credit, haven't been able to get it up for anyone since that night, and all we did was kiss."

God I can't even imagine being inside her, I'd want to die.

A slight smile creeps on her face.

"Oh, you think that's funny?" I buck my hips into hers.

She nods, biting her lip.

I glance down at her heaving chest. I want nothing more than to bury my face in her cleavage, suck on her tits, give her what she's asking for, make her scream my name while I fuck her senseless.

"This is too tight and too low too," I mutter leaning toward her ear. All of a sudden I'm hell and ready.

"So you keep saying."

I do the unthinkable by snaking my hands up from her hips to cup her tits, I can't help it, they're right there and ripe for the picking. She gasps at the contact watching my hands play with her as I begin to knead them, feeling the hard peaks beneath my thumbs as I rub her nipples, she squirms against the wall, making the most delicious noises.

"You know you could put that mouth to much better use," she breathes, her beautiful eyes only encourage me.

"Yeah?" I cock my head. "You think so babe?"

"Oh yeah."

I move back in and kiss her hard and heavy. I lift her and she wraps her legs around my waist as I walk us further along the side of the clubhouse to the far end so we're out of sight, it's not like I want to get caught dry humping Lily against the wall by anybody.

I leave her hitched against the bricks and her skirt rides right up around her hips as I press into her, we pull apart and she looks at me with pure lust, it's almost my undoing. I want to yank her top down and suck on her beautiful tits, but I don't want her exposed out here in case we get caught; so instead I dip my head to suck one peak through the material of her tank top and she moans at my touch.

I move to the other one and repeat the movement. She hangs onto my neck as I bring my hands up to cup her while she squirms beautifully beneath me; each move brushes my cock and I can barely contain what's going on in my jeans.

I imagine her in my bed as I fuck her all night long and my dick twitches violently. That's uncomfortable.

"Not gonna do you like this," I say hoarsely as her hands move to grip my hair. "Not gonna."

She ignores me, rubbing herself against my wood and it's driving me insane.

I shouldn't be doing this here.

I pluck at her nipples through her tank top and watch her get even more excited. God, I want them out so bad.

"Oh god," she groans. "Gunner…"

I run a hand up her hip and around to her inner thigh as her breath hitches.

I brace myself as my fingers pull her panties to the side and I immediately feel her wet heat. She's smooth, nothing there but skin, everything about her is turning me on like no other. She's so ready for me it takes all my composure to not just rip my jeans down and give it to her hard and fast, right now.

I run my fingers through her slick, hot pussy and she moans again. I find her clit and run my fingers over it, back and forward softly, her body tenses and she begins to unfold. I watch her cheeks go pink as I tease her, God I could do this all day.

She closes her eyes.

"Eyes on me," I say. "I want to see you when you come."

I rub around and around as she bites her lip, trying to hold on. I dip my middle finger inside her while I continue to play with her clit. I finger her in and out slowly, she's so tight, so fucking tight. I imagine it's my cock and I have to shut my eyes and count to ten.

"Gunner…" she breathes. I love hearing my name like that on her lips.

I can't get enough and I know I'm playing with fire as I continue to rub her. Moments later she tenses, then comes hard as I cover her mouth with mine to avoid her screams being heard as I kiss her through her climax.

She's so responsive to my touch. Her arms tighten and her orgasm has her clenching down on my finger as I ride her through it.

The knot in my chest tightens with possessiveness.

Shoulda' ran when I had the chance.

"Oh god, Gunner," she breathes into my neck when it's over, I smile against her skin.

"Touch my dick," I demand. She moves her hand to the unmistakable bulge in my jeans, her small hand caresses me and the friction has me weeping through my boxers. Fuck, I could come right now, especially after seeing that.

"Oh yeah babe, oh fuck yeah." I watch as she fumbles with my buckle and my top button. Jesus she's gonna get my dick out, if she does that then I know I'm done. I don't try to stop her though, instead I begin to insert another finger, but her hand suddenly grips my wrist as she bites her lip, stopping me.

"What?" I whisper, I stop moving immediately. "Did I hurt you?"

She shakes her head; her hand has also stopped rubbing my cock but that's probably a good thing since I'm about to explode. "What then babe? You don't like that?"

"It's not that." She looks down.

I've no idea what I've done wrong so I wait for her to say something…And I wait.

I kiss her forehead. "Babe, why you stoppin' me? Is it cause' we're out here in the open?"

"No…. I…" her eyes are wide and all of a sudden we're back there again, in the back storeroom, both young and reckless without a care in the world.

"Lil? Not gonna do you here I told you that, you deserve better than that, but I like playing with you, if you don't like it or I did something, you gotta tell me."

She lets out a long breath. "I do like it."

I give her a pointed look, trying to work out where she's going with this.

"I'm…"

I stare at her, still wrapped around me, my hand still in her panties, what *is* the problem?

I'm losing my mind here.

"Liliana!" I growl.

"I'm a virgin!" she blurts out.

My heart suddenly hammers in my chest loudly, louder than it's ever hammered before.

She's a what?

I must be hearing things.

"Huh?" Is all I can manage.

She tries to bury her face in my shoulder as I stare down at her.

"You heard me," her voice is muffled. "This is mortifying, please don't make me say it again."

I tilt her chin with a free hand so she's looking at me, her big blue eyes try to hide but I hold her chin firmly so she can't move.

"How is that possible?" I blurt out.

She puffs air into her flushed cheeks and bites her bottom lip again.

"I… I just never really felt that way about anybody…"

I look at her face for any sign of hilarity or dishonesty and there isn't any.

Fuck me sideways.

I know her. She doesn't lie. I scratch my head trying to understand, she's had boyfriends, she lived away from home while doing beauty school, she's twenty-three-years old-for fucks sake! She can't still be a virgin, *can she?*

Here I am about to defile her against the wall of a dirty clubhouse with my fingers and she's telling me this shit, I don't know whether to laugh or cry or jump for joy. All I can do is stare.

The gravity of the situation hits me though and it's like she just threw cold water on me as I look at her uncomprehending.

I can't move.

Fuck me dead.

For the first time in a long time, I'm completely lost for words.

12

LILY

I'M TEMPTED to wave my hand over his face to make sure he's still with me, but his breathing is just as ragged as mine, so I know his heart hasn't stopped. I can't help but feel a little bit smug that I got him so turned on, but now he looks like he's seen a ghost.

"Guns?" I call, for what feels like the hundredth time.

He pulls his hand out of my panties and tries to back away from me, I clutch onto his neck, not so fast.

"How is that possible?" he whispers again, confused.

I blink at him.

"What, that I'm still a virgin?" I stutter, stunned at his reaction.

He nods.

"I just told you... I never really met anyone I was that interested in...I guess?"

"So, all of high school, college..."

"I went to an all-girls high school, and it's not a crime, is it? To still be a virgin? To wait?"

I know this will be a bit shocking to him, I'm sure he wasn't exactly expecting it.

He pulls back and this time, I let him. I unwrap my legs and he sets me down. He watches me very deliberately, like I'm now made of glass.

"Gunner?" I say looking up at him. "What's wrong?"

"I'm just… I'm just processing it."

I roll my eyes, feeling tempted to thump him on the chest. "What, so now you don't want me because I'm not experienced enough for you?"

His arms cage me in against the wall as he stares at me. "Tell me the truth."

"I am!" I screech. "If I was going to lie about something, I'd make it far more interesting and far less embarrassing than that!"

He studies me carefully. "You never went this far with anyone? Like, ever?"

"I didn't say that."

God this is like hell. Torturous hell.

"But I almost took your virginity with my god damned two fingers," he stutters, incredulous.

He does not look happy about it.

I'm at a loss for words, and embarrassed as hell.

"I want to keep going, I just…"

"You just what?"

I gulp. "I just haven't had experience like you have, I want to do this, though, I don't want you to stop."

He runs his hands through his hair. "You should have told me."

"I just did."

He looks up at me and gives me a shake of his head. "Don't be a smart ass, I meant you should have told me earlier, before I did that."

"It's not like I go around announcing it to everyone," I start, annoyance in my tone. "I'm not sure why it even matters."

His eyes go wide. "You're not sure why it even matters?"

I shrug, unable to face him. "You know what I mean."

"Look at me."

I reluctantly lift my eyes.

"How far have you gone?"

My eyes go round. "Gunner! I'm not answering that."

The shame could kill me.

"Why not?"

"Because... it's *private.*"

He brushes my hair back off my shoulder. "You never stop surprising me, Liliana Marie."

I hope that's a good thing but I don't dare ask.

He sighs, his eyes softening. "I don't like there being secrets between us. You deserve better, your first time isn't meant to be like this, not with someone like me."

I gape at him for a solid ten seconds, my voice a whisper when I find my vocal cords. "It *is* supposed to be like this, other people's first times usually suck, it's rushed, inexperienced and usually in the backseat of a car. At least I know mine won't be like that, I know you know what you're doing or you should by now."

He cocks an eyebrow. "This isn't the time to be cute."

"I can be a bad girl," I say, looking up at him. "Let me show you."

He looks down at my skirt rucked up to my hips, then brushes his thumb over my bottom lip. "Your outfit proved that, baby doll."

"You don't like it?"

"Didn't say that."

"What *are* you saying?"

"I told you, it's too short and other guys have been checkin' you out all night, not to mention the dude you were bumping and grinding with had his hands all over your ass, that never used to bother me, until now."

I can't help but feel just a little bit satisfied. Took him long enough.

"Why's that?"

He shakes his head and sighs. "I don't know. I've never had this feeling before to be honest."

"Do you like the fact I'm a virgin?" I taunt. "Does it turn you on just a little bit?"

"It's every man's wet dream, isn't it?"

Something flashes in his eyes. It's a mixture of lust and something else....like he's trying to work something out but can't quite get there.

"Gunner?" I probe. "Tell me what you're thinking."

He shakes his head. "Another place, another time angel." He almost sounds sad.

I don't want my revelation to ruin the moment.

"So, can we go upstairs then?"

He laughs out loud. "Absolutely not, not to that shit hole."

"You just made me come, you can't just leave me like this."

He shakes his head and a slow smile spreads across his face. "What the fuck am I gonna do with you, Liliana?"

"I've got a few suggestions," I say, raising my eyebrows.

"I bet you have."

I run my hands up to his face and study him, my beautiful Gunner.

He's wrong; this *is* how it's meant to be. With someone you care about, someone you want, *someone you love.*

Even though he doesn't love me back, it's alright. I still want it to be him. I've always wanted it to be him, ever since I was eighteen and we did what we did. I've never stopped thinking about it.

"You said you think about it all the time."

He levels me with a gaze but stays quiet.

"You said it's like fucking paradise," I whisper.

He closes his eyes. "I never should have told you that."

"But you did."

He kisses me gently. "Babe, we both know I'm not capable of anything more, of what you really deserve and you know what I'm like, I tend to hurt women by being myself, not intentionally, I don't want to do that to you, it would kill me."

My heart lurches at his admission even though he's being honest. "I'm so sick of everyone thinking they know what's best for me! Mom. Steel. *Now you?* It doesn't matter what I do or where I go, I'll never be good enough, will I? I know you. I know that you're capable of more and that's not what I'm even asking, I'm just asking you to be my first, but I got it. You don't want to go there, got it loud and clear."

He pushes me back against the wall, his eyes darken. "You got it all wrong Lil, it's not that you're not good enough or that I don't want to go there, you know I do. It's the other way round. *I* don't deserve this; *I* don't deserve *you*. You think I'm something I'm not and here you are offering me yourself on a silver platter, it feels like I'm already committing the ultimate sin by touching you."

He couldn't be more wrong if he tried.

He may have been around the block several times but he's always treated me with respect. He's never said or done anything to make me think any less of him.

"Well, you know what? You do deserve it, we both do, the only sin you're committing is not giving in to what you really want, in fact it's not even a sin, it's a fucking tragedy."

"Lily."

"It's the truth, I've thought about it so many times too, Guns, which makes me sound desperate and pathetic I know, but nobody compares to you, they never could."

"You could never be desperate or pathetic." His knuckles brush my cheek. "But with you, things are different Lil, I don't know how to…" He trails off.

I wait without interrupting.

"I don't know how to make love to someone, that's what you want me to do, that's what this is about babe, but all I know how to do is fuck, I fuck babe, I fuck hard."

I stare at him. I literally don't know what to say. His words are filthy and delicious, and it sears me everywhere. My pussy clenches at his dirty words.

"Guns…"

He tilts my chin up. "You like me being vulgar, babe?"

I bite my lip.

"Better stop biting that lip." He pulls it with his thumb and I kiss the tip gently.

He continues to rub it and I bite the pad as he watches me.

"Careful," he growls. His eyes are hooded and I know he wants this as much as I do.

But I don't want to be careful, I want to be anything but. He watches me as he slowly pushes his thumb into my mouth and I suck the end.

A low growl permeates from his throat and it only spurs me on. I look up at him under my lashes and the look he's giving me shocks me to the core. It's hungry with lust.

I take his thumb deeper into my mouth as we stare at one another and I keep sucking. He mutters something undecipherable as I move him in my mouth back and forth, tantalizing him.

"You make me so hard," he mumbles, and I can feel it as he presses into me.

My skin feels hot, I'm shaking all over because I'm so ready for him. Nobody will ever make me feel like he does, when he looks at me, I want to die. I want to get lost in him and never resurface.

"Maybe we should reconvene?" I suggest hopefully. I move my hand between us to the bulge in his jeans and he hisses at the contact.

He looks down at my hand and I squeeze his hard length gently while I continue to suck his thumb and he lets out the most sexy, guttural noise. I love making him lose control, I love how he responds to me.

"Jesus, Lil."

"He isn't going to help you," I say as I pop his thumb out noisily, very pleased with myself.

He narrows his eyes but a smirk tugs at his lips. "For someone so innocent, you seem to know quite a bit about how to get a man aroused."

Butterflies flutter in my stomach as his admission and I go along with it. I like hearing that my little experience gets him aroused.

"I've got cable."

He bumps me with his hips. "We're not gonna need cable, babe."

He leans in and aggressively attacks my mouth with his, suddenly his tongue pushes its way in again just how I like it; it's hot and demanding. I hang onto his shoulders as our bodies mold together, we fit so perfectly.

My body comes alight with flames and I'm lost in a world of pleasure just from his mouth, I dare to imagine what the rest of his body parts can do.

It's then that my phone decides to ring noisily in my purse. I ignore it and pull him closer, our kisses getting hotter and hotter by the second. A small mewl escapes me and I know the slightest friction against my pussy will have me coming apart in seconds.

Annoyingly, my phone rings again and Gunner pulls back.

"You wanna answer that?"

I pull him back to me by the lapels of his jacket and don't answer. We continue kissing hungrily, my hand continues to rub up and down his growing length and he starts to pump his hips.

"Getting uncomfortable in there, babe," he breathes into my neck, biting my pulse point as a surge of moisture lubricates my panties.

"I want to get it out," I say, reaching for the zipper. To my surprise he doesn't stop me, what he does do is continue to gently bite my neck and then my shoulder, cursing and filthy talking while he does it. Everything he does sets me on fire.

Imagining seeing him naked for the first time is exhilarating and delicious, I want my mouth on him, on all of him.

My phone rings again. "Urgh!" I spit, annoyed.

"For fuck sakes, answer it," he growls, one hand moving to my breast as he squeezes it hungrily. He pulls back slightly, still touching me, as I reach around into my purse and pull my phone out.

I've missed three calls from Sienna. Oh shit.

"Uh oh," I say, panting.

"Who is it?"

"Sienna."

Which obviously means Steel. *Shit.* Maybe he's looking for us.

Gunner steps back and looks momentarily worried, I can't say I blame him, Steel is enough to make anybody feel scared.

"Better answer it."

I hit the answer button. "Hey Sienna."

"Lily! I've been calling you forever."

"Sorry, I couldn't hear over the music." She sounds panicked. "Is everything alright?"

"Are you still at church?"

There's a strange pause for a few moments and I know somethings wrong.

"Yes, why, what's wrong?"

"Cops just called Steel; there's been an attempted break in at the salon."

My eyes go wide. "Oh no, was anything taken?"

"Not that they're aware of, smashed a window and set off the alarms, I don't think they got inside, Steel is headed over there now."

"Oh shit, I can be over there in five."

"Are you okay to drive?"

"It's alright, Gunner's here, he seems sober enough to drive me."

The minute the words leave my mouth I could kick myself. Gunner's eyes go slightly round.

"Right," Sienna says, clearing her throat. "Well, best get over there sooner rather than later."

"Thanks Sienna."

I hang up.

Gunner's looking down at me with concern.

"The salon's been broken into," I blurt out.

"Oh shit, is anything missing?"

"I don't know, Sienna says she thinks nothing was taken, the alarm must have scared them off, I better get over there, Steel's dealing with the cops."

"I can drive, I haven't had much to drink," he says. I watch as he readjusts himself through his jeans. Damn it, and things were just getting hot and heavy. Maybe if we get this sorted out soon then we can take things upstairs at my place. *Yes!*

He holds his hand out.

"You trust me?"

I know he's not asking about me driving him, there's an underlying meaning.

"Yes," I reply, as I grab his hand and he hauls me off the wall. "Of course I do."

"Good, but I've no fucking idea how you're gonna mount my sled in that get up."

I giggle as we make our way back down the deserted pathway back to the bonfire.

Even being broken into can't sour my mood.

Nothing can when I'm with him.

13

GUNNER

I'VE NEVER HAD a woman on the back of my sled before. Never.

The sensation of having not just a woman, but Lily, pressed up against me and wrapped around my body is an entirely new sensation, one that has my chest tightening like I'm going to have a heart attack. I don't know what that's all about but, fuck me, I'm doomed. This girl is sure to be the death of me.

Her sucking my thumb almost threw me over the edge. Virgin or not I may have just taken her there and then, against the clubhouse wall. I'm still hard just thinking about it, imagining me in her mouth is enough to make a man drop to his knees and beg for mercy.

It's not the first time Lily has me feeling new and strange things. Things I don't really know what to do with. She has the power to beguile me, undo me, a power nobody has ever had over me, and that's very dangerous.

I don't know whether to run the other way or kamikaze towards her, but I'm treading a very fine line, that I know all too well.

Her touch is different from the other girls I've been with. Obviously, she's far less experienced than the girls I'm used to. Usually I'm quick to get upstairs, get going and get off quickly, but with Lily I want to take my time. I want to explore her body, every inch of it, please her, instead of just myself, see what she likes.

I want to give instead of take. It's like I've had Lily heroin and now I can't go back.

Everything that's good and pure about her seems to seep into my bones, making my blood boil, making every nerve ending in my body come alight. I wish I could turn it off, maybe if I could, I would, but maybe the sinner in me doesn't want to.

I shake my head, attempting to get rid of all of my errant thoughts. The last thing I need is to get emotionally involved. She's offered me her body, and on all levels that appeals to my bad side, the side that will have her screaming and begging me for more, but I know she feels more than she lets on. I know that for her it wouldn't just be a one-night fling.

It's wrong.

It's so very wrong.

But nobody lights the fire in me like she does.

The trouble is I meant what I said about being broken, I don't know if I can ever be fixed. Women always want more from me and I've never been that way inclined, up until now.

I sure as hell can't give her romance and the things that she probably wants and deserves. I'm not capable of any of that. I don't know how.

I think about Steel and how adamant he was about getting anyone permanent in his life, that was before Sienna came along. He was dead set against all that shit, the poster boy for cheap one-night thrills, now he's settled down and happy, and he pursued her, he *wanted* to get snagged.

He's hook, line, and sinker now and there's no question Sienna is good for him, they're good for each other.

None of the men in our club are easy to deal with. It takes a strong woman to be an ol' lady, and I can't help but feel a jolt of electricity when I think about Lily wearing my cut.

What the fucks got into me?

I mean, those are *not* normal thoughts. I never thought I'd have a girl on the back of my sled until today, and yet here we are, with me imagining Lily doing just that in my cut.

Sweet mother of God.

We speed through the deserted streets of Bracken Ridge towards the salon as I fight my inner demons which are on non-stop repeat.

I drive into the laneway and pull up behind the salon.

I immediately see Steel, he's talking with Jenkins, a police officer well known to the club. He gives me a chin lift then frowns when he sees Lily climbing off my sled, probably because her skirt's pushed up to her hips. Jesus fuck that's all I need.

I kick the stand down, cut the engine, and dismount. I let out a long, guilty breath as I make my way over to them.

"Oh my God!" Lily gasps, assessing the damage. There's a couple of higher windows smashed, and glass shattered all over the pavement below, maybe they planned on hoisting themselves up and getting in that way.

Why would anyone want to steal hair color supplies? Nobody keeps cash on the premises these days and most people pay with card, but then again desperate people and drug addicts will do anything to score.

"There's a camera at the front, facing the street," Steel tells Jenkins, "but not at the back."

He frowns and purses his lips; I know by this time tomorrow that's all going to be remedied.

His eyes flick to Lily, his brow furrows. I have a sinking

feeling he may be a psychic for a second and realize what we've been up to, but then I see his eyes assess her scantily clad outfit and I understand his obvious annoyance. She's overdone it tonight with that get up, it leaves little to the imagination and when it's her, it aint good.

"We'll need to get the footage, that's if they attempted the front first," Jenkins says, giving me a nod. "Once we have that we can go from there, see if we can get an I.D."

"What the hell?" Lily frowns as she takes in the damage.

"Be thankful they didn't get in, or that you weren't inside," Steel gruffs.

"Has she got locks on the apartment doors?" I ask, looking up toward the high second floor.

"Yeah, a bolt and a double lock to the upstairs," Steel replies.

"Better get more, just to be safe."

Lily spins on her heels. "I'm right here, you can just ask me you know!"

Steel looks down at her; they are so much alike yet so very different at the same time. In stature they are worlds apart; he's a giant and she's barely five-four, but they have the same dark hair, stormy eyes, and fiery temper, not to mention stubbornness personified. Of that I know both very well.

"What's up your ass?" Steel grunts.

"Oh nothing, my place just got broken into and there's glass everywhere," Lily cries, clamping her hand over her mouth in disbelief.

"Attempted break in," Jenkins interrupts, writing in his pad. "Lucky this place is like Fort Knox; the damage could have been a lot worse."

"If it ain't Fort Knox now it will be by tomorrow," I mutter. "You piss anyone off lately, Lil? Dye their hair the wrong color? Wax the wrong bit?"

She rolls her eyes and crosses her arms in front of her chest. "Ha-ha very funny."

"Are we done here?" Steel asks Jenkins.

"Yeah, I'll file a police report for the insurance, I'll come by tomorrow and give you a copy then and I'll retrieve the footage, we've dusted for fingerprints so even with a partial print it's something, hopefully they would've been dumb enough to not realize the camera was there."

"Appreciate it," Steel says, as Jenkins goes back toward his vehicle and climbs in.

When he's gone Steel turns to face me.

"We gotta board this place up tonight just in case they decide to come back."

"On it."

He turns to Lily. "You go get upstairs and get changed, put some clothes on and pack a bag, you're going to mom's tonight."

She pulls a face. "Why do I have to go to mom's?"

"Uh, maybe because your windows are all smashed and if someone's high on drugs, they may just be desperate enough to come back, I don't want you here alone."

Lily's eyes flick to mine.

Oh no, don't you dare.

To my relief she doesn't say anything, even if her eyes plead with me to step in.

"Hello?" Steel waves a big, meaty hand in front of her face. "Earth to Lily, are you with me?"

"Yeah, I heard you."

"So, go upstairs and pack a bag, am I talkin' fuckin' Chinese?"

She fishes out her keys from her purse as Steel rolls his eyes at me while her backs turned.

I just watch in absolute silence, there is no need to involve myself.

She unlocks the door and lets herself in quietly.

"And wash all that shit off your face!" Steel yells as she flips him the bird behind her back. "Come to think of it, burn that skirt while you're at it, we don't want mom thinkin' you're a lady of the night, she's too young to die of a heart attack."

He turns to me and points a finger in my face.

"You're lucky you know."

Oh shit, *here we go,* maybe he *is* psychic.

My throat goes dry as I think about what we just did and where I had my hands and my mouth. Another sensation I've not had in a while rises like bile in my throat, *guilt*. I'm like a fuckin' merry go round.

A huge part of me knows I never want to disappoint Steel. He taught me everything, from age seven; I look up to him, he trusts me.

"Oh yeah, why's that?"

He nods upwards. "Her! Be thankful Summer gives you no grief or gray hairs, you wanna swap sisters sometime and take her off my hands, I'm fine with that any day of the week."

I snort. "Yeah, she's a handful."

"You alright to drop her off at mom's? Kind of in the middle of somethin', need to get back to it, don't feel like babysitting tonight."

I smirk. "Yeah brother, but we gotta get some plywood or something for this first."

"I'll shoot home and get something out of the workshop, you watch her, make sure she's covered up when she comes back down and if she hasn't washed all that junk off her face drag her back upstairs and do it for her."

My eyes go wide at the thought as Steel assesses the glass once more, his back to me.

"I'm sure I'd rather not get in a shit fight with that alley cat," I snort.

"She's a good girl but she gets into trouble faster than you can blink, lucky she got you to get her home safe, askin' for trouble in that outfit."

Now is not the time to remind him that we don't usually mind or complain when women wear revealing outfits, I guess things are different when it's your sister.

I keep quiet. No need to put a target on my back unnecessarily, not tonight anyways.

I think about the night mine and Summer's life changed forever; when Hutch came to take us to safety, when Liliana wasn't even born yet.

Fuck.

I haven't thought about that night in a long time but lately it's resurfacing more and more.

I rub the back of my head and then my temples.

What have I done?

"Back in a few."

I nod as he moves toward his sled and fires her up.

Steel's workshop isn't far, maybe four blocks.

I lounge around in the doorway. There is no way I'm going up to her apartment, not a chance in hell, that is until I hear a blood curdling scream of my name, loud enough to wake the dead.

I move fast and take the stairs two at a time to get to her.

When I find her though, she's in her closet, in her underwear, unscathed. She's looking around the tiny space frowning.

"Jesus Lily, you gave me a goddamn heart attack, I thought there was someone up here attacking you!"

I want to spank her little ass, but that would only turn me on even more than I already am. Best not invoke the beast inside me.

"Took you long enough," she groans.

She twirls something around in her hand.

"What's that?"

"Pepper spray," she replies. "Steel makes sure I have it on my key ring at all times, so you see, I'm just fine defending myself, I have provisions."

"Hope you're not going to use that on me."

I glance around her bedroom; it's small but neat and tidy. She has a large bed that takes up most of the space and more pillows than I've ever seen in my life.

"Mom's on night shift," she whispers softly.

My eyebrows reach the top of my hairline as I turn back to her. "And?"

I try hard not to look at her almost naked body but fail miserably. Her breasts are a perfect handful, I can see the peeks of her nipples through the thin fabric and the almost sheer panties... *Jesus Christ.*

She lowers her voice. "We could finish where we left off?"

I baulk at her. "Are you actually serious right now?"

She shrugs as I stare at her wordlessly.

"Don't be a spoil sport," she says, sashaying towards me.

I swallow hard.

She throws her arms around my neck.

"You know what? You are a piece of work, here I was thinkin' you were some sort of fuckin' angel."

"I thought you liked women with a strong mind?"

"Your place just got broken into, your brother is about to come back with some very large tools, perfect for swinging at my head, and you're standing here in your underwear trying to seduce me."

She laughs out loud.

I cock an eyebrow. "This isn't funny Lil, put some goddamn clothes on, I'm gonna burst into flames just lookin' at you."

"You're such a party pooper," she pouts.

"And you've clearly had too many cocktails."

She turns and begins rummaging around in one of the drawers, then bends over and pulls out some sweats, muttering under her breath at me.

My head tilts sideways as I check out her ass.

Fuck.

I'd love nothing more than to come up behind her, rub my hard cock against her ass and fuck her from behind. I adjust myself in my jeans and turn away; if I don't, I'll end up doing just that and then Steel *will* bury me in the back yard with his shovel.

"Where are you going?" she stammers.

"Hear those straight pipes?"

She stops and tilts her head. "Oh."

"Oh alright, put some fuckin' clothes on, woman, and meet me downstairs, and wash that shit off your face or he'll just send you back up here again."

"You're so cute when you're bossy."

I turn to leave.

"You better get used to bossy," I call over my shoulder as I exit her bedroom. "And start listening. Especially to Steel, answering back is only gonna get you in more trouble."

"Answering back is only gonna get you in more trouble." I hear her mocking tone as I take the stairs down just as fast as I came up.

I run both hands through my hair. Goddamn it, she'll be the death of me.

I get to the back door just as Steel's pulling up.

We make short work of hammering the wood over the window, by the time we're done, Lily reappears with a small overnight bag. She's now dressed in a grey tracksuit with the Arizona Wildcats emblem on the pocket and down the leg. She's as cute as a button.

"I'll check the inside doors," Steel says, as he hands me his hammer.

"I checked them already," Lily replies, makeup-less and her hair now slung in a high ponytail.

He ignores her and pushes past and goes into the dimly lit room. "Should always leave the front reception lights on," he hollers over his shoulder. "Puts people off if it's lit up."

Lily clutches her bag as she looks up at me, she looks younger without all that gunk on her face. She's prettier without it, her skin is perfectly clear and there's a small smattering of freckles across her nose and cheeks. I don't know why she'd want to cover up such pretty skin.

"Most people scrub up alright, but you scrub down even better," I smirk, taking her bag off her shoulder.

"Please don't let him drive me."

"He has to get back home; I'll drop you off."

Steel's back in no time, he shuts the door, reaches for Lily's keys and deadbolts the back door.

"Guns is gonna drive you to mom's."

"Fine," she replies, crossing her arms over her chest. "Hey, thanks for coming to sort this out, Steel."

Steel grunts in her direction then looks toward me.

"I'll get Colt onto a new security system tomorrow, need more cameras. There's also too much easy access back here, we need a locked gate with pin pad access for the side entry, anyone can just wander down here whenever they feel like it."

"What about deliveries?" Lily stammers.

"They can come through the front," Steel replies. "Or you can code them in when they arrive."

Lily narrows her eyes, her temper flaring. "Don't I get a say in this?"

"No," we both say in unison.

"No flood lights here either," I agree, pointing up. "Anybody could be lurking around. I'll swing by tomorrow, get the security footage for Jenkins, help Colt if he needs it."

"Appreciate that brother."

We clench hands then he slaps me up the side of the head like he always does.

"Don't give him any shit," Steel says to Lily.

"Thanks for totally rearranging my shop," she retorts.

I give her an exasperated look, she of all people knows when not to push Steel's buttons, not that any time is a good time.

"It's a wakeup call, Lil," I say as we walk towards my sled. "Think yourself lucky you were at church and not here."

She gives me a blank look but mischief dances in her eyes, clearly, she's thinking about what we were doing at church.

"Amen brother." Steel mounts his sled and rubs his eyes, then he turns to Lily. "And I'm glad to see you're finally in some clothing that actually fits you."

"Since when do you get to pick my outfits?"

"What happened to your date?" Steel suddenly remembers, starting his engine.

"Left him at church, last I saw of him he and Colt were making plans to run away together."

I snort. "Better not let him hear you say that."

"Told you she's trouble," Steel mumbles. He revs his engine as it roars to life and takes off down the alleyway. He's right though, anyone could just come round the back here any time they wanted, it's not good and certainly not safe.

"Don't suppose you're going to defend me in any way?" she retorts sarcastically, jumping on behind me as I pass her a brain bucket.

"You're on your own there, cupcake."

"At least take the scenic route, will you? The night's still young."

"Anything else I can do for you, your royal highness?" I

start my engine, my sled rumbling beneath us, there's no greater sound, or so I thought until I heard Lily in the throes of passion. If she were going to be mine, which she isn't, I'd have to do something about that smart mouth of hers. She doesn't know when to quit.

"Yes, but apparently that isn't going to happen tonight."

I shake my head and chuckle despite myself.

"Shut up and hold on," I tell her as I take off onto the main street.

I wonder if my guilty conscience will get the better of me before my raging libido takes over, it's fifty-fifty right now, but facing Steel is like having an icy, cold bucket of water thrown on you. There is no way anything's taking place tonight.

I feel as much of a fraud as I ever have.

I want her, but I don't want to hurt her, and I will. I will because she can't know the truth about me, and deep down I know I will fuck up.

It's what I do. It's what everyone expects.

Trust me, she'll be no different. Just give it time.

14

GUNNER

The following week is long and dull and I haven't seen Liliana. It's not because I don't want to, duty calls, or rather Brock does.

Once a month Brock and Bones often go out of town to sales, industrial sheds, deceased estates, and business foreclosures and fill the truck to the brim with scrap metal, steel, wood, tools, used cars and car parts, and I get roped in when Bones can't be there, since he's hurt his back, I'm Brock's bitch for this trip.

Some laugh, they think it's just total junk, but they're making a fortune. It's true what they say about another person's trash is another person's treasure.

I help him out when I can, and I don't mind it, especially when they find old motorcycles and engines, lately I've been too busy to do much of anything.

I had a call from Teresa, she told me Sizzle is ecstatic with the photoshoot and the images have been selected. I also have to go over everything I want for Gunner After Dark with Deanna. The magazine comes out in a week and I've already been sponsored to do a calendar as well as the Tattooed Ink magazine shoot.

Things are looking up, finally.

This year has certainly been the year for me to make some good coin and fill the club's coffers.

I'm happy for it, not so much for me, but for what I plan to do for Summer.

She's been wanting to finish nursing school since as long as I can remember, but she's been putting it off, using one excuse after another. I know if I help her out financially then it'll make her decision easier. Though, she doesn't like being a charity case, it pains me to see her bartending and not finishing what she started. She can't work at the Stone Crow or the club for the rest of her life. She's smart, she could do anything.

"Steel's worried about the attempted break in," Brock tells me as we're almost at church. "Thinks it might be something more sinister, dude's paranoid, though we can't exactly rule out kids being shit heads either. I guess the best thing to do is keep an eye on Lily, the amped up security system won't hurt."

"Yeah, they didn't get shit from the footage and that back-alley area is fucked up."

"Did you ask Lily about anything else that may have been out of the ordinary lately?"

I shrug. "She hasn't pissed anyone off if that's what you mean, Jenkins put it down to some stoner, probably trying to break in to steal anything they can sell for quick cash."

Brock rubs his beard but doesn't say anything more.

Before we even get out of the truck, Rawlings, Angel's kid, comes bounding up to us.

"Uncle Brock! Uncle Gunner! Look what Hutch gave me!"

She's such a cutie. I have a bit of a soft spot for her, with her little blonde ringlets and her big blue eyes, she melts everyone's hearts. Brock scoops her up with one arm.

"What you got princess?" he laughs as she waves a pink Harley Davidson figurine in his face.

I'm not sure how elegant it is giving a kid a Harley Davidson, but it looks like Rawlings is gonna be a chip off the old block like her Momma.

"Woah, that's super cool kiddo," Brock says as she makes motorbike noises and runs the thing up and down his arm as we walk towards the back entry.

"You sure you're not tapping Momma bear?" I say out of the side of my mouth.

Rawlings looks at me and waves the motorcycle in my face. "Uncle Gunner?" she says in a tone that belongs to a twenty-one-year-old about to ask for my car keys and not a six-year-old.

"Yes, darlin?"

"What's tapping Momma bear mean?"

Brock almost chokes on his intake of breath and my eyes go wide.

"Umm, nothing princess, pretend you never heard that alright? Uncle Gunner will buy you a big scoop of ice cream if you don't tell on me."

Brock slaps me upside the head as we walk through the back doors. A few of the guys are playing pool and Ginger is doing some inventory. Angel is sitting at the bar, her back to us.

"Look what we found out in the parking lot." I smile sidling up to her and sling my arm around her shoulder. "Long time no see Angel, how you been?"

Brock sits Rawlings down on the stool next to Angel and moves behind the bar.

"Good babes, I hear you're putting some fires out at the

Sizzle Magazine HQ." She gives me an eyebrow waggle and I laugh out loud.

"I don't know about fires but I'm certainly being paid handsomely, who knew this old dog could rake in cash from dropping his pants? There's hope for me yet."

"There ain't no hope for you," Brock says, shaking his head.

"Mommy?" Rawlings asks, as Brock slides a shot of whiskey onto the bar in front of me.

"Yes honey?"

"Uncle Gunner's going to buy me the biggest scoop of ice cream," she says excitedly, jumping up and down on her stool.

"Oh, he is, is he?" she side eyes me and I shrug.

"Yeah, if I didn't say what the Momma bear was."

She frowns. "What are you talking about?"

"Shhh," I laugh leaning on the bar so Rawlings can see me. "Our little secret, remember? That's why there's ice cream involved."

She slaps her hand over her mouth then giggles behind it.

I roll my eyes.

"I have no idea what that's all about," Angel says, looking up at Brock.

He's looking down at her all serious. I glance at her again and it's then I know somethings going on.

He's gotta be tapping it. He and Angel go way back, and she's one hot chick, I can't say I blame him but she comes with a shitload of baggage and a kid to boot.

"Trust me when I say you don't wanna know." Brock slings his shot back then turns to Angel, "you need a brew?"

"I'm good," she replies. "I've got to get Rawlings home soon."

"You headin' down to New Orleans this weekend?" Ginger asks Angel. She shakes her head. "Nah hon, I don't really know Crystal all that well, and Rawlings has her recital on Saturday night."

"Oooh yes!" Rawlings squeals with delight, she's really loving that motorcycle, she wheels it all over the bar and over the coasters. "I've got to sing, right Mommy?"

"That's right honey, and I'm going to make a video of you to show everyone just how amazing you sound."

She jumps up and down again. "Uncle Brock, will you come and watch me?" she asks, looking up with those big blue eyes.

He leans down off the bar. "I'd love to kiddo, but I've got to go out of town this weekend."

She pulls the bottom lip out, then turns to me. "What about you, Uncle Gunner? Will you come watch me?"

Poor little kid, I actually feel like an asshat now. "I'm gonna be with Uncle Brock," I tell her, chucking the shot down my neck. "But when I come back, I'll have the biggest, bestest present for you to open, so you gotta be a good girl for your Momma, yeh?"

She bangs her bike up and down with excitement. "Yes! Mommy, did you hear that? Uncle Gunner's getting me a present!"

Angel smooths her hair down lovingly. "Well then you better be a good girl like he said until then, munchkin."

"I will be," she assures us. "I'll be the bestest ever!"

"Thanks for teaching her a word that doesn't exist in the English dictionary," Angel says out of the side of her mouth.

"Hey, bestest is a word, I use it all the time."

"Doesn't mean it's an actual word, Guns."

"Mommy I'm hungry," Rawlings moans, rubbing her eyes with her little fists.

"You just had some fruit," Angel tells her. "And we'll be having dinner soon."

Brock reaches behind him and produces a small bag of

potato chips; he opens the bag and hands it to Rawlings. She looks up at him like he's the messiah.

Angel gives him an annoyed look.

"What?" he questions with a shrug. "Kids hungry."

"Yeah, mom," Rawlings repeats, diving her hand into the bag and spilling half the chips on the floor. "Kid's hungry."

We all laugh as Angel stands to leave. "I gotta get this kid home, see you guys later."

"Later babes," I say as Brock just gives her a nod. "Bye Rawlings!"

"Bye!" she waves the pink bike at us with her hand as the other is clutching the potato chips.

Once they're gone, I turn to Brock.

"What the fuck, bro?"

He looks up at me and grabs the bottle, filling our shot glasses again. "What?"

I nod behind me. *"That!"*

"Nothing's going on there."

"Does she know that?"

"It's ancient history, I help out with Rawlings from time to time." He shrugs like it's nothing. He's such a bad liar. We all help out with Rawlings when we can, so that's the excuse of the decade.

"You can tell me bro, I won't say anything, you definitely not tappin' it?"

"Nothin' to tell and no I'm not."

"Need some pointers? I know what chicks like."

"Fuck off."

"Well, the vibes you two are giving off say more than words can."

He rolls his eyes and comes around to sit next to me. "Nothin' serious anyway, you happy now? Inspector Clueso."

I turn to look at him. "So, what then?"

"Just some flirtin' and shit."

"Shit like what?"

"Do I have to spell it out for you?"

"Kinda."

"Makin' out a bit, nothin' heavy, she's keeping me at arm's length, gettin' my dick tied up in knots cause' she won't let me have any."

Shit. "Isn't she up for it all of a sudden?"

"We don't roll like that anymore." He seems annoyed by that. "She's gone all good-girl on me."

I snort. "But you used to, what happened? She's a cool chick, seems to have her shit together now."

"That was before Rawlings," he sighs heavily. "And that douche bag she married."

We both pause, Angel's had it tough. She doesn't have much of a family to speak of and her old man treated her real bad. He doesn't have anything to do with Rawlings, in fact he skipped out when she was born.

The club's been her family ever since. Having Rawlings has tamed her, that's for sure; she was into some pretty wild shit back then.

"So, you can still do the friends with benefits thing?" I suggest.

He gives me a side eye. "Do people really do that shit?"

I shrug. "Fucked if I know, never been friends with a woman."

He slaps me upside the head again. "Anyway, you can talk."

"What's that supposed to mean?"

"What about you and Lil? Anything happen the other night? You been quiet as lamb about it, not like you. Chelsea said you disappeared."

Shit, am I that transparent?

"I had to go see to the break in at Lily's."

"Funny that huh?"

"I was the only one partially sober enough to drive her, before you start."

He grunts like he doesn't believe me. "Sure, dude."

I look around to see if anyone is in earshot, all this sneaking around is starting to grate on me.

"And don't even bother with the cute face bro, I know something's up." He goes on. "So, fess up."

I may as well come clean. "A little bit of somethin' might have happened," I admit. I trust Brock but I don't want him knowing any of the details. "I didn't plan it, swear to God."

"Fuck man."

"Yeah, she's a handful. She was grinding against some loser in front of the stage; I lost my shit."

"You better not be fucking her around, I mean it."

I glance at him. "You really think I'd do that?"

He side eyes me. "Not intentionally."

I've nobody to ask any of this shit to, so now seems like an opportune time.

"I've been feeling kind of weird lately."

He glances at me again, Brock's not exactly one for heart to hearts but I know he'll hear me out.

"What, your dick won't work?"

"Nothin' like that, but... She's got me feelin' all kinds of things I haven't felt before, things I don't know what to do with, emotions and shit."

He baulks. "You goin' soft?"

I grab my nuts. "Nah man, hard as."

He shakes his head. "Fuckin' women, they know how to mess with us, they get us right where it hurts."

I run a hand over my face. I'm not done yet.

"You're tellin' me. For example, you saw her, she comes in with her date on Saturday night all dressed up like she's got somewhere to be, and I get this sharp pain in my chest like I'm havin' a goddamn heart attack, then I realize I'm fuckin' jealous, like green eyed monster jealous, lucky her date wasn't around much, or I may have just floored him for lookin' at her sideways. I mean, what the fucks gotten into me?"

He shakes his head. "You got it bad, bro. Chicks fuck you up in the head, I'm tellin' you, if you know what's good for you, run away, run now while you can."

"Speaking from experience?" I chortle.

He ignores me. "And while we're on the subject, I'd fess up to Steel if you're even thinking about anything permanent with her, out of respect... oh, and yeah, your will to live."

I snort. "Yeah, then he can respectfully amputate my limbs, then my organs, one by one. I'm sure giving him the heads up on defiling his little sister is gonna go down a real treat, no matter how I broach it."

He grunts. "Best bein' up front, tellin' you now, it's easier in the long run. Mark my words." He brings the shot up to his lips again and throws it back. "And you better be certain that you understand what it means brother, cause if you fuck up, you won't just have Steel to deal with, but this entire club, Hutch included; just think about that before you do anything stupid."

I run a hand through my hair.

I'm certainly not gonna admit that I can't get it up at the moment for anyone except her. I don't want Brock to think I'm a total pussy, I still have a sliver of pride left.

The conversation though has done nothing for my inner turmoil.

Just then Hutch's door swings open and I give him a nod as he makes his way across to us.

"Glad to see you back," he says, nodding to Ginger for a glass. She pours him a couple of fingers from the top shelf and slides it over. "Thank you, darlin'." He turns back to us. "How'd it go? Get any good shit?"

"Great," Brock replies. "We got some fuckin' great shit man, just unloaded the trailer, took that as well, wanted to stop by and check on things before we unload the truck, plus I got some parts in the back to drop off to Steel."

"You all set for tomorrow?"

Tomorrow we head down to New Orleans for the wedding.

I stifle a yawn. "Yeah, but I could sleep for a hundred years."

"Toughen up princess, you're only gone for three nights and you'll be staying at the clubhouse. I've arranged it all with Cash, just make sure Deanna doesn't lead the other girls astray, you know how she can get."

"She sure as shit takes after her mom then," I say with a smirk.

"Trust me, she got her looks from her momma and her personality from me, that's what I'm afraid of."

"Fuckin' women," Brock grumbles.

I know he's thinking about Angel. I don't know why he fights it, they're good together, but maybe he just doesn't want to be tied down. I get that too, but it kinda seems like that's not the reason.

He's pushing forty, surely you can't be doing this shit forever. Even I draw the line somewhere.

"Can't live with em, can't fuckin' get a word in edgewise," Hutch mutters as we clink glasses. "God punished me with not only a smart kid but a beautiful one too, be warned boys if you ever have kids of your own, tie your daughters down and invest in a good fuckin' shot gun, you're gonna need it, it's why I'm old and gray cause she keeps me up at night worrying."

"Oh, is that the reason why?" I snicker.

He hits me upside the head, everyone seems to be doing that a lot lately.

"No girls comin' out of this," Brock cusses, grabbing his junk.

I splutter into my newly poured shot and almost choke on it.

"Yeah, not sure you have a choice in that, big guy." I slap him on the back. "Anyway, don't you just shoot blanks?"

"Sure as shit ain't got any fuckin' say," Hutch grumbles. "Deanna's more of a handful than I could have ever bargained for, must've been fuckin' devious in my past life, lord help the poor fella who takes her off my hands, he's in for one hell of a ride." He downs another shot, shaking his head, cussing some more.

"To women trouble." Brock knocks his shot glass into ours.

"Keep your balls hanging for as long as you can," Hutch mutters with a grimace.

"Amen to that."

15

LILY

I love New Orleans.

I always have, you can come here and be as weird as you like and nobody gives a shit.

I don't love flying but this is the best option, nobody wants to spend twenty-two hours in a car or on a motorcycle driving through multiple states.

I've also packed so much stuff you'd think we were going for three months. In my defense I need all my makeup and beauty supplies so I can get Crystal ready for her big day, and I intend on going all out.

I don't think I've been this excited for a long time, and it's not just about the wedding.

I know Gunner's been out of town, but I still haven't heard from him all week long. After what we did and what I confessed, it feels a little chilly. I am, truth be told, a little pissed at him.

We make out, he gets to third base-sure we got interrupted- then he splits and ghosts me without even so much as a text message. Typical biker behavior, out of sight out of mind.

GUNNER

It's his fault I'm even in this position to begin with.

I went to church with a date and I tried my best to give him a chance.

That was an obvious disaster, then Gunner drags me off the dance floor and devours me with his mouth and his hands. Now all I do is imagine that mouth everywhere and us in bed together every spare second I get.

It's like now that I've had a real taste of him, I want more, so much more.

I even packed all my good underwear, you know, just in case. I plan on pulling out all the stops this weekend.

If Gunner wants to pass me up again and again then he can go right ahead, I'm through with playing games, he either wants me or he doesn't.

I'm sure there's plenty of available men at the New Orleans chapter that would look at me twice and like what they see and won't give me the run around. Gunner can't just drag me away from other guys if he doesn't intend on following through himself.

I want him to do all those dirty things to me, I want him to do them all night long.

I've barely laid eyes on him since we boarded the plane, of course he was late as usual and almost missed the flight.

As predicted, the boys are not happy about having to drive hire cars, but Cash promised he has plenty of motorcycles in his possession for them to use when we get there.

When we arrive, there's about a hundred bikes parked in the lot. I knew this chapter was big but hell almighty.

The clubhouse is a large, old, brick building with huge iron gates all around the perimeter. It's in a quiet, industrial part of the business district. I guess you can make noise out here and nobody will care.

Gunner's also cut his hair since I saw him last. It's long on top and shaved at the sides, just how I like it, but he's also growing this short goatee, Charlie Hunnam style, and I'm not complaining. He suits being both clean shaven and with a beard, it wouldn't really matter with a face like his, the lucky bastard suits anything.

We haven't even emerged from the car and Crystal runs/waddles down the pathway from the open doors and just about bowls me over.

"Lily!" she squeals, holding onto me tight. "It's been like a hundred years!"

"I know," I laugh back, "and omg you're getting married!"

She squeals as we jump up and down with excitement, Deanna and Summer join in as we jump around stupidly.

I look down and see she's really starting to show.

"I can't believe you're going to have a baby!"

"I know," she laughs, rubbing her small bump. "I'm pretty freaked out, but I keep telling myself it's gonna be okay, and Rider is so amped up about it though we've no clue what the hell we're doing."

"You've got a good man there, Crystal, he loves you," Deanna says. "Has he got a twin brother by any chance?"

She laughs. "No, and God knows I've been through enough losers to find him."

"Send some hot dudes our way," Summer says with a sigh. "Bracken Ridge has no hot guys."

"Amen to that," Deanna chimes.

"I'll see what I can do," Crystal giggles. She really does have that baby glow going on.

"You boys going to just stand there or come help us?" Deanna yells to the boys, who exit their car and don't rush to help with our stuff. Typical.

Brock stubs out his cigarette with his boot but doesn't move.

"What do we look like? Fuckin' bell hops?"

"Are you supposed to be smoking in a rental?" I fling back at him over my shoulder.

"You look like the last of the chivalrous romantics," Deanna smirks.

I glance at Gunner, he's watching me.

I shake my hair out of my ponytail and straighten my spine. I didn't just dress in a patent leather skirt and tank top for nothing, he can read it and weep this weekend, and I don't have Steel riding my ass telling me what I can and can't wear either, Sienna convinced him to stay home, praise the lord.

His eyes assess me and I know he's judging my outfit; this skirt is way shorter than the one I had on at church and he had plenty to say about that. Well, he'll just have to learn, he can't tell me what to do or what to wear either. In fact, he's no right to comment on anything I wear, say, or do.

If I had any doubts about how he feels, it's kind of cleared up in those few short moments as our eyes meet, and that's why I'm so confused.

He looks at me like he wants to devour me whole.

The feeling I get shoots all the way through my body till I swear I feel it in my toes.

We haul our bags and suitcases out and Gunner makes his way towards us, he can't help it, out of all the boys he is the nicest to all the women. The others just treat us like idiots because they'd rather act like cavemen than to have anyone think they may have one decent bone in their stupid bodies.

"Well, well, what do we have here?" A booming voice sounds from the doorway. I look up from the trunk and Cash, the club Prez, is standing watching us with his hands on his hips.

I haven't seen him in years. He's aged well for a man in his late forties, his hair graying at the sides as is his beard, but he still looks damn fine, for an older guy.

He fills out his t-shirt and cut in all the right places. Deanna was right about him being a bit of a silver fox.

He bounds down the front steps and slaps Gunner, Bones, and Brock each on the back and they do that one-armed, handshake hug thing.

"Hey Cash!" Deanna calls, as me and Summer lug the heavy case filled with my beauty supplies up the pathway.

He looks up and then comes to greet us and swings Deanna into a big bear hug and whispers something in her ear, she giggles in response.

He nods to me. "Hey princess, haven't seen you in a while."

"Ditto, and thanks for letting us crash here for the weekend," I reply. "You're still looking good, Cash."

"Ah darlin', you're makin' me blush." He gives me a wink as I introduce Summer.

"How was your trip?"

"Urgh uneventful," Deanna replies once she's back on her feet. "Fuck Cash, you been working out?" She presses her fingers to his abs and he looks down at her with surprise.

"Leave it to you to be here two minutes and molest the first man you see," Brock hollers, shaking his head.

She ignores him. "Can't help it if I have good taste." She gives him a sly wink.

My eyes go wide as he laughs like he doesn't know what to do with her. Hurricane Deanna has landed.

"I can see that I have to keep a sharp eye on you this weekend, little miss."

Deanna is the world's biggest flirt and she dials it up several notches, smiling up at him under her lashes.

"As long as that's not all you're watching." I hear her whisper back.

I roll my eyes at her though I'm not one bit surprised.

Some of the club members come out to greet the boys but

Gunner still lingers close by. It's like he wants to say something.

Cash turns back to us. "You girls wanna come inside and make yourselves at home?"

"Love to." I pick up the beauty case as Gunner passes us with some of the heavier stuff.

Cash leans down and picks up Deanna's suitcase like it weighs nothing and leads the way to the clubhouse doors.

Crystal links her arm with mine and we follow the herd inside.

The clubhouse has an industrial feel with concrete floors, it smells a little smokey and has pool tables scattered around and a long bar, the shelves filled with every bottle imaginable. There are not many people around it being mid-afternoon, but we don't linger there and head up the stairs, down a long corridor.

"You know, I'm studying to be an interior designer," Deanna says to Cash. "And I'm really good at it, I've got an eye for detail. If you're ever thinking about an overhaul, just hit me up."

"What you tryin' to say?" He gives her the side eye. "My place not good enough?"

"No," she says innocently, "just, you know, it's never too late to think about upgrading the décor, a lick of paint here and a little bling there, could work wonders."

He shakes his head as we laugh. "A little bling?"

"Well not girly shit obviously, manly stuff, biker get up, I cater for all kinds and different tastes. I aim to please."

Somehow, I get the feeling she's not referring to interior decorating any more. Crystal and I giggle behind her.

"Never had a broad complain yet," he mutters. "You know, about my *décor*."

Crystal rolls her eyes. "That's because it's usually dark

when you drag the girls up here Cash, they don't notice the old-fashioned wallpaper."

He grunts. "Trust me darlin', I don't *drag* anyone anywhere, they come willingly." He pushes open one of the doors.

It's rustic inside, old wood floors and high ceilings. It's quaint.

"Hope it's alright that you girls have to share, there's only two doubles and the boys have the other rooms."

Of course, Gunner, Brock, and Bones all have to have separate rooms so they can bang any chick they like while they're here. I don't know why we can't just stay in a hotel.

"This is great, thank you," I reply as we all stand in the small space. While it's just a bedroom it is neat and tidy and surprisingly clean, though I guess Crystal had something to do with that because it smells like lavender and furniture polish.

"We'll all be getting ready at my place though, before the ceremony," Crystal reminds us. "We need a little girl time."

I'm so happy she's excited. I am too.

"It's gonna be great," I declare. "Don't worry, I'll pamper you rotten mama, I brought everything I possibly could."

She laughs excitedly.

"Sure fuckin' feels like it," Cash says, dumping Deanna's suitcase on the bed. "What you got in here, a dead body?"

"Everything but the kitchen sink," Summer replies. "I call shotgun!" She bounces on the middle of the bed.

"You can't call shotgun on a bed!" I tell her.

"Looks like it's you and me babe," Deanna says with a wink, then her eyes flick to Cash. "Unless I get any better offers."

I mean, could she make it any more obvious?

Cash visibly swallows and wisely doesn't say a word. It's probably better that way.

He's got at least twenty-years on her, not that there's anything wrong with an older guy, but he's just about best buddies with Hutch.

That could pose a problem, a very big problem. I don't know what she's thinking.

"I promised your old man I'd look after you girls," he says, giving me a wink. "So, you girls gonna play nice or am I gonna have to get my big guns out and scare all the bad boys away?"

"I'll be fine." Deanna waves him off. "I only go for men, not boys."

I bite my bottom lip.

"I don't know," Summer pipes up. "Don't bad boys do it better?"

Cash shakes his head, probably wondering what he's gotten himself into and that Hutch should have organized a hotel room.

"Sorry Cash, the girls don't get out much," I explain. "Being from a small town and all."

Cash grunts a laugh.

Gunner appears in the doorway. No doubt some chick accosted him on the way up because it doesn't take that long to bring bags up.

"I dropped your stuff off in the other room Liliana, or do you want it in here?" he asks me.

He only calls me Liliana when I'm in some kind of trouble or, on the rare occasion he's worried about me. He doesn't look very worried, however.

"In the other room is fine, thanks," I reply coolly, not looking at him.

"Where do we get a drink around here?" Deanna chimes.

"More like where are all the hot, sexy, single men in this chapter hiding?" I whisper to Crystal, knowing Gunner's right there and can hear every word.

"You know these guys party hard, just warning you," Crystal laughs with wide eyes. "Why do you think we moved out?"

"I thought it was because you were too loud?" I bump her with my hips.

"You're so bad, Lil!" she shakes her head. "I forgot some of the crazy shit we did."

"I plan on reliving some of it this weekend." I'm hammering it up just a little bit.

"I'll see what I can do then."

We laugh together as we head back downstairs to begin a magical weekend, one I hope we never forget.

~

"Jesus Christ!" Crystal cries as I rip the hair from her body with the waxing strip.

"He won't help you babe," I say. "This is what happens when you skip appointments."

"I can't take any more," she whines. "Seriously!"

"If you want to have sexy time on your honeymoon babe, trust me, he's gonna appreciate it."

"He's already knocked me up," Crystal rages on. "There's nothing he hasn't seen."

"Trust me when I say, guys love Brazilians."

I apply more wax and shake my head as she closes her eyes and puffs up her cheeks with air.

"Distract me then, how's your love life been?"

Of all the questions I *don't* want to answer. "Ugh, don't ask."

"Nobody on the horizon?"

"I'm too busy with work," I admit. "I did have a date last weekend, but he wanted in at the club more than he wanted me, spent all night hanging around the patched members asking questions about how many miles to the gallon, it was embarrassing."

"Ugh God, be thankful he's out of the picture, you can do way better, girl."

"Everyone keeps saying that, but this mystery man who's set to sweep me off my feet hasn't exactly surfaced yet."

All except one.

"You're not still crushing on Gunner?"

I sigh heavily. "That was a long time ago, I thought we were gonna hook up but now I'm not so sure."

"I sensed some hostility earlier, you wanna talk about it?"

I rip the wax off with the strip and she yelps.

"Well, for one he's being an absolute douchebag."

"Aren't they all, honey?"

"I'm starting to think so. He thinks he can just blow me off when it suits him, then when nobody's looking, he can come crawling back, make out with me, then leave again and I don't hear from him all week."

She opens her eyes. "Oh my God, did you guys…?"

"No, but things were getting pretty hot and heavy last Saturday night until the salon got broken into and we had to leave, he was all over me, then he didn't text or call or anything while he was out of town, like how hard is to send a text? If I send one then I just look desperate and needy."

She frowns. "My God, he's a total douchebag."

"I know, so what's a girl supposed to think? And I told him personal, private things about me and he goes and just blows me off like that so easily. I'm seriously so over his shit."

"You know the best way to get revenge?"

I look down at her as our eyes meet.

"No, what?"

"Make him wish it was him with his hands all over you."

I laugh candidly. "You sound like Deanna; her suggestion is use him for sex because he's not capable of anything more."

Crystal smiles sympathetically. "You have to consider the fact that she's right, I mean I don't know him all that well, but from what you've told me, he doesn't seem like the being tied down type, if that's what you want?"

"I know I'm tired of dating," I tell her. "He says he respects me, I mean, that's sweet and everything but it isn't like that's music to my ears, it's girl code for not gonna happen in this lifetime. If something was going to happen, wouldn't he have done it by now?"

I know I sound whiny but it's nice to vent to someone neutral, someone who'll give it to me straight without knowing all the details.

"That's because you obviously have feelings for him that run deeper than sex, that's when you run into complications, that's when you get hurt."

I apply the last of the wax with the spatula as I consider that thought.

"Things would be super awkward if we did friends with benefits," I tell her, my voice quiet. "Which is another one of Deanna's helpful suggestions, I just don't know if I can handle the thought of him being with other women as we wouldn't be exclusive obviously, I don't do the random hook up thing but he definitely does, of course. He's never even had a girlfriend."

"Oh Lily, why don't you just tell him how you feel? He obviously feels something too if you've come this far, some guys are just really bad at expressing how they feel out loud."

I sigh. "You're right. It's like he won't let himself be happy, you know. It's like he doesn't think he's worthy enough, I can see behind all of the bravado he puts on. He says he isn't capable of more but yet he shows me otherwise when we're together, when we're alone it's like we can do anything, conquer the world if we want."

"Sounds like you either need to throw him a fuck or forget it."

I sigh. "If only it were that simple."

"Maybe it is, Lil. You just have to take the emotion out of it and if you can't do that then walk away, it's that or risk being hurt."

I know she's right because it's not the first time I've heard it. I'm so sick of the fight or flight mode.

Suddenly there's a knock at the bathroom door.

"Who is it?" Crystal calls out.

"Deanna. You bitches almost done? We got tequila shots out here."

"Don't know if you noticed," Crystal yells through the door. "I can't drink in my condition."

"Yeah, but you can take us to the nearest strip joint and be the designated driver."

"You have got to be kidding me?" she squeaks. "Rider will never agree to that."

"We don't need his permission," she yells back brazenly. "Anyway, you can say you didn't know and that we dragged you there, blame me if you have to. It's your bachelorette party and we're goin' sweet cheeks, get your butt out here ASAP or I'll come in and haul your ass out myself."

We groan in unison because one thing's for sure, Deanna always gets her own way.

"There goes the neighborhood," I groan.

"She doesn't take no for an answer, does she?"

"I heard that!" Deanna yells as we both snort with laughter. "Hurry up or I'll break the door down."

We hear her stomp away.

"She is actually serious, isn't she?" Crystal cringes.

"Oh yes, you think this is painful, try drinking with her."

I don't care, I need a fun night out, it might take the edge off. In fact, it may be just the edge I need.

16

GUNNER

The girls have all gone out for dinner, so they say, and we're left to our own devices at the clubhouse. There's a big party organized for tonight, we're having a big farewell to bachelorhood for Rider, being his last night as a free man and all.

I lean against the bar as the festivities begin and people pour into church. The strippers are coming later, courtesy of some of the patched members.

Rider seems in good spirits, he's ecstatic to be getting married with a kid on the way, Crystal seems cool, though I don't know her well, they seem happy.

I keep thinking about Lily and why she's giving me the cold shoulder, though deep down, I know why.

I didn't purposely stay away from her, despite my inner turmoil over what we've been up to. Granted, it was shitty to not text her, but she's got fingers too, and a mobile phone. Today at the airport and at the clubhouse she's purposely ignored me and when she's had to acknowledge me, it's been short and curt. Even if I deserve it, I can't keep up with her mood swings.

The chair moves beside me and Cash slumps onto the stool.

"On the hard stuff already?" he nods to my half-filled glass of scotch.

"Fuck man I need it; those girls been drivin' me up the wall today, I don't know how I turned into their yes man, been hauling' shit all over New Orleans for them."

The girls had me running them all over town because they didn't have proper directions, they had to drop boxes of shit off at the restaurant for the tables and then I had to pick up dresses. Lily still managed to sit in the backseat and avoid talking to me.

"Fuckin' women," he snorts. "Did you really expect anything less, though?"

I laugh. "You got a ball n chain?"

"Nah man. Had an ol' lady years back, long story, needless to say it didn't work out. I miss it though, you know, havin' someone to come home to, share shit with, feelin' of a warm body next to me that's got my back. Must be getting' fuckin' old."

I chuckle and look at him over my glass, surprised. I'd never pick him for someone who actually wanted to be tied down.

One of the chicks serving at the bar drops two shots of tequila in front of Cash, he pushes the other glass towards me.

"Have a drink with me."

I take it as the chick watches me. She smiles and I glance down at her huge tits, barely contained in the top she's wearing. We both sling the shots back and he orders two more.

"You got some nice-lookin' women down here," I say, giving her a smirk. I wonder why my dick hasn't woken up though, that's still troubling. Normally a huge set of knockers and beautiful big lips will do the job nicely, but I'm limp as.

He lights up a cigarette as the broad pours two more, gives me a wink and moves on.

"No shit, but one wrong move and they'll have your balls in a vice."

"Isn't that all women?"

I sling the second shot down; the sweet burn soothes my soul and chases the demons away.

"I gotta ask you somethin' bro."

"Shoot."

"Deanna."

I glance at him. "Yeah, what about her?"

"She grew up, that's what."

I snicker. "Oh yeah."

"Hutch would fuckin' kill me, but she's been coming onto me pretty hard, she always like that?"

I shrug. "How would I know. She's always been direct, says what she feels, gets what she wants, she comes from a long line of hard asses, shit's ingrained into her I guess."

He takes another long drag. "She needs to stay away from me."

Unlike some of the guys in my chapter I very rarely judge, but if he starts something with Deanna, being Hutch's friend, it could pose a problem, stir bad blood between the clubs.

That shit's never good. It's why I'm trying and failing to stay away from Lily. I don't want bad blood with Steel or to be on the outs with Hutch.

Then again maybe I need to fight for what I want and grow a pair and take what's mine.

It could go either way.

"You worried about Hutch?"

"Fuckin' oath. We go way back."

I nod. "Yeah man, I wouldn't go there, but it's your club,

your rules, though I'm technically here to look out for her, for all the girls."

He nods like he understands. "You got women troubles too?"

"Am I that transparent?"

I watch as the chick who served us the shots bends over to get ice and I watch her skirt ride up so her G-string shows.

My dick doesn't even twitch, I got nothing.

"Nah, just figured you're sittin' up here all by your lonesome in the middle of a party with plenty of pussy going round, you got a face like a bag of rotten apples."

I laugh. "You're not far off."

"So, what gives?"

"Lily and me."

"Ah."

"Yeah. It's more complicated than I'd like it to be."

He snorts. "Ain't that the truth, brother."

I turn to him. "Have you ever figured them out?"

"Who? Women?"

"Yeah."

He grunts. "Fuck no, and if you want my advice or two cents worth then here it is; if you find yourself a good woman, a woman who's loyal, will stand by you, who'll let you play a few innings but has her own mind, grab onto her with both hands my friend, they don't come around too often."

Again, he surprises me with his admission.

"Never really thought about her like that, but you're right, she is all those things, that's why I can't do anything, I'll ruin her."

"What're you afraid of? Having one snatch for the rest of your life? I know one thing; you get too old for all the shit and drama, before you know it, fifty is knocking on the fuckin' door, your bones creek and you can't party like you used to. You're pissin' in the dark and makin' your own fuckin' food. Find a good woman before you're too old, and if you've found her then show her who she belongs to, trust me on that."

"Jesus, fuck," I laugh. "Think I need a stronger drink. I've never been monogamous. But ever since me and Lil have been fooling around, it's like she's ruined me for all other women, I can barely fuckin' get it up for anyone else, then she walks in a room and I'm drooling like a dog with a bone, feelin' all kinds of shit I shouldn't be feelin.'"

The cute chick tops up our shot glasses again and leans over to me.

"You wanna get out of here later?" she says close to my ear.

I raise my shot glass and down it but don't say a word. I just grin at her.

She grins back and blows me a kiss before moving on.

"Doesn't seem like you have much trouble with the ladies," he muses.

"I only have trouble with *one* lady," I grumble.

"Hate to break it to you, if it ain't Lily Steelman, it'll be some other chick, they should all come with a warning label."

I snort and down my shot. "You said a mouthful there, Prez."

Tag plonks down noisily on the stool on the other side of Cash. The Sergeant at Arms doesn't look happy, then again, I've never seen him smile.

If I thought Steel was a fuckin' mean son of a bitch, this guy makes him look like a boy scout.

He's six foot and wide; I don't think I've seen shoulders that big in a very long time, and he's got a reputation for being a hard ass, none of the women like him because he takes no shit. He looks disgruntled about something, but that's just his everyday face.

I don't get to hear what his complaint is as we're deafened by the music that suddenly blares out from the loudspeakers.

The party amps up and gets wild pretty fast, it's midnight and the lights are down and the crazy is in full swing.

I noticed the girls still aren't back.

I've texted Deanna with no reply, then Summer, who told me to get lost, and then I resorted to messaging Lily, still no answer. I doubt they're still having dinner and I doubt they're all playing charades back at Crystal's place.

Maybe I have a sixth sense too and it might just be for sniffing out trouble.

The front doors open suddenly and whoops and cat calls ring throughout the bar. I know by the noise that the strippers have arrived.

The boys move like Moses parting the Red Sea. The girls, clad in all kinds of costumes, parade on by, strutting their stuff. One has a biker's get up on with a vest half zipped up and a whip in her hand, one is dressed as a nurse with suspenders and a see-through dress, and another as a policewoman swinging handcuffs and a fake baton. The boys push Rider into the middle of a man-made ring and he gets shoved into a chair. The girls proceed to dance around him as the music starts up again and he shakes his head, gulping the last of his beer with a big grin on his face.

I don't know how much trouble he's gonna be in, but I hear my phone chime and go to retrieve it from my back pocket.

It's Deanna:

At a strip club. Send fire extinguishers.

Finally, an answer, but not one I was hoping for.

Me: *I fuckin' hope not.*

A message bounces back: *I'm moving to New Orleans FYI; this is off the charts HOT! Sayonara Bitches!*

I stare at the message and I know that Deanna isn't joking, it'd be right up her alley to organize this.

Me: Yeah, not sure your papa's gonna like that, babe

I turn back to the action and the strippers are getting into full swing, tops are coming off, hollers are getting louder, and boobs are getting shoved in Rider's face. I'll bet he's glad the girls aren't here so he can enjoy a lap dance or three without getting his ass whooped by his soon to be ol' lady.

We all watch the girls put on a show, and it's pretty damn hot, dollar bills are getting thrown and panties are coming off and Rider doesn't know what hit him. It's freaking crazy.

Brock slaps me on the back, taking a swig of beer.

"I love New Orleans," he yells in my ear over the throng.

"Don't you start."

He looks at me questioningly.

"Deanna," I explain, leaning to him so he can hear me. "She said the girls are at a strip joint."

He looks at it for a second then roars with laughter. "Fuck man. That'll be her doing."

"Don't tell Rider, he'll freak the fuck out."

"He's got a couple of prospects lookin' out for them," Brock informs me. "I already got them tailed, didn't know it was a strip joint."

I sigh with relief. I should have known an innocent night out of dinner and a movie wasn't going to be anything of the sort.

"Thanks for tellin' me, been worrying all night."

He rolls his eyes. "Not fuckin' stupid."

I feel a pair of hands, followed by arms, wrap around my waist and I look down behind me. The pretty girl from the bar looks up at me with a sly look in her eyes. Her top is barely hanging onto her tits, she's beautiful, and it seems she isn't shy about letting me know what she wants.

"Hey handsome."

Brock and my eyes meet. "Shit bro," he mutters.

"Hey yourself, what's your name?" I can't exactly ignore her though I don't know why, I'm just not in the mood for her, or for anyone. Except Lily.

"Whatever you want it to be," she purrs seductively.

Brock almost chokes into his beer.

"Sweet, well I'm Gunner, this is Brock."

She turns to look up at him and he gives her his best shit-eating grin.

"They make 'em pretty round here, Guns," he says, giving her a wink, as she looks between the two of us.

"Ever done a threesome?" she chirps. "You guys are both smokin' hot."

I splutter my scotch back into my glass, she grabs my ass with one hand and I wrap an arm around her.

I whisper in her ear. "I don't fuck in front of my brothers, sweetheart."

Nah that ain't and never will be my thing.

She pouts. "Aww, I like the look of both of you though, I don't like to choose."

Brock shakes his head. "How do you pick 'em bro?"

I smirk and suddenly she leans up to kiss me.

I'm a little stunned at her making the moves and being so forward, though I should be used to it by now, but it ain't my club, not my rules, and I don't wanna get my face punched in.

I also don't want her. Not even a little bit.

A commotion has me glancing over her head across the room.

The girls are back.

Just my luck I'm met with a pair of cool, blue eyes that assess me with a look of shock.

I want to pull away but a part of me wants to see Lily's reaction; to know if she really is that jealous.

She watches me and I don't take my eyes off her as I let *whatever-her-name-is* kiss me.

I take great delight in seeing her shocked face, her eyes narrow as she takes in the scene. Good, it'll teach her some manners on ignoring me all weekend and giving me the cold shoulder.

Here I was trying to be a nice guy, trying to do the decent thing while she throws her fuckin' virginity in my face, and what for? It's not gonna get me what I want being a nice guy, and it sure as hell ain't gonna feel good knowing some other dude's gonna get it.

I don't want this chick in front of me, my dick kicks in my jeans for the first time tonight and it ain't because of the kiss or the strippers, it's because Lily's eyes are staring right at me.

I grab the chick by the back of the head and slide my tongue in her mouth as she moans, all the while I stare at Lil, enjoying her obvious annoyance.

I can't look away and I'm a fucking prick for doing it. The chick's hands grab both my ass cheeks as I pull away look down at her.

"You fuck as good as you kiss?" she purrs like a kitten as we break away.

On any given day, a *normal* day I'd be off with her upstairs immediately, but I know I don't want that anymore. I want Lily.

"Not tonight baby doll, I already made plans."

I'm not a man. I'm a monster. I'm cutting her loose because I know that there's only one woman who is going to whet my appetite.

She pouts but then looks up to Brock hopefully. He grins down at her.

"I ain't goin' nowhere darlin'."

She cuddles up to his side as he reaches down and grabs her ass with his meaty hand as she giggles.

I look back up and Lily's gone.

I glance to the circle where Rider still sits, but now he has Crystal straddled in his lap and they're making out like long lost teenagers. She isn't one bit annoyed he just had strippers flouncing around all over him, they're working the crowd now and the boys are offering to buy them drinks while they milk the tips.

"Back in a bit," I call to Brock, who's whispering in the chick's ear, I'm long forgotten.

He nods, giving me a grin as I head to the bar. I get my drink refilled and make my way through the crowd. I'm gonna need a shit ton of alcohol to get through what I'm about to do.

I see Deanna on a stool further up the bar chatting with Cash; she's animated in whatever story she's telling and he's laughing with his head thrown back.

"Hey D," I say, sidling up to them.

"Hey Guns!" she gives me a big hug and I can tell she's well on her way to being pretty smashed.

"Did you really go to a strip club?" I look down at her.

"Freakin' A!" she laughs, jumping up and down on her seat. "It was so much fun, the dudes are all baby oiled up and they pick you out of the crowd and do a little dance for you in front of everyone, if you can call it a dance, more like sex with your clothes on. Poor Crystal, I thought she was going to have a heart attack!"

"Jesus," I mutter, giving Cash an eye roll as he watches her.

"Better not tell Rider what y'all got up to, he's a little on the jealous side," Cash winks.

"He can talk, he had boobs in his face when we walked in and Crystal didn't care." She shrugs.

One thing's for sure, she'll give Cash a run for his money, but he's a good guy. I know he won't take advantage of her.

I need to find Lily. "Have you seen Lil and Summer?" I interject.

"Summer's behind you," Deanna says.

I turn around and I see my sister talking with a couple of Crystal's friends, there's no worrying about her, she barely drinks and she definitely doesn't hook up.

"Lil was just here," Deanna continues, dancing in her chair to the music, "somebody gonna dance with me or what?"

I ignore her. "I gotta go check on Lil," I say to Cash.

He gives me a chin lift and I notice that Jett's leaning against the bar, watching the group of girls where Summer stands. I back slap him on the way past and he tries to punch me in the gut, but I keep walking, gotta find Lily pronto. I keep looking around but I don't see her anywhere.

I head towards the female bathroom to check there, my next stop will be upstairs in her room, if she got jacked off for good and took off then I got bigger problems.

I barge in there and a couple of girls turn to look at me from the mirrors.

"Sorry ladies," I say, giving them a lopsided grin.

"That's okay sugar." The first one says with a smile, applying lip gloss to overly filled lips. "Barge on in anytime you like."

I give her a wink.

"Liliana Marie, are you in here?" I bellow.

No answer.

I turn to the chick applying gloss. "Is there a cute little brunette wearing a gold halter neck dress in here?"

She points to one of the stalls behind her.

"Lucky bitch," she says, giving me a wink. "If she won't come out, I'll be right out there, honey."

The other girl snickers and begins fluffing up her hair.

I give lip gloss girl a chin lift as she leaves.

"Lily," I warn in a sing-song voice. "I know you're in there."

"Can't a girl pee in peace?" she whines finally.

"I'll give you five seconds."

"Ooh I'm so scared."

The remaining girl at the sink laughs. Great, now I'm a laughingstock, this won't do.

"She's from out of town," I explain in a hushed voice. "And she's about to be spanked for answering back to me."

"God, some girls have all the luck," the chick mutters as she leaves, pouting at me as she passes.

A few moments later, when we're all alone, the stall door jolts open.

Lily emerges and it's clear now what she's been doing in there. My heart sinks.

She's been crying. Her eyes are all red and puffy and her makeup's run slightly.

This is all I need.

I'm really not that great when chicks get emotional, well, I'm better than some of the brothers, but I generally don't like upsetting women. Especially not Lily.

I'm more of a lover than a fighter.

She's so sweet and innocent, and it calls to me on another level.

There is a part of me, a very dark part, that wants to take it all, fuck what anyone else thinks; take her and show her how much pleasure I can inflict on her body.

Then another part of me never wants to hurt her because I know that's all I can give her; my body. It's like I have this constant battle in my head between right and wrong.

But Sienna was right when she said that Lily is a grown ass woman, she can do what she wants and it seems she knows what she wants.

Me.

And I want it too.

I'm sick of fighting it.

I give in.

It's time I manned up.

I'm waving the white flag.

17

GUNNER

I stare at her.

"You okay?"

"Why would you care?" she replies, haughtily.

She goes to the sink, doesn't look at me, and proceeds to fix her makeup with a tissue.

Her dress is super low at the back, showing off her ivory skin and her curves.

"I do care, that's just it, Lil."

She stares in the mirror, avoiding my eyes. "You have a funny way of showing it Guns, with your tongue down another woman's throat."

I let out a long breath. "I don't want her," I say pointing to the door. "If I did, I wouldn't be in here with you now, would I?"

She glares at me from the mirror. "Didn't look like it to me, looked a lot like you were enjoying it, I'm so sick of playing these games. I'm not doing it anymore. You can go to hell for all I care, Gunner. Go fuck whoever you want because it's not going to be me."

She really is pissed. She takes no part at all in the fact that she's been bitchy to me this whole weekend and purposely ignored me.

I run a hand through my hair. "I was tryin' to get to you," I admit. "I wanted to make you feel something, *anything*. To see how you really felt about me, to see if this was really real."

I'm bad at this, at feelings and shit.

She looks lost for words for a moment. "Why would you do that? You know how I feel."

I shrug. "Cause I'm a sucker for punishment, obviously."

"Why did you ignore me all week?"

"Why did you ignore me?" I throw her words back at her.

"After almost boning me against the clubhouse wall and then the silent treatment, I figure chivalry isn't exactly your strong point." She proceeds to wash her hands in the sink and still won't look at me. "So, there is no point at all, especially having this conversation. It's a waste of time."

I fold my arms over my chest. "I wasn't purposely trying to piss you off, if that's what you mean, I got shit goin' on too. I had to go out of town."

"With you I never know where I stand." Her words actually cut me as I stare at her. "Maybe I never will."

I'm fucking this up royally, as always.

"You don't mean that."

"I'm sorry Guns," she whispers. "But I just can't do this anymore. I have to let you go."

Panic surges through me at her words. I didn't want this.

She pushes off from the sink and tries to march past me. I catch her by the wrist as she passes and pull her to my body.

"I'm tired of fighting it Lil, you want the truth?"

She stares up at me, unmoving.

Right now, I'm not sure if she does.

"I don't want *her*. She kissed me first and I saw you watching, so I did it for a reaction cause I'm a sick son of a bitch. Truth be told I'm mad at you, you didn't text me either, it works both ways, so don't go gettin' all dramatic on me because you're pissed off. I have a right to be pissed too."

I know we're acting like little kids but this ain't all about her.

Her chest rises rapidly. "You're unbelievable!"

She tries to wriggle away but I hold her arm behind her back and our fingers intertwine, I grab her free hand and move it up to cup my face. She could scratch my eyes out so it's a bold move.

"You know what you do to me by now, for fucks sakes… *this*, you're a fuckin' prick tease Lily and I'm done too."

She swallows hard. "What do you mean?"

I hold a finger up to her lips to quieten her.

"For a club girl who should know better, you sure have a lot to say for yourself with that little smart-ass mouth of yours, any other brother wouldn't put up with this shit. Any other brother would've taken what he wants and not thought twice about it."

"What are you gonna do about it?" she throws back at me. It's not the first time she's said that to me.

I also don't give her time to answer, I reach down and grasp her chin with my hand and before I can stop myself, I kiss her brutally.

My tongue finds its way into her mouth and pushes in violently as she whimpers at my touch. The sound is like music to my ears, I could never get enough of hearing it.

Instead of shoving me off and storming out like she was threatening to do she does the opposite, her arms snake up around my shoulders as I continue to kiss her until she's breathless and panting. I grind my dick into her and she moans a whole lot more.

Yeah, I'll show you what I want Liliana Marie, what I've always wanted.

There's no going back now.

She moves her hand to the bulge in my jeans and gives me a squeeze.

"Fuck Lil."

"Gunner…" she pants.

"Been thinkin' about this for a long time."

"But you said…"

I cut her off by yanking her by the hips and pushing her up against the wall, she shrieks as I go to town, eating her mouth, giving it all I got as I press my hard on into her stomach. She wanted to feel me, well, she's got it. Eat that shit up, baby.

"I can't fight it anymore, you can't make me," I say in her ear.

I've lost any kind of sense or reason I possessed before tasting her, that chapter's over.

Now I'm starting a new one.

Her only answer is a lustful mewl as I grin into her mouth.

I don't wait for her to be ready; I intertwine our fingers again and make my way to the door.

We're right near the stairs that lead up to my room. I'm fairly confident we can sneak up there unnoticed. Even better that Brock's now busy, I haven't seen Bones since earlier in the night.

I'm relieved to see nobody is paying any attention as we go out into the throng of the busy clubhouse.

I take the stairs, tugging her behind me, and we get to the landing in no time. I pull Lily inside my room with a sharp tug.

I'm impatient now.

I've waited long enough and she's a temptress who's pushed my buttons for way too long.

I lock the door behind us and she takes a step back, taking me in with huge eyes.

One of the things I love about her is her innocence. She's always had it, she's always had this little bit of trepidation about her, and it turns me on, big time.

Time to play.

"Heard you seen some strippers tonight?"

She bites her lip and then nods slowly.

I stare at her, unsmiling.

"They get you wet?"

She shakes her head. "Not like you do."

"Show me."

She swallows hard.

"Show me Lily, show me what gets you off."

She bites her lip again and it's so goddamn exciting that I reach for her, kiss her hard, shoving my tongue in her mouth and just as quickly I let her go again.

I want to watch her.

"Show me." I demand, hands on hips.

She reaches behind her and tugs at her straps and in a few seconds her dress falls to the floor. She's got no bra on, she stands there in just a lacey, black thong. Fuck me.

I run a hand through my hair staring at her, *all* of her.

I'm going to hell; this I know for sure.

Seeing her bare breasts for the first time has my cock growing twice its size instantly. It strains against my zipper painfully.

They're big, round and juicy, her nipples are already peaked and it makes my mouth water. I move one hand to the button of my jeans and let the fly loose because I need some goddamn room in there.

"Touch yourself," I tell her, my eyes skating over her delicate skin.

She moves her hands to her breasts and begins to knead them, pushing them up and together, I watch her perfect nipples pucker as she plays with her herself. I want to suck on them, tease them with my mouth, show her what she's been missing out on for all these years.

Oh yeah, I'm gonna show her alright.

I take another step forward.

"Wanna come all over those," I say darkly.

Her eyes go wide.

"Touch your pussy."

Her breath hitches.

The thought that I'm gonna get to be her first, go all the way this time and teach her what I like excites me even more. She's no idea the pleasure I can inflict on her body, now that I've got her all to myself there's nothing gonna stop me.

I stand and wait for her to follow my orders.

For once she seems to be listening.

I watch as she snakes a hand into the front of her lace panties and begins caressing herself. I stand there staring at her, wondering if I'm in the twilight zone.

She's a fucking apparition.

I pull my cut off along with my shirt and toss them on the floor. Her eyes dip down my body and I unzip my jeans, I reach down and yank my boots off, then pull my jeans and jocks down in one foul swoop, my cock springs free finally and her eyes go wide as she stares at it.

I stand there naked letting her see all of me. Her eyes, hungry in response, take me in with lustful whimpers. It's a nice sound, I could never tire of hearing it.

She bites her lip, her eyes on my cock like she can't look away.

I raise an eyebrow in question and heat noticeably rises in her cheeks.

I sheath my cock a couple of times as I move toward her. I walk her back to the bed.

I can see lust mixed with a little bit of fear in her eyes, but she's got nothing to worry about; I'm gonna take it slow with her, get her ready for me.

I push her down onto the bed then kneel down in front of her and bury my head between her tits and grasp them with my hands, testing their weight, squeezing them gently.

"Fuck, these are beautiful," I murmur into her skin.

She keeps moving her hand in her panties as I take a nipple in my mouth and suck on it, squeezing the other one, I taunt her greedily then switch to lavish the other one with the same attention. I suckle both back and forth as she moans and I lick her with my tongue.

God she's so sweet.

I play with her tits as my eyes dip to her hand working herself over down south; I spread her legs a little wider, like a good girl she lets me. I suck her hard, holding her breasts to my mouth with both hands as she wriggles around in pleasure.

"I love how big these are, so fuckin' hot," I tell her between sucks. Her free hand goes into my hair and she pulls gently.

My dick's so hard I can barely contain blowin' right here, right now, as I continue my assault on her senses, I know we're gonna be good together. I want to taste her sweet honey though; I can't wait any more.

I yank her hand out of her panties and then pull them to the side and spread her legs, she's bare, no hair at all and I groan in pleasure looking at her sweetness. I run my fingers through her slick heat, she's dripping wet.

"Fuck." Is all I can manage. She grasps my hair in both her hands as I spread her legs even wider, rubbing her back and forth with my fingers. Finally, I yank her panties down all the way and throw them behind me.

I dip my head and lick her through her slick center, looking up as she watches me. I do it nice and slow with my tongue, back and forth. She practically jolts off the bed at my touch, gasping with the sensation.

"Anyone ever done this?" I ask, softly.

She shakes her head.

Good.

Another first.

I never really eat chicks out, I've never really enjoyed it or cared enough to give them it, until now that is. It's like my whole mission in life is to please her, I'll do anything to make her scream my name.

Adrenaline pumps through my body.

"Oh God, Gunner!" she all but screams and I've barely touched her.

I know she's close just from me using my tongue, I chuckle into her flesh.

I dance my tongue over her sweet little nub and flick it back and forth, spreading her slickness all over, she tastes so damn fine. I feel her shudder beneath me.

It only spurs me on.

I part her with my fingers and latch onto her clit and suck it; looking up at her I'm delighted that she's got her eyes closed and she rubs herself against my mouth as I fuck her with my tongue. She tenses, her cheeks pink with excitement and a few moments later she comes loudly as I ride her through it, inserting a finger as she climaxes, calling my name wildly and it's the most glorious sound I've ever fuckin' heard or seen.

I'm so hard, pre-cum drips out of me; I'm thrilled to know my dick's still working after being soft all goddamn week. Thought I had a problem but no, it seems I'm just hot for her and only her.

My how the mighty have fallen.

"We're just gettin' warmed up, angel," I say, into her thigh. "I've got so much more planned for you, baby girl."

She surprises me by sitting up and beckoning me to her like a siren. "I want to suck you, Guns, I want all of you."

Not gonna argue with that but I still stare at her, never in a million years did I think I'd ever hear those words come out of her mouth.

I'm corrupting her already.

It's so dirty and forbidden, and so utterly addictive.

I waste no time standing as she takes my length in one hand and grips it firmly, *woah holy hell*, my cock is so ready. She moves forward down the bed and I watch as she takes the tip into her mouth. I hiss at the contact. She swirls her tongue around the end and I jerk as her big eyes look up at me.

I've never seen anything so beautiful.

"Goddamn," I mutter, closing my eyes momentarily.

"You like that, Guns?"

"Oh yeah babe, but I'm not gonna last watchin' you do that."

She smiles, taking my cock further into her mouth, holds me at the base as I clutch my hand over hers and show her how to milk me at the same time, just how I like it, at the right pressure and speed; oh yeah, showing her is the best part.

She sucks me off as I watch her pretty little mouth take me, and I know the sight is gonna be ingrained into my brain for the rest of time.

There could never be anything greater.

I hold her head as I move my hips, fucking her mouth but not trying to ramrod her too much. I can't help it, her lips wrapped around me are undeniably addictive. I know I'll never have my fill of her. Never.

I'm marking her.

Making her mine.

I'm her first in so many ways, and in some ways she's mine too.

Nobody else has been here except me and God that feels so fuckin' good.

I have to stop and seriously control myself from rolling her back and taking what I want. This is supposed to be special for her, I wanna do her right and make this about *her*, not me.

I clutch the side of her head aggressively and I marvel at her gag reflex, instead of wanting air she clutches my ass with her fingernails and digs right on in, encouraging me further as I assault her perfect mouth. I know I'll never be able to look at her the same way again.

I can't hold it and I want to make her mine. I need to be inside her, but I'm too far gone this round.

I start to come as my cock hits the back of her throat and she rides me through my orgasm, halfway through I pull out and squirt all over her tits, throwing my head back as I call her name wildly, pulling my cock hard till I'm drained dry.

It's so erotic and so primal I'm sure I've shocked her.

I like shocking her.

It could become a new favorite pastime.

There may never be anything sweeter in the world than her watching me come undone.

18

LILY

Gunner looks down at me as he wipes the mess he made off my chest with a face washer. I move backwards on the bed as he looms over me, a glimmer in his eyes that I definitely like the look of.

That was without a doubt the hottest, sexiest thing I've ever seen.

I've never had anyone go down on me before and I know I like it; I like it *a lot*.

"That was so hot, babe," he says, his eyes dancing with delight. "I love watchin' you."

I hold my arms out toward him and he hovers over me, our tongues clash and collide as we devour each other, our hands everywhere. I feel his pecs and his shoulders and marvel at how hard his body feels under my hands, every cell in my body is on fire for him.

It's always been him; it always will be, this only confirms it and makes it that much harder to let him go when I have to.

I don't want to think about that part.

He moves his mouth to my neck, his torture is never

ending, every kiss sets me on fire with an intensity I've never known.

I pull on his hair as he sucks my tits again, pulling on my nipples with his teeth and I now know what he meant about only being able to fuck. This is what this is; raw, passionate, primal, like he's got a rite of passage to my body. He owns all the tickets and I've got no say in the matter.

He looks up at me with his sapphire eyes, his hands cup my breasts as I lie there in absolute agonizing desire for him.

We sizzle together, there is no doubt about it. He flicks my nipples with his thumbs as I groan. His dick presses into my leg and I reach down to fondle him.

He hisses at my touch.

"I liked sucking you off, Guns," I tell him softly. I think he likes dirty talk; it turns him on.

"Yeah baby?"

"You taste so good, I wanna suck it again, over and over."

He grunts into my skin at my navel then reaches down to my pussy.

His touch is exquisite, like nothing I could ever have imagined. Not for the first time I know I'm lucky I waited. It was worth it.

"I wanna be inside you so bad babe, but gotta make sure you're really ready for me, don't want it to hurt."

"I'm ready," I moan.

"No, you're ready when I say you're ready."

He rubs me back and forth then inserts a finger inside me, gently, pushing it in and out as I spread my legs wide. I need him so bad. His thumb rubs my clit and I feel him insert another finger, stretching me, rocking me back and forth, finger fucking me as I close my eyes and hold on.

I moan his name incoherently. I'm so close to climax again and everything he touches is super sensitive. I picture his illicit mouth between my legs again, *oh my god.* That was off the charts.

"Let go baby, let me hear you."

He flicks my clit back and forth with his thumb and I explode again like there's no tomorrow, he rides me through it, his mouth on my throat as I cling to him and come hard, clenching around his fingers.

This man knows his way around a woman's body, and I know by the intensity that he wants to take me hard and fast, and probably would, if not for the fact he thinks he has to be gentle with me.

He doesn't. I'm not made of glass.

I don't even know what I mutter but he chuckles into my skin when I'm finally coming down from the high.

"Gonna take you babe," he whispers softly.

I watch as he gets up, goes over to his jeans and rips out a foil packet.

"You need to put this on me, I'll show you how."

I gape at him.

"Don't look so worried, it's easy."

He grabs my hand and helps me roll it onto the tip.

His dick is long and thick, and it feels perfect. Once it's rolled all the way, I unashamedly pull him back down to me with force.

We kiss for a long time, his dick hitting the inside of my thigh. I know I've never been this turned on or horny ever in my life, but then again, I've never gone this far before.

I feel him reach between us, his dick in his hand as he moves the tip up and down my folds, spreading my slickness everywhere. Then he lines me up and I close my eyes.

Yes!

"You okay, babe?"

I nod.

"Let me hear you say it."

"Yes. I'm ready."

"You gotta tell me if you want me to stop, you got me?"

"I won't." I squeeze his butt cheeks, hoping he'll get on with it. "I want it, I want you."

He smirks. "I know, but it's important you tell me if I hurt you, got me?"

I nod. "Yes, I heard you, hurry up."

He chuckles shaking his head then he pushes into me slowly.

I'm so hot for him that I arch my back and try to encourage him to take me deeper.

He mutters incoherently into my neck.

It's a beautiful sound.

I don't want him to hold back, so I grab his ass and pull him closer. With one sharp thrust he sinks into me deeper, a searing pain shoots through me at the intrusion.

It's so tight and he fills every inch of me. I let out a strangled moan as he stops, looking down at me.

I smile up at him and he kisses me softly.

"Baby, you okay?"

I nod. "Everything's perfect."

"I want you to know that this means the world to me. I still don't deserve it, but I'm glad it's me, babes."

I love you.

"I'm glad it's you too, Guns."

He moves again, slowly in and out, ever so slow as if he's testing the waters. He's being so sweet it melts my heart even more. I could combust just watching him watch me.

"So tight," he whispers, holding his body off me with his hands on the mattress. "You sure you're alright?"

I try not to eye roll with his attentiveness.

I grab his butt cheeks instead and encourage him. "For the third time, yes, now fuck me, please."

He grins then thrusts a little bit harder.

God his hips can move.

"Fuck, babe," he mutters, the heady rhythm is intoxicating as he milks my body so easily, so effortlessly, it's like my body is made for him.

He dips his head and takes a nipple into his mouth and sucks on it, looking up at me as I wrap my legs around him and he spreads my knees wider. The tension inside me builds higher and higher. The angle he's pumping me brushes every sensitive nerve ending in my body, taking me to new heights, he increases the pressure and the intensity.

I'm lost in a blur of thrusts and pleasure, my pain long forgotten. The orgasm rips through my body like a runaway freight train. I've never come so hard in my life. He continues pumping me until I'm all the way over the line, it's soft and sensuous and dirty all rolled into one.

"I want you to ride me," he says, pulling out and rolling us over so he's on the bottom and I'm on top. I straddle his hips and he reaches up and pulls me closer, sitting up so we're face to face. His lips find mine as does his tongue, we kiss like lovers, like two people who've known each other their whole lives, two people that have nothing left but reckless abandon. And I wouldn't want it any other way.

He holds his cock at the base and I hover over it, he helps me as I sink down slowly, holding my hips. He's watching where we're joined and groans as I get lower and lower until I'm all the way down.

It's tight, it's pain, but it's worth it. So worth it.

He grasps my hips harder and moves me up and down on him slowly.

"Fuck, Lil," he moans.

"Gunner..." I whisper. The tight sensation has me squeezing my eyes shut.

I never want this to end.

I rest my hands on his chest as he lies back and watches me, his hands behind his head as he grins.

"Fuck, you ridin' me is a sight for sore eyes."

I can't do anything except keep my eyes closed and moan, him watching me is too much.

"Touch yourself," he tells me.

I cup my tits and push them together.

He grunts as I back and forth, faster and faster, rocking my hips. The primal look in his eyes has me seeing stars, not to mention how good he feels beneath me.

Suddenly, he sits up, so we're face to face again. He moves his mouth to kiss me harshly, his tongue wild and furious, he moves to my neck, then my tits as he sucks on a nipple.

I feel his hand move between us as he rubs then pinches my clit. At his illicit touch I lose control and come even harder as he bounces me up and down, sucks my nipple, and pinches my clit all at once. I call his name like a wild animal, holding his shoulders as I throw my head back.

"I wish I could last all night," he grunts. "But I can't, your pussy's milkin' me good, babe."

I smile but he doesn't let up, he bounces me faster and faster, thrusting his hips upwards. I hold onto his shoulders, my tits now bouncing in his face as the bed hits the wall with fury back and forth.

Suddenly he rolls us back over so he's on top again, he holds the back of my thighs while he comes to his knees, holding my ass slightly off the bed as he pounds into me hard and fast. He's so deep I see stars, hitting every inch of me to the hilt. I can't hold on and by the look on his face, neither can he.

I sail into oblivion unashamed as he continues to pump, groaning, until I feel his dick twitch and he comes violently inside me calling out my name.

After a long moment, he finally stills. A few seconds later he collapses on top of me and breathes heavily into my neck.

"Oh, my fuckin' god," he groans, and I admit, I feel pretty pleased with myself.

"Yeah," I pant, my breath coming hard and fast, like the rest of me. He pulls out of me slowly, but I still wince. He flops down beside me, bringing me with him as I rest my head on his shoulder. His breathing ragged and uneven.

I love how undone I make him.

"You alright, babe? For real?"

I nod into his side. "I'm perfect, Guns, you're perfect."

He kisses my hair. "Did it hurt?"

I shake my head. Well, *maybe a little.*

He laughs, stretching both hands behind his head, in no hurry to move as I watch his perfect face break into a smile.

"I took your virginity," he declares. "I'm the luckiest son of a bitch in the world."

I giggle into his skin.

"Glad I waited for you, huh?"

I feel him move to look down at me. "So glad Lil," he kisses my hair. "I don't deserve you but I'm glad."

I snuggle into him as we catch our breath.

"I loved it, I want more," I declare, knowing my body isn't done with him yet. Far from it.

He chuckles. "You wanna have a shower, freshen up sweetheart?"

"If you're coming then, yes."

He smiles down at me and kisses me chastely. He rolls off the bed and as I get up, I see blood between my legs. Shoot, that's embarrassing.

There's a tiny bathroom attached to the bedroom with a small shower. I hear Gunner run the water and I follow him in. He holds the shower curtain aside for me to climb in. The hot water feels good on my skin as I step in and quickly wash myself between my legs before he can see, a few moments later he climbs in behind me, he kisses the top of my shoulder and cups the side of my face.

"You did good, Lil."

I smile up at him, I feel so elated. I begin working the soap around to wash my body.

"Let me do that for you."

He takes the bar from me and slowly moves it all over my body, caressing my breasts and stomach, taking a lot of care. His touch sends ripples right through me, it's so intimate.

So unnerving.

He's so sweet like this, this is the Gunner I know and love.

"You're perfect, Lily," he whispers in my ear as I lean back against him. "So perfect."

He washes me slowly, taking his time.

I feel his erection at the top of my ass as he turns me around. "You ready again so soon?" I giggle.

"You need a rest, babes," he chuckles. "It just won't stay down when you're around, can't help it."

I reach over my head to pull him down to me.

"Shut up and fuck me."

He grins into my neck. "Your insatiable, glad I do it for you."

"You know you do."

He nibbles my pulse. "Put your hands on the tiles."

A thrill runs through me and I do as he says as he runs the tip of his cock through my folds back and forth. I close my eyes, oh yeah, I'm ready. He disappears suddenly, then comes back seconds later and I hear him roll on a wrap.

He cups my breasts in whispers into my skin. "I love your body Lily, can't believe it took me this long to see you naked. Kickin' myself."

"Me either," I sigh, lolling my head to one side. "Bit slow on taking the reins, aren't you?"

"Gonna make up for lost time, babe."

It's like music to my ears.

Without warning he pushes into me, his hands come along side mine on the tiles as he groans. I stick my ass out further and he moves his hands to my hips and begins to move in and out agonizingly slow.

"Gonna make you beg for it," he whispers.

I need all of him, and he takes me, over and over as we both find another heady and heart-thrumming release.

~

I WAKE and the first thing I hit is a warm body.

I open my eyes and see Guns pressed up against me, he's very cuddly in bed, he couldn't keep his hands off me even in his sleep. After the shower we did it again in his bed.

The way he moves his hips…I know I'll never forget last night as long as I live.

I really am feeling it, though. *Ouch.*

I watch him sleep; his beautiful, tanned face is like an angel. His dusty blonde hair falls onto his face and I admire his beautiful body without any interruption.

Last night was, *wow.* I have no words. I always knew we would be good together, but I never expected *that.*

He stirs a few moments later and reaches for me, pulling me to him, murmuring my name as I stare at his angelic perfection.

He cracks one eye open as I avert my eyes. I don't want to be caught staring.

"Hey babe," he whispers hoarsely, "you awake?"

Phew, got away with it.

"Yeah," I whisper back. "I should have probably gone back to my own room, but it's still early, doubt anybody will be up."

"To catch us?" he snickers.

"Well, you're not a prospect anymore, so at least Brock can't beat your ass."

"True, but if it gets back to Steel, could be a different story."

"Do you have any last words then?" I giggle quietly.

He turns to look at me. "I'll die happy if this is it, Lil."

My heart warms at his words, I know I shouldn't read into it, but the smoldering look he's giving me is off the charts.

"Last night…" I begin, but swallow hard before continuing, "last night was awesome Guns, like seeing stars awesome. You were so tender, so patient with me."

"There you go already ruining my reputation."

"No but I think those stamina and girth rumors are definitely accurate."

He snorts. "Girth? Who says that?"

"You're a jerk." I tease.

He pulls me to him and kisses the top of my forehead. "Glad you liked it. And to think I held back."

"Held back?" I squeak.

"I fuck, remember," he laughs at my wide eyes.

"Oh." I realize, the fire burns in my core just remembering some of the flashbacks from last night.

"You alright?"

I snuggle into his side. "Never been better."

He smirks, closing his eyes again. "I meant, are you sore?"

I bite my lip, shy at his words in the light of day.

"A little, but you did *a lot* to me last night."

"Couldn't help it, you've got a hot little body babe and a hot little pussy."

I warm at his words. "I hope I didn't disappoint you."

I mean, I have nothing to compare to, so I don't know. I think he enjoyed himself as much as I did.

"You could never disappoint me, you did perfect babe," he yawns and raises an arm behind his head. "Could do with some coffee, though."

"Right, because the other girls get you coffee in the morning?"

"Nah they cook me a full breakfast." He grins as I swat him with one hand.

"For future reference, I like it strong with cream and two sugars."

"You know I'm not going to go make you coffee."

His lips twitch. "You could do something about the tent under the sheets though, babe?"

I lift the sheets and see what he's talking about.

"I really like that thing."

"That *thing?*" He pretends to be hurt, pressing his hand to his heart, his eyes still closed. "It's not that big but it's still got feelings."

I roll my eyes and roll over his body to straddle him. He's big enough. Not too big, not too small, just right.

"I think it's absolutely perfect," I murmur, leaning down and kissing the tip softly. "But you have to say pretty please with a cherry on top."

He runs a hand down the side of my head and caresses my face, being naked in front of him feels so natural. I don't have any inhibitions around him when we're like this.

"Pretty please with no cherry on top because I just popped that cherry," he laughs, then leans up to kiss me quickly. "Fuck. I like havin' you on top."

"You like me everywhere," I mutter into his hair as he kisses my neck, his body hard and warm under me.

"Yeah, I do and you're still talkin'…"

I shove him back down and he rests both hands behind his head as he watches me move my way south of the border. I tease his belly button and the smattering of hair with my tongue, sucking it into my mouth, lapping him eagerly.

His cock hangs upright between his legs, like he didn't pump me all night long, nope here he is, raring to go again.

"One thing's for sure," I whisper, licking the tip again. "Some rules are meant to be broken."

He pumps his hips. "Don't you know it, ahhh babe."

I take more of him into my mouth and cup his balls as I lower my mouth. His salty taste is so wickedly good, and I don't know if I'm any good at this, but he seems to like it.

I move my mouth up and down, hollowing my cheeks as I suck and blow him good, he makes delicious noises and I remember him coming all over me last night and I get an ache between my legs.

I grasp him with one hand and begin to work him over, he leans forward and puts his hand over mine and pulls faster. "Like this, babe."

I love it when he teaches me, it feels special, like it's our dirty little secret.

When I get the rhythm going, he sits back again with arms behind his head, I can't get enough of his body. He's a machine.

I'm sore but I want him between my thighs again.

I move up and down, wanting to make it good for him, I cup his balls tighter and he makes the most delicious sound in the back of his throat.

"Gonna come, babe…"

He closes his eyes, jerking his hips as he fucks my mouth and then shoots his load down my throat and I take it all. He's still breathing hard when I'm done cleaning him up and I kiss him gently letting him go.

"Fuck Lil." His hands grip the sheets. "You get me so rock hard, c'mere."

He pulls me back down and I lie on his chest as he kisses the top of my head.

"I like it when you lose control," I whisper, feeling pretty fantastic about making him lose it so easily.

"That right, babe?"

"Umm hmm," I reply as he takes a few moments to slow his breathing.

"You know what I like better than coffee, angel?"

"No," I giggle, knowing this is going to be good. "What?"

He smirks and flips onto his front and moves over me swiftly. "Honey."

It's official.

I'm ruined for any other man.

19

GUNNER

I stare at the bride and groom and how happy they are; Crystal is pregnant with a child that's actually wanted with a man who loves her, hell, cherishes her.

I wonder how some people get so lucky and have it all, and then there's people like my birth mom who shouldn't ever have been allowed to bear a child, let alone two.

Every now and again, in my waking moments, my brain decides to take a trip down memory lane, and I have to physically stop myself from going there.

My nightmares are enough.

I jolted awake in a panic last night, I felt as if I were choking. Luckily Lily didn't wake up, she's a deep sleeper. I clearly didn't think about having her in my bed when I woke up as I was too lost in the moment.

I think about the last time I broke down some months back; I drunkenly shot at empty bottles on top of my mom's grave. I shouldn't call her that, she was nothing but a parasite, and then there was *him*. I can't even think his name let alone say it. The anger surges inside me but I push it back down.

Don't go there.

What haunts me the most was not being able to protect Summer, we were just kids. Innocent. We didn't deserve it.

I realize I've clenched my fists and I'm probably wearing a scowl. I don't know why I seem to sabotage any happy situation or moment with bad thoughts. Maybe it's just how I'm wired.

People clap and cheer as I snap out of my reverie.

The happy couple have a big, get-a-room kiss at the makeshift altar and everyone cheers louder and louder.

I glance over at Lily, she's smiling and happy, her hair's up and she's wearing a dark blue dress that brings out the color in her eyes. She looks so pretty.

I haven't been able to stop thinking about her, not after what we did.

I can't get over it, how perfect she is, how her body moves with mine so easily, how she gets me off in super record time – okay that's not great for my reputation – but I've never gone several rounds with a woman in years, not since my early teens.

A curl forms on my lips at the thought of what we got up to last night, and this morning. Dirty little thing.

It's always the quiet ones.

I can't do anything right now, obviously, but just the thought of what I'm *going* to do has me excited all over again. Yeah, this is definitely not going to be a one-night thing.

My eyes are firmly on the prize.

Suddenly her eyes flick to mine mid laugh and I'm caught staring.

I give her a chin lift and she bites her lip and smiles. The gesture goes straight to where I don't need it to. I don't think there's any blood left in my head, it's all rushed south of the border as I plan out what I'm gonna do to her later. Doggie-style comes to mind, her facing the mirror, *oh holy Jesus.*

"...another one bites the dust..." Tag grunts out next to me. I glance sideways at him. He watches the commotion with a frown.

"I dunno, I think they look quite content to me."

He side eyes me. Tag's a man of few words, a lot like Steel in that way. But they are total opposites. Tag's got short, military style hair and a dark, close cut beard, and he's on some serious roids. And he definitely ain't got no ol' lady.

"Need a fuckin' drink," he mutters.

The wedding reception's being held at one of the taverns downtown that has a restaurant and an outdoor area adjoining the bar. The girls spent all afternoon yesterday setting it up all pretty.

Summer sidles up next to me.

"What did you get up to last night?" she asks. "I barely saw you."

"This and that," I mutter. "What about you?"

"Had a catch up with some of the girls."

"So I heard."

She shrugs. "Stripper joint was okay; they don't really do it for me though."

I look at her sideways, as does Tag.

"You're the only woman in history who's ever said that you know."

She rolls her eyes. "I spent most of the night making sure Deanna didn't put all her cash into the underpants of strange men."

I visibly shudder.

Over the top of her head, I look up and see Jett leaning against a tree, having a smoke. He's talking to Bones. He looks our way every now and again.

It hasn't escaped me that he seems to be a little bit interested in my sister on both trips to Bracken Ridge and this weekend.

I nod towards him. "Has he been making any moves?"

I like him, but I'll cut him if I have to.

She shakes her head. "No, he's really nice, we talked a little bit but that's all, he's kind of quiet."

Summer's not the kind of girl you pick up. I know a lot of it has to do with our childhood, hence nobody's ever really been given a chance. She keeps her guard up more than I do.

Tag grunts.

Talked?

"What the fuck that brother got to talk about?" Tag spits.

If I got the horns, then she definitely got the halo.

"He doesn't just talk, he's a good listener," she tells us as we both snort.

"Ruinin' a man's reputation," Tag grumbles. "Nobody in this club wants to be remembered for *being a good listener.* Fuck me."

"Maybe you should get in touch with your feminine side a bit more, Tag?" she offers.

I roll my lips inward at her taunts.

Just like all the girls belonging to the BRMC, she's a little bit lippy and she probably should mind her manners.

"My fuckin' what, woman?"

"It wouldn't hurt you to be a little less tense, I mean, there's like a vein sticking out of your forehead right now." She frowns at him and I shake my head. She's got guts.

"It's there because you're fuckin' annoying me."

"Just pointing out the obvious," she sighs. "You know, like Luna."

He grunts. "Why are we talkin' about Luna?"

Who the fuck is Luna?

"We're not, but it's a beautiful day, we just witnessed a beautiful wedding, it wouldn't hurt you to realize that she's right there, she likes you, and she's hot as fuck."

Tag grunts again, clearly not impressed.

I glance down at my sister. "You meddling again?"

She shrugs. "No, but it seems some of the men in this club aren't very perceptive."

"You don't have a whole lot of control over your women, do you?" he mumbles to me.

I hold my hands up. "Hey, she's my sister, and she's been hanging around Deanna too long."

Summer doesn't let up. "Right, you're one of those misogynistic types who wants a woman who's submissive, cooks and cleans and won't say boo to you, it's hell or high water if a woman comes along who challenges you."

He looks down at her menacingly. "I have no idea what the fuck you just said, but you talk way too much, now button it."

She rolls her eyes. "Still single are you, Tag?"

He glares at her. "Yep, and that's how it's gonna stay cause' that's how I like it."

He stalks off leaving us standing there.

Way to go, sis.

"You know how to clear a room," I say out of the side of my mouth. "Or in this case, a field."

"He knows what I'm talking about," she maintains. "Like most idiot men he can't see what's right in front of him. Luna's been catching his attention for a while and he won't do anything about it, he's been an asshat to her and she's really sweet."

I turn to her. "You should stay out of other people's business. Probably not a good idea to get involved or disrespect him in his own club."

She shrugs. "I don't care and we're not in the club, we're outdoors, it's neutral territory, it's not like I'm gonna see him again."

"Don't be a smart ass."

"Well, at least I got him thinking."

I shake my head. "While we're on the subject, why not Jett?"

She looks at me sharply. "What do you mean?"

"Well, he seems like a good guy."

Truth be told I'd probably slip him a fifty if he even made it out of the driveway.

Not gonna happen in this lifetime.

"I'm not interested. I mean he's cute and all, but he lives down here, remember, not a good idea, long distance situations rarely ever work."

There's always some excuse.

I don't wanna think about my sister in uncompromising situations, but hell, she hasn't had a boyfriend since high school.

I turn to her as we begin walking with the crowd towards our sleds to get to the reception. The bride and groom take off on a Harley Davidson with cans attached to the exhaust pipe. The girls are in a hired limo going to have photos taken, so I'm not gonna see Lily until later.

"When are you gonna be interested?" I push.

She turns to me and looks at me dangerously. "You know I don't do relationships, Gunner," she whispers angrily. "I… I just don't find that many men attractive, and I'm too busy."

Yeah, unlike me, she wears her heart on her sleeve. She's never gotten over her demons, I guess neither of us have.

"You're always too busy. And I'm not talkin' about that, nothin' wrong with goin' on a date, testing the waters, you gonna stay single forever?"

"Are you?" she shoots back.

I shake my head, she's so difficult to talk to. I wonder how Jett's a good listener, more like he left last night with his ears bleeding.

"What do you want?" I ask, facing her.

"You getting all deep and meaningful on me?" she shakes her head and stares ahead.

"No, but I worry."

"You know you don't have to worry, I'm fine." Her voice is softer.

It goes without saying that I always will.

She'll always be that little six-year-old I hid in the closet. Some things never leave you; some things will remain etched into your soul forever.

"You wanna finish nursing school?"

She looks at me sharply, I've hit a nerve. "One day," she stammers. "When I can afford it, why are you asking about that?"

I hold her by the elbow. "Been thinkin'," I say, knowing I have to broach this subject someday, may as well be now.

"Really, did it hurt?"

I roll my eyes. "Very funny, I mean about school…"

"Yeah, what about it?" she narrows her eyes, she's always suspicious, of everything, even me. It makes me sad. I have no ulterior motives. I want to see her happy and successful, not pulling pints and pouring shots at the bar forever with slobs trying their luck.

"I know you all make fun of me because of the shit I do."

"You mean like that *women's only* magazine shoot?" she pretends to vomit. "God that was so gross."

"Yes, the very one, I might not mention that I'm doin' a calendar next year but that's not important right now," I snicker. "The point is, it was good scratch and I've made quite a tidy sum."

"Good for you."

"Well, it's good for both of us."

She puts her hands on her hips as she turns to me. "What's going on, Guns?"

I gulp down every fear I have knowing how resistant she is to change.

"I wanna help you finish nursing school." There. I said it.

I've been saving hard for a couple of years now for this moment.

She needs this. She needs to do something for herself, something she's passionate about.

She stares at me blankly. "How do you mean?"

"Financially, I've got some savings and I wanna help you through school." I shift awkwardly. "It's time baby girl, it's time for you to spread your wings like you always wanted. I'm in a position now to help you make that happen and that's what I'm gonna do."

She waves a hand at me. "Stop Gunner, I can't do that, I'm saving up and I'm going to have enough in a couple of year's time myself, I don't need your charity."

My heart breaks for her. It breaks because this is me and her. She never accepts anything.

It's like her pride gets in the way.

"No babe, I've saved up for the two of us, gonna get me my own place and I wanna help with your tuition; anyways, it's done, so yeah."

She stares at me blankly. "What's done?"

"Happy early birthday present from me and mom."

Mom isn't well off but she's given us more in love and kindness than anything monetary value can possibly buy.

"My birthday isn't until next month," she reminds me, her eyebrows furrow, waiting for me to come out with a joke. That joke isn't coming this time.

"Yeah well, it came early, I got you the money, if it's what you still want. Or if you want to do somethin' else, that's okay too."

She gapes at me. "Gunner?"

"Yeah, sweet cheeks?"

"You can't do that," she whispers. "I won't let you, it's too much." I don't miss the tears forming in her eyes.

I nudge her with my shoulder. "I can, and I just did, was gonna wait until your birthday but you'll just chicken out and the new semester starts soon, so you may wanna get yourself enrolled."

"You're actually serious?"

Her hands go to her throat as she takes in my words.

"I'm dead set, it'd be perfect, you'd start in the new year."

"Gunner, I can't accept this!"

"Well, you can and you will. I didn't drop my clothes and pose with a fire reel hiding my dick so you could work as a bartender for the rest of your life, you're too good for that shit."

She looks a little insulted. "I like bar work."

I give her a pointed look. "But it's not your passion Sums, you know it's not."

She looks down at her feet. "You did all those crappy shoots and sold shots of your body to put me through school?"

I give her a sideways grin. "Wasn't so bad, got a lot of chicks…"

She puts her hands over her ears. "Ewww, please God, no."

I laugh out loud.

"Seriously, I can't Gunner, surely you can put the money to better use?"

"It's done," I reiterate as we reach my sled. "Think about what *you* want for once, and not what everyone else wants, who cares about church? You have this thing where you always have to be there for everyone else. You don't want to let anyone down and I get it, but you don't have to do that anymore, you need to start thinking about you and your future and what makes *you* happy. That's all I want for you, to be happy."

She kicks the dirt with her sandal. "I'm not unhappy, that's almost the same thing."

My heart lurches in my chest. "Summer."

She holds up her hand. "I feel bad now."

"What for?" I cock my head sideways.

"Bagging you out over the shoot and everything else stupid you did."

"I wouldn't expect anything less." I grin.

She places her hand on my arm. "You're a good brother, Guns, the best. For what it's worth I'm glad it's you and me, it'll always be us, right?"

"Of course, we stick together. You need help, you talk to me, always."

She looks up at me. "Thanks, Guns."

I glance at her, this is hard for her, to talk. "You're a good sister, kid. We did okay."

She acts like she hates me but I know I'm her most favorite person alive. She just doesn't know how to show it.

"God, we're not gonna hug now, are we?"

"I certainly hope not," I grumble, scuffing up her hair instead. She shrieks as I laugh; she swats my hand away, shoving me back. "Promise me you'll enroll."

Our eyes meet and that little lost girl in those deep blue depths stare back at me. All of a sudden, she is that little girl again and I'm seven years old, trying to keep her safe. It was too much for a little kid, but I'd do it all over again in a heartbeat.

I'd die trying to protect her.

"I can't promise, Guns."

I smile wistfully. "I'm sorry sis, for what it's worth, for the cards we got dealt, but you gotta start livin' life, baby girl, you can't give up on your dreams or on what you want, and if you don't know what it is, then you better start figuring it out. Life doesn't go on forever."

She nods. "I know."

There's no two ways about it, she's doing it. I'm not gonna accept any more excuses.

"Love ya, sis."

She smiles, a tear slides down her face as I wipe it away with my thumb. "Love you too, you big pair of smelly old boots, and you still didn't tell me where you were last night."

There's no way I'm telling her about Lily.

"Trust me when I say you're better off not knowing." I give her a wink.

She wrinkles her nose. "Eww."

Unlike Summer, I love sex. I enjoy it and now that I've had Lily, the connection we have makes it feel all that much sweeter. I can't get her off my mind night and day. I can't wait to get her back in bed and in between her legs.

The way she's so elegant and beautiful without even trying has my heart thumping in my chest, never felt that before.

For once in my life, I feel like I've done something right.

I lean toward Summer's ear and nod toward Jett.

"You know they have an awesome program down here in New Orleans." I grin. "Or so I've heard."

She pushes me by the shoulder. "Not going there, Gunner, not going there."

20

LILY

My feet are killing me as we finish up the locomotion across the dance floor. Tonight has been a blast, I've not had this much fun in forever. The party's pretty wild but everyone's cutting loose and having a good time, and Crystal's face has been a picture of happiness.

Gunner's been staring at me all night and I'm dying to get him out on the dance floor, but most of the guys here aren't really up for kicking up their heels, and he's no exception.

Random girls have been coming up to him all night, that's not unusual, but he just smiles and keeps drinking his beer and turns his attention back to me.

He likes to watch. I'm slowly figuring that out.

It's as I'm making my way to the bathroom that I feel a pair of hands on my hips. I turn quickly and Gunner's right behind me.

"Hey," he says, looking down at me, full of mischief.

"Hey yourself," I reply, biting my lip.

He pulls me into the men's room and once the doors shut, he pulls me to him and kisses me hard, his tongue in my mouth and I can tell by his kiss that he's missed not touching me, and it's only been a few hours.

When he pulls back, we're both breathing ragged.

"I've wanted to do that all day," he tells me, sagging back against the wall. "Fuckin' annoying not being able to touch you when I want to."

I smile at him, overjoyed at his reaction.

I reach up to run my hand through his hair. "You look so handsome."

He smirks, pulling me against his body.

"You look so sexy in that dress, babe, can't keep my eyes off you, when's it acceptable to sneak away?"

I laugh as he plants a light kiss on my lips.

"You're naughty dragging me in here, anyone could just come in."

He waggles his eyebrows. "I like a bit of excitement, a bit of risqué."

"Not in a men's bathroom," I admonish. In reality, he could lead me anywhere and I'd follow.

He leans down to my ear. "How sore are you?"

I feel a shiver run through me as his hot, dirty words. "A little," I breathe.

He places a kiss on the side of my temple. "Too sore to… do stuff?"

I shake my head. "Never."

He sighs with relief just as the door swings open and we jump apart. I quickly slide out of the men's room with him in tow, not meeting the eyes of the patron, hoping it isn't one of the boys from our club.

We don't get stopped or questioned and it's hours later when we finally get away. I sneak down the hall to Gunner's room while the party continues downstairs when we get back.

Gunner barely waits until I'm inside before he pounces

on me, kissing me with reverence and unzips my dress slowly; it drops in a pool at my feet so I'm naked before him.

He swallows hard. "You mean to tell me you've had no underwear on all day?" he rubs his chin with one hand and I have to say, I'm liking the whole facial hair thing he's got going on. It's especially nice when his head is between my legs.

I shake my head.

He's already shirtless but wears his jeans, they're slung low on his hips and the top button and zipper are down. His hair's slicked all back off his face with gel and he looks as delicious as he does dangerous.

"Like what you see?" I tease as he just stares at me then moves his eyes down my body. I thought I would feel self-conscious with someone like Gunner assessing me completely naked, but I am surprisingly confident upon his scrutiny, especially when I see the hungry look in his eyes.

His hands grasp my hair as I moan as he moves them to my ass, grinding me into his junk. Our lips meet and it's a sweet dance of lust and want; he sure knows how to kiss and I feel it all the way down to my toes.

He pulls back then sinks down the foot of the bed so he's sitting on the floor. I look down at him, unsure what he's doing.

"Lift up your leg, rest it on the bed frame," he says, his voice hoarse.

I do as he says as a thrill of excitement runs through me.

My pussy is right in his face as he stares at me hungrily. "Jesus, you're so beautiful."

He blows softly on my wet heat and then parts me with his fingers and licks me.

"Waited all day to taste you," he whispers.

I moan in sheer ecstasy at his gentle touch.

I move over him further as he continues to lick me. Then

he moves his mouth to my clit as he sucks on it without mercy, his beard feels tingly on my skin and it only adds to the sensation. God how I've dreamed about this.

I gasp as he puts one finger inside me and begins to move it in and out as I brace my hands against the bedpost to stop myself from falling.

He looks up at me from below and it's almost my undoing. I watch as he hitches his jeans off his hips and spreads his legs, his cock straight and hard as he touches himself while continuing to devour me with his tongue.

"Oh god Gunner," I moan. I can feel the climax building.

He pushes another finger inside and I start to ride his hand, my boobs bounce together as he watches me from below; his tongue going to town as I moan out a long, drawn out orgasm as my skin burns and heats like I'm on fire.

When I'm coherent again, he grins up at me, still fisting his shaft.

I stare down at this man in wonder, what he does to my body is insane, it should be illegal.

He stands, then presses up against me, his hard bulge is like a piece of steel. He brings his mouth to mine and dips his tongue inside as I wait for what he's got planned next.

As if reading my mind, he smirks, then spins me around so I'm facing the bed. He positions both my hands against the end of the bed frame and runs his hands down the side of my body and rests them on my hips.

"Spread your legs, babe."

I do as he says, and he runs a palm back up my spine and pushes my body forwards so I'm on my elbows. He holds my hips as my ass sticks up in the air. He shoves his jeans down the rest of the way, rolls on a wrap, and without warning, he thrusts into me as I gasp.

He gives my ass a little spank as I wiggle against him, taking the few seconds he gives me to adjust to him.

"You feel that, babe?" he moans as he pulls out and then slams back into me again.

He moves his hands to cup my breasts and pulls on both my nipples. I buck at the contact, leaning my head back as he bites my neck gently, it stings and sends shock waves through me as I push back into him.

He moves in and out of me faster and faster, it's clear he can't hold on much more than I can, and a feeling of joy courses through my body.

He pushes me faster, our skin slapping together harshly, then one hand reaches around and rubs my clit; I'm so wet, he gets me like this every single time.

I let out a loud mewl as he bangs me harder and harder. I see stars as I come hard, calling his name, it's enough to tip him over the edge too as he finds his own loud and incoherent release. He lowers me down onto the mattress and falls on top of me.

"Guns!" I yelp.

He pulls out then rolls next to me, his breath ragged as he sighs.

"Love how your pussy milks me so tight," he says as I shake my head into the duvet. "Can't get enough of it."

"You're such a romantic post coital," I laugh.

He traces his fingers down my shoulder as I lie on my front, him on his back.

"Maybe I don't want to give you back tomorrow," I hear him whisper, our time together here is coming to an abrupt close.

"So, don't," I say, as I close my eyes and give in to the tired wash of exhaustion that comes over me.

We lie together in the dark and I realize I'm under the covers now. At some point in the night, he's moved me from the foot of the bed to the top. The party is long since over and there is no sound or movement, just the steady thrum of my own heartbeat as Gunner touches me, rubbing his knuckles over my bare shoulder.

"Have you been to sleep yet?" I yawn, snuggling further into his warm skin.

I feel the bed move as he kisses the top of my head. "Can't sleep, babe."

"Why not?"

A few moments of silence follow. "I asked Summer about goin' back to nursing school today," he says, his voice low and soft. "It's something she's wanted to do for a long time, now she'll just come up with any excuse to not do it."

"She'd be amazing," I agree.

"She's afraid of change." He plays with the ends of my hair like we've done this our whole lives.

I sit up on my elbow. "She'd be great at anything she wants to do. Jett's got his eye on her but she's keeping him at arms length. How come she never dates?"

His hand stops stroking my arm as his body stiffens.

"I don't know," he mutters. "She doesn't like many guys."

"Oh," I shrug, I can tell he wants to drop the subject. I'm not sure why. I know he's protective, all the boys in the club are, but still, it was just a question.

I remember the night that Steel called me when Gunner was drunk and he'd passed out at my mom's house. He'd been muttering all kinds of weird stuff.

He mentioned his mom several times but I couldn't make out what he was saying. I wince at the memory he has no recollection of.

"What are you thinking?" he asks when silence falls between us.

Maybe I should broach it?

"That night that you got really drunk," I admit.

He chuckles. "Which one?"

I turn to look up at him. "The night Steel called me, at the graveyard."

His eyes meet mine. "What about it?"

"Nothing, I just haven't seen you like that before." I definitely haven't seen him that inebriated, or emotional.

He turns and stares up at the ceiling for a long time. "What did I say?"

I shrug. "A lot of stuff that didn't make sense, mainly dribble."

"I shouldn't get like that, but it was the anniversary of my... of my birth mom's death..." he cracks his neck side to side. "It always brings out the worst in me around that time, sometimes I lose control, I'm not proud of it."

My eyes go round. He's never spoken much of her out loud. Something in my bones chills me and I don't know why. Maybe I'm reacting to his body language and how rigid he's gone talking about this.

"I'm sorry," I whisper, for whatever it is he's thinking.

"Don't be, she was a junkie and a whore."

I'm shocked at the venom in his words.

"How is Gloria?" I squeak, this is a safe subject. His adoptive mom is a really nice lady and he adores her.

"She's awesome babe, she loves Miami. I should go visit her soon, work on the tan."

I think about me and Gunner going away together. I know it's not likely to happen, but one can dream. I imagine having him all to myself and it's a very indulgent thought.

"You so should, that would be fun."

He looks down at me. "She's always liked you."

He looks so earnest that a lump forms in my throat.

This is going to kill me. Leaving him. I don't want to.

"That's cause I'm an angel," I smirk.

He shakes his head then a wide grin creases across his face, he leans down to kiss me. "Not anymore, hate to break it to ya, but I corrupted you good and proper."

My heart thuds. "Maybe I like being corrupted."

He looks back up at the ceiling and continues stroking me gently, something's on his mind. I wish he'd let me in, his secrets are safe with me.

"Penny for your thoughts?" I kiss his shoulder, his skin's so warm and soft.

His lips twitch. "I was thinking about how bad I used to be."

I frown. "You've never been bad."

He laughs ruefully. "Oh yeah babe I have, I used to be a very angry person. I didn't treat women very nice either, I used them, sure, they probably used me right on back, but it's what I knew, it was all I knew how to be." His voice is barely a whisper.

"What changed things?"

"Hutch," he states without qualm. "He saved my life in more ways than one, your mom too and Kirsty, I owe them everything for what they did for me and Summer, I can't ever repay them for the shit that went down back then."

"You were a child, Guns."

He winces then closes his eyes. "You're right I was, it wasn't supposed to be like that."

I gulp. "Do you want to talk about it?"

He shakes his head and whispers, "No."

There's so much I don't know about him and I want to know it all but at the same point I don't want to push him. I'm from a broken home too, I get it.

"You're doing good though," I smile at him. "Especially the shoot, and the salon, your jewelry line, your mom's proud of you, we all are."

He looks far away. "I've got so much to be thankful for and so many good people around me now."

I swallow hard.

I wish I could just blurt it out and ask him what's going to happen when we get home, but maybe a part of me doesn't want to know. Maybe it's best to stay in this little bubble for a few more hours before we have to leave and not think too far ahead. It's not like he's mentioned anything about us or if he wants to keep this going.

I don't want to think about if he doesn't.

I think about the sweet butts at church, especially Chelsea and I want to gag. I don't know how I'll handle it when girls are all over him again.

I've never had such raw emotions or cared so much about anybody. I know it isn't healthy, that he's my undoing, but like a moth to a flame I'm drawn to him.

It's like I can't help it.

We're magnets.

"You're amazing, Guns," I sigh into his skin as he kisses my hair. *I love you.* "I've had the best weekend of my life."

He looks down at me, a ghost of a smile on his lips, it doesn't touch his *eyes* and I wonder what he's truly thinking.

"Me too babe," he murmurs. "Me too."

21

GUNNER

"Put your back into it," Brock hollers as I flip him the bird. I'm not exactly cut out for manual labor. I'm more of a hands-off kinda guy when it comes to heavy lifting.

"Shouldn't you have a loader or somethin' to cart this shit around?"

We're lifting heavy blocks from one side of the scrap yard to the other.

"Broken," he informs me. "Gettin' it fixed and I got more shit comin' in this week, but I need this moved."

I grunt my disapproval; this is what you get for being a nice guy.

He's also been ribbing me a whole lot about what went down in New Orleans, seems as if I wasn't as subtle as I'd like to think.

I know I can't do too much at home with Steel being around, and while it's only been a few days since we got back, all I've been thinking about is Lily.

They say this happens. When you let chicks get too close, let them sneak into your heart and trust me, I haven't let one get *this* close. All the flirting and shit I do is just surface stuff, it's nothing meaningful.

With Lily I feel like I could bare my soul to her, even the deep, dark stuff nobody knows about; stuff I can't even deal with.

With her, things feel different. They don't feel anything like when I'm with other girls. I want to tell her things, I want so much more than I should or have the right to.

This felt so different than just a dirty weekend, but what a weekend it was.

I've definitely had Lily heroin.

I'm counting down the days, hours, seconds until I can see her again.

If I thought I could actually have a taste of her then give her up, I was sorely mistaken.

Her goddam body drives me wild. It's all I can think about. I can't fathom how she's not let anyone touch her before, claim her, take her.

Our connection is off the charts. I feel a surge of protectiveness towards her that seems to be controlling my every thought.

I know deep down I'm not good for her.

My own demons still lurk in the shadows. I don't know how she would react if she knew what happened to me. Would she find it hard to look at me knowing all of that? Knowing that I'd been molested by my own stepfather?

It's dirty. I'm ashamed of it.

Even though I'm almost thirty years old, shame still fills me as I think about what happened and how that part of my life is like a serial nightmare that plays on repeat. How long it took me to trust being in the presence of another man before I'd come out of my shell. It took me two years to even speak properly.

I shudder at my wayward thoughts and why this is all coming up again now.

"My grandma moves quicker than you," Brock calls out, hands on hips, breaking my reverie. "And she's been dead for ten years."

"Funny, fucker," I mutter. "You know I'd love to know what the prospects are doing right now, why not get Lee or Jaxon over here to do this shit? These hands are not cut out for this kind of manual labor."

"Shut your pie-hole, the quicker we get this done the quicker you can go off to the beauty parlor and get your bits waxed."

Yeah, yeah. You have one incident with some fake tan and nobody lets you hear the end of it.

"You're just full of good humor today Brock, what happened, did someone wake up on the wrong side of the bed?"

Despite what he thinks, I'm observant. I know what his problem is, and it stands about five-foot-eight inches, wheat blonde, has pale, tattooed skin and green eyes. *Angel.*

He's been acting weird for weeks now, and she's been showing up more and more at church.

Time for some pay back of my own cause shit stirring is what I do best.

"Just shut up for five minutes, if you worked as fast as you talked then we'd have this done in no time," Brock grumbles.

"Talk to me bro, what's got ya balls all tied up in a knot this time?"

He snorts and lifts another block on top of another, I swear we're gonna need a chiropractor after the day's out.

"My balls are just fine, thanks for the concern."

Time to go in for the kill. "You heard Angel's seeing someone?"

He lets out a bigger grunt.

Bingo.

This is why he's a little bit extra on the grumpy side.

"But it's early days, bro," I add with a smirk. "You've still got time to get on in there, show her what's she's missin' out on and all that shit."

He doesn't look up. He keeps lifting, each brick gets a little more oomph than the next. "Well, she didn't seem to care about missin' out the first time 'round."

"Sometimes it takes a few goes round the block to get it right."

He looks up at me, his face full of surprise. "All of a sudden you're an expert on the subject; fuck man, didn't realize that you're Dr. fuckin' bleeding heart with all the answers."

Ooh touchy. I hold my hands out in surrender. "No need to get aggravated, I was just trying to help."

"Like a hole in the head," he mutters. She's got him well and truly wound up tight, like only a female can.

I imagine Lily going out on a date now and a weird, possessive shudder begins to permeate through my body. No, I don't think I like that idea at all.

Shit.

Am I fucked now?

"What's her problem anyway? Why won't she go all the way again?"

Brock's definitely irritated, but I think he may wanna talk about it. He would have punched me and stalked off by now if he didn't. While we had that conversation at church about it, it seems things have taken a downward spiral.

He sighs loudly. "Says it'll ruin our friendship."

I blink a couple of times to make sure I heard right. I guess the woman's got a point.

"So, no friends with benefits then?"

He laughs like that's a huge fat joke. "That's not gonna

happen. Anyway, I'm too fuckin' old for the mind games. She says if things don't work this time, then we'll just hate each others guts, or some shit."

I guess that is kind of smart. Boning your on/off best friend probably isn't a very wise thing to do in the long run, even if you do have history.

"Things were so much fuckin' easier when we were younger."

He side eyes me. "I got a few years on you, bro, but thanks for the compliment."

"You're not gettin' any younger, brother." I agree, earning me an arched brow. "Need a good woman to look after your sorry ass and wheel you around when you're old, wipe your ass and feed you and shit."

He shakes his head like I'm ridiculous.

Then it occurs to me. "Wait a minute…"

Brock looks up at me.

I know him too well. "You're gonna get rid of the guy, aren't you?" In the philosophical sense of course. I'm sure he wouldn't just whack the guy for taking her out for dinner.

A smirk creases at the corner of his mouth. "Now we're gettin' somewhere."

I stop what I'm doing and laugh out loud. "You sick fucker, what did you do, threaten him?"

Brock rolls his eyes. "He's a pencil pusher, no way Angel's gonna fall for that, she needs someone with a little more backbone, plus the guy's shady. What kind of man works in an office and wears a suit for a living? He's definitely got ulterior motives right there."

I shake my head. "Cuz he wears a suit," I sputter a laugh. "It ain't so bad, beats gettin' torched out here in the blazing sun, maybe the guy's smart."

He grunts again. "Well, let's just say there won't be a second date."

I shake my head. "For someone who says they ain't got it bad, you seem to care an awful lot about who she's dating, and you're forgetting one vital point, brother."

"Oh yeah, what's that?"

"She's gonna kick your ass for scaring him off." I laugh at the very thought. She's a tough nut.

I don't have an issue with women being headstrong. I like how Lily runs her own business, she's not reliant on anybody, I admire that, it shows she's got smarts.

"That's something we can both agree on," Brock mutters just as the delivery truck pulls up just in time as I lift the last block. "She'll thank me for it later. And I like a little bit of rough foreplay, kicking my ass may be just what I need."

I pretend to block my ears. "You owe me a beer, or three," I tell him, trying to shrug that thought off. "Definitely not cut out for this kind of lifting shit."

"I've had a chihuahua that made less noise than you do."

"Sexual frustration can bring out all kinds of emotions in a man," I laugh, standing. "Takin' it out on the rest of us won't help you."

I duck as his arm flies out to try and swing one at me but I'm too fast for him.

"Always were a fast little fucker." He could beat me in a fight hands down, but catching me, yeah, he'd have zero chance of that. I've always been light on my feet.

"You taught me," I remind him as I dodge an elbow. "If you can remember that far back."

∼

I STARE at Lily across the room of church. She's organizing some charity event with Summer and Deanna, they're using the bar area to brainstorm because it's quiet during the day, though I really wish the other two would piss off so I could haul Lily upstairs to my room instead and have a quickie.

As much as I've tried this week, I haven't been able to switch her off. I even went to her place last night and we fucked into the wee hours of morning in her sweet, sunny bedroom.

I smirk at the memory of being in her bed, oh and her shower, oh yeah and the kitchen counter.

I'll never be able to make a sandwich again without thinking about her ass planted on the laminate.

It's then that Angel decides to barge through the door looking like she's about to explode.

Oh great. So, it seems she's found out about Brock's little stunt. Didn't know if he'd actually go through with his threats.

I, of course, play completely dumb.

"Hey babes, what's got your panties all in a twist?"

The girls all look up as she stands there, hands on hips, steam could pour out of her ears, she looks that wild.

"Any of you seen Brock?"

I know where he is, but I don't know if I want to be responsible for the recovery of his body if I give away his location.

"Tried the yard?" I sing out helpfully, knowing he's not there.

She gives me a withering look. "Of course I tried there, it's the first place I went."

Ooh, she's snitchy.

"What's wrong?" Deanna asks as Summer and Lily shrug at one another.

"What's wrong? *What's wrong?* I'll tell you what's wrong! I had an amazing date the other night and the guy was really nice, and sweet, and... and... fucking Brock's gone and ruined it all! I'll have his fucking balls for this, you hear me?

On a platter!" She throws her hands up in the air and stalks over to the bar.

"Need a shot?" Summer asks, reaching for the tequila.

"What I need is a gun with a silencer."

I burst out laughing as she side-eyes me like a she-devil.

"What happened?" Lily questions, her brow creasing.

"He only went and told the guy he'd cut his balls off and ram them down his throat if he came near me again!"

The girls shriek in horror, Lily slaps her forehead.

I refrain from grinning, knowing that's not helpful. "Now, now," I say, walking towards them. "Violence isn't always the answer, I'm sure there's a reasonable explanation for why he supposedly did what he did."

I tried to warn him, but oh no, nobody wants to take my advice. Too bad, Brock. You've done it now.

"Supposedly? Ha! The reasonable explanation is that he's a dead man walking, does anybody know how hard it is to find a nice guy in this town? One that doesn't even mind that you have a kid?"

All three girls raise their hands.

"Well, aside from the kid part." Summer smiles sympathetically.

I cock an eyebrow at Lily's raised hand and she rolls her eyes.

"Okay, bad example, I don't know who he thinks he is! I mean, I haven't been on a date in a looong time, and he comes along throwing his weight around like he's got some claim over me or something! I'm so done with him!"

I stand and watch her get more furious by the second. If I were Brock, I'd emigrate, but Canada wouldn't be far enough.

"He's got a major jones for you," Deanna sighs, like this isn't already common knowledge.

"It's his way of getting back at you, if he can't have you

then nobody can, total asshole move and totally predictable; why do you boys act like cavemen?"

All the girls turn to look at me.

I hold up my hands. "Hey, wait a minute, since when do I act like a caveman?"

"That's a good point," Lily agrees, sticking up for me. "Gunner is the only one who doesn't treat us like we're dumb asses."

I try not to stare at her sexy mouth and give myself away. "Thank you, Lily."

Angel ignores all of us, her rage is past the point of boiling. "I don't understand how he thinks he can just waltz into my life when he feels like it and start trying to run it, typical archaic biker bullshit is what it is." She throws a shot down her throat and wipes her mouth with the back of her hand. "I'm seriously going to kill him."

"It's a boy's club around here," Summer complains. "They all stick together, why don't you make yourself useful, Gunner, and tell us where Brock is?"

"Why?" I laugh. "So you can go lynch him?"

Angel turns with hands on her hips, her devil eyes scorn me. "Do you know where he is?"

She could cut glass with those eyeballs. I contemplate lying, but really, I wouldn't mind seeing Brock get his ass kicked by Angel, it'd make up for all the shit he's done to me over the years.

"I can't say for sure," I reply, pretending to think. "But last I heard he was over at Steel's trying to get some parts for the loader."

Angel gives me a very smug and equally scary smile, like she may actually go over there with a silencer. "Thank you, Gunner, that wasn't so hard was it?"

I purse my lips and this time I don't hold back my grin. "You gotta ask yourself a couple of questions babe, why did he chase this dude away? And secondly, why are you so mad about it?"

She shakes her head. "He did it because he's an asshole, and I'm mad because I liked the guy."

I shake my head as I lean on the side of the bar. "Some may say that he did it to protect you."

She snorts angrily. "I don't need his fucking protection, I don't need anything from him, you're mistaking me for a damsel in distress, Guns, and we both know I've never been that."

I cock a brow at her tone, even though I know it's true.

"He's always had a thing, we all know that," Summer continues. "Don't be so hard on him Angel, maybe he wishes it were him going on a second date?"

Angel laughs without humor. "Well, he's got a pretty funny way of showing it, doesn't he?"

"Neanderthal," Lily replies sagely. "Look it up in the dictionary, he's there next to Steel."

Deanna snorts a laugh. "You're not wrong there."

"Now, now ladies, let's not get dramatic." I don't know why I always feel compelled to play devil's advocate. "He's only got your best interests at heart. Brock's never done you wrong baby girl, maybe his actions are somewhat questionable, but he means well."

She regards me coolly. "Well, you tell him if you see him before I do that it's probably for the best that I shove my foot up his ass when I get hold of him!"

She doesn't wait for a reply, she stomps off in the direction she came in to go hunt him down.

I shake my head in her wake.

"Jesus, he's fucked," I mutter.

"He shouldn't go messing in her business." Deanna points out. "She's a big girl, she can handle herself. If he's so concerned about it then he should have the decency to tell her himself."

I lean on the bar. "Since when do any of us have any decency? And you're forgetting the men in this club don't have to do shit, babe."

Deanna gives me the middle finger.

"You know what Angel's like." Summer reminds me, as if I needed it. "She won't submit to a man."

"Nobody's sayin' she's gotta submit to anyone."

All three pairs of eyes glare at me.

"What I mean is, no woman in this club does anything against her will," I go on, before they decide to lynch me too. "Before you all go gettin' your panties in a twist."

"It's still shitty." Deanna maintains.

I turn to look at Deanna, suddenly remembering what I had to rib her about.

"Hey that reminds me" I say with a nonchalant tone. "You and Cash looked pretty cozy down in New Orleans this past weekend, you like older dudes?"

Lily and then Summer turn to look at her.

"What?" They both stammer in unison.

Deanna gives me a withering look.

"I think he's pretty smitten, at least, that's what he said." I give her a wink as she pretends nothin's going on. I know her too well.

"When did he say that?" Deanna questions, suddenly interested.

But this conversation has gone on far too long and I have to go. My work here is done, and I have to go rescue Brock from near and certain death.

"Would you look at the time," I say in an exaggerated fashion as I push off the bar. "Gotta go save me a V.P., that is if there's anything left of him by the time I get there."

I feel the daggers in my back as I leave them to it and

Deanna to explain, since it seems neither of the girls know anything about her little escapade with the New Orleans Prez. I grin as I swagger out to my sled.

I don't even get to start the engine when my phone buzzes. I reach for my back pocket and I grin even wider when I see it's a text from Lily.

We still on for tonight?

Oh yeah, we're on, baby girl.

I type back as I climb aboard my sled.

Only if you promise not to wear panties.

I don't wait for a reply. She's a minx. She knows what I like and that's her with nothing on.

As smitten as I am, I can't let a brother go down in a blaze of glory. Plus, I really wanna see Angel kick his ass.

I shove my phone inside my jacket and roar off to avenge Brock's murder.

22

GUNNER

A LOUD CRASH wakes me from my sleep. I listen closely then I smell him. He always smells like smoke and bourbon. My skin crawls.

If he's crashing around, he'll be too drunk to do anything, it doesn't stop me from jumping from the top bunk to hide Amanda though. She's sound asleep, it's amazing what you can sleep through when you try, we're good at it by now.

Another bang.

He's taking it out on mommy. I gave up trying to defend her long ago, I'm only seven. I can't beat him.

Amanda stirs in my arms as I roll her towards me and lift her tiny body, she opens her eyes momentarily. I tell her to be quiet, we know the routine; be as small and quiet as possible. Don't come out no matter what you hear. I open the closet door and place her inside, a blanket already laid out beneath her. She's a good girl, she'll stay here out of the way.

I'm scared, but I won't let him see.

People are starting to notice the bruises. My teacher at school asked me how I got them, and I said I fell off the swing. Whatever happens; we can never tell. He said mommy will go to jail and then we'll be all alone with nobody to care for us.

GUNNER

A loud bang has me jumping in fright, it halts me in my tracks. I hear voices, male voices, and lots of loud stomping through the house. My stomach drops... what if he's brought some friends around? I contemplate opening the window and escaping, but it's too late now.

I glance toward the cupboard where my baby sister lies, as long as she's alright, that's all that matters... I have to be brave for her. I'm all she has.

The shouting gets louder, mommy screams. I hear yelling, cursing and a lot of pounding... something smashes, then there's total silence.

I run back to the bunk and hide myself on the bottom of Amanda's bed in the corner. If I stay really still, they may not find me.

I wait and listen carefully. Everything's gone quiet now.

Suddenly the door swings open and I ball my hands into fists. I don't know this figure approaching, but it's not him; that doesn't make him any less dangerous.

I don't know what he's doing here. I try not to shake, that won't help me, it'll only make things worse.

"Joshua?" I hear the man's voice call out.

Strangely, it sounds familiar, then; "It's Hutch."

I stay completely still. It's the man from the motorcycle club.

"You don't have to hide or be afraid, son, you can come out. I'm not gonna hurt you."

He comes closer into the room but doesn't turn on the light. I see his boots cross the dirty, carpeted floor. He stops afoot of the bed.

"We're going to get you and Amanda out of here buddy," he tells me, softly.

My eyes go wide. What does he mean?

He comes to the very end of the bunk and then crouches down. His piercing eyes find me quickly, but he keeps his distance.

"You don't have to hide any more Joshua, you hear me? I'm not gonna do anything to hurt you. It's okay to come out, bud, I promise."

I tremble but I don't speak.

"Where's your sister?" he asks when I don't respond.

I shake my head. Never! I want to yell... but this man is good, isn't he? He rides a loud motorcycle and mommy used to drink at his club. He's always been nice to me. But men are bad. Men do bad things.

"It's alright Joshua, you remember Helen, the nurse from the hospital?"

I nod my head. She's a kind lady, she helped me when I broke my arm.

"She's going to come in with Kirsty, she's a friend of mine too, and they're going to help you and Amanda, buddy. You're going to go with them and have some dinner and watch some tv, does that sound okay?"

I stare at him.

Something crosses his eyes but I can't place it. He looks sad, almost.

He runs a hand over his face, and I stare at him; still, I can't look away.

I look to the closet and then back to him. I try not to tremble.

"Did you hide your sister?"

"NO!" I yell at him.

He holds his hands up. "It's okay, it's okay, nobody's ever going to hurt you or Amanda again, I promise you but we need to get outa here. If I let Helen in here, will you show her where Amanda is?"

I don't know if this is a trick; mommy says not to trust strangers, but getting out of this cold, stinking place and getting something to eat sounds really good.

I can't stay here.

We can't stay here.

I find myself nodding.

He smiles. "Good boy." He turns to the door and walks over to it. I hear male voices and I strain to hear what's being said...

"Take that dead beat fucker out the back until the kids are safe." I hear Hutch say.

"Gotcha, Prez."

"And take Brock with you, this'll be a learning experience for him, time to prove what it takes to be a man."

The other man chuckles. "You want us to start without you?"

"Fuck no, I want him to feel everything I'm gonna inflict on him, just make sure he's tied up and gagged."

"Already on it. And the woman?"

"I'll deal with her myself."

I know they're talking about him and mommy.

A few moments later, Helen comes in. She holds out her hands to me and I hesitate, but I know we have to go.

I don't want to stay here.

She smiles kindly as I shuffle to the end of the bed. She brushes my hair back off my face softly. "Such a good boy Joshua, you're going to be okay. Can you show me where Amanda is? Then we can go and eat and you can have a lovely hot shower and watch some tv."

I stare at her and she smiles kindly. "It's alright sweetheart, nobody is going to hurt you ever again." She has tears in her eyes and I look at them curiously.

I hesitate but then I find myself pointing to the closet. She smiles again and tells me how big and brave I am.

She opens the door tentatively and Amanda peers out at her.

"Hello Amanda, I'm Helen," she says softly. "Me and you and your brother are all going to go on a car ride to my house, there won't be any more shouting. You'll be safe there; we're going to get some burgers and you can watch some tv and get nice and warm."

Amanda sucks her thumb into her mouth and her eyes go to me for approval.

She won't go anywhere without Ted. I reach near her pillow for her favorite stuffed animal.

Helen's eyes well up with tears when I bring Ted to her. She *looks like she's going to cry. I don't know what she's sad for, mommy cries a lot but that's when she gets hurt.*

As if reading my mind, she glances at me. "You're going to be safe now Joshua, you hear me?" *she whispers softly.* "I'll never let anybody touch you, but we have to go now."

I just stare at her.

Somebody's told.

She knows.

Hutch knows.

I hang my head in shame.

"Are we going to be in trouble?" *I blurt out, my voice barely a whisper.*

She shakes her head. "No! My darling angel you're not, neither of you have done anything wrong, don't ever think that."

She helps Amanda out and we go to leave, I tug on her sleeve and point to our things in the closet.

"Jayson is going to pack it all up and bring it over, he's my son, you met him a while back remember? He's a good boy."

I do remember, he threw the football to me and showed me how to pitch.

I nod again.

She holds Amanda in her arms and I walk next to her.

I don't know where mommy is, and I don't dare ask.

He's nowhere to be seen but the furniture is broken and there's glass everywhere.

We get out of the front and over to a big car and another lady gets out. Hutch comes around the side of the house.

"This is my friend Kirsty," *Helen says as the other lady smiles warmly.* "She's going to come with us and help me take care of you tonight, we'll stop for burgers on the way."

My stomach growls at the thought, it's been a few days since we had anything to eat. We've never had store bought burgers before.

My eyes light up.

"Hi Joshua," Kirsty says gently. She's a tall, blonde lady with long nails and bright lips. "Hi Amanda, are we all set to go?"

I nod and just as I do Amanda starts to cry. The women look at each other and Helen holds her close to her chest, I notice then the bump at her tummy. I watch as Hutch plants a kiss on the side of Kirsty's head. I stare at them. I've never seen a man, especially a mean looking man like him, be gentle like this.

"Get gone out of here while I take care of this," he says to her softly.

Helen opens the door and slides Amanda inside, she gets in with her, she holds her tummy with one hand and softly rubs it. "You want to ride shot-gun Josh?"

I nod enthusiastically. This car is cool.

I turn to Hutch. "Where's mommy?" I ask quietly.

He looks down at me. "You don't need to worry about that right now, son, I meant what I said back there." He thumbs towards the house. "You need to be a good boy and go with the ladies now, everything's going to be okay."

"Do we have to come back?" I stammer, barely getting the words out.

He stares at me for a long while, something crosses over his face that I can't place, then he softens as he clears his throat. "You'll never have to come back here again Josh, you or Amanda, you hear me? Never. That's my promise to you."

I turn to climb in the car.

He turns to Kirsty and pushes her hair back off her face and nuzzles her nose with his.

I've never seen a man treat a woman like this. He's gentle with her, nothing like what I've seen with mommy. She screams and cries a lot. She gets called a lot of bad names.

"How long will you be?" she asks, looking up at him with big eyes.

"As long as it takes."

"Hutch..."

"Don't go getting your knickers in a knot, woman, now get gone, I know what I'm doing."

"Do you?"

He pecks her on the forehead. "You don't even need to ask me that."

They kiss and I quickly hightail it into the car before they catch me staring.

"Buckle up Joshua," Helen tells me from the back seat.

I do as she asks.

Kirsty comes around the side of the car and climbs in. I turn around in my seat to check on Amanda, my gaze shoots to Helen's tummy again.

She sees where I am looking and laughs softly. "It's a little girl, she's due in a few months."

Amanda has stopped crying.

"Hands up, who wants burgers?" Kirsty sings out happily.

I turn to Kirsty and shoot my hand up, I can't see if Amanda does but I shoot up another just in case.

The women both laugh.

Kirsty starts the engine and we begin to roll out.

I jump as I hear a gunshot, I start to turn my head.

"Never look back, Joshua," Helen says as I turn back to the front quickly. "There's nothing back there for you anymore."

Another shot rings out into the night as I close my eyes and I know I'll remember this night for the rest of my life.

∼

I WAKE UP WITH A JOLT. Someone is shaking me. I shoot up out of bed and then I hear a shriek. I grasp whoever it is and roll over disorientated.

I keep hearing; "Gunner it's me, it's Lily, it's Lily…" in a panicked tone.

I stop what I'm doing and realize I'm not in my own bed.

I'm in Lily's. We fucked and I fell asleep in her arms. It all comes back to me quickly.

Jesus H. Christ.

She looks up at me terrified. I let her wrists go. I go to push off her and she holds onto my biceps, stopping me in my tracks as I look back at her confused.

"Lily, I'm sorry..."

"It was just a bad dream," she whispers. "It's alright, I'm here."

I stare at her. "Fuck, I hurt you." I'm disgusted with myself. I've never hurt a woman physically in my life.

"You just startled me," she says, breathless. "I'm fine."

The last thing I would ever want to do is hurt her. I could never live with myself if I did, accident or not.

"You're not fine, I could've hurt you!"

"But you didn't."

I run a hand over my face. "I'm sorry, sometimes I have these... bad dreams, they come and go."

"Gunner, this isn't the first time this has happened."

I'm lost in her eyes, the last thing I wanted to ever do was see sympathy staring back at me.

I can't tell her.

"What do you mean?" I thought she hadn't noticed the other times I'd woken up in a panic.

She raises her hand to stroke my face. "You have a lot of bad dreams, Guns. You..."

"I what?" My heart hammers in my chest.

"You called for your mom," she whispers. She sounds sad and I know this dream must have been bad, of course it was, I almost choked her. This isn't what I wanted, and this is exactly why I don't stay over.

I blink up at her.

"What else did I do?" I really don't know if I want the answer.

"You sometimes say some other names."

"Whose name?"

My throat feels dry as I watch her, she bites her lip, unsure if to tell me.

"I want to know," I encourage. *But do I want to know?*

She visibly swallows. "You called out for Amanda."

I wait to see if there's more.

"And you…" she stops.

My chest feels like it may cave in from the pressure but I wait.

"And you kept saying for Rick to stop."

My heart rate accelerates and I drop my head.

I haven't heard his name in over twenty years.

"Please…" I state. "I don't want to talk about that."

"Gunner, do you actually sleep properly *any* night of the week?"

I stare back at her. "I get what I need."

"Why?" she whispers. "Why do you wake up shouting and screaming every night? You can tell me."

I shake my head sadly. "No princess, I can't."

She soothes my cheek gently; I melt into her touch. "I won't think any less of you."

"There's nothing to tell. I don't want to talk about it, please let it drop."

She stares at me. "What do you want? What can I do to take this away?"

I look at her beautiful face. I shouldn't be here. I shouldn't be defiling her. She's too sweet and innocent. But it won't stop me from having her.

I want her more than ever.

"You," I state.

She smiles tentatively and I kiss her lips gently. She raises her hands to my face and runs her fingers through my hair. I love it when she does this. With her, I forget everything.

I've never spent any time in a woman's bed other than to fuck, and nine times out of ten it's at my place. But since I started this thing with her, things have changed. *I've* changed. And I'm sick of having this battle with myself.

I have to confess to Steel.

I want her to be mine.

"So, have me."

I kiss her jaw, her chin. I move my lips to her neck and work my way down to her nightdress and pull the straps down, her plump, beautiful breasts fall out. I kiss them each tenderly, my dick hard at the sight of her face alone, this just makes it all that much sweeter. I suck gently on each bud and she arches her back up into me. I could spend all day worshipping her perfect tits.

I don't warm her up because one feel of my hand between her legs tells me she's wet and ready for me, like she always is.

"You're so fucking perfect, Lil."

She moans as I slowly rub her sweet center and spread her wetness around. I line myself up and enter her slowly, we both sigh at the same time, the feeling intense and tight.

I don't know how I can give her up. I don't want to. I fucking won't.

I rock my hips back and forth, I want to make it up to her, show her I would never hurt her deliberately. It's maddening seeing and hearing her come apart from what I do to her.

I own her body.

She owns mine.

There is nothing more to it.

I love her.

Fuck.

Where did that come from?

I don't love anyone, not like this.

I roll my hips gently, thrusting slowly.

I know that she knows I'm making love to her, this isn't fucking, and I finally get it now.

That's what they say when you fall for someone, *everything* changes. I used to think people like that were losers, that they didn't know what they were talking about, hopeless romantics. But ever since we got back from New Orleans, things have changed.

She rocks her hips, trying to quicken the pace but I stop and kiss her gently, my tongue goes into her mouth and she gasps at my sensual touch.

We fit. I know that much.

I'm not often very soft in bed. I like it rough, but with her, with her everything is uncharted.

She bumps my hips and I smile against her mouth and begin again, rocking my hips back and forth gently, pushing in and out of her with maddening slowness. My hands dig into the mattress and her legs wrap around me. I want her orgasm to go on and on and I know at this pace it will. When she grabs the bed sheets, and then my ass, I know she's close.

"Oh Gunner…" she moans, but I don't quicken, I give her just a little bit of a harder thrust at the end and she falls over the edge. I could never get sick of watching her come undone, it's the best sound I've ever heard when she says my name like that. I let go too, emptying myself inside her, it's so slow and exhilarating that I lose myself, yet again.

I also realize for the first time ever that I didn't use a wrap and I don't fucking care. She's on birth control and I want nothing between us.

She's mine.

I've made her mine. There ain't no two ways about it.

"I love you." I'm sure I hear her say as I collapse on top of her and bury my face into her neck.

There is nothing else. Just her.

23

LILY

DEANNA and I stand outside the salon and assess the damage as the prospects clean dry paint off my shop window.

"I can't believe this," Deanna says, her hand over her mouth.

"You and me both, seems someone's got it in for me."

"What about the security footage?"

"They had a mask on," I sigh. "Cops can't get a proper I.D."

"Was it just one person?"

"According to the footage, yes, they got a partial plate number from the curb but nothing concrete."

White paint is splattered everywhere. I've had to cancel today's appointments and reschedule them until the mess is cleaned up.

"I don't get what you get out of doing this?" she goes on, as annoyed as I am. "Like seriously?"

"I know, it's totally fucked." I can't take any more. "You want a coffee?"

"Love one."

We step inside and I turn the coffee machine on in the staff lunchroom.

"Oh, and the gigs up, Steelman," she says as I grab a couple of mugs from the cupboard. "You can fool everyone else but you can't fool me."

I look at her quizzically. "What have I done now?"

"I saw Gunner's sled pulling out of here in the wee hours of morning, that's what."

I pale under her scrutiny and my throat goes dry.

"What happened to *just one time?*"

I bite my lip. Deanna got it out of me, what we did in New Orleans, but I haven't exactly told her we've kept at it since then. Gunner will kill me if he knows I told Deanna.

I'm worried about him.

His sleeping patterns and nightmares aren't normal.

Night tremors. Sweating. Calling weird things out and people's names. Shaking. And then there's the anger like the other night. I can't deny that was a little disturbing.

Something strange happens every night and he won't talk about it.

The fact that he barely remembers his dreams or what he does when he's asleep is more than cause for concern.

I googled his symptoms and most of the searches suggest PTSD.

"That kind of went out the window," I admit.

"Now you're at it like rabbits, huh?" she grins.

I try to play coy. "You could say that."

"I knew he'd be good in bed, it's in the swagger."

I pop a pod into the machine and turn to face her. "He's *really* freaking good."

She rolls her lips inwards. "I want *all* the details, every last one." She rubs her hands together excitedly.

"You already had details, the first time." I remind her.

"And you still never told me what really went on with you and Cash when we were down south."

"Nothing went on." She shrugs. "I got too drunk to remember anything. I woke up on his bed but I was fully clothed with nothing to show for my trouble except a massive hangover."

I give her a pout. "Aww, that's kind of sweet, though. That he obviously took care of you and didn't leave you drunk somewhere."

"Yeah, he let me pass out with dignity, that makes me feel so much better about making an idiot out of myself!"

I laugh. "Least he's not a creep."

"I know and I'm pissed at myself for getting that hammered."

"Only because you wanted to jump his bones?"

"That's precisely why." She points at me. "Never underestimate the power of an older man, they know all the moves, know how to do it right. They been round the block and rumor has it they got amazing staying power."

"I did not know that." I admit.

"It's true. I have a sixth sense for these things."

I hand her the first coffee then put another pod in the contraption.

"He is pretty hot, for an older guy, would you really have slept with him though?" I don't know why I bother asking, I know the answer.

"I don't think we would have done any sleeping." She winks.

I roll my eyes. "TMI."

"Anyway, stop deflecting, I wanna hear more about you and Gunner."

"What about her and Gunner?"

We both jump as Steel suddenly appears in the doorway,

my heart leaps in my chest wondering how much he overheard.

Typical Steel; he just appears like an apparition without any warning.

I know he knows how to be invisible and quiet from his military training, but this is ridiculous.

Even Deanna pales a little under his scrutiny.

"Jesus, Steel!" I press my hand to my chest. "You scared the shit out of me!"

My brother, however, is not fazed. "Why is the backdoor just wide open for anyone to just come wandering in? After that break in and the paint situation you ought to be more careful, it's like an open invitation to the neighborhood to come and rob you."

"The cops were here, remember."

He grunts, taking up all of the room in the doorway, blocking any escape.

"I didn't put that fuckin' security system in so you can just leave back doors open and unlocked and not protect yourself," he continues as I try not to cringe into the wall. "I'm puttin' a prospect in here, full time until we get to the bottom of this and why this shit keeps happening."

"Steel! That's completely ridiculous. I know things have been a little weird around here lately, but let's not get carried away."

"Yeah, it's ridiculous until your face appears on the side of a milk carton."

"It's vandals, that's all. It happens. And when I catch the little shits, there's gonna be hell to pay."

He glares at me. "What's goin' on with Gunner?" As if his formidable presence isn't enough, he crosses his arms across his chest and waits for my answer.

I have to think quickly.

"Umm, I'm just pissed with him about the jewelry launch."

"Why's that?"

"He's ordered all this shit and I've nowhere to store it, he needs to get his own freaking storage container or something instead of cluttering up my shop."

"That it?"

"I just said so, didn't I?"

We face each other and he glances towards Deanna who remains completely still, like moving an inch will alert him to the fact I'm lying through my teeth.

He rubs his chin. "I need a favor."

I almost breathe a sigh of relief. "Isn't that the only reason for your regular visits?" I fire back.

I can't believe I've gotten away with it.

"You're gettin' a bit lippy, I heard Summer had quite a bit to say to Tag while she was down south, too, he wasn't impressed. Told me that the girls of the club need a little lesson in discipline and manners."

"What a douche," Deanna mutters.

"Take it up with her," I reply. "Anyway, he would have deserved it, he's worse than you are."

"I guess the men in that club have bigger mouths than the men in this club," Deanna pipes up as I snort.

"Should be showin' respect when you're in another clubhouse."

"We did, I personally did shots off some dude passed out on the pool table." Deanna smiles up at him as he meets her gaze with a look that could cut glass.

"Yeah, I heard all about the male strippers."

"Don't blame me," she warns. "That was all Crystal's doing, and anyway, the guys had strippers, so why can't we?"

I bite on my bottom lip at her lies, knowing Crystal had nothing to do with organizing the strip joint. Well, what Steel doesn't know can't hurt him.

"Trouble with you girls is you never listen, and you never do as you're told."

"I bet Sienna doesn't do as she's told, from what we've heard." Deanna goads him. It's never a good idea to challenge my brother but that's on her. I'm staying right out of it.

He stares at her. "Heard you were flirting with Cash, big time."

She stands her ground. "I flirt with everyone Steel, not my fault if he's still got the goods."

He frowns. "Playin' with fire there, I'm sure if he wanted to be nagged to death, he would have taken you up on the offer, clearly he didn't."

She glares back at him.

"Steel," I interrupt. "What favor do you want? I've got shit to do."

He turns his glare back to me, clearly we've pushed his buttons enough.

"I wanna take Sienna away next weekend and I need you to watch Lola and Rocky."

Oh. That's not so bad.

"Yeah of course, I love those two little fur balls."

"Ooh romantic getaway, things sound serious Steel," Deanna sing-songs. "Do I hear wedding bells?"

We both burst out laughing.

"Anyone ever tell you that that smart mouth of yours is gonna get you in trouble one day."

"One can only hope," she replies with enthusiasm.

He shakes his head again, unimpressed.

"What happened to Cassidy?" I suddenly remember Sienna saying she'd left town. The further I lead us away from Gunner the better.

Steel shrugs. "She went back home for a while, probably a good thing, she's been pretty fucked up since shit went down."

"I don't know, she seemed pretty sweet on Colt." Deanna shrugs.

"Clingy, more like," Steel mutters. "Sometimes shit happens when it's traumatic, they latch on, don't know how to let go, it fucks you up in the head."

I stare at my brother, it's hard to imagine him being anything but the hard man that he is standing there, but I know he has a soft side. One that you rarely ever see. It was only a few years ago when he'd been pretty fucked up himself; his divorce, recovering from his deployment, night tremors, taking it out with alcohol.

My mind flicks to Gunner again and I have half a mind to ask Steel about PTSD, only I can't, because then he'll definitely know something's up.

Steel waves a hand in front of my face. "Hello in there?"

I realize he's asked me a question and I'm lost in a daydream.

"Oh, shit sorry, I spazzed out for a second."

"Are you good for next weekend? I need to book somethin' and it's non-refundable."

"Of course, I'd be happy to." Anything to get him off my back.

He gives me a chin lift.

"Where are you taking Sienna?" Deanna asks.

Avoid the topic of Gunner complete.

Girls, one. Steel, zero.

"There's a lodge up in Wattle Canyon, overlooks the mountains, she likes that kind of shit, it's quiet and isolated, plus there's no internet or phone service, so we'll have to keep ourselves busy for the whole weekend, somehow."

"Very romantic," I say almost choking.

"Yeah, she can scream for miles and nobody will hear," Deanna adds. "Good thinking."

Eww.

"Thanks for that visual." I cringe into my coffee.

He points at me. "Keep the back door fuckin' locked, and I'm sending Lee down here during the day and Jaxon during the night."

"What?" I squeak. "I don't want him in my apartment."

He rolls his eyes as if I'm stupid. "He won't be in your apartment, dummy; he'll be outside watching the premises."

"Oh." I reply.

He shakes his head in an exasperated fashion then turns and leaves without another word.

Fuck you, Steel, Deanna mouths.

He slams the back door loudly behind him.

"Okay, maybe he can read our thoughts, but his bullshit radar has gone soft since Sienna," Deanna remarks.

"Tell me about it," I sigh. "This is exactly why we shouldn't be discussing *you know who,* anymore out in public, or at all."

"In all seriousness Lil, you better be sure your heart's not involved in this thing; it is just sex, right? A good time, nothing more?" she moves closer to me, concern in her eyes.

"Of course." I nod. She doesn't seem convinced.

"I just don't want you getting hurt." She rubs my shoulder with one hand and I can't help but feel in the pit of my stomach that she could be right. I mean, I told him I loved him, and he didn't say it back.

This little bubble we've been in is just that, it can burst at any time.

"I won't, it's fun, that's all." I wish to God I really believed that.

She shakes her head. "Just don't fall in love with him."

I smile weakly, little does she know, the damage is already done.

GUNNER

I can't find Gunner. He wasn't in bed when I woke up. He came over, we had dinner and made out on the couch, then we did it on the couch, twice.

We can't seem to get enough of each other. The sex just gets more incredible and thrilling every time I'm in his arms. He loves to kiss me over every inch of my body, and I mean every inch.

I've never known what it felt like to be truly adored, truly desired by someone. Now I do and I find myself not wanting to give him back, as if I ever stood a chance. I just don't know if he feels the same way.

I know he feels something, but he hasn't said anything about *us*. It's still early days, and it's only a few weeks since we got back from down south so I know I'm jumping the gun, but I can't help how I feel. I knew going into this that there was every chance I wouldn't want to let go and now look at me.

I know he hasn't left because his cut is still on the floor from earlier, he wouldn't leave without it.

I don't see him anywhere, I check the bathroom, then the kitchen. My apartment is silent and still. Yet, I know he's here, somewhere.

I walk back into the bedroom and call out his name. A few moments later I see a shadow in the corner of the bedroom. He's huddled in a ball, shaking.

I rush over to him.

"Gunner?" I go to shake him but then remember what happened the last time I did that, so I keep my distance. "Gunner, can you hear me?"

I jump up and go to the bed and grab the throw. He's completely naked and shaking uncontrollably.

"Guns, what's wrong?" Panic rises in my voice. I don't know what to do.

His eyes glance up at me and I can see he's been crying. My heart leaps into my chest.

"Please Gunner, please let me in."

He stares at me vacantly. "I can't Lily," he whispers.

It hits me then.

I knew something was up before, but I know for sure now that something is, terribly, terribly wrong. To the point that he's now having some kind of panic attack on the floor.

"Just breathe in and out, slowly," I tell him, trying to remember something from the first aid course I took a while ago. "It will pass, I'm here, I'm always going to be here."

I sit in front of him while he slows his breathing. God knows how long he's been sitting here riding this out. My stomach twists in knots.

"I love you," he says out of nowhere. My eyes go wide at his admission. "I'm gonna fuck this up baby girl, I know I am. You won't want me anymore. How could you?"

I reach to caress his face with my hand softly. "That's where you're wrong Guns, you underestimate me if that's what you really think. I've wanted you since I was a little girl, I've always had a crush and as I got older it only intensified."

We stare at each other.

His voice is so quiet. "I destroy everything baby, this will be no different, you'll see."

"Stop it," I tell him, gently. "You have so much good inside you, Gunner. I know you have. I see it, I feel it. You make me feel like I'm the only woman in the entire universe, when you look at me like you do, I want to combust, when you touch me, I want to die. You did all of that. *You.*"

I hate how he looks so vacant, so broken. I want to take this pain away but I can't. I don't know how or where to even start.

I just have to listen, be here for him, and hope he will let me in.

"There's nothing without you," he whispers. "You're everything to me Lily, I didn't know... I didn't know it could be like this."

I hold his cheek in my palm. He's so vulnerable. So angelic. Not the aloof, fun-loving, hot sexy biker I'm used to who's so full of confidence.

"I'm all yours, I'm not going anywhere," I whisper back.

A ghost of a smile crosses his face as I gently move toward him and kiss his forehead, then each cheek, feeling the wet stains on his face that he hasn't even bothered to wipe.

Oh Gunner. I don't know how to help you.

"I can't be fixed."

"I don't want to fix you." I smooth back his hair. "I love you just how you are, no matter what, nothing you say could ever make me feel differently."

I kiss his lips gently, tasting the salt on his skin.

"I love you, Lily," he whispers.

"I love you too, Gunner."

"I want to go back to bed."

I nod, moving to stand, he follows me, and we fold around each other under the covers. He's still cold, his skin's all clammy but once he wraps himself around me, he stops shaking.

"I'll never stop wanting you," I whisper as we cling to one another. "Never."

I fall asleep to the sound of his soft, rhythmic breathing and he doesn't let go of me.

All night long.

24

GUNNER

"You may as well have just gone the whole nine yards, Guns. From where I'm standing though, a pinky finger would've sufficed in covering the goods, instead of your hands." Bones thinks he's hilarious as he flicks through my images for Sizzle on the iPad.

"Didn't know you were that way inclined brother, if you'd like a physical inspection, I can drop my pants right now, spare your curiosity."

He shakes his head. "Funny fucker. What's the coin for this sort of thing?"

"Depends." I shrug. "With royalties from Gunner After Dark, maybe like ten k."

He whistles through his teeth.

"Fuckin' pretty boys."

I laugh. "You jealous? Want me to hook you up?"

"Yeah right, they'd probably pay me *not* to pose. But I'd need a fire hydrant, not a pinkie finger."

I snort into my beer. It's been almost three weeks since New Orleans, things with Lily are good, aside from my nightmares, but I've been going home most nights so I don't wake her. She's getting more and more suspicious about what's going on with me. The last thing I want is her finding out more information.

It killed me to hear *his* name come out of her mouth. I wanted to wash it out with soap and tell her to never speak that name ever again. I never want to taint her beautiful lips by spouting poison like that.

I close my eyes at the memory. I never want to hurt her. It would kill me to see any kind of sadness in her eyes that I had caused and she'd only feel sorry for me. I don't want that.

I'm about to ask Bones how his back's feeling since he's been out of action, but the doors barge open and Steel marches in, wearing his usual frown, except this time it's directed at me and he looks like he's about to unleash hell.

"You!" he points at me. Oh boy, this oughta be good. "We gotta talk, fuckface."

I stop mid-sip and a slight course of fear runs through me that he might know about me and Lily, but that's impossible, we've been careful.

Ever since I realized I want more than just sex with Lily I've been thinking about how to approach Steel, I just haven't found the right time.

Everything's changed since New Orleans.

He knows me better than anyone and I doubt he'll appreciate my sincerity, but I am just that. I've real feelings for her, this isn't just fucking.

"Yeah?" I nod. "What's up?"

Maybe there's a chance he doesn't know? I've been in trouble so many times, it could just be Steel doing his thing.

He comes towards me, it's then I see his jaw ticking. That sets me on edge a little.

"You got some shit to move out of Lily's salon?"

I almost sag in relief. "What are you talkin' about? I only got one workstation bro, can't take up that much room."

"What about all your jewelry supplies comin' in?"

I don't know if this is a trick question. "I've got them at D's already, I don't even keep them at the salon."

He stares at me then his nostrils flair.

I don't see the punch coming but it knocks me backwards off my stool.

I blink once, twice, then hang onto the side of the bar. My head may roll off my shoulders from the impact.

"Think I was born yesterday, fucker?"

"What the fuck, bro?" I spit, tasting blood in my mouth. That fuckin' hurt.

He points at me as Bones attempts to hold him back.

"She spun me some fuckin' fairy tale about bein' pissed at you for havin' your shit lying around when her and D were talkin', could tell she was lying. Could smell a rat a mile away.

You also ain't been takin' any sweet butts upstairs the last few weeks, in fact, you've been hidin' out since you went down south. That's not like you. Tag mentioned somethin' in passin' bout seein' you with Lil, then low and behold, I see your sled leaving Lily's apartment in the early hours of mornin', that seems odd since you don't fuckin' live there. You bangin' my sister, bro? Think very fuckin' hard about your answer."

I feel all the tension in my body rise to the surface.

So, we've been sprung.

Oh, holy fuck.

I should have known this was too good to be true. I should have known the small shred of happiness I've found couldn't last. It never does. I always find a way to ruin things. Should've fessed up like Brock told me weeks ago. No matter what I say though, Steel won't believe shit.

I hold up my hands as he towers over me.

"This isn't what it looks like, Steel."

"Oh yeah?" He goes to swing again but I duck and he misses, further infuriating him. "How does it look exactly?"

"We should go outside, talk about this privately."

"Oh? You wanna settle this man to man, do ya?" his snicker indicates he liked that idea, then he'd get to kick my ass, knowing he'll win.

"I don't think that's a good idea, Guns," Bones adds quickly. "Why don't we go into the meeting room and discuss it there, like civilized people."

Who is he kidding?

Civilized?

Neither of us have ever been that.

The prospects have stopped playing pool and Ginger comes over to where we're standing, ready to throw cold water, or something, on us; she looks as worried as I feel.

"Don't wanna discuss nothin' anywhere except here, I want you," he points at me again, "to tell me the fuckin' truth!"

I let out a breath and drop my eyes. I can't lie to him.

"It didn't happen like how you think."

He pushes me in the chest and I let him. "Yeah? Then let me know how I *think* it went down and then I can kill you accordingly, either way ain't gonna be good, so much for brotherhood."

This was never gonna be easy, no matter which way we played it.

I realize I'm an idiot, Steel notices everything.

He shoves me again and this time I shove him right back. "You wanna fuckin' listen to me, bro, or not? I got shit to say."

"You had every chance in the book to fuckin' go there and you still chose to sneak around behind my back!" he roars.

The last thing I wanted was for it to come to this. I didn't know until Lily and I slept together in New Orleans that I even wanted this myself. I seriously doubt he'll give a shit about how I feel; that I actually do love her, that I adore her. That I feel different when I'm around her, that I don't want another woman. No, he doesn't want to hear any of that shit. He just wants to beat my ass.

"Steel." Bones clutches his shoulder, trying to get him to calm down, he shrugs him off.

"We got together yes," I start, hoping he won't hit me again, my jaw is fuckin' killing me. "But it wasn't something we planned, it just sort of happened. She's special, she's fuckin' amazing and I planned on tellin' you once I figured it out myself."

He narrows his eyes. "Sort of happened?"

"Yeah, I swear to God."

"How long?"

"Since we went down south," I say. When he frowns, I quickly add; "I'm not shittin' you bro, nothing happened between us until then, I wouldn't lie about that."

"Why her? You ain't got enough pussy around here, you have to go chasing Lily? She's a good girl, she won't recover when you're done with her."

"It just happened, Steel." It sounds lame but I don't know how else to describe it, nor do I wish to tell him it was her who initially pursued me. He won't want to hear that. "I swear to God I didn't plan this, neither of us did, and... I won't be done with her..."

We stand toe to toe.

He ignores all the good things I say because he's pissed and now he just wants to fight me.

"It's not even that, it's the fact you've been lyin' to my face for weeks, her too. That I had to find out by catching you sneaking around like a couple of kids. So much for bro code; no sleepin' with club sisters. I guess the rules don't apply to you, they never have, right Guns?"

I stare right back at him. "Did anyone ever tell you you're not the easiest motherfucker in the world to talk to?"

"Don't get fuckin' cute, it won't help you. I'm not in this club to be fuckin' easy. If I let everything that goes on around here slide, we'd all be fucked."

"She's a grown woman, Steel, we both know that she's capable of making her own decisions."

"Says you, who'd do exactly the same thing if a brother moved in on Summer. You'd be the first one to come down on him."

I shake my head. "No, I wouldn't. I'd be man enough to let her make her own decisions knowing she's smart and has a brain in her head."

His eyes go wide. "I'm not man enough huh?" he pushes me again. "You wanna say that again and follow it up you little punk?"

"You know what?" I throw at him. "Yeah, I wanna take this outside, you been sayin' you're gonna kick the shit out of me since I was a teenager, well, now's your chance big guy, let's fuckin' go at it."

He shakes his head like he knows I'm a dead man.

I push past him and storm to the door. If I'm about to die then at least it won't have been for nothing. I've had the best few weeks of my entire life.

"Gunner," Bones calls. "You don't have to do this."

I flip him the bird and I know Steel will be hot on my heels. No way he'll be backing out of a fight, any chance to assert his authority is a good one. It's like talkin' to a brick wall.

I make for the door and sure enough, as soon as I turn, he's right behind me.

"You gonna say I don't deserve her?" I spit. "You know what, Steel? I fuckin' know that, tried to tell her that, but we both want this. Somethin' happened to me, somethin' I've never felt before and if I knew what it even was then I'd tell you, but I fuckin' don't."

He swings and I duck backwards, missing me only infuriates him further.

"Yeah, you defiled a club sister, *my* sister and didn't give two shits about it, great goin' asshole."

I hear the doors open behind us and see Bones in my periphery, along with the prospects and anybody else who wants to witness my beating and imminent death.

"With all due respect Steel, she's capable of knowing what she wants, she's not a kid anymore. I wouldn't disrespect her…" I interject, he slams me in the ribs before I can finish, finding his target easily. I swing back and miss.

"You wanna believe the shit you spout go right ahead, after all the fuckin' years we've known each other, you expect me to believe any of it?"

I've actually never seen him so livid.

"Steel, she's different, as soon as I knew that she wasn't just another…"

"Another what? Notch on your belt? Come on Guns, we both know what you're like, that you can't give her what she needs, that you're not capable of anything concrete, you love em' and leave em', that's what you do and it's what you do best."

I know it's true but the words spilling from his mouth still hit below the belt. I never wanted Steel's disappointment, never. But here it is on a silver platter.

How I thought we could go under the radar I'll never know.

"She was never that. Give me some credit."

"Credit?" he spits.

"Things have changed," I tell him as he circles around me. He's unpredictable, the hit could come any which way. "Things changed the minute we spent time together. I didn't know what to do about it or why I wanted it, all I know is I do. I don't want that old life anymore, I want... I want *her*."

He clips me on the side of the face but not with full force as I manage to dodge backwards just in time. It leaves him open for a split second and I take my opportunity. I swing and cop him right on the chin.

We're like a couple of teenagers in the school yard fighting over a spilt milkshake.

"You've no fuckin' right to tell me what to do anyway," I yell at him. "I'm a fuckin' grown man and I can make my own decisions without asking for permission, so can Lily. We know what we're doing."

It's bold but he has to hear it.

He shakes his head. "Shoulda come to me, out of respect."

"I'm fuckin' sorry Steel, but this is our decision, not yours. Dude, don't make this harder than it already is."

"I'll fuckin' show you hard, pretty boy."

Fists are flying, and I'm glad I'm at least getting some hits in. I clop him in the ribs and I hear him curse.

Somewhere behind me I hear Bones calling, and other voices too, probably the prospects.

To avoid any more hits, I ram into him headfirst in the guts, trying to knock him over, which is near impossible because he's bigger than me, however he stumbles off-guard for a moment and I manage to trip him. It's a cheap move. He grabs onto me and brings me with him as we both fall onto the ground. If he pins me down, it's over.

"Stop it! Stop it!" I hear a woman calling and someone begins tugging on my cut from behind.

"Steel, that's enough!" comes another voice.

Steel shoves me off him and then trips me as I try to stand, I land on my ass.

I see Sienna standing in front of him and Lily is the one tugging at my cut.

Steel sits up on his elbows. "Finally got a fuckin' hit in, took you long enough," he barks. "Also took you long enough to fuckin' stand up to me and prove you've actually got some balls."

"What the hell's going on?" Lily yells.

"Ask your boyfriend," Steel says, flexing his jaw. I'm glad to see I split his lip. "He seems to have all the fuckin' answers to everything."

"Steel!" Sienna chastises. "What the hell's gotten into you?"

He glares at her but doesn't answer.

"For God's sakes, Lily is a grown woman, she can see whoever she wants to, she doesn't need your permission and she certainly doesn't need you gallantly defending her honor when it's not even asked for!"

He does not look very happy about being chewed out by his ol' lady. I'd laugh if I weren't in so much pain. "Don't you start! You don't know shit about this and it's not women's…"

"What Steel?" she demands. "What? It's not *women's business*? Is that what you were going to say? For heavens sakes, pull your head out of your ass. You can't control Lily or Gunner's life, there's being protective then there's this, whatever *this* is."

I hear the prospects snicker and Steel turns and glares at them. "Get the fuck back inside!" he booms, as they scatter quickly, laughing as they go. "Sienna, keep out of it, I mean it, it's between me and him and the brotherhood I thought we had."

She looks far from scared which I find amusing.

"We still have it," I groan as Lily fusses over me. "If you could listen for half a second, I've been tryin' to tell you how I feel, never fuckin' easy for me, but you heard what I said, I meant it, every damn word."

I hear Hutch's sled as he pulls up, his ride's a beast. He

climbs off, raises his sunglasses and looks down at us as he gets closer. "What the fuck's going on here?"

"Long story," Bones replies. "The boys had a disagreement; we're just sortin' it out."

He scratches his chin, assessing the situation. "What sort of disagreement?"

Lily looks at me, then at Steel.

"Why don't you ask Gunner?" Steel mutters.

"I'm askin' you."

"Fucker's been bangin' Lily."

Lily gasps, mortified. "Steel!" she yells.

"Bro." Bones shakes his head.

"I can't believe you just said that." Sienna facepalms her forehead in disbelief.

I don't know why they're so shocked, I've said a lot worse.

He turns to me. "Gunner? What's goin' on?"

I shake my head. "We're just talkin', sortin' shit out between ourselves."

"Doesn't look like there's much talkin' goin on."

He glances up at Lily, to her credit she straightens her spine and looks him right back in the eyes, true Steelman style.

He grunts then brings his gaze back to me, then Steel. "Well, you better stay out here and work it out," he barks, sparing Lily any further humiliation or interrogation. "You let it get this far then you gotta finish it, don't either of you come inside until you've beaten it out of each other cause I don't wanna hear your petty shit, that's a promise. Too old for this shit."

He stalks off towards the doors and disappears inside, muttering under his breath.

Lily kicks Steel's boot. "Thanks for that, big brother, way to go."

He narrows his eyes. "We'll talk about this later, me and Guns aren't finished here, not by a long shot."

"No we won't," she replies, hands on hips. "Beating the shit out of him isn't going to change how I feel."

Sienna crouches down in front of Steel, we're both still on the ground. "You're acting like a couple of idiots," she admonishes. "Punching the shit out of each other, honestly. I knew you were all a bunch of cavemen when I first got here, but I certainly didn't expect you to turn on one another when something happens that you don't agree with."

"For the record, I never said I didn't approve." Steel wipes the blood from his mouth with the back of his hand. "Or that I wouldn't, it's the fact two people I care about lied to me, and *he* couldn't come to me like a man, that's the fuckin' point, woman!"

"I should have come to you, I agree with that, should've fessed up, I went about it all wrong, Steel," I say, rubbing my jaw. "But like I said, Lily's a big girl and she's capable of knowing what she wants, and you gotta let her, you can't be makin' her choices for her."

The words come out freely, because for the first time in my life I want to try for something. I want to try for happiness. I want to make Lily happy; I want to be the sunshine in her life that she is to mine.

He points at me again. "I get a say because I'm the Sergeant at Arms of this club. I remember the oath I took when I got fuckin' patched in, brother."

"Are they a security threat?" Sienna asks, sarcastically.

I snicker but regret it when pain shoots through my jaw.

He looks up at her. "Why are you questioning me, woman? Don't you gotta be somewhere else? Done chewin' me out in front of everyone?"

She puts her hands on her hips. "Stop beating your chest and leave them be. You're not exactly the easier person to talk to, Steel. Excluding Lily, if either of you have anything intelligent to say, which I doubt, I'll be in the bar." She stalks off as Steel stares after her.

He runs a hand through his hair. Seeing him being dressed down by his woman is a short lived, sweet victory.

"This is your fault!" he says, looking over at me. "Now she's apparently runnin' the M.C. and I've got you to thank for it."

"She did own it once," I remind him. He doesn't find the funny side.

"She's right," Lily replies in a softer tone. "Nobody tells you anything, Steel, because we get our heads chewed off if we do. It's better to just sneak around than to come to you like an adult and expect an adult conversation; and might I remind you that you're not my father, I'm a grown adult and I'm capable of making my own decisions, good, bad or otherwise."

He grunts. "I may not be your father, but I'm the only father figure you've ever had. This is the thanks I get for tryin' to protect you."

"Steel, you've protected me my whole life and I'm thankful for that. Not to mention I 've got Hutch, I've got Brock, I've had all the boys in this club look out for me, too. But it's high time you stop treating me as if I'm a child."

He comes to a full seated position. Dusting off his cut.

"For what it's worth, I'm sorry," I say to break the silence. I may never get the feeling back in my face, it's numb. "I should have been man enough to come to you the minute I knew I had feelings, *real* feelings for her and told you, and accepted that you wouldn't be happy about it."

Lily glances at me. She gives me a small smile, it's the first time I've admitted anything deep and meaningful to her face other than the other night. "You do?"

I nod. "Yeah, babe."

Steel shakes his head. "I think I'm going to vomit."

Lily reaches for my cheek, looking concerned. "The bruises are already starting to form."

"He fuckin' hits like a girl," I scoff.

We both know that's not true.

Steel kicks dirt in my direction. "I can give you a couple more bitch slaps if you like."

Lily caresses my skin with her delicate hands. "He fucked you up pretty bad, Guns."

I look up at her. "It's alright, not my face that I need workin' babe."

Steel shakes his head. "You just can't help yourself, can you?"

Lily smiles at me.

"I love her," I say to Steel while staring at Lily. "And I don't know what kind of boyfriend I'm gonna make, but I'm gonna give it my all, not gonna dick her around, I'm not gonna be doin' shit anywhere else. Just her."

Her eyes warm at my words. "Gunner... I love you so much, I always have."

We go to kiss, not caring Steel's sitting right there, he can't do any worse to me. I know the fight in him is over. He grasps onto my shoulder, using it to help him stand, as Lily and I break apart.

"Pass me a fuckin' bucket, no need to go rubbin' it in my face, and you still didn't ask permission to date my sister, but it's your funeral, Guns."

"This mean we're okay?"

He baulks.

Maybe not.

I go to stand too, linking Lily's hand with mine.

"Can I date your sister?" I ask as I pull her into body and wrap my arm around her.

"No." Steel says firmly. He looks down at her, he doesn't

smile but his eyes crinkle slightly. "If he hurts you, then you'll get to pick the spot where he's buried. Deal?"

She nods. "Deal."

"No more fuckin' lyin' to me."

She nods again.

His eyes shoot to mine. "You got a lot to live up to, I'm watchin' you, sunshine."

He turns on his heels and makes towards the club house without another word.

"I want to be cremated!" I yell after him.

I turn back to Lily and she snuggles her face into my neck.

"I'm so sorry he did that to you," she whispers. "Does it hurt really bad?"

"It's alright." I grin. "Not my first rodeo with Steel. Nothin' a bag of frozen peas won't fix."

"He'll cool down when he gets used to the idea, you know how he is. He'll calm down when he sees how happy I am, how happy *we* are."

I snort. "This is Steel we're talkin' about."

She brushes my hair back off my forehead. "You're a good guy, Gunner. I know you think you're not but you are."

I kiss the top of her head. "We can agree to disagree on that, babe. Come on, I need a stiff drink, speaking of stiff, stick your hand in my pants and make sure it's still working."

She does just that and then looks up at me triumphant as her hand slides into the hem of my jeans. "Yes," she whispers. "Definitely working."

I feel myself twitch in her hand and I immediately pull her hand out. The last thing I need is round two with Steel when he sees Lily touching my dick in public, there's only so much a man can take. He needs to digest what's gone down in his own time.

I laugh out loud.

Lily pulls away and looks up at me. "What's so funny?"

We walk towards the clubhouse doors.

"Sienna going to town on his ass."

Lily giggles. "She's the only one he'll pretend to listen to."

"Remind me to never get on her bad side."

She cuddles into my side and I kiss the side of her head.

"I don't wanna even think about what would have happened if you two had kept at it."

"Easy. I would have sprayed him with mace."

She laughs into my cut. "Right. I'll believe that when I see it."

25

LILY

I HANG up the phone from the insurance company. I've had to report the vandalism and file a claim for repairs to the front of the shop. I look down as I feel little Rocky at my feet, he nudges me with his nose.

I'm dog-sitting Rocky and Lola for the weekend since Steel and Sienna have gone out of town. I bend down and pick him up, he's so small and loves his cuddles, it makes me want to get a dog of my own.

Things have been a little strained around the club since word got around about me and Gunner. I can't say Steel's been over the moon about it, but he's handled the aftermath a little better than what I thought he would. He's kept his distance, as if it's just hitting home that I'm not a little girl anymore.

Change has always been hard for him and I know he cares about me, but he's over the top.

Gunner's been very attentive, almost *too* attentive. I've wanted the guy for as long as I can remember and the moment I get him, I can't wait to send him away for an evening so I can have a moment to myself.

I'm definitely not complaining, even though I wish he'd stay over more now that we don't have to sneak around. He won't let me stay in his room at church, he says it'll be too high a fall from grace going up there and it might make me change my mind about him.

As if it ever could.

The past is in the past and that's where it's going to stay. I knew Gunner had a reputation long before we ever got together, there is no point pretending he doesn't. I can only hope that I'm enough for him to not want to stray.

The thought leaves a tight pain in my chest.

I've never been good imagining him with other women, but he's given me no reason to be jealous. Then again, I've stayed away from church as much as possible but if I see Chelsea or Tiffany anywhere near him, I'm quite sure I'll punch them in the face.

There's only so much a person can take.

He also hasn't claimed me at the table, I've always known that I'd wear his cut in a heartbeat, if he asked me to. He has asked me to go on a club run with the boys next weekend, the weather should be good to go on a long ride up into the mountains.

I know having me on the back of his sled is sending a message and hope only blooms in my chest at the thought.

Lost in my reverie, it's almost six and Katy should be finished with her last appointment downstairs. I give Rocky a little bit of roast chicken and leave some for Lola in her bowl. She's gone off under the bed somewhere to sleep.

I make my way downstairs just as the customer is paying at the register.

I dump some towels in the dryer and tidy up the staff lunchroom.

The salon is as busy as ever and I've just hired another beautician to do waxing and tinting appointments. My priority for the business is getting on top of my paperwork and keeping everything fresh and relevant. I've also got to keep ahead of the game with marketing. If business keeps up like it has been, then I may have to hire a receptionist, something I never thought I would do this early in the game.

I smile to myself when I think about how happy mom was when I told her Gunner and I were dating, though dating is probably not the right word for what we're doing.

She's always had a soft spot for him. At least mom's on board with us, even if Steel is still on the fence. I can't say I totally blame him. Gunner's reputation is pretty bad and I get why Steel's acting like he is. This is how he shows he cares.

Katy's locking the money in the safe and turning the lights off when I finish in the lunchroom.

"It's been crazy today," she says. "The phone hasn't stopped. Gunner's appointments are all booked out for the next few weeks, we're turning people away, don't suppose you can put him on for any more shifts? Seems to be the flavor of the month."

I laugh. "I might have to convince him, though I'm pretty sure he knows he's popular."

Ever since Sizzle went live, Gunner's media popularity has increased to astonishing amounts. He's been offered multiple deals for other shoots and even a calendar, I can't wait to get my hands on that one. I don't mind other women looking at him online, as long as I'm the only one in his bed.

"Surely Brock can see he's more useful to us here," Katy muses. "And it's air conditioned."

That I can't disagree with, Gunner isn't great at manual labor.

"It's getting him to show up on time that's the problem," I admit. Everyone knows he's late to everything.

"I'm sure you can find a way to convince him," she says playfully.

"Trust me when I say, the way to a man's heart is through his stomach, nowhere else."

God only knows what he's been feeding himself all these years. I've reintroduced him to vegetables.

"Well, he seems to like it, whatever you're doing."

I try not to blush as I think about the things we got up to this morning. There's one way to wake up, then there's Gunner with his head between your legs.

The truth is he lets me play an innings, not like some of the other brothers.

He isn't made like that. He always lets me speak my mind, do what I want, be independent.

I don't need to ask permission.

Even when I do get a bit lippy, he just comes at me with that grin of his and if I'm really bad he'll torture me with his beautiful mouth. He's not really kinky but he likes pushing my body to new limits. I love everything he does, my body is his to do what he wants with and teaching me has been the best part of getting to know one another.

"Well, that's me, I'll see you tomorrow," Katy says with a wave, opening the front door.

"Have a good night," I call after her.

I go back out to check the back door, the last thing I need is Steel ragging on me again about unlocked doors. I'm just halfway down the corridor when I hear the doorbell jingle.

"Did you forget something, Katy?" I call out.

When I don't get a reply, I turn back and see a woman standing there.

She looks a little out of place because she's wearing baggy clothes and looks very disheveled. She may need a little more than a wash and blow dry.

"Oh sorry," I say with a smile. "We've just closed up; did you want to make an appointment?"

I round the counter to go grab the appointment book.

I glance up when she doesn't answer.

She watches me with strange eyes and a sudden thrill of panic runs through me. Her eyes don't look normal, she looks kind of out of it.

"Is everything okay?" I ask quietly.

She shakes her head. "No, Lily everything is not okay." Her voice is monotone. Cold. It sends chills up my spine.

How the hell does she know my name?

"I'm sorry, do we know each other?"

"No," she whispers. "But our paths have crossed."

She's freaking me the fuck out.

"I'm sorry, I don't remember, but I meet a lot of people."

"Of course you wouldn't remember," she hisses.

"Please tell me what you want," I demand. I want her gone. That feeling in my gut doesn't feel good.

"You killed him," she says slowly.

I stare at her. "W…what?"

She continues to look at me strangely, as if trying to fathom something out.

"I think you need to leave." I tell her firmly.

"It was you! You let him die you stupid bitch!" she uncurls one hand from her pocket and right before me she pulls out a big knife and points it in my direction. "You don't even remember do you? Why would you? Girls like you can have anyone they want, anyone! And you took him from me, you took him! Why would you do that?"

My eyes go wide as my heart kicks up about ten thousand notches. "Ummm. I don't know what you're talking about, there's obviously been some kind of mistake…."

She grimaces and moves closer to me, trying to round the counter and trap me.

I have nothing at all to use as a weapon.

"There is no mistake. Because of you he went to prison.

You ruined his life! You think you can just ruin people and get away with it? That you won't have to pay?"

Fear courses through me. She's talking about the guy who almost raped me a few months back.

Jesus fucking Christ.

Who is this woman?

"Are you his girlfriend?" I whisper.

She nods, her head slow and controlled, calculating. "Hung himself in prison, you took him away from me, now I'll never see him again." A tear falls from her eye.

"Your boyfriend was a rapist and a felon." I fire back at her. Okay she's holding a knife and it probably isn't smart to anger her further, but I can't stop my mouth. "He drugged girls, raped them, kidnapped them and sold them in a human trafficking syndicate, sounds like a real stand up kinda guy."

"You're a liar!" she hurls at me. She's still moving towards me slowly, like she's trapping a defenseless deer. I know she'll cut me the first chance she gets.

"You don't want to do this," I warn her. "We can talk about it; you don't have to come at me with a knife."

The last thing I need is playing nice to this crazy woman, but I have to do something.

"You need to suffer too, like how he did."

I want to tell her she's wrong. She's so very wrong. *I'm* the victim here, not him. She's clearly deranged if she thinks I'm the one who's guilty.

"I'm going to end you." Her words chill me to the bone.

I need to stall.

"Are you the one who's been terrorizing my shop?"

She smiles without humor. "I liked scaring you, you seem to have a lot of bikers at your disposal, ready to come and save you, but where are they now? Where are any of them when it matters? I've been watching you for a while, waiting for my chance to strike, seems I timed it perfectly."

Imagining her watching the salon, watching me, it makes me feel nauseous.

I've never wanted Gunner so badly in my life but he's out for most of the night. There's nobody coming anytime soon.

"My boyfriend is due home any moment," I tell her quickly. "Then what will you do? Take him on too?"

She shakes her head. "I don't think so, in fact, I think I have you all to myself for a little while. Didn't you hear me? I've been watching you."

I step back instinctively as she slowly comes toward me. I don't think I've ever felt this kind of panic, fear, and adrenaline all at once before. I want to tackle her but I know if I do, she'll slice me with that knife.

"I'm sure we can talk about this? Maybe if you hear my side of the story then you won't be so hell bent on threatening me and holding a knife in my face."

"The time for talking is over," she says. "You're so tough when they're all around to protect you, yet now when it's needed, you're just weak and pathetic, just like I knew you would be."

"Is that why he prayed on me?"

She shrugs. "You got what you deserved, it might pay you a lesson to keep your hands off another woman's man, maybe if you weren't such a whore then things could have turned out differently for you and I wouldn't have to do this."

She's clearly lost her mind.

How can I reason with crazy?

The thumping in my ears doesn't help. I need to think and fast.

"I got away, remember. He didn't get away with it, maybe he finally got what was coming to him after all the damage he's done and the people he's hurt."

I got away; other girls weren't so lucky.

Her nostrils flair at my words and I quickly make a move

grabbing the first thing I can use as a weapon; the mobile credit card machine. I lob it at her head, it makes contact and bounces off, smashing to the floor in pieces. It momentarily distracts her.

I make a run for it but she grabs onto my arm, pulling me back. I feel a sharp sting of steel and pain shoots down my arm where the blade cuts me.

I turn back and push her, falling over in the process, she's on me in seconds, waving the knife around. I hold her back by the forearms but she's stronger than me, the blade comes close to my face as I wriggle backwards. I manage to get to my feet and kick her in the shins, she goes down cursing and I try to wrestle the knife from her fist. She hangs onto it for dear life as I smack her arm over and over as she tries to claw at me and eventually the blade slips free, clanging to the ground.

Her hand grabs a fistful of my hair and yanks my head back.

I kick the knife away. Using my elbow, I whack her in the stomach with fury as she buckles over and let's go of my hair. I quickly dive for the apartment door, knowing I can lock myself inside. I just reach the handle when she lunges at me from behind. I swing the door open as she pulls backwards and fall on top of her.

Before I can even scream something has my attention and I dart my eyes to the door.

I see Lola.

Sweet, innocent, beautiful Lola. She's wearing a glittery headband that I put on just hours before. She lost one of her ears in a dog fighting syndicate, long before Steel rescued her. She's the sweetest girl I know, gentle for a pit-bull, or so I thought until this moment. She growls menacingly as I struggle and reach out to her instinctively.

The chick's arm wraps around my throat and she squeezes tightly, cutting off my oxygen.

It all happens in a blur.

One minute I'm being dragged backwards, the next Lola is barking and growling louder than I've ever heard her.

I watch as she dives from the bottom of the stairs and bounces onto the floor leaping over my head with a snarl, snapping her jaw as she makes contact with the woman choking me.

A blood curdling scream rings out on contact and her arms around me go slack. I scramble to crawl away, turning I see Lola mauling her arm and she's got a big bite mark on her neck that's drawing blood. I try to call Lola back, fuck, if this crazy bitch picks up the knife again Lola could get hurt.

I crawl backwards, keeping my eyes on them, I reach into my back pocket and pull my phone out. I dial Gunner on speed dial. He doesn't answer. *Fuck!!!*

I try his number again and he picks up on the third ring.

"Sorry babe, I was in the can."

"G...Gunn...Gunner..." I manage, but it feels like I've lost my powers of speech.

"What's wrong?" he asks, immediately on edge.

"Lola!" I cry. "The...there's a wom...an...she's got a...kn... knife...hurry...please hurry...she's going to...hurt her..."

"Fuck!" he yells as I watch Lola tear at the woman's arm, she's locked on and not letting go. "Get out of the salon Lily, do it now!"

"I...I can't..."

"Fucking do it!"

I hang up the phone and I'm about to run when I see Rocky peering from the steps around the corner, shaking. I scoop him up and head to the front door, I swing it open and call for Lola. She looks up at me as I call her again.

"Lola!" I yell. "Come here girl! Now!"

I hope to God she listens to me. I can't leave her here.

She lets go and runs over to me. I push out the door with her hot on my heels and we run down the street.

The shops are all shut up as I run and run and run and I don't stop. Somewhere across town I hear police sirens and then the sound of straight pipes.

I don't know where I run to but when I come to the park I dive into the bushes and my phone buzzes again.

"Lily?"

I cry down the phone, unable to form words.

"Where are you?"

"The park," I blubber. "I'm in the park down the street."

The phone clicks off and moments later I hear the rumbling sound of motorcycles as they get louder and louder.

Fear, panic, and pain run through my body as I clutch little Rocky to my chest. Lola is at my feet, whimpering. I know I'm bleeding badly but I'm so scared she got up and will come looking for us that I don't come out until I hear Gunner call my name.

When he does, I stumble my way through the shrub and collapse into his arms.

"Fucking hell, Lil!"

"Shit," Rubble mutters. He reaches to take Rocky out of my arms quickly.

"What the fuck happened?"

"Gunner...Oh Gunner..." I cry into his cut as he holds me.

"You're bleeding." He turns to Rubble. "We need a fucking ambulance!"

"On it."

I look down and I can't believe the large wound that is gaping open from my wrist to my elbow. "Lola..." I cry. "Is...is Lola...hurt? Sh...she attacked her..."

I watch Bones bend down and check her over as she sits

there calmly, her tail wagging like nothing's wrong. "Nah, not her blood, she's all good."

I sob into Gunners cut. "She saved me, Gunner, she saved me."

Rubble's barking some orders down the phone as I hear more police sirens. Gunner rips off his bandana and proceeds to wrap my arm up. Pain shoots through me as I wince and I can't feel my fingers.

"Had to call it in." He kisses the top of my head. "Can't fuck around with shit like this, angel. I should have fuckin' been there."

I stare at what he's doing, unable to feel anything up my entire arm.

"Gunner…"

"Maybe we should take her, be fuckin' quicker," Rubble says, tucking Rocky into his jacket. He's started to shake, poor thing, he's probably terrified.

"She can't hold onto me, she's lost a lot of blood."

I start to sag. "Gunner? I feel weird…"

I hear a string of curse words, Lola whimpers and Rocky barks as I feel my body get lighter and lighter, and then I don't feel anything anymore.

The pain, the adrenaline, the fear, it takes over my entire body and mind until the darkness swallows me whole.

26

GUNNER

I'VE NEVER BEEN SO scared in my life.

I thought I knew what pain was like. I thought I knew how to react in a time of crisis, but it turns out when someone you love gets hurt, it's a whole different ball game.

Lily lost a lot of blood and the knife hit several arteries and tendons, but it's not life threatening, thank God. She may have limited mobility in her wrist and her hand for some time. The doctor said time will tell, when she starts to heal, they'll know just how badly it will impair her.

When she passed out, so many fears of losing her flashed through my mind. It just cemented the fact that I don't ever want to lose her. I don't ever want to let her down either but it seems I've succeeded in that by not being there when she needed me.

I sit beside her hospital bed looking at my phone. I've tried Steel and Sienna a thousand times but they're out of range at the mountain retreat they went to for the weekend.

No doubt I'll get a severe ear bashing from Steel, and I deserve it. This time he can kick my ass and I won't put up a fight.

The fucking lunatic walked right in the front door! My mind goes over it again and again but how could we have known? She lurked in the shadows, waiting for the right opportunity.

I run a hand over my face and slide my phone onto the side table next to me.

Lily's been out of it after her surgery and she's been sleeping for a while. I just want her to wake so I can tell her again and again how much she means to me.

Bones took Rocky and Lola to his place and the pigs dealt with the psycho chick who Lola had just about mauled to pieces. She's not a killer dog, in fact, she's never done anything like that in her life. But it seems she was in over-protective mode where Lily's concerned.

Typical Steelman.

Without Lola I don't know what would have happened.

The door opens suddenly and Hutch walks in.

"How is she?" he nods, looking at the bed.

"Sleeping off the anesthetic."

"How'd the surgery go?"

I pinch the bridge of my nose so I don't lose it. "She may have limited mobility in her arm and hand, it's too early to say."

"Jesus fuckin' Christ." He runs a hand through his hair and looks up at the ceiling.

"We couldn't have seen this comin'," I tell him. "Thought the attempted break in and the paint was just kids being shit heads, turns out she's been stalking her all this time."

He moves over to the other side of the bed. She looks so small and fragile yet I know she's as fierce as a storm.

"You get a hold of Steel?"

"Nah, not yet, he's still out of range. I'll keep tryin'."

He nods. "I've always treated her like she's the baby, always tried to look out for her, it feels like a kick in the

301

teeth when one of your kids goes down, and she is like my kid, fuck knows I worry about her as much as I do my own."

"We all do, especially after what happened at the Crow."

"Don't remind me, fucker got what was comin' to him."

"Wish we could have gotten hold of him first," I grumble. "Could've at least drawn the process out for him."

"An eye for an eye, son."

I stare up at him.

He looks at me, holding my gaze. "What?"

My mind goes to that night that we got bundled up in Kirsty's car.

All of a sudden, I have to know.

"Was it you?"

We stare at one another.

"Guns, what the fuck you on about?"

"That night," I reply, unable to stop myself. "When you came to get Summer and me. Were you the one who ended him?"

He opens his mouth to speak then closes it again. It's been over twenty years and we've never so much as spoken a word about that night.

He looks away for a moment but holds his stance at the side of Lily's bed.

"You askin' me that now?"

"Yeah."

He rubs his chin. "What does it change?"

"Nothin', but it might satisfy my curiosity."

"You curious after all this time?"

I shrug. "I never wanted to know, until now."

He stares at me. "One thing you have to understand Guns, and you will if you ever have kids of your own one day; there isn't anything you won't do for them, nothin'. When Deanna was born, I held her in my hands and swore I'd never let anything happen to her. It cut me deep what happened to you both, it always will. Granted, you weren't mine, but you were an innocent little boy and Summer..." he trails off, shaking his head at the memory.

It's always been hard for him. Our story would make a grown man weep because it is so fucked up.

"You didn't deserve what that monster did to you, son, and when I found out it was true and he'd done it before, something inside me snapped. I vowed I would never let anything happen to any kid I knew ever again. The only way to put these parasites out of their misery is to give them a helpin' hand so they can't hurt anyone else. Jail's too fuckin' good for them,"

"Is that what you did Hutch? Did you pull the trigger?"

"He got the slip on Brock, he was a little wet behind the ears back then."

He looks over my head at the wall, his eyes distant.

"I wanted to cut him, keep him there for hours. Inflict worse on him than what he did to you and Summer." He trails off and closes his eyes momentarily. "Then when he got a punch in on Brock, I shot him in the kneecap."

I remember the shots as clear as day. My body feels numb remembering it.

"There were two shots."

"He's got two kneecaps, don't he?"

I smile without humor. "Lily wasn't even born then."

He looks down at her again. "I vowed that night, when I shot him, that I'd be a better man, that I'd do anything I could to protect those I loved, though I didn't know either of you well back then, I knew right from fuckin' wrong, I knew that no deed like that can go unpunished. And I had the power to do it. I don't regret it. I'd do it again in a heartbeat."

"You saved us." I stare at him. "You did that for us."

He shakes his head. "No kid, you did more than I ever could, you had to endure it without a single hope in hell's chance of gettin' away, my only regret is not knowing about it sooner."

I know I need to get help; I've known it for a while.

Sure, I'd talked to someone when I was seven, for a while, but it wasn't until my late teenage years when all of this fucked up shit came back to haunt me. When I was out of control. And I know I haven't really dealt with it properly since.

I'll do it. I'll do it for her. I want to be better and prove to her I'll do whatever it takes to give her a good life. I can only do that by combatting my demons once and for all.

"You're a good man," I say, my throat hoarse. "You're the father I should have had, the person who showed me what it's like to be a real man."

He glances at me. "That means a lot, Guns. I stand by what I did, always will, and since we're talkin' man to man, you gotta promise me somethin'."

I can't help but to sit up a little straighter. "Anything."

He points down at Lily. "You take care of her, don't ever let there be a reason for me to come bang your door down and shove my fist down your throat. I may be an old man but I'll still kick your ass if you fuck this up."

I smirk. "I think I can do that."

He nods. "Don't let me down, girls like Lily are few and far between. It's your job now to protect her, to keep her safe. She's a good girl."

"Yeah, I did a great job of that tonight, didn't I?" I can't help the anger in my tone.

"Not your fault that someone walked through the front door, Guns. Coulda happened to any one of us."

"She was so scared." I remember her trembling as she fell

into my arms and I wish I could take all of the pain away, all the fear. "She fucking scared me."

"She's gonna be fine, she's one tough little cookie. She's a Steelman, she knows how to survive."

There's a knock at the door suddenly and a few moments later, Helen appears in the doorway in her uniform.

"Still out cold," I say as she passes me a Styrofoam cup of coffee.

"Would you like something, Hutch?" she offers, looking down at Lily with teary eyes. Helen is honestly the best person I know.

"I'm good darlin', we're all just waiting for Lil to come out of the anesthetic, then we'll breathe a little easier."

"Nice of you to come down."

"Of course, the girls are all in the waiting room, but I told them no visitors until she's up to it."

"Appreciate that."

He gives me another nod then points at me. "I meant what I said."

"I won't disappoint you." I promise.

Helen pats me on the arm. "I've got to finish rounds, be back a little later."

I nod and they leave the room, leaving just the two of us together.

I lay my head on the side of her bed, my brain reels at what's happened these last few hours and how fragile life really is.

I don't want to take another minute of it without her in my thoughts, without her in my future. I don't know why it took me this long to get to this conclusion. I guess I had to open my heart and let her in. Now I see things much more clearly.

I end up sweet talking the nurses into letting me stay the

night on a makeshift bed. I want to be as close to her as possible.

Hours later I hear movement and crack an eye open. I haven't slept a wink. I wanted to be here when the drugs wore off properly.

"Hey," I hear her whisper. Her voice sounds a little rough.

I throw the blanket off and rush to her side.

"Liliana, you tryin' to give me a fuckin' heart attack? I thought you'd never wake up."

She smiles. "I'm really bad under anesthetic."

I brush her hair off her face as I help her sit up. She glances at her arm, all bandaged up and winces.

"Are you in pain? I can call a nurse."

She shakes her head. "I'm alright, is my arm gonna be okay?"

The doctor did explain it to her and Helen earlier but she was far from being fully conscious.

"They don't know for sure if you'll get full mobility but they're hopeful."

She nods, tears in her eyes. "I'm lucky to be alive, I'm lucky in so many ways."

"Thank God for Lola."

"Lola, oh my God. Is she okay?"

I nod. "She's fine, baby girl. She's our hero."

"How's Steel taking it? Bet he's pissed."

I caress her cheek with my thumb. "Haven't gotten hold of them yet. Left a message at the hotel, though there's nothin' they can do even if they do come back now. Steel will have my head for this though and I deserve it."

"It's not your fault," she whispers. "The woman's crazy."

I smile at her and hand her the pitcher of water and she takes a sip. "You don't need to worry about that now, angel."

"I'm so glad you were there so fast. I was so scared, Guns."

"I know." A rush of protectiveness surges through me at the thought of someone doing this to her.

The woman has been arrested and is being treated in the hospital under strict police guard. "But I'm not lettin' you out of my sight from now on, that I can promise you."

She groans. "I love you Guns, but seriously, you have to let me live my life. I'm not made of glass, yeah this sucked big time, but I won't let it stop me from doing what I want to do, especially when she just walked right in the front door."

I kiss her forehead. "Always the little hot head."

"I'm not a hot head! I just don't want you all going ape shit over this. I'm hoping my crazy stalking days are finally over." She attempts a smile but winces again.

"I'm calling the nurse."

She grabs the sleeve of my cut. "No, Guns. I just need a distraction."

I meet her gaze and shake my head. "Don't give me that look. You're not gettin' *that* kind of distraction, your mom could walk in here any time not to mention one of the other nurses or the doctor, we both know I'm not a five-minute kinda guy."

I peck her quickly on the mouth but that's all she's getting.

She laughs. "You're definitely not."

I pull back. "I'm sorry Lil, for what it's worth, that this had to happen to you, you don't deserve it, any of it."

"I got away. I lived. I survived. That's all that matters."

I rub her cheek back and forth with my thumb. I never want there to be any secrets between us.

"While you were out, I talked to Hutch."

"Oh no."

I kiss her chastely. "No, it's not bad. He gave us his blessing; said he'd kill me if I hurt you. Nothin' I haven't heard before. We talked about some other shit too, shit to do with me."

She looks at me wide eyed. "Gunner, you don't have to."

I shake my head. "I can't go into all the details right now Lily, but maybe in time I will." I puff up my cheeks with air and let it go. "There are things you should know about me, before you decide if you wanna make me your ol' man."

She bites her lip, tears forming in her eyes. "There's nothing you can say that will change how I feel about you."

I close my eyes momentarily. "You say that now."

"Don't." She reaches out and I let her touch my cheek. "You know that's not true."

I never wanted her to know, now I *need* her to know. I want her to know that the reason I'm broken isn't because of her. If anything, she's my savior.

"When I was seven... my step-father.... he... he... did some stuff... to me and Summer."

She gasps. She's not an idiot and I suspect she knew something to this degree a long time ago. I can't tell her the graphics, though I'm sure she can work it out.

"It's why I have the night terrors and panic attacks, I guess I still haven't exactly fought all my demons from back then, and it creeps back in when I least expect it."

Tears spill down her face. "My beautiful Gunner, I'm so sorry."

I smile. "I was called Joshua back then, fuck it feels like so long ago, like all of the shit that went down was someone else's life, you know?"

"Joshua," she breathes, testing the words.

It sounds nice coming from her mouth. Delicate and soothing, not harsh and horrible like I remember.

"Please don't say anything to anyone, nobody knows aside from Hutch, Steel, and your mom, and with Summer, that ain't my story to tell."

"I won't, I promise."

"Just know that parts of me are hollow Lil, parts of me don't work right, like my heart. Sometimes I love so deep and other times I don't even know if my heart beats or has any feeling at all."

She shakes her head. "That isn't true, you're a good man, you're beautiful, smart, and funny and you always make everyone else feel good whenever you're around. Don't ever say that. I know how big your heart is. I feel it."

I kiss the tip of her nose. "And here I was paying Teresa to be my PR person."

I wipe her tears away.

"I'm so sorry that happened to you, you were just little kids."

"Hutch saved us, I owe him everything, this is why the brotherhood is so important to me. Why I didn't want to get involved with you and fuck it up. I can't disappoint any of them, I can't let them down. Hutch is the only father figure I've ever known, and Steel's like my own flesh and blood brother, that's why I've been so hard on the respect thing. It's taken me so long to get to this point and I never want to go back and start again. Family is everything to me. Even though Summer is the only flesh and blood family I have, the club has done more for me than I can ever repay them for. I don't ever want to lose them, or lose you."

"You won't, this changes nothing Gunner, nothing at all. I'm just so sorry this happened to you and you're still suffering all these years later."

I look into her wide eyes, so full of love for me. I can see it reflecting back because that's exactly how I feel about her. "I'm gonna get some help babe, I promise, I'll talk to someone. I don't want medication; I've been down that track and it didn't work for me. But I'm not gonna sweep it under the rug, there are good therapists out there and natural alternatives to help with stress and anxiety, I can do this, I want to do it."

"I know you can," she says, her voice breaking. "And you'll never have to do it alone ever again."

"I want you to know I'm gonna claim you at the table, you want that?"

She stares at me wide eyed. "Are you sure?"

"My heart's never beat so strongly about anything. Nobody else can have you, I want you to know you're mine, in every sense of the word, but…"

She waits, tears in her eyes.

"You can't repeat this outside of this room, promise me."

"I promise, Guns, you've got my loyalty, now and always."

I smile and bite my bottom lip, this is gonna be hard to say but here goes nothing; "You are mine yes, but you don't belong to me. I know I'm not supposed to say that, it's not what the brothers would want, they find out they'll think I'm a pussy boy and you wear the pants, but the truth is, I love you because you have your own mind. You belong to yourself first, I'll never ask you to put me above you, never. You always have a choice, always babe, you got me?"

"I love you," she whispers.

I kiss her on the lips, the kiss becomes urgent as she pulls onto the lapels of my cut, trying to bring me closer. I pull back.

"Naughty, naughty, I might have to tell the nurse you're misbehaving."

"Go lock the door," she whispers.

I chuckle. "To think you were as pure as the driven snow before I corrupted you."

"I liked every minute of you corrupting me."

"Good, cause you got a lot more to learn from me, sweetheart."

The sound of her laugh is all I need to settle my nerves and chase my demons away. It's all I'll ever want.

I finally found my forever, it may have taken me a little while to realize it and see what was right in front of me, but better late than never.

I'd do it all over again if I had to.

And I will never regret a single second of it.

EPILOGUE

FIVE YEARS LATER

LILY

I REACH DOWN to my growing bump and hum softly as I watch Gunner in the surf. I love the beach. Living in Arizona we don't get to see it too often, but when we vacation in Florida where we visit Gunner's mom, I love nothing more than to read a book all day and listen to the sound of the ocean. It brings me so much peace, so much comfort.

Not long after the stabbing at the salon, Gunner declared me his ol' lady, it got voted in at the gavel and I've been wearing his cut ever since. I love wearing it. I love being his. Although my cut is pink, much to the disgust of the other brothers, Gunner doesn't seem to mind one bit.

Things with us have gone from strength to strength and they continue to flourish. We've had our ups and downs but Gunner's never gone back on his word.

He's my everything, just as I always knew he would be.

My soulmate.

My reason for being.

It took some time but he worked through therapy and got stronger mentally, while he'll never

forget, he's put his childhood in the past where it belongs.

When I first found out I was pregnant, Gunner was more shocked than I was. It wasn't planned, obviously, and we'd discussed kids briefly. Me being- I wanted one someday, him being- he really didn't know what kind of father he'd make or if he wanted kids.

Of course, I always knew he'd make a great father, kids love him. We're not finding out the baby's gender until the day I give birth, we wanted to save it, something for just us.

I watch as he runs out of the waves, towards me. He's still the most gorgeous man I've ever seen, and he still turns heads. His sandy blonde hair, it's longer now, he's sporting a beard and his tattoos now cover his arms and most of his back, he's still a bad-boy rebel and he always will be. Some things will just never change.

He shakes water over me from his hair as I squeal under the umbrella.

"Gunner, its freezing!"

He flops down on the towel next to me and kisses me, then moves to my tummy and kisses that too.

"You look so hot in a bikini and a bump it's not even funny."

I laugh. "Now I know you're lying."

He grins up at me, turning on his side and rubs a hand over my skin. "I'm fuckin' not, I think we should get gone, mom's out for lunch, we could get some alone time in before she gets back." He gives me a sly wink.

Oh yeah, ever since I got pregnant, he's been even more insatiable. At first, he wasn't really sure about having sex while I was carrying, in fact, he was totally off the idea. But after chatting to Lucy all about it and how it can't harm the baby, he did a complete turnaround.

I don't know why he loves me pregnant; I feel fat and sore most days and my feet kill me nonstop but he doesn't seem to care, he dotes on me more than ever.

"I'm enjoying the sun too much to go back just yet." I pout.

He gives me a pointed look. "A man has his needs, and I've got this thing here…" he looks down at his groin and then grabs his junk, clearly hard through his shorts and I snort a laugh.

"God, I can't take you anywhere."

He rolls up and hovers over me, kissing my neck then my jaw then my lips. He always knows how to turn me on, nothing has dulled over the years, it's only gotten better.

"Bet if I sneak a hand in your bikini bottoms nobody will see."

I go to grab his hand that's lurking dangerously in that area. "Gunner! There are families around."

"You know I like adventure, babe. The risk of bein' caught is enticing."

I swat his hand again. "Fine, we'll go home, but please note that for the record you owe me another day at the beach."

He grins, happy to have won so easily, then pecks me quickly and stands, then he begins packing up all our shit as quick as he can. "But don't go wearing that bikini again or we wouldn't be in this mess in the first place."

I laugh. "I love you, you filthy animal."

He grins as he rolls the towel up that he was just laying on.

"You're gonna love me a whole lot more when I get you on your back."

"Is that all you think about?" I giggle.

He pretends to think. "Yeah, pretty much. Glad you picked me, babe? Told ya to run when you had the chance."

I sit up and put my book away. "You know I am."

He's everything I could have ever hoped for.

He leans over and kisses me chastely. "Shut up then and let's go."

Nothing in the world could be sweeter than this.

∼

GUNNER

"Just one more push!" the doctor tells Lily as I stand there holding her hand, watching her do this amazing thing that I never, ever thought I'd be doing.

So many emotions have run through me when she first told me she was pregnant.

Did I even want to be a father?

I don't even know what kind of father I'd make for fucks sakes, but I've vowed to myself, Lily, and to the unborn kid that I'm gonna do my darndest to give he or she the life they deserve. The childhood I never had.

If it kills me then that's what they'll have.

I'll make sure nobody will ever hurt them, that's my job now. That's all that matters.

She's my rock, I can't believe she's doing this or that it's even possible, though she's squeezing my hand like she may crush it.

"You're doin' great babe, just one more push and we'll have our baby."

Our baby.

She's given me everything I could possibly want, now she's giving me our first child. I don't know how I even got this lucky.

She groans and her face screws up and she wails as she pushes hard.

All of a sudden there's a moment of silence, then a baby cries.

I go numb.

They fuss around for a second as time seems to stop.

A few moments later the doctor lays the baby on Lily's stomach and we both look down at it.

"Congratulations, it's a boy."

Oh Fuck.

I have a son.

Lily gasps. He's so tiny and his face is all screwed up as he wriggles around.

She cries as she holds him and I feel like I might faint.

The nurse quickly cleans his face up as he's covered in goo.

"We have a son," I whisper.

Lily cries as she kisses his tiny head. "Holy shit, Gunner."

I kiss her forehead as I stare at him. He has a flock of light hair. "Looks like he's got my hair."

"I hope he has your looks too," she whispers as I turn and we kiss.

I snort. "I hope he has yours, mama."

"Would you like to cut the cord, dad?" the doctor says.

I look at Lily, she's crying and nodding at the same time. "Please, Gunner."

"It won't hurt him?"

The nurse smiles like I'm an idiot and passes me the tools, showing me what to do. "No, not at all. Won't feel a thing."

I nod.

I've done some pretty intense shit in all my life but I've never done anything like this before. I feel like I'm treading in unchartered waters but I gotta step up. I gotta prove to Lily I can do this.

I cut the cord and the baby wriggles around, the nurse

quickly takes him to wipe him over and weigh him and then he's back again all swaddled up.

"Gunner, why don't you hold him?" Lily says, softly.

My heart hammers in my chest. "What if I drop him?"

"He'll be a tough nut if he's anything like his dad."

His dad.

Holy shit.

She passes him to me and he's stopped crying, his little eyes are closed as he sleeps. A surge of joy, love, and pride sweeps through me.

We did this.

We have a baby.

"I can't believe you did this," I whisper as I look at Lily.

She smiles. "*We* did it, Romeo."

I grin back. "I love you so much, Liliana Marie."

"Not as much as I do you."

"You got any names, what does he look like?"

She looks up at me with those beguiling eyes, my heart almost stops every time she looks at me like this, but this time it's something else. "Can we call him Joshua?"

We've discussed baby names but she's never mentioned this once.

I stare at her.

"Why would you want to?"

Lily smiles softly. "Well, it'll be after his amazing, beautiful, wonderful father, the man I fell for and waited for, the man I admire more and more each day, the kind of man I want him to be one day. That's why."

Tears well in my eyes and I don't wanna lose it in front of the doctor and nurses.

I nod.

"Maybe Joshua James." I manage, since James was my first choice. He needs a good strong name.

"I love that." Lily looks down at him with pride. "Joshua James."

I kiss his tiny forehead as he sleeps soundly in my arms.

I pass him back and Lily and I just stare at him for a long time.

"I might go let the others know, the waiting room's pretty crowded, you up for a coupla visitors?"

She nods enthusiastically.

I kiss her again and make my way out to the double doors.

All heads turn to me as I make my exit.

All the girls are there as well as Helen, Kirsty, Hutch, Steel, Sienna, and all the boys and ol' ladies, Lily's closest friends too.

I stand at the doors until Brock yells out; "Come on fucker, what is it?"

I grin. "It's a boy!"

A loud roar and cheers and applause break out. Bones, Brock, Rubble, and Hutch all come at me, patting me on the back, shaking my hand and telling me it's great news and good luck gettin' no sleep and no sex from now on.

Kisses and hugs come at me from all the girls.

Steel looms over me and I look up. He clutches my shoulder and gives it a shake.

"Proud of you, fuckface."

"Thanks dude, that means a lot."

"You name him yet?"

I nod. "Lily wants to name him Joshua."

Steel nods.

"So, we decided on Joshua James."

Helen butts in again for another hug and kisses me and squeezes me. "My first grandbaby!"

Kirsty stands next to her, beaming. "I can't wait to spoil him rotten! Finally, another baby to add to the brood."

Steel grins at me. "You did good."

I nod. "Thanks, bro, but she did most of the work." I wink and he shakes his head, leans down and kisses Sienna on the forehead. She's holding a giant bouquet of flowers.

"Are we allowed to see her yet?" Sienna squeals.

"I think so, but the doc said only like four or five at a time, they've even brought security in." I nod over to the door and sure enough, a security guard is hovering close by.

I guess we are a room full of bikers, after all.

I hear a bottle of champagne pop and more cheers erupt.

"I gotta get back." I look down at Helen. "Grandma, you wanna do the first honor of meeting him?"

She dabs her eyes with a tissue. "I'd love to."

I nod to Steel and Sienna. "You guys too."

Sienna jumps up and down and claps her hands.

They follow behind me and when I go through the door and see my beautiful Liliana holding our son, I know that nothing in this world will ever be as great as this moment.

I always thought that running away from commitment was what I should have been doing, avoiding my feelings and going from girl to girl without consequence, but that can only go on for so long. That never made me happy.

I stare at the two of them in wonder.

I'm home now.

I'm stronger. Happier. I'm in love.

I love my life.

Finally, I have purpose.

I've no regrets. Everything we fought for was worth it.

A man can't get any luckier or ask for any more than that.

In her world, I'm King. And her world is the only world that matters.

THE END

ACKNOWLEDGMENTS

Gunner wasn't always the easiest to write at times, he had me laughing and crying and feeling everything in between. From the very first book I wrote in this series (Steel), I knew Gunner was going to be special. He just stole my heart and it's been a joy bringing him and Lily to life. I hope I didn't disappoint.

Thank you to all the amazing people who have supported me yet again with my 3rd published book in 6 months– I'm so beyond grateful.

To all the amazing bloggers and FB and IG friends who share, like and comment on my posts, thank you so much! Without your support and help I don't know where I'd be.

Thank you to my other indie author friends (you know who you are) for your kind messages and advice, we got this!

Thank you to my amazing PA Savannah – check her out at @peachykeenas on IG. peachykeenauthorservices@gmail.com – thanks for all you do keeping me organized.

Thank you to LJ from Mayhem Cover Creations for Gunners' amazing cover and my website, you do a fabulous job

Thank you to my side-kick D (also my proofreader, twin sister and shoulder to cry on) you're amazing, thank you for not letting me quit!

I'm also very excited to announce that Brock will be book #3 in this series!!

It will be released later in the year 2021, date to be confirmed. Pre order link below at the bottom.

Please take a few moments to leave an Amazon and Goodreads review if you enjoyed Gunner, this helps me so much as a new indie author!

Happy reading my friends!

All my love xx MF xx

ABOUT THE AUTHOR

Mackenzy Fox is an author of contemporary, romantic and erotic themed romance novels. When she's not writing she loves vegan cooking, walking her beloved pooch's, reading books and is an expert on online shopping.

She's slightly obsessed with drinking tea, testing bubbly Moscato, watching home decorating shows and has a black belt in origami. She strives to live a quiet and introverted life in Western Australia's North West with her hubby, twin sister and her dogs.

Find Mackenzy at:

Facebook: https://www.facebook.com/mackenzy.foxauthor.5

Instagram: https://www.instagram.com/mackenzyfoxbooks/

Linktree: https://linktr.ee/mackenzyfox

Goodreads: https://bit.ly/2TKp7ck

My website: https://mackenzyfox.com

COMING SOON

COMING SOON BROCK – BOOK 3
Preorder today!

ABOUT BROCK– Bracken Ridge Rebels MC Book 3

Bracken Ridge Arizona, where the Rebels M.C. rule and the only thing they ride or die for more than their club is their women, this is Brock's story:

Brock: For years I've let it slide. What she does to me, how she makes me feel.

I've brushed it off like an annoying habit that comes back every now and again to haunt me. We came together once, then we drifted apart.

It's the story of my life.

We were best friends, but back then we were a lot of things. She was the fire in my blood, the elixir in my veins. My world fell at her feet, before it fell spectacularly apart.

She thinks she can run from the M.C. she thinks she can run from me.

Little does she know that this old dog ain't learnin' any new tricks.

I've got my eyes on the prize. She will be my ol' lady, I'll make sure of it.

I let her slip away once before, but I have no intension of doing that again.

She's mine, and I'm gonna make her realize it once and for all.

Angel: Nobody owns me. I don't want to be someone's property, and in the M.C. when you're a woman; that's all you are. Property.

I belong to myself.

My life's been no fairytale, I've had to grow up fast, learn hard lessons, dust myself off and start again.

Now I've got my daughter to think of things have changed.

I can't fall for him. What Brock and I had was a long time ago.

What we had was lust, infatuation, nothing more. We were a couple of kids and now it's ancient history.

We're not the same people we were then.

I have to protect my heart; it can't be broken again.

He can't have what was never his to take. I won't let him.

BROCK EXCERPT:

BROCK

TWO MONTHS AGO...

THE SCREECH of tires outside my office alert me to the fact that Angel's arrived.

I know the sound of her vintage Mustang anywhere.

Of course, I already knew she was on her way over here, got this the heads up from Gunner.

She's pissed that I threatened her date, I told him to fuck the hell off or I'd rearrange his face if he came ever came around her again.

She's ungrateful truth be told. And I'm a jealous prick.

The two definitely don't mix but here we are.

Still, she's got a right to be pissed, I suppose, but I'm saving her heartache in the long run, she just doesn't know it yet.

The guy wasn't her type to begin with; your typical asshole who wears a suit, slicks his hair back and rides in a fancy car he paid way too much for, an unworthy asshole at that. I get she doesn't wanna haul her cookies all the way over to church to find herself a man, but this is scraping the barrel.

The guy had no balls.

"Brock!" I hear from the lot out front.

I sigh into my cold cup of coffee. I can't wait for the screaming match that's about to unfold. One thing about Angel, she can't be controlled.

I knew that back when we were fifteen.

She'll speak her mind; she'll stand up for herself. I respect that, truly I do, but it doesn't mean I'm gonna be okay with some other guy fucking her. Nah.

She bursts through the door as I continue to stare at my computer screen, ignoring her.

"Brock!" she yells again, like I'm hard of fuckin' hearing.

I glance up. "I don't think they heard you over the other side of the Canyon, Ange."

I'm delighted to see she's furious. Yeah, I'm a misogynistic son of a bitch.

Her long, pale blonde hair hangs behind her back like a cloak, her bluntly cut bangs could literally cut glass.

She's tall, curvy in all the right places, has pale skin with piercing green eyes that I've never seen on another women, not that I tend to look in their eyes when I'm doing what I need to do. I prefer them reverse cowgirl truth be told.

But Angel. She's different.

Yeah, I could stare into her eyes while I fuck her all night long. Trouble is she won't let me.

I'm in the fuckin' friends zone and I've been tryin' for a mighty long time to get the hell out. A while back we got close, not so close as I scored a home run, but we were flirting and touching and stuff, then she goes all cold turkey on me and says she doesn't want to 'ruin the friendship.' So, we stopped. Now she's had me on a short leash ever since.

I don't like being tamed, doesn't suit my nature.

Fuckin' females.

Talk about flogging a dead man's horse.

"Don't play coy with me," she spits. "I've been running all over town looking for you!"

"Well," I sigh, like she's a nuisance. "You found me."

I don't need to glance up to know she's got steam coming out her ears. She's so fuckin' cute when she's angry.

I try very hard not to burst out laughing at her annoyance. That won't help me, it'll only dig me further into a bigger hole.

"I know what you did."

"Last summer?"

She comes closer as I start typing an email; or pretend to.

She's wearing ripped jeans, a black tight tank and boots up to her knees. The woman's a fuckin' goddess. My dick stirs in my jeans at the thought of doing it with her in my office, over my desk.

I don't know why I torture myself. It's never gonna happen.

Then again, they do say angry sex is the best sex, don't they?

"Don't be cute, Brock, in case you haven't noticed I'm not in the mood."

I can't help my smirk. "That time of the month?" That should get her going.

"You really are a sexist, chauvinistic pig, aren't you? Why would I expect anything less."

"Answered your own question then," I smile.

"You're an asshole."

I glance up from my screen. "Jesus Ange, the vein in your forehead looks like it's about to pop out of your skin any minute."

"You have no right to interfere with my life! You drove my date away!" she yells, I can tell by the quick rise and fall of her chest that she's not kidding. Not that I need to be staring at her chest, her beautiful cleavage does nothing to calm my raging hard on.

She's as mad as an alley cat. She means business.

"Whatever you think I've done, I can assure you, I've only done to protect you."

She shakes her head. "Protection I didn't want, nor did I ask for!"

I shrug. I don't give a shit. The guy wasn't worthy of her, I don't know what else to say.

"I don't know why you've got your knickers in a twist, the guy was an asshole, drives a fuckin' Mazda."

She may shoot lightening from her eyeballs, she's that fired up. "That's not your call, where do you honestly get off? If anything, it's you who's the asshole! You can't run around like you've got some stupid claim over me, Brock."

I wouldn't normally let a broad come and yell at me like this, but Angel and I have a history, we go way back. And this is what it's like with us.

We fight.

We used to kiss and make up.

We used to do a lot of wild shit.

The fucking used to be goddamn spectacular, but it's been years.

Seeing her like this doesn't turn me off, far from it. I'm more turned on than ever.

I'm a sick fuck, what can I say.

"You know how I get off so that a mute point, anyway, how is looking out for your best interests being an asshole?"

"You're sick you know that? You've got a problem if you've got nothing better to do than spy on me and scare the men in my life."

"Men? So there's more than one?"

"That's none of your fucking business!" she cries, poking me in the chest.

I look down at her finger that jabs me back and forth.

"Careful babe, you know that counts as foreplay for me."

"You wish."

I've made no secret to her that I wanna give things another go, or at the very least get to third base, but she just can't let me past go.

I know she has feelings for me, it's why she keeps coming back, which is why I can't let her ruin her life with some other schmuck. Not happening. Not on my watch.

I've always had a protective urge over her and ever since she has Rawlings it's only grown stronger.

"In any case, do you really want a man who can't stand up for you?" I raise my eyebrows in question and begin to stand, she immediately backs off. "Do you really want a grease monkey in suit who runs at the first sign of trouble? A real man would fight me, tell me to fuck off, not run the other way and hide under his desk. You deserve better than than, a simple thank you would have been nice."

She shakes her head as she takes another step back. I round the desk and lean back against the wood leisurely and cross my feet at the ankles.

"A simple thank you?" she spits. "I doubt any man on the planet is going to fight you, tell you to fuck off or *not* run the other way, you're intimidating, and wearing an M.C. cut, hell you probably ran him off the road with your stupid motorcycle."

I wave a finger at her. "I'll have you know that's a Harley FXSTB soft tail night train you're dissing off, one of the most classy, luxurious, bad ass bikes around, should wash your mouth out with soap or put you over my knee for that comment."

She does not look impressed.

"Oh, you'd like that wouldn't you?"

I stare at her.

I know what I do to women when I look at them like this.

Let's call it my 'fuck me' face. Yeah, I can turn on the charms when I want to.

She can say what she wants, but she's affected by me. I know her too well.

If she was really that pissed and wanted rid of me, she'd have stomped out of the office by now.

"I can't imagine anything more disgusting!"

I snort. "Yeah, right. I bet you lay in bed every night thinking about what we used to get up to, don't you Angel? Bet that's what gets you off when you're with another man instead of me."

Her cheeks flush slightly but she stands firm. "Ha! Like you'd have the faintest idea what gets me off, the last thing I do in bed, Brock Altman, is think of you!"

Another lie.

I don't stalk the woman but I know she hasn't had *that* many dates.

Like most of the girls associated with the club, they're busy, they have businesses or jobs that keep them tied to the desk. I'd really prefer her tied to my bed, especially in this rage.

"You sure about that?"

She crosses her arms over her chest and stares back at me defiantly.

"Positive."

"Your panties wet?"

Her eyes go wide. "You'll never find out."

I smirk. "All you have to do is ask, babe, you know I'll give you what you want, how you want it, how I know you need it."

"You don't know anything about what I need."

"I know how you like to be touched," I remind her. "My memories not that far gone. I know just how to hit it right, I know you like those titties being played with, know how you used to scream my name."

She snorts. "Things have changed since high school Brock, women don't like to be thrown over a man's shoulder and dragged upstairs like some fucking sweet butt anymore, that's how it goes with you isn't it? Caveman style?"

"Don't seem to remember you complainin' or being dragged anywhere."

She tilts her head upwards, as if pretending none of it ever happened. "Maybe your memory is fading, or maybe I was just young and stupid back then, I didn't know any better."

I roll my eyes. "You keep tellin' yourself that," I say, slyly. "If you say it enough times you might start to believe it."

I can almost see her stamping her foot and stalking off, but she always likes to have the last word. I know how to get right under her skin.

"Leave me the hell alone, Brock. I mean it!"

I raise both my palms in surrender. "Fine."

"If you do this again…"

"You'll what?"

"I'm not kidding around."

"Me either."

She stands there as I take a long, hard look down her body. She's one fine specimen of a woman, especially in that tight tank top.

I'd love nothing more than to touch her, feel her, make her come -right here, right now. Since I apparently don't know how to please her, I'd love to prove her wrong.

"Stop looking at me like that," she replies.

Mission accomplished.

I don't give her the satisfaction of a smile.

"Like what?"

"Like you want to fuck me."

"That wouldn't be a lie, babe. You know what you do to me."

She closes her eyes momentarily. "Brock," she whispers.

Just like that, her anger dissipates.

It never lasts, she knows what we had, what we could have again, but she won't let herself.

Some asshole hurt her, not me, a different asshole. And now I'm payin' the price for his mistake.

I push off the desk.

She glances up as I come towards her.

"Please."

"Please what?" I stand toe to toe.

"Please don't."

I brush my fingers across her shoulder, her chest rising rapidly.

I move my other hand to the back of her neck as I whisper in her ear. "You really mean that Angel? Say the words, I'll fuck off, if that's what you want, you just gotta say it loud and clear, or…"

She smells so sweet, like vanilla. The very scent of her makes my dick painfully hard. Imagining her on her knees before makes me want to explode.

But we have to do things her way. That's how this dance works, how it's always worked.

And I'll play along if it gets me what I want, and what I want is her. Now.

"Or what?" her voice sounds husky, raw, like mine.

"Or we could fuck."

I feel her chest beat against mine at my words. She can't deny what's happening here.

"You know we can't."

I pull back so our foreheads press together. "You know we can."

I want to kiss her, devour her. It's been years since I felt her lips on mine. Since I sank my cock into her sweet pussy.

The more she pushes me away, the closer I want to get. The more I need to get.

She's got to want this as much as I do, though.

"Brock, you know how this complicates things."

I hover my lips just away from hers.

"I can keep a secret, if that's what you want. Just one time, for old times sakes."

She shakes her head. "You know it'll change things."

"We can keep it casual."

She laughs. "Yeah right, as soon as I meet another guy, you'll bury him."

Fuck I want her.

I'll say anything right about now if it gets me inside.

My heart thrums dangerously in my chest and I'm ready to rock and roll.

"Only if he's not worthy."

"You think everyone's not worthy."

"There you go then."

She bites her lip. "I should go."

She makes no effort to move.

She's beautiful, so goddamn beautiful.

Nobody is good enough for her, especially me.

I move my head to her ear and whisper, "Wanna see if your wet first, then you can go."

If she doesn't want it, she can stop me.

A guttural sound leaves her throat and it really isn't fair. She of all people should know I remember everything.

She likes this, the dirty talk.

"You think your suit and tie ass swipe knows how to fuck

you properly? You think he knows your body better than I do?"

"Brock, we can't…."

I move my mouth to her neck and bite gently on her pulse point, she just about convulses in my arms.

"How longs it been since someone fucked you properly?" I say into her skin.

Her hands grip my biceps, her touch sends heat through my body like an electric current.

"I….it's…..been a while," she admits……….

COMING IN 2021!!!!

PRE ORDER HERE:

ALSO BY MACKENZY FOX

<u>Bracken Ridge Rebels MC:</u>

Steel

Gunner

<u>Bad Boys of New York:</u>

Jaxon

Printed in Great Britain
by Amazon